Fighting the Shadows

The Story of Elizabeth Welborn

SUE THOMSON

Barefoot Press

First published 2025
by Barefoot Press
Copyright © 2025 Sue Thomson

Edited by Holly Proctor
Cover design, text design and typesetting by WorkingType Studio.
Cover image © Unsplash

Paperback ISBN 978-0-646-70610-8
Ebook: 978-0-646-71147-8

Contents

This book tells the story of the life of my fourth great-grandmother, who was transported to Australia from Ireland as Elizabeth Church. However, while she was transported from Ireland, DNA tells us that she was born in North Carolina, in what is now the United States of America. In the early 1800s, Elizabeth travelled from North Carolina to Dublin and then to Australia, an epic journey for a woman in those days, even if not entirely on her own terms.

While the story's bare bones are historically correct, I have imagined the details, as their lives were not significant enough in the grand scheme of life in the nineteenth century to have been recorded. Even worse for Elizabeth was to have been born female, where not even your crimes were enough to etch your name in the history books.

But life for women in the colony of New South Wales, extending to what we now know as Tasmania, was harsh and unforgiving, demanding immense strength and resilience. Men comprised approximately 80 per cent of the population in 1811 when Elizabeth first landed in Botany Bay, leaving women highly vulnerable. In addition, female convicts were widely viewed as either a drain on resources (Hirst, 1983) or a moral and social threat to the colony. Governor Lachlan Macquarie remarked, "Let it be remembered how much misery and vice are likely to prevail in a society in which women bear no proportion to the men ... To this, in great measure, the prevalence of prostitution is reasonable to be attributed" (Shaw, 1977, pp. 100–101).

For women like Elizabeth, survival meant enduring gruelling work, overcrowded conditions, and the constant threat of exploitation or violence. It meant bearing children year after year, often with little time to recover, and making do with what little they had. These women didn't live lives of comfort or privilege; they faced daily battles against hardship and uncertainty. Yet, despite these struggles, they persevered—raising families, building communities and supporting each other through shared burdens.

Whether convict or free, women existed in a society dominated by men, where they were often valued more for their labour or potential as wives than as individuals. But our foremothers were resilient, determined and resourceful, carving out lives in a land as wild and untamed as their circumstances. Their survival required physical endurance and an unyielding spirit, and their struggles laid the foundation of our society today.

From those first generations born on Australian soil—the so-called currency children, viewed by some as inferior to their British-born counterparts—come all of us, their descendants. These women and their families fought for what they built, and what they built is worth remembering, for it shaped the identity of a nation forged through resilience and hope.

I have aimed to include every detail possible from the combined genealogical research of many cousins and to provide enough extra information to understand the historical context of the family's lives. Readers should note that events are depicted in this context, and they may include scenes that some readers may find distressing, such as sexual and domestic violence, stillbirth and murder. In this book, I have also barely touched on the tension between the original inhabitants of this country and the colonial invaders. Many other books go into this in more depth, and so I have left that field to those; however, it is part of our country's history that has too long been ignored. Although it is inappropriate today, the term "blacks" was commonly used during this period to describe Indigenous people in Australia (and similarly "Indians" to describe Indigenous people in North America)—probably in a descriptive rather than derogatory manner — and is used in this book without inverted commas to be consistent with this.

Elizabeth was a pioneer of this beautiful country we, their descendants, call home. She lived in Paramatta during Sydney's first twenty years of settlement, moved to Port Dalrymple, which became Launceston, a fledgling town of about 1,300 people, and possibly lived in Melbourne within the first five years of John Fawkner's establishment of a settlement on the Yarra River.

Elizabeth and John had nine children and 61 grandchildren. At least nine of these grandchildren didn't make it to their second birthday. However, the ones who reached adulthood produced a total of 275 great-grandchildren, largely thanks to Annie, with 94 grandchildren, and Ellen, with 60 grandchildren.

For those interested in learning what happened to Elizabeth's children, I've included descendant charts for each of them, along with any other information I have about their lives, in the Epilogue.

And me? I'm descended from Elizabeth's daughter Bridget. She was married (perhaps) to Sam Hockey, and they had one child, Isabella. Isabella married William Walter Guy in 1855 in Geelong, and they lived out their lives in Staffordshire Reef, Victoria. The house in which their large family lived was still standing only a few years ago.

A photograph of Isabella Hockey, c.1855

The family house at Staffordshire Reef, c.1990

A photograph of the Guy family, c.1858: (L to R) Samuel Hockey, William Walter Guy, Isabella Guy nee Hockey, Emily Guy

Acknowledgments

The numerous conversations between my cousins Karen King-Cain, Julie Allen and I inspired this book. We've spent countless hours, together and separately, delving into the intricacies of our family's history and more recently DNA, trying to piece together the complex puzzle that traces our roots.

I would like to extend my heartfelt gratitude to my partner, Michael, whose unwavering support and encouragement motivated me during times of doubt when I considered giving up. I am also immensely thankful to my mother, Gwen, for meticulously reading of every draft of this work, as well as to Karen, Julie, Catherine and Gail for their time and valuable feedback on various drafts.

This book was written on the lands of the *Wurundjeri* and *Bunarong* people.

Family tree — Elizabeth Wellborn

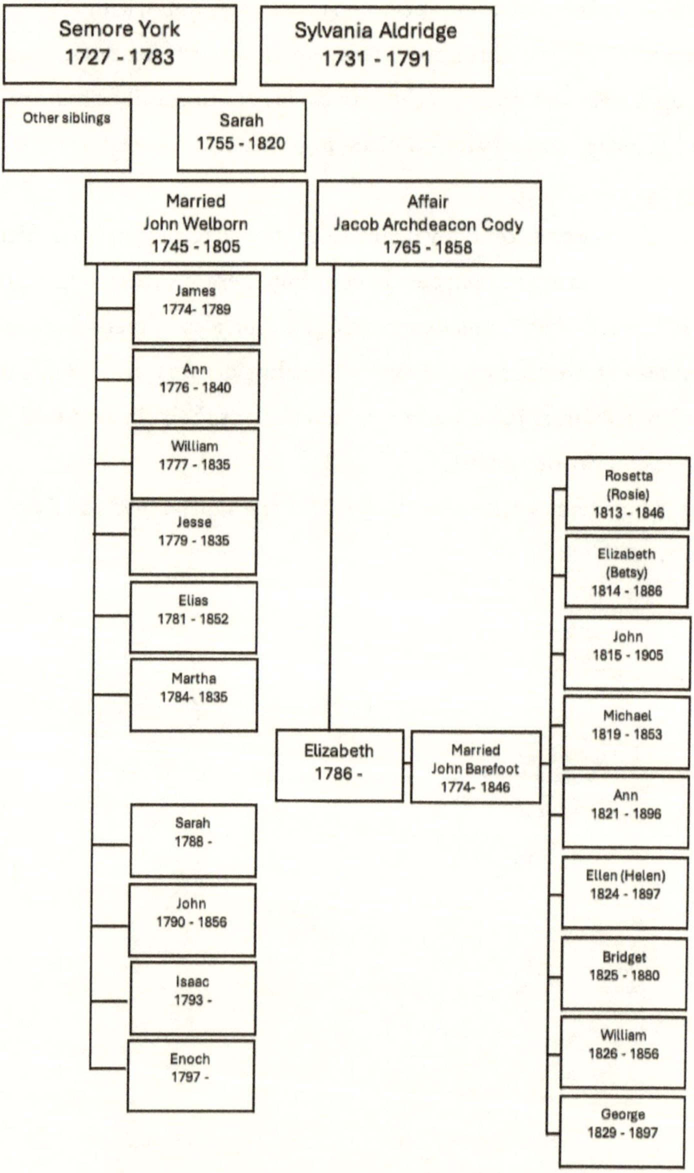

Chapter 1

Sandy Creek, North Carolina, 1803

My father hissed at me as I stood to leave the church service. "Elizabeth Welborn, you sit yourself back down right now." I could hear the anger in his voice, and I bit my lips to stop myself from crying, but I did not sit down; I strode out of the church ahead of the others attending the service that morning. The icy wind bit at my face as I stepped outside, but it was nothing compared to the icy turmoil in my heart. Anger, confusion, and a profound sense of injustice swirled together, leaving me more unsettled than usual.

A few days earlier, it had been even colder, a bleak winter's day in our small community of Sandy Creek, North Carolina. The world outside was a desolate expanse of white; the ground was blanketed in a thick, unyielding layer of snow. Inside their little home, my Aunt Martha had been weighed down by the ceaseless demands of caring for eight children, a task rendered even more daunting because more than half of them were sick with various ailments. Because of these demands, she did not attend the foot-washing ceremony that morning. In our Baptist Church, this ceremony was supposed to be a spiritual experience that the congregation found fulfilling and uplifting, but for my aunt, it was just another task she couldn't face that day. However, she knew that by not attending, there would be consequences. We all knew it, and surely enough, that lapse did not escape our pastor's notice and his subsequent wrath.

I loved my Aunt Martha. While I often felt like an outsider within my family, she was always welcoming and accepted me for who I was. My father often joked that I was a throwback to another generation, both in looks and temperament. I have brown eyes and a deep red tinge to my hair, while all my siblings have sandy blonde hair and blue eyes, like our parents. I was often in trouble for being contrary and rebellious, while my siblings were compliant and easy-going. Aunt Martha was a kind, generous person who was expansive in her love of family.

Because of this incident with my aunt, I did not want to attend the church service on the following Sunday. I said as much that morning, and my father was furious.

"You are still a child, just sixteen, and you cannot make this decision. This community expects you to attend church with us. No arguments."

So, with a heavy heart, I walked into the church with my parents. I sat beside my father on the hard wooden pews, shivering with the cold. I looked around me – at my sisters and brothers filling the rest of the pew. I folded my hands in my lap, my fingers tracing the frayed edge of my shawl. The pastor's voice boomed from the pulpit, stern and unwavering, as though his words could scour away every sin in the room. My mind wandered as I glanced out the small, frosted window. A blue jay flitted past, its brilliant cobalt feathers bright against the grey sky, and I felt an ache of longing—a longing for something more, something beyond the bounds of this little church and this tiny life I led.

As the pastor continued his sermon, his voice thundered in the small chapel. He aimed his words squarely at my aunt, speaking with righteous indignation and condemning her for what he perceived as her neglect and sin.

A surge of indignation and defiance welled within me, a fiery torrent I struggled to contain. How could the pastor be so blind to her struggles? How could he, a man of God, lack such compassion and understanding? My fists clenched, and my teeth dug into my lip as I fought to hold back the angry words that threatened to spill forth.

When the sermon finally ended, the congregation rose to their feet as the pastor began the final hymn. I mouthed the words without feeling, my voice blending in with those around me. When the hymn was over, my father's gaze found mine. His look was sharp, and his words stern as he told me to sit and wait until others had left. I lowered my head, my cheeks burning, but ignored him and strode out.

As we filed out into the chilly air, I moved ahead of my family. My younger sister, Sarah, skipped ahead to join me and tugged at my sleeve. "What's wrong?" she whispered, her blue eyes wide with curiosity.

"Nothing," I replied, though my chest felt tight. How could I explain the anger I felt at the pastor, at the injustice of the situation, at the restless thoughts that had begun to take root in my mind? Thoughts of freedom, of escape, of finding my own path beyond the community's rules and expectations. In my heart, I knew I wanted more than endless sermons, rough wooden pews, and cornfields. I wanted to choose for myself, to decide what I believed in, who I would become, and where my life would lead me. But I also couldn't see how this would happen.

In the days following the incident, I made a resolute decision: I would not set foot in that church again. At first, my parents told others I was unwell, a story that bought them a brief reprieve from the inevitable gossip. But as time dragged on and my supposed illness showed no signs of abating, it was apparent that I was perfectly healthy. By the second week, there was no hiding the truth: I was deliberately avoiding the church and, more specifically, the pastor's scathing rebukes.

"You're not fooling anyone," Mother said one evening as we sat by the fire. Her voice was low, but there was no mistaking the edge of frustration in it. "People are starting to talk, and it's not just about you. It's about all of us."

I looked up from the mending in my lap, meeting her gaze. "Let them talk. I won't sit there and listen to him tear people apart for not being perfect."

Father looked up, his face lined with concern. "It's not just about the pastor, girl. It's about our place in this community. You're making things harder for all of us."

I set the needle down and folded the fabric. "He humiliated Aunt Martha in front of everyone. She couldn't go to a ceremony because she was caring for her sick children. And what did he do? Condemned her for it. Is that what our faith teaches? To kick people when they're down?"

Mother sighed, rubbing her temples. "It's not that simple. The pastor has his ways, but turning your back on the church isn't the answer. We need to stand together, not tear each other apart."

"But it's tearing me apart," I replied, my voice trembling with the intensity of my emotions. "How can I believe in something that punishes rather than helps? I can't do it, Mother. I can't pretend everything's fine when it isn't."

Father's jaw tightened. "Your defiance is disgracing this family. We've always been respected here, but now ..."

"Now people look at you with pity and disdain?" I finished for him, my tone sharper than I intended. "I'm sorry if that's hard to bear, but I can't go back. I won't."

The tension in the room was thick enough to choke on, the crackling fire the only sound in the oppressive silence that followed. I knew I was causing them pain, but the thought of returning to that church, of sitting in that pew and listening to that man, filled me with a revulsion I couldn't ignore.

And I was angry, too—angry at the lies spun to appease the pastor and maintain appearances. A few years ago, my older sister Ann had been forced into a hurried marriage because she was expecting a child. Had the pastor known, his condemnation would have been swift and unrelenting, delivered in the form of a fiery sermon and the looming threat of shunning from the congregation.

The truth was, in our small community, it wasn't exactly rare for children to be conceived before marriage, though no one dared admit it aloud. Behind closed doors, the girls involved were the subject of harsh whispers, their names tarnished while the men slipped by with nary a word of reproach. The church called it a grave sin, but the hypocrisy stung far worse to me.

So, Ann—just twenty years old—was rushed into marriage. There wasn't much choice in the matter; the baby made sure of that. Now Ann was a wife and a mother of three, with a fourth on its way. Whenever I visited, I couldn't tell if Ann was happy or just resigned, but she wore her new life like a heavy quilt—keeping her warm, perhaps, but weighing her down all the same. She was still young, but the demands of the children were overwhelming, and I found her in tears on more than one occasion.

History repeated itself when my sister Martha, then sixteen, married quickly—her baby arrived just a few months after their marriage. So, my sister, just two years older than me, was already firmly set on the path of wife and mother. Her youth quickly gave way to the responsibilities of adulthood, and I found myself continually questioning the inevitability of my own journey.

Over the next few days, the house felt cold, not from the weather but from the silence that hung between my parents and me. Of an evening after supper, the family would usually sit in front of the fire, sewing or just talking about what was happening on the farm. Mother would often tell us stories of our grandparents, who were all gone before I was born.

Mother's father was a captain in the war with the British—on the side of the British. Apparently, he was quite dashing in his uniform and was taken captive and put in jail by the Americans. On the other hand, Father was a colonel in the Continental army, fighting against the British. But when the war ended, they put aside their political differences and worked the land together.

Mother told us stories about how our families were born in England in the very olden days but came on ships to America, as it was supposed to be a new land full of opportunities. We heard stories about their travels down the Great Wagon Road from Pennsylvania through Virginia to

North Carolina sometime this century. The stories included meetings with Indians, wild animals, and even robbers.

One story that was often requested seemed to fire the imagination of all of us children. Mother would tell it in a way that would draw us into the story and make us imagine being on the wagon with our great-grandfather.

"My grandfather, Jeremiah York, left Pennsylvania with his family along the Great Wagon Road, accompanied by about ten other families in wagons. One evening, as the sun set, Grandfather and his family ended up separated from the others and were trying to reach them before they settled for the night. Suddenly, a group of Indians appeared from the shadows, their faces decorated with war paint and holding clubs and tomahawks. Grandfather jumped down from his wagon and went toward the men, raising his hands in an open position to indicate he was unarmed. At that time, Indians often scalped or killed travellers who were alone, so this act was quite courageous. The Indians appreciated his gesture and offered them food for their journey." We children would shout with excitement whenever she mentioned scalping!

As well as talking to us about our grandparents and great-grandparents, Mother would also speak to us about our brother James, who died when I was a very young girl. Father and my older brothers James and William had been to visit a town nearby, Raleigh, to trade some of our farm produce for other supplies, but they came home with more than just those. They came home with influenza, which was spreading rapidly worldwide. It started with a fever, wheezing, coughing, and aching joints, and while Father and William started to recover a week later, poor James just got worse and worse. The rattling noise and his cries of pain as he struggled for air were horrible. There wasn't much we could do—Mother tried dosing him with linseed, but it didn't really help. Everyone in the community prayed, but that didn't do anything either—James died. He was fifteen, the same age as I am now. It made me sad to think that James never got the chance to grow up in this family that was full of warm, loving people, but it always made me feel better to know that he had not been forgotten. But there were no stories now, just a cold silence.

Chapter 2

Sandy Creek, North Carolina, 1803

My behaviour seemed to bleed into every interaction my parents had with the community. Other women responded to Mother's usual friendly banter at services with cold, curt replies. Father, once greeted with hearty handshakes, now received only stiff nods and narrowed eyes. It affected my younger sister, too.

"Why do you have to be so stubborn?" my Sarah asked one afternoon, her voice barely above a whisper as we worked side by side in the garden. "It's bad enough you're making everyone talk, but now none of my friends will even look at me."

I paused, wiping the sweat from my brow, and turned to her. "I'm sorry, Sarah. I really am. But I can't go back. It's not about being stubborn. It's about doing what's right."

Sarah shook her head, her eyes sad. "But what about us? What about the family? Can't you just ... pretend?"

The question lingered in the air, and for a moment, I considered it. Could I pretend for their sake? The thought of standing in that church and forcing myself to believe in something that felt wrong made my stomach turn.

"I don't see how I can," I finally said, my voice firm. "I wish I could make this easier for you, for everyone. But I can't pretend to be something I'm not."

And so, the days turned into weeks, and my absence from the church became the new normal. The community's whispers grew louder, the judgment sharper, and I could see how it affected my family. Each cold shoulder and each disapproving glance made my parents and sister more withdrawn from the others around them. Even though I still felt that my cause was just, I began to have misgivings about the broader effect this was having on my family.

One evening, as I sat alone on the porch, watching the stars blink into existence in the darkening sky, Aunt Martha came out to join me. She wrapped her shawl tightly around her shoulders, the chill in the air biting. Her presence was always a comfort, though tonight, there was an edge to her that I couldn't quite place.

"You're causing quite a stir, you know," she said, her tone light but carrying an undercurrent of something more profound.

"I know," I replied, my eyes fixed on the endless canvas above. The stars seemed to flicker like tiny beacons, their light barely reaching the earth. "But I can't help it. I feel I can't go back there, not after what happened to you."

Aunt Martha fell quiet for a long moment, her breath visible in the cool air. Then, with a deep sigh, she spoke again. "I appreciate what you're doing, Elizabeth. But you must understand, it's a heavy burden. More than you know."

I turned to face her, the weight of her words sinking in, though I wasn't ready to back down. "Aunt Martha," I said, my voice steady but firm, "you know I can't just pretend everything's fine. Not after what they did to you. I won't go back, not after the way they've treated us."

She paused, her worn hands clasped tightly on her lap, her gaze distant as if wrestling with memories she wished would stay buried. "I know, child. I know. But there's something you need to understand. I've been accepted back into the church. I've found peace in it again despite everything. It's an important part if our lives here in Sandy Creek, something bigger than the pain we've suffered."

The words stung. I had always believed that the church was supposed to be a place of refuge, a sanctuary, but it had turned its back on us when we needed it most. Still, Aunt Martha's voice held a quiet wisdom that could not be ignored.

"I understand," I said slowly, though a part of me still bristled at the thought of returning to that place. "But I can't just let them pretend like nothing happened. How can we move forward if we act like all if this is behind us?"

Aunt Martha's eyes softened, the lines around them deepening as she considered my words. She reached out and gently placed her hand over mine, her touch warm and grounding. "I understand, Elizabeth. I do. But remember, there are more ways to stand up for what you believe in than just refusing to go to church. Sometimes, the most powerful resistance isn't loud, isn't in open defiance. It's in the quiet strength we carry within us, in the way we choose to live our lives, even when others would rather us break."

Her words lingered in the cool night air, settling in the space between us. I wanted to argue, to protest that silence would only let them win, that passivity would only make us complicit. But something in her eyes, something in the way she held my hand, told me that she wasn't asking me to surrender. She was asking me to find another path, one I hadn't yet seen.

The stars overhead seemed to pulse softly as if they were waiting for me to decide. The weight of the moment pressed down on me, but for the first time in a long while, I felt a flicker of hope, a quiet understanding that there were many ways to fight—and perhaps, some of the hardest battles were the ones we fought quietly, in the spaces between the words.

After thinking about this conversation for several days, I relented and returned to church attendance, and life for my family returned pretty much to normal. Folks started talking to them again, and they were invited back into the social life in our small community. I swallowed the bitter pill of resentment that I felt after the whole incident and tried to get on with my life. However, I knew that things would never be the same for me and that the church and its pastor no longer garnered the same respect they once had.

We went to church at least once a week, and I despised it afterwards even more than I did before the incident with my aunt. I would sit there, listening to the pastor droning on and on, daydreaming about freedom and a different life. But what would that different life look like? I had grown up knowing nothing else but the life before me; my only contact with the outside world was when we encountered travellers making their way to the western states. Our parents taught us what we needed to know at home—for the boys, how to plant crops and manage a farm; for the girls, how to sew, cook, and care for children. I sat there and thought that maybe I wanted something different—but I did not know what that might be.

I had never been more than a mile away from our house, and I wondered whether I would ever go further than that. To Raleigh, maybe even to Wilmington, which I had heard about from my uncle Jem, who travelled there fairly often. He described it as a "den of iniquity". He said there were many sailors there, and where there were sailors, there was alcohol and loose women. I wasn't too sure what this all meant or what a loose woman was, but his face was very stern when he said it, so I assumed it was not good.

In addition to my sisters marrying and moving into their own homes, my brothers William and Jesse left our community, heading north to the new territories of Kentucky and Indiana. I overheard a conversation between my parents and brothers when William first talked about going.

"There are so many opportunities out there, Father," he said, "The new territories are opening up, and we can get big land grants." Jesse agreed with him, and before long, they had packed up their lives and headed off in search of opportunities to build their own farms and start new lives. Though it was sad to see them leave, knowing I was unlikely ever to see them again, my sadness was tinged with envy, knowing they would experience the new world and adventures I could only dream of. It was also tinged with more than a little crossness —with all of them gone, there was so much more work on the farm for those still at home—after all, the work still needed to be done.

My parents were farmers, same as all our folk and neighbours. It's not an easy life; from the time we were about five, we children had to help out on the farm, each of us with our assigned chores. Father planted corn as our main crop, while Mother tended the house garden, where we grew vegetables that we could eat. We had a few cows, some for milking and some for meat. Father also hunted deer, keeping an eye peeled for bears or wildcats, which live in the forests surrounding our farm. We traded with others in our community and occasionally with others in Raleigh or Wilmington.

There were only two books in our home. The first, of course, was the Bible, and inside the front cover, Mother had carefully inscribed our names and birth dates—she could read and write, though Father could not. None of us children ever learned to do either. Mother was always too busy to teach us something so complicated. When we asked, she'd say that we would all grow up to be farmers, so what use would we have for reading and writing anyway?

The other book we had in our home was called an atlas, and it was the most fantastic treasure trove of pictures of different places all over the world. I would often lie in front of the fire at night, poring over its pages, with Mother reading me the names of countries when I asked her. I remember thinking that there was so much out there. The world is such a big place; even as a small child, I recall it filled me with wonder.

Chapter 3

Sandy Creek, North Carolina, 1804

There remained an underlying tension between my parents and myself. My father still resented my disobeying them over something he considered important. This tension peaked one morning when, to my shock and dismay, I overheard a hushed conversation between them. They were discussing the unsettling idea of arranging a marriage for me with a distant cousin. I knew this would happen sooner or later; I was now eighteen, and many girls my age were married and had started families.

My father's voice carried a tone of finality as he declared, "It will be a turning point for Elizabeth. She needs discipline, and I can't do it anymore. Wilbur should be able to take her in hand and make her into a proper wife." I heard a strange snorting sound, and my mother's laugh rang out. "John Welborn—you are indeed a very hopeful man! Do you think that Wilbur is brave enough to tame Elizabeth?" She snorted again, then continued, "I doubt very much that he has any idea how to deal with a girl like her." My father grunted, and seemingly, the matter was left at that. I knew, however, that it was not the end of the conversation.

The thought of marriage to anyone filled me with dread, and the idea of this marriage, in particular, made me feel a bit sick. I only remember meeting Wilbur once before, many years ago, and really, all I remembered was that he was much older than me, a man when I was still a child. Growing up on a farm with plenty of livestock and gossiping with my sisters, I had no illusions about what happened between a man and woman—before or after marriage. And I had been attracted to boys my age that I had met when they came to help on the farm for harvest, but Wilbur? No, it was unthinkable. The idea of being bound to him for the rest of my life, consigned to breeding and domesticity, was utterly terrifying.

I waited for my parents to speak to me about this, and I didn't have to wait long. The following day, they drew me into the sitting room after breakfast. Father's face was set and stern, while Mother sat quietly, her eyes steady on my face. "Elizabeth," Father started, "we have decided that it is time you were wed. And we think your cousin Wilbur would be a good match for you. He has his own small farm and is agreeable to the marriage, although it has been quite some time since he has seen you."

Unable to contain my disgust, I jumped to my feet. "I won't do it," I declared, my voice shaking with fear and defiance. "You can't make me marry Wilbur!"

My father's face twisted in an unexpected outburst of fury. "Ungrateful child!" he shouted, his voice echoing through the house. "You have no idea what you're refusing!"

Mother's hand trembled as she reached out to him, her calm voice a sharp contrast to his anger. "Please, John," she murmured, "shouting won't help us here." She turned back to me, her eyes now pleading. "Elizabeth, dear, this isn't just about you. It's about the future of this family. Wilbur is a good man, dependable. With him, you'd have stability, security—something every woman needs."

I clenched my fists, my nails biting into my palms. "But I don't love him, Mother! How can you expect me to spend my life with someone I don't know?" My voice cracked on the last word, tears stinging my eyes, but I refused to let them fall.

Father leaned forward, his hands braced on the back of the chair. "Love?" he scoffed. "You speak as if love puts bread on the table or keeps a roof over your head. You're a woman, Elizabeth. You have duties—to your family, to your future. Romantic notions will do nothing but lead you astray."

The room felt smaller with every word they spoke, the walls pressing in on me, stealing the air from my lungs. "If that's the life you want for me, then I don't want it," I whispered, my voice barely audible but filled with defiance.

Father's mouth opened as if to retort, but Mother silenced him with a glance. She rose slowly and crossed the room to me, her hand soft against my cheek. "You're young," she said, her voice almost kind now, "and you don't understand yet. But you will, my dear. In time, you'll see we're doing this for your own good."

But I wasn't sure I would ever see it that way. My father stormed out of the room, heading to the fields to work off his anger with me.

"Let him go," my mother said, her voice weary.

He worked there all day, his figure a solitary silhouette against the fading light. When he finally returned home late that night, long after everyone else had gone to bed, his demeanour had changed. He seemed resigned, as if he had come to a decision. My concern grew, sensing that his decision would heavily affect my future. His anger had subsided, and he beckoned my mother and me to the porch, where we stood under the crisp late summer air.

"Elizabeth," he began, his voice grave and laden with unspoken weight, "I know you do not understand, but this marriage is in your best interests. Wilbur is a practical choice—he has land, a future, and the means to provide for you. I'm prepared to go ahead slowly with the marriage plans, to give you time to adjust to the idea but go ahead they must."

I felt like a heavy door had closed behind me, locking me in. My father's words left no room for argument, yet his offer of delay was a faint crack of light—a chance, however slim, to find another way. Trapped for now, I nodded stiffly, not trusting my voice to speak.

Mother let out a soft sigh of relief, her shoulders relaxing slightly.

"Good," she said, almost to herself. "We'll send for Wilbur so you can spend time together before finalising arrangements. It will give you a chance to see that he's kind and steady."

Kind and steady. As if those words could sweeten the bitter taste of being handed over like a parcel. I bit my tongue to keep from saying something that would only inflame my father's temper further. For now, I had to play along.

"May I be excused?" I asked, my voice carefully measured.

Father waved a dismissive hand, already turning his attention to other things. Mother gave me a searching look but said nothing.

Once outside the room, I let out a shaky breath, my composure crumbling as I hurried to the sanctuary of my bedroom. I closed the door behind me and leaned against it, my heart pounding. The idea of marrying Wilbur felt like a noose tightening around my neck.

I crossed to the small window and stared out at the fields stretching beyond our house. Somewhere out there, freedom existed—a life where I could make my own choices, not live according to someone else's plan. But how could I reach it? What could I say or do to make my parents reconsider?

Pacing the room, I turned over possibilities in my mind. Perhaps they would relent if I could prove there was another way—another future that didn't involve Wilbur. But time was short, and I had no clear path forward.

A soft knock at the door startled me from my thoughts. "Elizabeth?" It was Sarah, her voice hesitant.

"Come in," I called, brushing a hand across my face to compose myself.

She slipped inside, her wide eyes full of concern. "I heard Father," she said quietly. "Are you really going to marry Cousin Wilbur?"

"For now," I said, forcing a small smile, "I'm going to think."

I spent many nights lying awake in bed, staring at the dark ceiling, my mind racing in circles. I was desperate to think of an alternative, but for the life of me, I couldn't find a solution my parents might agree to. Every idea crumbled under the weight of their expectations. The main problem was that my world was so small, and I didn't know anything beyond the lives I saw around me. For the women in our community, those lives were straightforward: marry and have children. Work on the farm, plant crops, milk cows, sew clothing, cook meals. Rise before dawn, collapse into bed after sunset, and do it all again the next day. There was no deviation, no room for dreaming. The cycle was as endless and unyielding as the seasons.

The thought of that life—of tying myself to a man like Wilbur, of slipping into the same monotonous existence—filled me with dread. It wasn't that I thought myself above it; it was just that I couldn't imagine being content with it. But what was the alternative?

I toyed with the idea of leaving for a town, maybe Raleigh. I'd heard whispers of women finding work there as housemaids or in small shops. It wasn't glamorous, but it was independence—my own money, my own choices. Yet, even as the thought crossed my mind, I dismissed it almost as quickly. My father would never allow it. To him, the very idea of a daughter living alone in a town was unthinkable, a breach of propriety that would shame our family.

And if I defied him? If I ran away? The thought chilled me. Where would I go? How would I survive on my own? I had no connections, no skills beyond what I'd learned at home. The world outside our farm was vast and unfamiliar, and while part of me longed for it, another part quailed at the risks.

I knew, deep down, that I was trapped. My choices were dictated not by my desires but by the expectations of my family and the society we lived in. Yet that didn't stop my mind from racing. Night after night, I tried to imagine a different life, one where I could carve out my own path. But every road I envisioned led back to the same place: home, where my parents waited, ready to steer me down the path they had already chosen for me.

And so I lay awake, torn between the desire for freedom and the fear of losing everything I had ever known.

Life on the farm continued as if nothing had been said, yet I couldn't shake the feeling that a threat loomed just beneath the surface, like a storm cloud waiting to break. There was always plenty of work to do, and in some ways, this was a blessing. The endless tasks—feeding the animals, weeding the vegetable patch, churning butter—filled the hours and left little time for conversation or even deep reflection. As we moved into the harvest season, the fields demanded every ounce of our energy, and my thoughts of flight, of rebellion, and even of the impending marriage were pushed to the back of my mind.

Chapter 4

Sandy Creek, North Carolina, 1805

That fragile peace was shattered one crisp afternoon when Cousin Wilbur arrived. His appearance was heralded by the clattering of wagon wheels and the impatient whinny of a tired horse. I looked up from where I was bundling sheaves of wheat and saw the figure of a man stepping down from the wagon. His broad shoulders filled the doorway of the barn as he entered, his hat in hand and a polite smile on his face.

"Elizabeth," he greeted me with a nod, his voice gruff but not unkind. "It's been some time."

"Wilbur," I replied stiffly, brushing dirt from my hands and rising to meet him. His presence, solid and immovable as a tree trunk, sent a ripple of unease through me.

Up close, I could see the years etched into his face. He wasn't unattractive, but there was a weariness about him, a man who had spent his life in the relentless toil of farm work. His hands were large and calloused, his clothes practical and neat. He looked exactly like what he was—a farmer, steady and dependable, the kind of man my father thought would make a good husband.

The conversation over supper was awkward and stilted. Wilbur spoke of his farm, a modest plot of land that he hoped to expand one day, and the work he'd been doing to prepare for the coming winter. My parents hung on his every word, nodding approvingly, while I picked at my food, my thoughts swirling.

He seemed kind enough, I supposed, and he wasn't arrogant or cruel. But there was a dullness to him, a complete lack of curiosity about anything beyond the boundaries of his small world. He talked of soil quality and crop yields, but not once did he ask about me—my thoughts, my interests, my dreams.

After the meal, he approached me as I was clearing the table. "I'll walk with you a while," he said, more a statement than a request.

I hesitated but nodded, knowing my parents would expect it. Outside, the evening air was cool and smelled of freshly cut hay. We strolled in silence for a time, the only sound the crunch of gravel under our feet.

"You've grown," he said finally, breaking the quiet, "into a fine young woman. I remember you as a girl, always running wild."

I forced a smile, unsure how to respond. "That was a long time ago."

He nodded, as if satisfied. "Your father tells me you're a good worker. That's important. A farm needs a strong woman to keep it running."

There it was—the future he saw for me, laid out so plainly. No talk of companionship, of partnership, of anything beyond the practicalities of farm life.

I glanced at him, searching for something—some spark, some sign that he might be different than he appeared. But his expression was calm, untroubled. He seemed entirely content with the arrangement, oblivious to the turmoil churning within me.

That night, as I lay in bed, I stared at the ceiling, the weight of inevitability pressing down on me. Wilbur's visit had only solidified what I already knew: to him, I was just another part of the farm, like a plough or a cow—a useful addition to his life, not a person with dreams of her own.

The storm cloud that had loomed on the horizon now felt as though it was right above me, ready to burst. If I didn't find a way out soon, I feared I would be swept away entirely.

The next morning, I could barely focus on the chores. The conversation with Wilbur replayed in my mind, his words playing on a loop. I couldn't let this happen—not like this. The thought of being bound to him, to that life, filled me with dread so sharp it threatened to choke me.

As the day wore on, I resolved to speak to my parents. I didn't have a plan, exactly, only the raw, urgent need to make them see that I wasn't ready.

After supper, as the table was cleared and the house quieted, I found them sitting by the hearth. My father was smoking his pipe, staring into the flames, while my mother mended one of his shirts. They looked up as I hesitated in the doorway, my heart pounding.

"Can we talk?" I asked, my voice trembling despite my best efforts to steady it.

My father frowned but set his pipe aside. My mother's hands stilled, her needle poised mid-air. "What is it, Elizabeth?"

I stepped closer, folding my hands tightly in front of me. "It's about Wilbur. About the marriage."

At once, their expressions shifted—my father's to a deep scowl, my mother's to quiet worry.

"I'm not ready," I said quickly, before I could lose my nerve. "I know you think this is what's best for me, but I need more time. I—I don't think I can marry him right now."

The silence that followed was deafening. My father leaned forward, his elbows on his knees, and fixed me with a hard stare. "Not ready?" he repeated, his voice low and dangerous. "What nonsense is this Elizabeth? Many girls your age are already married with children. What more time do you need?"

I swallowed hard, feeling the heat rise to my face. "I just—" I hesitated, searching for the right words. "I don't know if I want to marry at all. At least, not yet. Maybe not Wilbur."

My father's hand slammed down on the arm of his chair, making me flinch. "Not marry?" he thundered. "And what would you do instead? Linger here, a burden to this family, while your mother and I grow old and you waste your life away?"

"John, please," my mother interjected softly, but he waved her off.

"This is foolishness," he continued, his voice rising. "We've given you a good life, Elizabeth, a secure future. Wilbur is a decent man, a hardworking man. Do you think offers like his grow on trees?"

I bit my lip, tears welling in my eyes. "I don't love him," I whispered.

My father snorted, a sound of pure contempt. "Love? What does love have to do with it? You think your mother and I married for love? Marriage is about duty, about survival. Love comes later—if it comes at all."

My mother finally spoke, her voice calm but firm. "Elizabeth, dear, we understand this is difficult. But your father is right. Wilbur is a good match. You'll have a home, a family, a future. What more could you want?"

I shook my head, the words tumbling out before I could stop them. "I want a choice! I want something more than a life that's already been decided for me!"

My father stood abruptly, towering over me. "Enough!" he barked. "This conversation is over. You'll marry Wilbur, and that's the end of it."

Tears streaming down my face, I fled the room, their voices chasing me down to my room.

That night, as I lay in bed, I felt utterly defeated. They didn't understand—they couldn't. To them, my hesitation was foolish, selfish, even. I pressed my face into the pillow to muffle my sobs, the weight of their expectations crushing me.

But beneath the despair, a small ember of defiance flickered. They might not understand now, but I would find a way to make them see—or I would find a way out on my own.

Wilbur's visit concluded without any firm plans being made, and I watched him ride off with a heart full of relief. For now, at least, the dreaded decision had been postponed. But as I turned back toward the house, my father's steady gaze met mine, one eyebrow raised. The reprieve was temporary; I could see that plainly. This battle was far from over.

"Come, Elizabeth," he said, his voice gruff but not unkind. "Walk with me."

We strolled through the fields, the late afternoon sun casting long shadows over the crops. Father pointed out the progress of the wheat and the corn, commenting on the yield we might expect this season. I responded dutifully, but the weight of unspoken words hung heavy in the air. I knew this talk of farming was merely a prelude to something far more serious.

Finally, as we reached the edge of the property, he stopped. The breeze rustled through the trees, carrying with it the faint scent of earth and grass. He turned to me, his face lined with an expression I couldn't quite read—part sorrow, part resolve.

"It's time for you to know the truth, Elizabeth," he said, his voice low and steady. "The real reason I've been pushing you to marry."

A flicker of curiosity stirred in me, mingling with a growing sense of dread. "What is it, Father?" I asked, my voice barely above a whisper.

He sighed deeply, his shoulders sagging under an invisible weight. "My health is failing," he admitted, his eyes fixed on the horizon. "I've been to the doctor in Raleigh, and the news is not good. My time in this world grows short."

The words hit me like a blow. I stared at him, my breath caught in my throat.

"I've kept it from you," he continued, his tone thick with emotion, "because I didn't want to burden you. But you're old enough now to understand. I want to see you settled, Elizabeth, before I'm gone. I want to know you're cared for, that you'll have a home and a husband to support you."

Tears pricked at the corners of my eyes, but I blinked them away. "Father," I said, my voice trembling, "why didn't you tell me sooner?"

"I thought I could spare you," he said simply, his gaze finally meeting mine. "I thought I still had plenty of time, but that's not the case, and my time is slipping away faster than I'd hoped."

For a moment, I didn't know what to say. My defiance, my dreams of freedom—they all seemed so small and selfish in the face of his quiet confession. Yet, the thought of marrying Wilbur, of surrendering to a life I didn't want, was no easier to accept.

"I understand why you want this," I said carefully, my heart aching with the effort to balance honesty and compassion. "But Father, I'm not ready. I—I don't know if I'll ever be ready for a life with Wilbur."

His face softened, and for the first time, I saw not the stern, unyielding man I'd grown up with, but a man grappling with the limits of his own strength.

"I don't want to force you into something you'll resent," he said, his voice quieter now. "But I need you to think about this, Elizabeth. Truly think. Life is not always about what we want—it's about what we need to survive."

As we turned back toward the house and my mother joined us, his words echoed in my mind. I understood his fears and his desire to secure my future. But even as my heart ached for him, I knew that his vision of my life and my own were worlds apart.

A wave of dread washed over me. My father, who, to my young eyes, had always seemed robust, was speaking of his impending death. His words lingered heavily in the air, enveloping me in disbelief and bewilderment. What would we do without him? My older brothers, Will and Jesse, had left for Indiana and Kentucky. Elias had packed up his new wife and child the year before and set out for the frontier of Ohio. My three younger brothers were still children, unable to take over a man's role on our farm. My older sisters were living with their husbands on their own small farms. Although they were nearby, they could not manage our farm as well as their own.

Feeling cornered, I could see no other option but to go along with his wishes. I agreed to the marriage, albeit reluctantly. Father greeted my agreement with a wry smile. "Good luck to Wilbur," he said to my mother, his voice tinged with a mix of irony and affection. "He'll be needing it with this one. I have never known a child so wilful and stubborn. It must be a throwback to an ancestor."

At this last comment, I noticed a strange expression flit across my mother's face. It was fleeting but enough to hint at some unspoken history. Before I could question her, Father broke the moment. "Tomorrow, we'll start making the arrangements," he said, his voice tinged with finality.

But Father lived for only three more weeks. It wasn't enough time to finalise the marriage arrangements, and so he passed away without seeing his wish for me fulfilled. Out of respect for our mourning, discussions of my marriage were temporarily set aside, granting me a reprieve that, while cloaked in grief, I couldn't help but feel relieved by.

Though I outwardly expressed regret at the delay, inwardly, I felt a deep sense of relief. Father's passing, while devastating, provided an unexpected pause—precious time to breathe before I was inevitably pushed toward a future I could not bear to face.

The morning after Father's burial, the house was steeped in silence. My mother and I sat together in the kitchen, a rare moment of stillness between us. Her hands rested on the table, worn and calloused from years of work, as she studied me with quiet intent.

"I know," she began softly, breaking the silence, "that you're relieved the wedding plans have been put on hold."

I blinked, caught off guard by her frankness.

"Tell me," she continued, her voice steady but gentle, "what made you agree to marry Wilbur in the first place?"

My throat tightened, and for a moment, I couldn't answer. Finally, I looked down at my hands, twisting them in my lap. "I didn't want to," I admitted, my voice trembling. "But I couldn't bear to disappoint Father— not in his last days."

Mother sighed; the sound heavy with understanding. Her face softened, and for the first time in weeks, I saw a flicker of something in her eyes that felt like compassion.

"Your father saw marriage as a way to protect you," she said gently. "He wanted to know you'd be cared for when he was no longer here. But I think he underestimated you, Elizabeth."

I glanced up at her, startled by her words.

"You're stronger than he gave you credit for," she continued, her tone unwavering. "Perhaps it's time you think about what you want—not just what others expect of you. Let's talk again in a few weeks, when you've had some time to think about this without your father's influence."

Her words lingered in the air, both tender and empowering. For the first time, I felt the faintest spark of possibility—a chance to truly consider my own desires, to imagine a life shaped by my choices rather than obligations. It was a startling thought, one that left me grappling with equal parts hope and uncertainty.

Days turned into weeks, and though the farm had an eerie sense of quiet without Father's presence, life continued its relentless march forward. One evening, as I finished my chores, Mother approached me, her expression a mix of determination and vulnerability. "It's time, Elizabeth, to talk about this marriage," she said, leading me to our small sitting room.

"Mother, I can't marry Wilbur," I blurted out before she could say anything else. "He's not the life I want. I can't imagine a future with—"

"Elizabeth," she interrupted gently, placing her hand on mine. "I understand."

My relief must have been evident. "You knew I would say this, didn't you?"

She nodded, a semblance of a smile forming on her lips. "You certainly have made your feelings quite clear over the last couple of years since the marriage was first suggested, and I got the feeling after Wilbur's visit that things had not changed. I agree that it might not be what's best for you. And, perhaps, we should have considered your feelings more seriously from the start."

Relief washed over me, but along with it, confusion. "Then what will we do?"

Mother took a deep breath. "For now, we take one day at a time. Your father's passing has shown us that life's plans rarely unfold as we predict. We'll manage the farm as best we can, and I'll help you find a path that aligns with your own heart."

Tears welled in my eyes. "Thank you, Mother."

She squeezed my hand, her eyes soft but determined. "And remember, Elizabeth, whatever comes next, face it with the same strength and spirit that's carried you this far. You are more resilient than you know."

That night, for the first time in what felt like a long while, I fell asleep with a sense of hope. The future remained uncertain, but I was beginning to see that uncertainty could also be a canvas for my own ambitions and dreams.

But what did I want to do? What could I do? All the women I knew did the same thing—got married, had children, and kept having children until they either could not have anymore, or they died. Is that what I wanted? At this point, the answer was no. I wanted to see more of the world outside Sandy Creek; I wanted to meet different people and try things I'd never tried before. But how could I do this—I had no idea what the next steps should be.

Chapter 5

Sandy Creek, North Carolina, 1806

Mother and I sat together one evening, going through the never-ending pile of mending and sewing that having children in the house seemed to entail. The flickering firelight revealed the lines on her worn face, markers of the burdens she bore through the years. I could feel tension hanging thick in the air, so strong it was almost suffocating. There was something on my mother's mind, and she seemed to be struggling with how to start a conversation with me. Finally, she lifted her head to speak, her eyes boring into mine as if she were battling inner turmoil, struggling to divulge a deep-seated truth she had kept hidden.

"You've always been ... different from the other children," she began tentatively, her voice whispering through the silence.

I nodded in agreement. "Yes," I said softly. "I've sometimes felt like an outsider, even though I love my brothers and sisters. Father used to say I seemed to belong to another time, another place."

Mother's gaze intensified, her words gaining weight. "That may be true," she conceded, her voice trembling. "But actually, you are very much like your true father. Which was not John Welborn."

Her words hung heavy in the air, enveloping the room in a deafening silence. My heart skipped a beat as her revelation sunk in. Disbelief and shock washed over me, and I felt as if the very foundation of my identity had been shaken to its core. I grappled with the reality that her statement suggested. How could this be?

"What ...? How ...?" I struggled to find the right question to ask, so enormous was my shock, and I knew that my voice was barely audible. The room felt stifling, the weight of her revelation pressing down on me like a suffocating blanket of uncertainty. Who was this "true father" she spoke of? How could I resemble someone other than the man I had always known as my father? What other secrets had been hidden from me?

Mother's gaze remained fixed on me. Her eyes were filled with apprehension and a silent plea for understanding. The silence between us stretched, pregnant with unspoken truths and uncharted territory.

Mother licked her lips and began to speak again. "Your father's name was Jacob Cody. He was just a little older than you are now when we met, much younger than me. Jacob was visiting kin nearby, helping with their farm. He came by one day to speak with John about the corn fields, but John had gone to market that day and didn't get home until late that night. Jacob followed me around as I worked, and we talked about so many things ... and well ... it was a long time ago. It's a little hard to remember exactly what happened ... but he was so sweet and handsome and interesting ..." her voice trailed off, but her cheeks were on fire.

"And ...?" I prompted, feeling an odd mixture of dread and curiosity. "So you broke God's law and lay with a man other than the one you were wed to in the church?" I burst out, unable to conceal my disbelief. While I wasn't particularly concerned about God's law or the church, it was astonishing to hear my pious mother admit to such a transgression. If the pastor or congregation had found out, they would have excommunicated her, shunned her from the community, and ruined her life.

"Not on that specific day," she responded, her voice tinged with sadness. "But he returned several times. He had such beautiful eyes; they were brown like yours with thick black eyelashes, and they were so full of longing—for me! And his mouth—my eyes were drawn to his lips. One day in the barn, when John was away, and all you children were off doing whatever children do, his arm brushed against my breast and ...

oh, Elizabeth, I felt something I had never experienced with John. It was as if a fire burned through me. It was so clear that he felt the same way. He kissed me, and, well … we made love right there and then in the barn."

I stared at her, struggling to reconcile this revelation with the image of my mother that I had known my whole life. "What happened next?" I asked, my voice barely above a whisper.

"We tried to stay away from each other. I knew this was wrong," she said with a distant look in her eyes. "But it was impossible not to be with him whenever it was possible. We met whenever we could. It was risky, and I lived in constant fear of being caught. But I couldn't resist him. He was only here for two weeks before he left, and I never saw him again. But soon after he left, I discovered I was pregnant. The child might have been John's, or it might have been Jacob's."

The room seemed to close in on me. I took a deep breath in an attempt to steady myself. "Did Father … did John know?" I asked, my voice trembling.

She shook her head. "I don't believe he ever suspected. He met Jacob a few times, but they had little to do with each other. I'm pretty sure that he truly thought you were his. I was careful to ensure the timing aligned with when he lay with me. But when you were born, I knew. Every time I looked at you, I saw Jacob. You have his eyes, and the shape of your mouth is the same."

A chill ran down my spine. Throughout my life, I had always felt like something was missing, a part of my identity that didn't quite fit. Now, I finally understood why.

"Jacob wanted me to leave with him," she whispered. "But I couldn't abandon our family. It would have destroyed our lives. We would have been cast out by the church, by everyone we know. So I stayed and tried to make the best of our life."

Her confession lingered heavily in the air, charging the atmosphere between us. I didn't know what to say or how to process this revelation.

Emotions whirled inside me—anger, confusion, sorrow, and an odd sense of relief.

"What do we do now?" I finally mustered the courage to ask.

"I don't know," she admitted. "At the very least, I wanted to tell you the truth. You deserve to know where you come from and who your real father was. But for now, we must keep this secret. It's for both our sakes."

I nodded, fully aware of the weight and importance of her words. Our lives had been built upon this secret and exposing it would shatter everything. However, knowing the truth offered me a fresh perspective and an opportunity to understand my place in the world.

We sat in silence for a while, each of us lost in our thoughts. The fire crackled in the hearth, casting dancing shadows on the walls. Finally, Mother spoke again.

"I don't want you to feel as though your entire life is a lie, Elizabeth. You are loved, and you have brought great joy and strength to this family."

To be truthful, I didn't feel like this. I felt bewildered and confused, yes, but I knew my family loved me. My mother's confession had placed a missing piece into the puzzle of who I was, and I felt a little happier knowing where I had actually come from.

In the days that followed, I found myself reflecting on my childhood, searching for any signs or memories that might cast light on my true parentage. I sought comfort in the familiar routines of farm life, drawing strength from the land and the rhythm of the seasons.

One evening, as we sat at the dinner table, the quiet chatter of my younger brothers filling the room, Mother gently placed her hand over mine.

"Elizabeth," she began, "I've spoken to Wilbur's parents and explained that you are not in a position to marry at the moment, and they have agreed that we should wait for a while. I think you need to give yourself some time to come to terms with everything you've learned. You've been through so much lately, although they just think it's about losing your father."

I looked at her, surprised by her unexpected understanding. "Do you really think that's wise, Mother? What will people say?"

"Let them talk," she said firmly. "What's important is your happiness. We have faced worse and come through it. We can handle this, too."

I nodded slowly, feeling a mixture of relief and anxiety. Her support was a lifeline, but the path ahead was still murky.

In the following weeks, we focused on the daily tasks that needed our attention. Mother and I managed the farm with renewed vigour, supported by my younger brothers and the occasional help from neighbours. It was hard without Father, but it provided a much-needed distraction from the emotional turmoil that had taken hold of my heart. Each day was a battle, not just with the soil and the demands of the farm, but with the questions that now plagued my mind. Who was I really? How could I reconcile this new identity with the life I had lived until now?

Mother, for her part, was a constant source of strength, though I could see the worry etched into her face. She tried to carry on as if nothing had changed, but there was an unspoken understanding between us. The secret we now shared bound us in a way that was both comforting and suffocating.

One afternoon, while we were working in the garden, I decided to broach the topic that had been weighing on me the most.

"Mother," I began cautiously, "what do you think Jacob would have wanted for me? If he had stayed … if he had known me … what kind of life do you think I would have had?"

She paused, her hands buried in the earth, and looked up at me, her eyes filled with a mixture of sorrow and longing. "I think he would have wanted you to be happy, Elizabeth. He would have wanted you to be free to choose your own path, to live a life that brought you joy. Even though what we did was wrong, Jacob was a good man. He had a kind heart."

I nodded, her words resonating deeply within me. But they also brought with them a sense of loss, a yearning for something that could never be.

"And what about John? If he were still here … would he have ever forgiven you if he knew?" I asked hesitantly.

Mother's expression softened, a sad smile tugging at the corners of her lips. "Your father was a hard man in many ways, but he had a strong sense of duty. I don't know if he would have forgiven me, but I believe he would have tried to understand. He loved you, Elizabeth, in the way he knew how. He was proud of you, and that would never have changed, no matter what." She lifted her hands out of the garden bed and dusted the soil off them, and looked me in the eye. "Your father and I got married when I was just eighteen," she said. "I liked him, but I didn't even really know him then. Fortunately for me, he was a good man, and we had a happy life, but that is not always the case, I know. But there was no wild spark, no passionate love like in stories. Our marriage, like most I suppose, was about companionship and having children."

In some ways, her words were a balm to my troubled soul, but they also deepened the sense of responsibility I felt toward the family name, the legacy I had always thought was mine. And her revelations about marriage were interesting.

That evening, as I lay in bed, staring up at the ceiling, I made a decision. My siblings were spreading out across the country as new land became available, and Jacob's relatives had left the area many years before, making it impossible for me to find him. There was nothing left for me in Sandy Creek. I wanted to follow my heart and go somewhere else, to find out who I was and what I could do.

Chapter 6

Sandy Creek, North Carolina, 1806

My mother's brother, Jeremiah York, who we called Uncle Jem, was going to Wilmington to sell our crops and buy provisions, and Mother talked to him about us making the trip with him. I had already decided that this would be a one-way journey; I wouldn't be returning to the farm. Instead, I intended to look for any work opportunity possible.

In his will, my father, as I still thought of the man who had raised me, had left me a cow and calf, my bed and bedding, and half a dozen pewter plates. I would have to leave the bedding at home, but I wanted to get a little money for the cow and calf and sell the plates, although they were likely not worth much.

The days leading up to our departure blurred together in a whirlwind of activity. Uncle Jem arrived with his sturdy wagon, its paint chipped but reliable, and together, we set about loading it with the essentials. Crates of corn and sacks of grain were stacked with precision, while jars of preserved fruits, wrapped carefully in cloth, were nestled into corners. The cattle destined for sale were tied securely to the back of the wagon, their occasional lowing punctuating the crisp autumn air.

In the quiet moments between the bustle, I packed my clothes into a small, weathered trunk. Each item folded carefully felt like a fragment of the life I was leaving behind. As I latched the trunk shut, a mixture of fear and excitement coursed through me. This was not only a trip to Wilmington; it was my chance to escape the narrow path laid out for me and find something more.

The morning of our departure arrived with a clear, calm sky. The soft hues of pink and orange painted the horizon, their beauty almost mocking the storm of emotions swirling inside me. I stood in the yard, clutching my shawl tightly against the early chill, the enormity of the moment pressing down on me.

"Elizabeth, are you ready?" Uncle Jem's voice broke through my thoughts, tinged with a blend of impatience and understanding. He stood beside the wagon, reins in hand, a reassuring presence amidst my uncertainty.

Behind me, what remained of my family had gathered to say their goodbyes. Tears streamed down Sarah's face as I pulled her into a tight embrace. Despite our constant squabbles, she had always been my closest confidante, my anchor in this chaotic world. Her trembling frame felt fragile in my arms.

"I don't understand why you're doing this," she whispered, her voice cracking. "Why you'd leave us?"

"I have to, Sarah," I murmured, my own voice shaking. "There's a world out there, something more than this."

She pulled back to look at me, her face streaked with tears and nodded reluctantly. "Take care of yourself," she said, her words a plea rather than a command.

"I will," I promised, though my heart ached with the uncertainty of it.

My little brother John, now sixteen and taller than me, stood with his arms crossed, his face a mixture of pride and worry. His deep voice, still unfamiliar in its richness, was steady as he said, "You'll do fine out there, Lizzie. I hope you find what you're looking for." But when I hugged him, his bravado faltered, and I felt the tremor in his shoulders.

Just thirteen but trying to act older, Isaac stood awkwardly beside him. He gave me a shy grin, his boyish freckles at odds with his attempts to appear grown. When I went to embrace him, he muttered, "Don't forget us, okay?"

"Never," I replied, my throat tightening.

Finally, little Enoch clung to my skirts, his wide eyes brimming with unshed tears. At nine, he still carried childhood innocence, and as I hugged him, he whispered, "Will you come back, Lizzie?"

I couldn't answer him. Instead, I kissed his cheek and held him tightly, wishing I could shield him from the pain of my departure.

As I climbed onto the wagon, I looked back at them one last time. The farm, bathed in the soft morning light, seemed so much smaller than it ever had before, and the faces of my family, etched with worry and love, felt like they belonged to a world I was leaving behind forever.

Uncle Jem snapped the reins, and the wagon lurched forward. My family's figures grew smaller with each turn of the wheels, their hands raised in a final farewell. Tears stung my eyes, but as the road stretched out before me, a fragile thread of hope wove itself through my sadness. This journey was my chance—a terrifying, exhilarating leap into the unknown.

"Take care of each other," I said, my voice cracking. "I'll always carry you with me, no matter where I go."

With one last glance at their tear-streaked faces, I took a deep breath and climbed into the wagon. As we rolled away, the sound of hoof beats and wagon wheels mingling with the morning birdsong, I felt their love and hope surrounding me, giving me the strength to face whatever lay ahead.

"Yes," I replied, turning away from the familiar landscape. "I'm ready."

Waving goodbye to my family, I turned to face the road ahead. As we neared the edge of the farm, my heart felt like someone was squeezing it. "Uncle Jem, could we stop for a moment?" I asked, my voice trembling slightly. He nodded, understanding, and brought the wagon to a halt.

I took one last, lingering look back at the home that had sheltered me all these years. The fields stretched out like a patchwork quilt, a testament to my father's life in so many ways. Taking a deep breath, the weight of the past few years lifted from my shoulders, and I turned to face the future.

Chapter 7

Sandy Creek to Wilmington, North Carolina, 1806

The journey from Sandy Creek to Wilmington stretched over four days, and each one was a unique chapter in my unfolding story. As the wagon trundled along the well-worn dirt roads, I watched the landscapes change and my spirits lifted with each passing mile.

On the first day, we left behind the familiar sights of Sandy Creek. Rustic barns and ploughed fields dotted the rolling farmlands, filling the air with their earthy fragrance. The sun hung high in the sky, casting long shadows over the landscape. There were other travellers along the way—farmers driving their cattle, children chasing each other by the roadside, and merchants hauling their goods to market.

As night descended, we made camp beside a tranquil river, its presence a lovely relief after the day's travel. At first, there was just silence, but gradually my ears tuned into the subtle symphony of the night. The gentle babble of the river, the soft swoosh of water slipping over smooth stones—it all wove together like a soothing lullaby, lulling both body and mind.

Above us, a tapestry of stars blanketed the sky, shining brightly despite the light of the flickering campfire. The fire's warmth seeped into my skin, its dancing flames casting shifting shadows on the ground. Uncle Jem leaned back on his elbows, his face alight with the joy of storytelling. He spun tales of his past travels, his words painting vivid pictures of far-off places and adventures. His voice carried a sense of wonder that ignited my own anticipation for what lay ahead, even as nervousness lingered at the edges of my thoughts.

Later that night, the campfire burned low, and the night seemed to stretch infinitely. My eyes grew heavy, yet my senses remained alert. A sudden, distant howl, sharp and haunting, cut through the stillness. The sound sent a shiver down my spine, and the fine hairs on my arms stood on end. Wolves. Their calls echoed through the woods, a reminder of the wildness surrounding us—beautiful and untamed but also tinged with danger.

The thick forests we travelled through on the second day marked the midpoint of our journey. Towering pines and oaks crowded close to the narrow path, their leaves rustling in the wind. The air was cooler and smelled of pine and wet soil. We crossed several wooden bridges spanning swift streams, the water below sparkling in the dappled sunlight. As we pressed on, the occasional deer or rabbit darted across our path, adding a touch of wild beauty to our trek. At night my dreams were punctuated with howls from wolves or the hooting of owls.

By the end of the third day, the landscape began to flatten and open up. We travelled through marshlands and low-lying fields, where the ground was soft and the air tinged with the scent of salt. The sound of distant waves grew louder, mingling with the calls of seabirds. We encountered more people now—traders and fishermen heading to the coast, their carts laden with goods and fish.

On the last day, I could barely breathe with anticipation and excitement. The air now grew thick with the salty tang of the sea, and the distant cries of seagulls told us that we were almost at Wilmington. We travelled along a well-trodden coastal road for the last stretch of our journey, where the horizon revealed the blue expanse of the Atlantic Ocean. As we neared the city, more homes and businesses appeared, marking the threshold between rural life and urban bustle.

Arriving in Wilmington felt like stepping into another world for a farm girl from rural North Carolina! The city was alive with energy and purpose. Ships from distant lands crowded the harbour, their tall masts reaching skyward, and their hulls laden with goods both exotic and prosaic. I wrinkled my nose as the smells of the town tickled the hairs inside my nose. There was the overall smell of the sea mingled with a thousand other scents. The pungent aroma of spices, the sweet fragrance of ripening fruits, the comforting warmth of freshly baked bread, not to mention the smells of people from many other countries. All of this was overlaid with the smell of the tar and pitch they used to waterproof the ships and the smoke from the many blacksmiths' forges.

As we rolled along the dusty streets towards the port, wooden and brick buildings gave way to market stalls, overflowing with so many things—vividly coloured fabrics from the Indies, baskets overflowing with tropical fruits, and glistening seafood fresh from the ocean. Vendors shouted their wares, shouting over each other and with each other, in a symphony of sound that was beautiful to my ears.

People of all kinds navigated the bustling streets, their faces purposeful and determined. Sailors in worn, rough clothes rubbed shoulders with finely dressed merchants, and children darted through the crowd, laughing and playing. And there were people of all colours, speaking languages I had never before heard.

Uncle Jem expertly navigated the wagon through the bustling streets of Wilmington, guiding us toward a quieter part of town. The noises of the market—vendors calling out, haggling with customers, and the general hum of busy life—gradually softened to a murmur as we made our way to a quieter, calmer area.

We soon arrived at a quaint inn with a faded, handpainted sign swinging gently in the breeze. The smell of roasting meat and freshly baked bread wafted out from the inn's kitchen, inviting and warm. Uncle Jem pulled the wagon to a stop and began to unhitch the horses.

"This is where I usually stay when I come to Wilmington," he said. "In fact, the last time I came here, I was with your father. Let's get you settled in," he said with a reassuring smile. "We have plenty of time to unload the goods."

The innkeeper, a stout man with a bright red nose and a welcoming smile, greeted us as we stepped inside. The interior of the inn was cosy, with wooden beams overhead and a large hearth crackling with a cheerful fire.

"Good afternoon, Mr York! Good to see you again! And who do you have with you this time? Is your brother following you in?" he asked, wiping his hands on his apron.

"Sadly Thomas, my brother died not that long ago. I'm here with his widow, Mrs Welborn, and my niece Elizabeth, so a couple of your rooms, please," Uncle Jem replied. Thomas murmured his commiserations to us and reached behind the counter to grab a couple of room keys.

Mother and I followed Uncle Jem up a creaking, narrow staircase to two simple, but comfortable rooms. Each room had a small window overlooking the quiet street below, where the last rays of the setting sun danced on the cobblestones. Inside each room was a sturdy bed with fresh linens, a wooden dresser, and, happily, a big jug of water and a gleaming porcelain wash bowl. "Ah, this looks like heaven after camping out for a few nights!" Mother exclaimed, her eyes twinkling with relief at the prospect of a proper wash and a soft bed.

Uncle Jem set down our travel bags and stretched his back, grimacing slightly as he did. "It will be nice to wash the dust of the road off," he echoed, running a hand through his greying hair, which had collected its fair share of dirt and grime from the journey.

"You two make yourselves comfortable," he continued, his face softening into a smile. "Dinner will be served in an hour, down in the dining room. The cook here does a roast that rivals anything back in Sandy Creek."

Mother and I exchanged grateful glances. The promise of a warm meal, not cooked over a campfire but prepared in a proper kitchen, and by someone else, was incredibly enticing. I moved towards the wash bowl, eager to splash the cool water on my face and rid myself of the travel's fatigue.

As I poured the water into the basin, the sensation of it running through my fingers was revitalising. I splashed my face, feeling the grime and exhaustion melt away. For a moment, I stood there, eyes closed, savouring the simple pleasure of being clean.

Mother, meanwhile, had already begun unpacking a few essentials, her hands moving deftly despite the tiredness they betrayed. "This inn surely knows how to charm its guests," she said with a contented sigh, glancing around the room. "I feel like I could sleep for a week in that bed."

I couldn't help but agree. The bed, the linens, the peaceful atmosphere— it all felt like a luxurious sanctuary compared to the nights spent under the stars, with the hard ground as a mattress and the whispering wind as our lullaby.

After freshening up, we descended the staircase, our footsteps muffled by the worn carpet. The rich aroma of roasting meat wafted up to greet us, making my stomach rumble in anticipation. As we entered the dining room, the coziness of the inn enveloped us. The room was lit by the inviting glow of oil lamps that hung from the beam-studded ceiling.

We took our seats at a wooden table near the fireplace, the crackling fire casting a warm, flickering light. Other guests were already engaged in lively discussions, their clinks of cutlery and of drinking vessels clinking together added to the atmosphere. Uncle Jem joined us shortly, his face relaxed and content.

Thomas approached our table with a tray laden with dishes. "Welcome again, folks. We have a lovely roast with all the fixings, fresh bread, and a bit of apple cobbler for dessert. What can I get you to drink?"

"Just water for us," Uncle Jem responded, his tone cheerful and matter-of-fact. Mother nodded in agreement. Drinking alcohol was one of the things frowned on in our community.

As Thomas made his way back to the kitchen, I couldn't help but let my eyes wander toward a nearby table where the apple-laden smell of cider wafted from a tall, frosty mug. My curiosity was piqued, and I found myself wondering what it might taste like—sweet, tart, refreshing? However, I quickly dismissed the thought, not wanting to disappoint Mother or Uncle Jem.

By the time we finished the apple cobbler, a satisfying heaviness settled in both body and spirit, a contentment that arises from a delicious meal and the warm company of family. The chatter in the dining room had mellowed to a soothing hum, and as the fire's glow dimmed, the inn seemed to settle into a peaceful quiet.

After dinner, we retreated to our rooms, the weight of the day's journey finally catching up with us. As I lay down on the soft, welcoming bed, the world outside seemed to drift away. The room was quiet, save for the occasional creak of the old inn settling and the distant sound of horses' hooves on the cobblestones below.

Before sleep took over, I glanced towards the window, the moon casting a silvery glow over the street outside. At that moment, I felt both anxious and excited. I had left behind everything I had ever known for a future that was uncertain, I just had to hope that it was also full of possibilities.

"Goodnight, Mother," I whispered, as I snuggled up to her, thinking that this may be the last time I did so. Her soft murmur in response was enough to lull me into a peaceful sleep, with dreams filled with the promise of new beginnings and the adventures that lay ahead in this bustling port city.

The adventure of Wilmington had only just begun, and I was ready to welcome it with open arms.

Chapter 8

Wilmington, North Carolina, 1806

The next morning, we packed up and climbed back into the wagon. Uncle Jem took us through the busy streets to a merchant's warehouse where we would sell our crops and, hopefully, my cattle. While my mother and uncle negotiated with the buyers, I took the opportunity to explore the streets around the warehouse, savouring the newfound sense of freedom and possibility. Everywhere I looked was a hive of activity—people loading and unloading wagons, discussing crops or livestock or the weather. The air crackled with the vibrant pulse of trade as transactions were made and deals were struck. The presence of sailors, with their stories of adventures on far-off shores, added to the allure of the scene.

After what seemed like an eternity, my mother returned. Uncle Jem had managed to sell my cow and calf for a reasonable price. Mother handed me the money in a neck purse. "Wear this under your outer garments," she instructed. "It's not a lot of money, but you may need it at some stage. I've also put something special in there for you to remember me by. My mother gave it to me when I got married. But you need to remember to be careful of pickpockets ... and scoundrels." Adding "and scoundrels" was pure Mother—she always warned us about "scoundrels", although she never entirely defined one. She continued, "You will need to keep your wits about you when I am no longer around. You have no male kin here to look after you, and there are so many men ..." Her voice trailed off as she looked around at sailors, labourers, wealthy men, and poor men, men of all different colours and sizes. "Please be vigilant, Elizabeth," she started again, "this is not a place for unaccompanied women." I hung the purse around my neck, under my clothes as instructed, vowing that I would look later to see what this "special" memento was.

We wandered through the bustling marketplace together, browsing through linens and other items. Despite Mother's warnings, I felt a sense of liberation, so different from our everyday life in Sandy Creek. I wished our time together here could continue, but I knew Mother would be eager to return to the farm to care for the younger children and grandchildren. As if reading my thoughts, Mother said, "Before I leave, we need to find you a position here in Wilmington. I want to make sure I know where you'll be so I can ask Jem or someone else to check on you in the spring."

We walked through the marketplace with a renewed sense of purpose, speaking to different vendors about job opportunities. Most were friendly but needed more information beyond day-to-day work in shops or stalls. I received a promising lead when we talked to a kind woman selling handmade linens.

"What about finding a position as a housemaid?" she asked, pondering for a moment. "I may know a family that could use someone like you. The Church family on Chestnut Street has three young children and has been looking for help."

"Thank you," I said, feeling a surge of hope. "Can you tell me where to find them?"

She provided us with detailed directions, and after expressing our gratitude, we headed toward Chestnut Street. The streets of Wilmington were a labyrinth, but the anticipation of a new opportunity guided our steps. When we arrived at the Church residence, a modest yet well-maintained house with a small garden, I took a deep breath as Mother knocked on the door.

A middle-aged woman with kind eyes opened the door. "Can I help you?" she asked in a gentle voice.

"Good morning, ma'am," my mother replied. "My name is Mrs Welborn. I am a widow, and my daughter Elizabeth here is seeking employment caring for children or as a housemaid. She is young, strong, and capable of handling nearly any task."

Mrs Church studied me for a moment before a smile formed on her face. "Come in, both of you. Let's have a talk."

We stepped inside, and she led us to a cozy sitting room filled with the sweet smell of freshly baked bread. "Please, take a seat," Mrs Church said, motioning to a pair of cushioned chairs.

I could feel my heart pounding as my mother and I settled down. Mother spoke first. "Elizabeth is hardworking and has helped raise her younger siblings. She's also had experience with farm work and household chores. She can cook and darn as well."

Mrs Church nodded thoughtfully. "Well, we have three children—a boy and two girls—all under the age of nine. We've been looking for someone trustworthy to help with their care and with some light housework. Could you start as soon as possible?"

"Yes, ma'am," I replied, my voice steady with determination. "I'm ready to begin whenever you need me."

Mrs Church looked pleased. "Wonderful. We can discuss the details further, but I think you would be a perfect fit for our family."

I glanced at my mother, who smiled, reassured by this promising turn of events. Mrs Church continued, "We will pay you, of course, although the wages are not high, and, of course, you will live in, as it will be easier when you are caring for the children. We have a small guest room that we can set aside for you. Can you bring your things over later this afternoon?"

"Yes, we can do that," replied Mother, while I squeaked "Yes, thank you, Mrs Church," feeling a wave of relief wash over me. The uncertainty of my future felt a little more secure, and I had a good feeling about things—Mrs Church had a kind face. And my excitement when she mentioned a wage as well as room and board — I had never had any money of my own.

After spending a few more minutes discussing the terms and details, Mother and I left the Church residence, feeling a sense of accomplishment. As we walked back towards the market to meet Uncle Jem, Mother turned to me, her eyes filled with both pride and a hint of sadness.

"I think you'll do well here, Elizabeth," she said, her voice warm yet tinged with sadness. "This seems like a good family, and they seem kind." Tears were shining in her eyes as she continued, "All my children seem to be growing up and flying the coop! I know I still have Annie and Martha at home, and their babies, but you are my special girl, and I will miss you." I hugged her fiercely, thinking about how she had kept the secret about my father for my whole life to protect me, how she had given up the possibility of passionate love to protect our family.

I felt a sense of possibility that I had never dared to consider while living in Sandy Creek. The world beyond our small farm seemed vast and full of opportunities waiting to be seized.

While Mother and I had been finding me employment, Uncle Jem had been gathering supplies for the farm, and when we found him, the cart was all loaded up for his return to Sandy Creek. He took me back to the Church residence with my little trunk full of possessions. As I prepared to say goodbye to both of them, the gravity of the moment weighed heavily on my heart. It was the first time I would be entirely on my own, away from the familiar comfort of my family and home.

Mother hugged me tightly, her embrace filled with unspoken emotions. "Be safe, my darling. And always remember, you are loved and missed by all of us."

"I will, Mother," I said, my voice choked with emotion. "Take care of yourself and the rest of the family. I'll come visit when I can."

With a final wave, I watched them climb onto the wagon and head back towards Sandy Creek. As they disappeared from sight, I turned towards the house, feeling a blend of fear and excitement for what lay ahead.

That first night was a bit of a blur — the children were fed and bathed when I arrived and there was barely time for the briefest of introductions before they headed off to bed. There would be time for that the next morning.

After talking to Mrs Church about plans for the following day, I climbed the creaky stairs to my attic room. For the first time in my life, I would sleep in a room by myself, in a bed all my own. The novelty of solitude was both thrilling and unnerving.

Stripping down to my shift, I washed my face with the cool water from the tall pitcher on the dresser. As I removed the small neck purse that Mother had given me, curiosity won the day. Other than the all-important coins, it held something small and shiny.

I retrieved it and stared in wonder—it was a small, silver locket, worn with age and imbued with an undeniable air of history. I had never seen it before. Gently, I opened the delicate clasp and revealed a tiny portrait of a woman, her features captured in exquisite detail. It must be my grandmother, I thought, or perhaps it was even older—a treasure passed down through generations. The woman's nose and the shape of her chin bore a striking resemblance to my mother and me.

There was no chain to wear it around my neck, but I felt an immediate bond with this heirloom. Carefully, I tucked it back into the neck purse, knowing it would be safe there, close to me.

Chapter 9

Wilmington, North Carolina, 1806

At first, life in the Church household seemed little different from life on the farm, although I was constantly aware that just beyond the blue front door was a whole wide world of possibilities. The thought was quite overwhelming at times, so the routine of the household and the familiarity of caring for children provided a sense of comfort amidst the sea of unknowns.

The children—Emily, George, and little Sophie—carried on with their daily tasks with disciplined regularity. Emily, at nine, woke with the dawn to help me with breakfast preparations. She was quite a serious little thing, often found with her nose buried in a book when she had no chores to finish. I envied her skill at reading and wished I could do the same. George, only two years younger, was full of boundless energy and an insatiable curiosity. His sandy hair and perpetually dirty hands a reflection of his adventurous spirit. Sophie, at four, had an infectious laugh and chubby cheeks that melted hearts. People often found her scampering after the chickens in the yard, her giggles ringing through the air.

When I had unpacked my trunk, I had looked at my clothing—a couple of shifts, one dress and a couple of pinafores, and my one pair of shoes—and realised that what was suitable and sufficient for the farm would not be suitable and sufficient for my new life in town. But that could wait for a little while.

Every Sunday, Mrs Church would hand me my weekly wage wrapped in a square of paper, and I would carefully add it to the little neck purse Mother had given me.

Similar to the farm, each day started with a hearty breakfast of freshly baked bread, oatmeal, and sweet jams. Once the table was cleared, the children attended to their chores; Emily helping wash and dry the breakfast dishes, George bringing in a load of wood for the fire, and Sophie gathering eggs. She did this with enthusiastic determination, treating each hen as her personal pet.

My role was to help with the household chores wherever possible, supervise the children's meals and chores, and just to generally make myself useful. As usual in a household with children, there was always laundry to wash and then fold when it was dry, and one day when I was folding laundry with Mrs Church, she raised the issue of my clothing.

"Elizabeth," she began, her tone gentle, "I've noticed that you only have one dress and a couple of pinafores to wear. It's high time we remedy that."

Surprised, I blinked at her. "But, Mrs Church, I don't have enough money ..." I started.

"No, no," she interrupted with a kind smile. "I don't mean for you to buy them. I have a dressmaker in town, and I'll ask her to make you a new dress and a couple of pinafores. I don't mean to be rude, but the ones that you have are quite old and a little ragged. We are not wealthy people, but we do have a certain standing here in Wilmington, and I can't have you looking like the poor cousin that's come to stay." I laughed a little to myself, thinking about how Mother had always bought large bolts of cloth to make us clothes—usually brown, sturdy, and long-lasting. In our community it was thought of as frivolous to focus on one's clothes, and, while Mother had a "best" dress for occasions, these were few and far between on a farm, and none of us children had ever had anything other than plain dresses and pinafores. We had also always made them ourselves, using the same pattern in different sizes depending on our age, and then, of course, there were always hand-me-downs in a big family.

The thought of having a dress made by a dressmaker dazzled me with its extravagance!

The very next morning, Mrs Church and I set off for town with the children, who were chattering excitedly. Our destination was a small dressmaker's shop run by Miss Violet, a woman renowned for her skill and eye for detail. As we arrived, the bell above the door tinkled softly, announcing our entrance.

Miss Violet, a petite woman with silver-streaked hair and warm, twinkling eyes, greeted us with a welcoming smile. "Good morning, Mrs Church. And who might this young lady be?"

"This is Elizabeth," Mrs Church replied, resting a hand on my shoulder. "She's my new housemaid, and she could use some new clothes."

Miss Violet nodded knowingly. "Of course, of course. Let's see what we can do for you, Elizabeth." She led us to the back of the shop, which was filled with bolts of fabric in every colour and pattern imaginable.

"We'll start with your measurements," Miss Violet said, pulling a tape measure from her apron pocket. As she measured me, she chatted away, making me feel at ease. "What colours do you like, dear?"

"I've always been fond of shades of blue," I admitted shyly. No one had ever asked me this question before.

"Blue it is, then," she declared, selecting a roll of soft, sky-blue cotton. She also picked out a floral print fabric for a new pinafore, the bright colours and delicate patterns serving as a cheerful contrast to the sombre tones of my current outfit.

As Miss Violet began to measure and cut the fabric, the children explored the shop, touching the fabrics and marvelling at the variety of colours and patterns.

"Elizabeth, come look at this," Emily called out, holding up a piece of vibrant silk. George had already wrapped himself in a roll of gingham, pretending to be a king, while Sophie twirled around with a scrap of lace like a princess.

"Settle down, children," Mrs Church said gently, though she couldn't help but smile at their antics.

Miss Violet finished her task with deft precision, her hands moving gracefully as she worked. "These fabrics will make lovely garments for you, Elizabeth," she said with a warm smile. "Come back next week, and they should be ready for you to try on."

"Thank you, Miss Violet," I said, feeling a mixture of gratitude and excitement. "I can't wait."

As we left the shop, the bell tinkled again, and Miss Violet waved us off with a cheerful, "See you soon!"

During the journey back to the house, the children excitedly chattered about the new clothes and their impromptu fashion show in the dressmaker's shop. Mrs Church walked beside me, her expression a mix of satisfaction and relief.

"Thank you, Mrs Church," I said quietly. "I'm so grateful for your kindness."

She smiled and patted my shoulder. "You're part of the family now, Elizabeth. It's the least we can do for you."

The week seemed to pass quickly, in eager anticipation. Finally, the day arrived for us to return to Miss Violet's shop. The bell above the door tinkled its little tune as we entered, and Miss Violet greeted us with a beaming smile.

"Ah, there you are! Elizabeth, your new clothes are ready," she announced, pulling out the finished garments. The dress was even more beautiful than I had imagined, the soft blue fabric smoothly draping and the floral pinafore adding a burst of colour.

"Try them on, dear," Miss Violet urged.

I changed into my new dress and stepped out to find admiring eyes fixed on me. The children clapped excitedly, and I felt a warmth spread through me, a mixture of pride and gratitude. Mrs Church's eyes sparkled with approval as she took in the sight.

"Elizabeth, you look lovely," she said softly, her voice filled with genuine warmth. "Miss Violet, you've done a wonderful job."

"Thank you, Mrs Church. And thank you, Miss Violet," I replied, my voice tinged with emotion. "These are the nicest clothes I've ever had."

Miss Violet chuckled, clearly pleased with her work. "It's always a joy to see someone so happy with something I've made. Wear them well, Elizabeth."

As we gathered the remaining garments and prepared to leave, Miss Violet handed me a small package. "A little gift," she explained. "Some extra fabric and a few sewing essentials. Just in case you need to make a repair or want to try your hand at making something of your own."

"Thank you, Miss Violet," I said again, deeply touched by her generosity.

I slept peacefully and soundly that night, with the new blue dress and the pretty patterned pinafore hanging where I could see them.

Chapter 10

Wilmington, North Carolina, 1806

I had been in the Church household for about a month and there had been no sign of Mr Church in all this time. Mrs Church had vaguely said that "he was away on a business trip", but I had not got any idea of what his business was. The lack of specifics left a veil of mystery over his activities, but as long as I was employed and the household ran smoothly, I didn't question it.

However, when he returned the following week, an almost tangible shadow hung over the household. Mr Church was an imposing figure, and his presence altered the tenor of the house, starkly contrasting with the simple, cheerful life to which I had grown accustomed. His tall, gaunt frame and piercing dark eyes held an intensity that made the air around him feel heavy. He moved with a cautious vigilance, as if continually looking over his shoulder, which set everyone on edge. The ambiguity surrounding his business dealings seemed to cloak him in a shroud of unease. While the children seemed to be happy he was home, they were more subdued than I had seen them.

One night, long after the children had gone to bed and the house had settled into its night-time quiet, I heard the low hum of urgent whispering from the kitchen. Curiosity tugged at me, and I crept silently down the stairs, each creaky step feeling like a thunderclap in the stillness. I reached the door and pressed my ear against it, straining to hear the muffled voices within.

"We can't keep going like this," Mr Church's voice was a hurried hiss, laced with an edge of desperation. "They are closing in. I need to find a way out."

Mrs Church responded softly, her voice a gentle counterbalance to his agitation. "What about the children? What about Elizabeth? She knows nothing."

"She can't know," he snapped back, the frustration clear in his tone. "It's too dangerous. We need to keep her in the dark."

A chill ran down my spine as I pieced together their fragmented conversation. Whatever Mr Church was involved in, it was clearly very close to catching up with him, and who knew what would happen then? And who were "They"? Quietly, I retreated up the stairs, my heartbeat echoing in my ears. The weight of their words filled me with a simmering unease, visions of unknown threats lurking in every shadow keeping sleep at bay that night.

I finally fell asleep in the early hours of the morning, after going through a hundred scenarios in my mind to explain what I had overheard. As a consequence, I was a little late in rising the next morning, waking with purplish bruises under my eyes. Downstairs, everything seemed to be normal. Mrs Church and Emily were finishing their breakfast when I came in. Mrs Church gave me a searching look and asked, "Are you feeling well Elizabeth? You look very peaky this morning."

"I'm fine, thank you Mrs Church," I replied, "I didn't sleep well last night. It must have been all the excitement of yesterday." The older woman nodded understandingly, and I felt a pang of guilt for the lie.

Sophie giggled from her corner of the room, where she was arranging her dolls in a neat row. "Lizzie, look! My dolls are going to a tea party!" she exclaimed, her innocent eyes sparkling.

"That's wonderful, Sophie," I said, forcing a smile. The children's joyful chatter offered a temporary reprieve from the weight of my thoughts.

Just then, Mr Church entered the kitchen. The room's atmosphere seemed to freeze as his dark eyes scanned each of us. His presence was an unwelcome reminder that something bad seemed to lurk just beneath the surface of our everyday lives.

"Elizabeth, I need to speak with you," he snapped, his tone leaving no room for refusal.

"Yes, sir," I answered, following him to a quiet corner of the room.

"I'll need you to try to keep the children out of the way today," he instructed, his voice low. "There may be visitors. Don't speak to them unless necessary, and keep the children occupied and quiet."

"Of course, Mr Church," I said, my stomach knotting with anxiety.

The rest of the morning was a blur of activity. Despite my efforts to keep the routine, the air crackled with an underlying tension. Emily focused intently on her tasks and her reading, her movements even more precise than usual, while George darted in and out, his antics slightly subdued. Even little Sophie seemed to sense the unease, her usually boisterous play more muted.

In the middle of the afternoon, the expected visitors arrived. Through the parlour window, I watched as a group of stern-looking men approached the house. Their faces were hard, and their eyes scanned the property with a level of scrutiny that made me shiver. Mr Church stepped out to greet them, his posture tense and his face set in a rigid mask of politeness. From my hidden vantage point, I could make out pieces of their hushed conversation.

"Mr Church," one of the men said, tipping his hat slightly. "We've been looking for you. We need to ask some questions about your recent activities."

Mr Church's voice was calm, but I could hear the strain beneath it. "Gentlemen, I'm more than happy to cooperate, but I must ask what this is concerning?"

"Let's not waste time, Church," another man interjected, his voice edged with impatience. "We have reason to believe you've been engaging in some ... questionable trade practices. We just want the truth."

Mrs Church emerged from the house then, her face pale but composed.

"Please, sirs, come inside," she said softly. "We'll discuss everything there."

A quick glance towards the kitchen revealed Emily, George, and Sophie engrossed in a game near the hearth. I asked Emily to take them upstairs, whispering urgently, "Quickly now, take George and Sophie to your room and stay there until I come for you."

Emily's eyes widened, but she nodded, grabbing George's hand and scooping Sophie into her arms. They slipped out of the kitchen and up the stairs just as the men were being ushered inside.

With the children safely hidden, I strained to listen to the tense conversation unfolding in the parlour. Snatches of heated dialogue reached my ears, but it was difficult to piece together the full picture.

"... can't prove anything ..." Mr Church's voice was defiant.

"... documents say otherwise ..." one man replied sharply.

In an attempt to distract myself from the growing anxiety, I busied myself with cleaning and preparing the vegetables for that night's dinner. Who were these men? The minutes crawled by, each one more agonising than the last.

Finally, the front door opened, and the men departed, their expressions a mixture of frustration and determination. I heard more whispered voices from the sitting room, Mrs Church's voice sounding anxious and almost afraid, Mr Church sounding as though he was trying to soothe her. Several minutes later, Mrs Church came into the kitchen, looking pale and drawn. When they heard their mother, the children came down from their rooms, looking puzzled. Emily asked curiously, "Who were those men, Mother? Why did they sound angry?"

Mrs Church said softly, "They were policemen, Emily, and they were a little angry, but your father has explained everything that they needed to know, and all will be fine. Dinner will be ready soon. You children go wash up."

As the children scampered off to wash their hands, I went to help Mrs Church with the final preparations for dinner. Mrs Church's hands were steady, but I could see the tension in her eyes. I looked at her but didn't know what questions to ask. I was a housemaid, after all, not a real member of the family, and I wasn't really sure of what my place in all this was. I'd never really encountered relationships as complex as these were, and I didn't really understand how to process the feelings inside me.

"Elizabeth," she began softly, "thank you for taking care of the children today. It was … necessary that they be out of the way."

I nodded, sensing the weight of her words. "Is everything all right, Mrs Church?"

She paused, her hands stilling for a moment. "Things are complicated, as you might have noticed," she said. "Mr Church has … certain business dealings that may have been … misconstrued." I wasn't sure what her words meant, but I could feel the underlying danger.

Dinner that evening was subdued. The children chattered about their day, while Mr Church, silent and brooding, picked at his meal. His eyes frequently shifted towards me, as if gauging my intentions. It made the back of my neck prickle, but I forced myself to remain calm and collected.

After dinner, as the children readied for bed, Mrs Church called me into the parlour, where Mr Church was waiting. The room was dimly lit, the fire in the hearth casting flickering shadows on the walls.

"Elizabeth," Mr Church began, his voice low and deliberate, "there are matters at play here that you do not understand, and it's best you remain unaware, for your safety and for the safety of the children." Mrs Church was looking distressed, and I nodded to show my understanding, although I didn't understand at all.

"We are going to have to leave here," he continued, "straight away. Early tomorrow morning."

"Elizabeth, can you please pack a small bag for each of the children—a few clothes, and whatever small toys they are most fond of, some books for Emily? And of course, for yourself as well," Mrs Church asked. "We need to travel fairly light." I nodded, feeling a churn of anxiety in my stomach. I wanted to protest, to ask for explanations, but the urgency in Mr Church's voice and the distress in Mrs Church's eyes left no room for questions. I had no choice but to comply.

"Yes, ma'am," I responded softly.

The house was eerily silent as I moved swiftly through the rooms, packing for the children. I selected sturdy clothes for Emily, George, and Sophie, ensuring they had warm layers and practical footwear. I tucked Emily's favourite books into her bag and placed a small, cherished doll in Sophie's. George's bag carried a couple of toy soldiers he adored, old but precious.

I packed a small bag of my own, including the new dress and pinafore that Miss Violet had made and a couple of essentials. Each item felt like a painful reminder of the precariousness of my situation. My heart ached when I thought of my mother and uncle, who would have no idea where I was or if I was safe. But as Mr Church had said, there seemed to be no other option.

The night passed in a restless haze, sleep eluding me as my mind raced with fear and uncertainty. When the first light of dawn filtered through the curtains, I rose and dressed quickly, feeling the weight of the impending departure pressing down on me.

"Elizabeth," Mr Church began quietly when she entered the parlour, "Thank you for your help. We'll be leaving in a few minutes."

Mrs Church, with her face displaying calm determination, had already dressed and was ready. "Are you all set, Elizabeth?" she asked, her voice steady despite the quiver in her hands.

"Yes, ma'am. I have packed the children's bags, and I'm ready to go."

Together, we woke the children, who sleepily complied with the hurried instructions. Mrs Church and I had hurriedly prepared a simple breakfast while Mr Church loaded a few essential items into the carriage outside. The children, still groggy from sleep, sensed the tension and moved quietly, their usual morning chatter replaced by anxious whispers.

Usually, they would have been busy interrogating each of us about why they were out of bed so early, why there were bags packed, where were they going, but this morning, sensing the tension, perhaps, there were no questions asked out loud, even though I could see the questions in their eyes.

"Come, children," Mrs Church instructed softly but firmly. "Eat quickly. We need to leave soon."

While the children tried to eat, I quickly made final preparations. I helped Sophie button her coat and tied George's shoelaces, my hands trembling slightly with the rush of it all. Emily helped her younger siblings and kept them calm, though I could see the worry on her face too.

As we finished the last bite of our hurried meal, Mr Church appeared in the doorway, his expression stern and determined. "Time to go," he announced, his voice brooking no delay.

With bags in hand and hearts pounding, we hurried to the carriage. The early morning light was faint, struggling to pierce through the heavy clouds that threatened rain. Mrs Church lifted Sophie into the carriage while I helped George and Emily scramble onto the seats. I clambered in after them, the tension crackling in the confined space.

Mr Church took his place at the reins, and with a sharp "Hya!" to the horses, we set off into the misty dawn. The landscape outside the carriage blurred into a swirling cloak of grey, reflecting the uncertainty that loomed over us. The sound of the wheels on the cobblestoned road was a constant reminder of the urgency that drove us forward.

As we travelled, the first fat drops of rain fell, soon turning into a steady, dreary drizzle. The children huddled close to Mrs Church and me, drawing comfort from the warmth of our bodies. Emily held my hand tightly, her small fingers cold and trembling.

"Where are we going, Elizabeth?" she whispered, her voice barely audible above the rain. "I don't know, Emily," I replied softly, squeezing her hand reassuringly. "But we'll stay together, and we'll be all right."

Shortly afterwards, the carriage came to a stop. My heart skipped a beat as I looked out the window and saw where we were. The docks stretched out before us, bustling with activity and crowded with ships of all sizes. I had never been on a ship, never even seen the ocean other than a few glimpses when we had arrived in Wilmington.

Mrs Church must have noticed my stunned expression as she gently placed a hand on my shoulder. "It will be fine, dear. Just stay close," she reassured me.

"Where are we going, Mother?" Emily asked, her voice tinged with uncertainty as she clung to Mrs Church's side. Mrs Church exchanged a quick glance with Mr Church before answering. "We're going to a safe place, Emily. Somewhere we can start fresh."

My heart pounded as we approached the gangplank. The rain had started to fall in a steady drizzle, soaking through our clothes as we hurried to board the ship. With each step, I felt the ground shifting beneath my feet, the weight of the unknown pressing down on me. Where were we going?

Chapter 11

Wilmington, North Carolina to the Unknown, 1806

As we settled into our cramped quarters, the reality of our situation began to sink in. The cabin was damp and musty, with narrow bunks and barely enough space for our few belongings. I unpacked a few items, trying to create a sense of order and normalcy for the children.

"Come, sit down," I coaxed softly to George, who seemed particularly uneasy. "Let's look at your soldiers."

George did this, his eyes brightening slightly as he retrieved his toy soldiers from his bag. Sophie clung to her doll, and Emily opened one of her books, trying to distract herself from the tension in the air.

Mr Church reappeared; his urgency softened slightly by the sight of his family settling in. "The journey will be long, but we must trust it will be worth it," he said, though it seemed more of a reminder to himself than reassurance to the others.

I nodded, my thoughts racing. I didn't know where we were going—maybe to New York, I thought, trying to remember places to which we could sail from Wilmington. I thought of my mother and uncle, wondering desperately what they would feel when they discovered I was gone. A pang of guilt mixed with fear settled in my heart. Deep down, I knew that they needed my presence here, but I was beginning to feel very anxious. The waters ahead were unknown, and the thought of the journey ahead was as daunting as the mysteries surrounding Mr Church's ominous words.

The moment the ship began to move, I felt the unfamiliar sensation of the ground shifting beneath my feet. It was unsettling, but I forced myself to stay calm for the children's sake. The children clung to me and Mrs Church, their eyes wide with fear and curiosity. I wrapped my arms around them, offering as much comfort as possible.

We stood on the ship's deck, watching as Wilmington shrank into the distance. The town's rooftops and church spires disappeared behind us as we glided up the Cape Fear River. On either side, dense forests pressed right up to the riverbanks, their towering pines and oaks casting shifting shadows over the dark water. The air was filled with the calls of birds flitting between the trees, some with bright plumage I had never seen before. On their impossibly long legs, great blue herons foraged on the riverbanks, standing silently, watching, then stabbing at fish passing by with their sharp beaks. The sight was mesmerising, wild and untamed, making me shiver with awe and unease.

As the river broadened and the morning mist began to lift, I caught sight of something that sent a chill down my spine. Several enormous, lizard-like creatures were lying on an open bank, half-hidden by reeds. They basked lazily in the sun, their dark, scaly bodies glistening. My breath caught when one shifted and slowly opened its mouth in a long, lazy yawn, revealing rows of jagged, bone-white teeth. I had never seen so many teeth on any animal before, and the sheer size of its gaping maw sent a shudder through me.

"Gators," muttered one of the sailors nearby, spitting over the railing. He glanced at me with a half-smile, noting my wide eyes. "They won't bother us here, miss, but best not fall in."

I nodded, trying to mask my fear. I'd heard about alligators before but had never seen one in the flesh, and the creature's reality was so much more startling than my imagination of one! The image of those sharp teeth stayed with me, a stark reminder that the river, with all its beauty, held dangers lurking beneath the surface.

The river widened as we reached its mouth, and the forests gave way to open, marshy land with long grass swaying in the wind. Dunes and scrubby vegetation lined the coast as we navigated around Cape Fear. The sailors were on alert here—the shoals were quite dangerous. We made it through them without incident, and then the vista of the open ocean was right there in front of us. Looking back at the land with some trepidation, I thought about everything I was leaving behind—my family, the life I knew ... everything. In front of me was a vast unknown, in more ways than one.

The movement of the ship was a strange new sensation. Sailing along the river, the ship's rocking had grown rhythmic, and the children gradually relaxed in my embrace. Emily, ever curious, ventured to the small porthole, peering out at the endless expanse of water. Using the small space creatively, George busied himself with an elaborate battle between his soldiers. Nestled against me, Sophie drifted into a fitful sleep, her tiny hand clutching her beloved doll. But despite the children's relative ease, the ship's constant motion continued to make me anxious.

As we sailed into the Atlantic Ocean, the ocean grew rougher, and the waves rose higher. The gentle, comforting sway quickly turned into a relentless, nauseating rhythm. After a couple of hours at sea, I was violently sick. Every lurch and roll of the ship felt like a blow, draining my strength and leaving me weak and trembling. I couldn't eat, and even drinking water became a struggle. The children noticed my discomfort, and their fear increased, making me feel guilty for not being strong enough. As we got further away and could no longer see land, the waves grew higher and higher, and my illness increased.

Mrs Church noticed my pallor and came to my side, her worry evident. "Elizabeth, you look terribly unwell. Come, lie down."

With her help, I stumbled to my bunk and collapsed onto the narrow mattress. The room seemed to spin around me, the musty smell only adding to my nausea. Mrs Church placed a damp cloth on my forehead, her touch gentle and reassuring.

"Just rest," she soothed. "We'll find a way to help with the sickness."

Emily hovered nearby, her eyes wide with concern. "Will Elizabeth be all right, Mother?"

"She'll be fine, Emily," Mrs Church reassured. "It's just seasickness. It happens to many people."

The days crawled by in a haze of nausea and discomfort. I could barely lift my head, each movement sending waves of sickness through me. The children took turns sitting by my side, their presence a small comfort amidst the misery.

Sophie stayed especially close, her small hand patting mine in an attempt to comfort me. "Lizzie, you'll feel better soon," she whispered, her innocent optimism shining through.

"Thank you, Sophie," I whispered, forcing a small smile despite my queasiness.

Throughout the days that followed, I depended heavily on the Church family. Mrs Church and Emily did their best to keep me hydrated, bringing me small sips of water and occasionally coaxing me to eat bits of dry bread. Mr Church, who initially appeared stern and distant, softened as he saw my struggle.

Despite my misery, I was impressed by the children's kindness towards one another. Emily kept herself busy reading and sharing stories with her younger siblings, trying to keep their spirits high. George stayed ever-vigilant, often sitting by my side and sharing tales of his imaginary battles. With her ever-present doll, Sophie offered simple but heartfelt reassurance that I would feel better soon. They reminded me so much of my own family, and at that moment, I missed my brothers and sisters with a searing pain.

The ship's rocking, which had initially seemed like an endless torment, began to blend into the background noise of our new reality. While I certainly had not got my "sea legs", I was not as sick as I had been earlier, even managing to keep light meals down. I could go up onto the deck for short periods, getting some fresh air and sunshine on my face, which made me feel a great deal better. The vast, seemingly endless ocean stretching out in every direction was awe-inspiring and terrifying.

A week passed, then two, and I realised we were probably not going to New York or Canada. The ocean stretched out endlessly in front of us, and we had been travelling in a roughly northeasterly direction since we left Wilmington. I closed my eyes and tried to think about what was east of America—Europe … maybe England—but the realisation that we had left the country and were heading somewhere new made my stomach drop with fear.

Finally, after what felt like an eternity at sea, a loud cry went up from the deck. "Land ho!" The shout reverberated through the ship, jolting everyone from their weary listlessness. My heart leapt into my throat as I hurried to the deck, the children close behind me.

On the horizon, the sight of land emerged slowly from the mist. Imposingly tall cliffs rose out of the sea, and beyond them, a sweep of green hills looked so lush after the endless grey and blue ocean and sky that they hurt my eyes. I gripped the railing with numb hands, the salt sprays stinging my face as I watched the coastline get closer and closer. I could see distant villages, smoke curling from their chimneys in the early morning light. Gulls and other birds wheeled overhead, and small fishing boats bobbed at anchor closer to shore.

Finally, the ship slowed as we approached the mouth of a river. The wind carried the faint smell of smoke and something sharp and unfamiliar. A pilot boat came to meet us and led us into the harbour.

I stood still as the rest of the passengers began to move about, fetching their bags and calling to one another. My heart beat quickly, and I felt half-excited and half-scared because I knew we were close now.

The river was wide but crowded, with big ships, small boats, and everything in between. Sailors shouted to one another, and I could hear the creak of wood and the splash of oars. The riverbanks were lined with buildings that grew taller and closer together the further we sailed. At first, it was cottages and small warehouses, with children playing in the mud near the water, but then the city rose before me, bigger and busier than anything I'd ever seen.

"Where are we?" I asked Mrs Church, apprehension and curiosity wrestling within me.

"This is Dublin," she replied calmly.

"Dublin, as in Dublin in Ireland?" I squeaked, feeling as though my eyes were about to pop out of my head. My mind spun with confusion. Ireland? Mrs Church seemed to sense my turmoil and placed a reassuring hand on my shoulder.

"Don't worry, Elizabeth. I'll explain everything later."

I clutched the thin shawl around my shoulders, trying to take it all in. The buildings I was looking at now along the quays were grander than any I'd seen back home—tall and delicate, with stone facades and rows of windows that seemed to look down on me. The Custom House was the most impressive of all, with its shining dome rising like a crown above the river.

But beneath all that grandeur, the noise and smell of the city hit me hard. The air was thick with smoke, fish, and the reek of something rotting, and the streets were alive with movement. Carriages rattled over cobblestones, their wheels clattering like gunfire, and people crowded every corner—men in tall hats striding briskly, women with baskets on their arms shouting out wares I couldn't understand, and barefoot children darting between them, chasing one another or begging for coins.

It was too much. I'd thought Wilmington was a busy place, with its docks and market square, but this—this was a world apart. I shrank back a little, pressing closer to the ship's side, afraid someone would see just how out of place I was.

"You there, girl, mind yourself!" a sailor barked as he pushed past me, throwing ropes down to men on the quay. The thud of our ship bumping gently against the dock made my stomach twist with nerves. I hadn't realised I'd grown used to the constant roll of the sea until it stopped.

I knew I should be gathering my things like the others, but I couldn't move, couldn't tear my eyes from the chaos of the docks. Men with thick, rough accents hauled crates and barrels off ships, their muscles straining under the weight. Horses stamped and snorted as carts were loaded up, the drivers cursing and cracking whips. A woman with a baby on her hip stood nearby, shouting something to a man I guessed was her husband, her voice swallowed up by the noise around her.

And everywhere—everywhere—there were beggars. Thin women in ragged shawls sat huddled against walls, hands outstretched. Dirty children, not much older than my youngest brother back home, ran up to sailors with wide eyes, pleading for food or pennies. I looked away quickly, ashamed that I didn't know where to look or what to do.

It felt like I'd stepped into another world, a world that didn't know me or care I was there. I suddenly missed the quiet hum of insects in the Carolina fields, the creak of our porch swing, and the smell of pine trees after a rainstorm.

But there was no turning back now. The Churches had brought me here for reasons I didn't fully understand, and this city—this vast, noisy, terrible place—was where I'd have to make myself useful.

"Come on, girl!" someone shouted behind me. I started and turned, grabbing the little bundle of my belongings. My heart was still racing as I stepped onto the gangplank, my feet unsteady on the wooden boards.

As I walked into the noise and smoke and strangeness of Dublin, I held my head high and tried to look like I belonged there, even though my knees felt weak and my hands wouldn't stop trembling. I told myself I was strong, that I'd weathered a long sea voyage and could weather this too. Fear and bewilderment churned within me, but I managed to maintain my composure for the children's sake.

It was so good to be back on solid ground again. I wasn't sure that my legs would ever feel solid again, that I wouldn't feel like I was swaying with the waves. Mr Church led the way away from the ship, with a porter trotting behind with our bags in a barrow. I clasped the children's hands, trying to take in our new surroundings.

As we navigated through the crowded streets, I felt overwhelmed by the scale of everything compared to what I had grown up with. The buildings, the people, the language—everything was new and overwhelming. Eventually, Mr Church brought us to a modest inn where we were assigned rooms. Exhausted from the day's excitement, the children fell asleep almost immediately.

That evening, as I sat by the window observing the unfamiliar city, Mrs Church joined me. "I understand that this may be confusing," she said softly. "However, we had no other option. Mr Church's business ... he fell in with the wrong people, placing us all in danger. Moving here was the only way to ensure the safety of our children."

I nodded, trying to process what she was saying. "But why Ireland? Why such a great distance?" I asked, seeking clarity.

Mrs Church let out a weary sigh, her expression reflecting her exhaustion and worry. "Ireland allows us to start anew, far from the dangers that pursued us. It may not be a permanent solution, but it grants us a chance for security."

The enormity of her words weighed heavily on me. I could see the toll it had taken on her—there was a fragility to her strength that both moved and concerned me.

"I trust you, Mrs Church," I whispered, though my heart still ached with uncertainty. "I just ... I never imagined ending up so far from everything I know."

She gave me a faint, encouraging smile. "None of us expected this journey, but we must make the best of it. For the children and for ourselves."

We sat in silence for a moment, the noises from the bustling streets below a distant hum and the soft breathing of the children providing a calming backdrop. I looked out the window again, taking in the unfamiliar sights. The cobblestone streets and the clang of church bells felt alien and oddly comforting in their rhythm.

Dublin's energy slowly settled as night fell, leaving the city wrapped in peaceful quiet. The children were fast asleep, their faces softened by the innocence of their dreams. I watched over them for a while, my thoughts a swirling mix of past and future, of fears and hopes. How on earth would I let my mother know where I was now that I was on the other side of an ocean from her? Would I ever see any of my family again? I lay down in the bed and snuggled up to Emily as I had so recently snuggled up to my mother. Her little body was warm and comforting, and I fell into a troubled sleep.

Chapter 12

Dublin, Ireland, 1806

Despite the initial oddness, the people of Dublin proved to be kind and welcoming. Their warm smiles and open hearts gradually eased my worries, and I became more at ease with the bustling streets and the melodic Irish accents that filled the air, even though they sometimes spoke so quickly and with such a strong accent that I just couldn't catch what they were saying! The city felt alive with its own rhythm, so different and vibrant compared to the quiet familiarity of Sandy Creek. At times, I had to pinch myself to be certain it wasn't all just a dream.

The local markets were a feast for the senses. They overflowed with vibrant flowers in every colour of the rainbow, freshly caught fish still shimmering with sea spray, and an impressive variety of food—some quite exotic compared to the simple, hearty fare I grew up with back home. The rich aroma of fresh bread blended with the sweet scent of ripe berries, creating a tantalising mix that lured passers-by.

One crisp morning, as I strolled through the market with Mrs Church and the children, a cheerful vendor called out to us. His voice was as warm as his smile, and his hands were busy arranging baskets of plump strawberries.

"Good morning, ladies! Care for a taste?" he asked, extending a handful of the glistening fruit.

Emily, her eyes wide with wonder, shyly took one and bit into it, her face lighting up with delight. "Thank you, sir!" she exclaimed, her usual reserve momentarily forgotten.

The vendor chuckled. "You're very welcome, little miss. There's plenty more where that came from."

As we moved through the market, George became entranced by a stall selling wooden toys and intricate carvings. "Look, Mama! Can we get one?" he asked, his eyes pleading as he clutched a small, carved horse.

Mrs Church smiled and nodded. "Why not? It's been a while since we had such simple pleasures," she said, handing the vendor a few coins.

The toy seller, an elderly man with twinkling blue eyes, gave George a nod of approval. "Take good care of it, mate. It's crafted with care and just a touch of magic."

Days turned into weeks, and the initial fear from our rapid exit from Wilmington began to ease. We found ourselves lulled into a fragile sense of security, finding moments of peace in the simple routines of our new life.

However, that fragile sense of security was shattered just a few months later as the warm summer days began to cool down with the arrival of fall. One afternoon, after a trip to the market, I returned to find our rooms at the inn hauntingly empty, with only my clothes and my small trunk in the room I had shared with the children.

Feeling puzzled and with a sinking sensation in my stomach, I hurried downstairs to find the innkeeper's wife. "I just went up to our rooms, and there's no one there—do you know what's happened?"

Her brow furrowed. "Oh dear, poppet," she said, her voice laced with sympathy. "You're in a bit of a pickle. Just after you left, the police came to the inn to arrest Mr Church. If that was even his real name," she sniffed, shaking her head. "He wasn't here, but after the police left, the Missus packed up all their belongings and took the children—where to, I don't know, my dear. She left this note for you."

She handed me a small note, but I shook my head and felt a rush of embarrassment. "I'm sorry, I can't read," I admitted softly, my shoulders slumping under the weight of this added blow. The innkeeper's wife gave me a sympathetic look and gently took the note back. Her expression softened, and she gave me a comforting pat on the arm. "Ah, don't worry, love," she said kindly. "Let's see what it says."

She gently took the note back and unfolded it, squinting slightly as she read aloud: "Elizabeth, I'm so sorry we had to leave in such a rush and that we had to leave you behind. The children, Mr Church and I are safe for now, but we must keep moving. I can't say where we are going for your own safety but trust that we will try to find a way to contact you. Please take care of yourself, and know you are in our thoughts. I have left you a little money—all we can spare. — Mrs Church."

My heart clenched at the words. The only family I had in this foreign land was gone, leaving me adrift in a sea of uncertainty. But the kindness in the innkeeper's wife's eyes gave me a small measure of comfort.

"Thank you," I whispered, trying to hold back the tears.

Left alone for a few moments, I tried to process what I had just heard. Fear and loneliness washed over me, but there was also a small spark of determination. I had to find a way to survive and figure out my next steps.

The innkeeper's wife came back with the coin purse that Mrs Church had left and handed it to me. "It's not much, but it should help you for now. Your room is paid for until the end of the week, so you've got a bit of breathing space while you figure out what to do next. Take care, poppet, and I hope you find the strength you need."

I clutched the purse tightly, feeling its slight weight in my hand. "Thank you," I managed to say to the innkeeper's wife, my voice barely above a whisper. "I ... I need to gather my thoughts."

I stepped outside, the cool autumn air biting against my skin, contrasting sharply with the warmth inside the inn. The streets of Dublin, which had once felt vibrant and welcoming, now seemed vast and intimidating. People passed by in a blur, their faces unfamiliar and indifferent. I wandered aimlessly for several hours, drawn by the sounds of the bustling market. The sights and smells that had once enchanted me now felt distant and surreal. I found a quiet corner by a church and sat on a bench, my mind racing.

"What am I going to do?" I whispered to myself, the weight of my predicament settling heavily on my shoulders. I fought against the rising tide of panic, trying to quell the fear that loomed large and unyielding. With no familiar face to turn to and no place to seek refuge, my situation felt increasingly desperate.

I had the room at the inn for a few more days, but beyond that, the future looked bleak. My belongings were few—a change of clothes, the small pouch of coins Mrs Church had left me, and what I had managed to save in Wilmington. My fingers traced the neck purse Mother had sewn, the hidden funds inside feeling like a flimsy lifeline in a vast sea of uncertainty. I touched the locket through the fabric of the bag, seeking the comfort of that small, familiar token. The cool metal beneath my fingertips provided a glimmer of solace, reminding me of my roots and the strength of the women who came before me. Bolstered by that small comfort, I took a deep breath, ready to face whatever came next.

Chapter 13

Dublin, Ireland, 1806

I spent the remainder of that week wandering from stall to stall in the market, inquiring about work of any kind. The bustling marketplace, filled with the sounds of vendors shouting their goods and customers bargaining, started to feel like a maze of disappointment.

Every inquiry received the same response: no work was available. It seemed that in Dublin, competition for jobs was fierce, with women of all ages searching for the same elusive opportunities, and I had no actual skills to speak of, certainly none that a dozen other girls didn't also have.

By the end of the week, it was clear that my little stash of money wouldn't last long. I knew I would have to move to a cheaper inn. During my fruitless job hunt, I kept an eye out for something more affordable and found a rooming house in the Liberties. I had to share a room with about six others. The beds were old and saggy, and there were bugs everywhere. I woke up scratching in the morning, my arms and legs covered in bites. But it was cheap and would help me stretch my money for a couple more weeks. The rooming house provided two meals a day—simple, stodgy fare, but enough to sustain me.

My pretty blue dress and flowery pinafore looked a bit worse for wear, but if I gave them a good brush at night, they didn't look too shabby. Keeping up a presentable appearance was important if I wanted to find work.

A month later, despite my best efforts, I still hadn't found a job, and my funds were running dangerously low. Desperation set in, so I decided to seek the mercy of the innkeeper with whom I had stayed while living with the Church family. She was aware of my situation, and I hoped she might show some sympathy.

I approached her, my heart pounding with anxiety. "Ma'am, I've been searching for work tirelessly, but I have found nothing," I explained, my voice shaky. "I have almost no money left. Please, I'm begging you for a job, any job."

The innkeeper gazed at me with a blend of pity and hesitation. "Given your situation, yes, love. Just for tonight, mind you. This ain't a charity," she cautioned. "And you'll need to pitch in the kitchen to earn your keep."

She instructed the cook to put me to work and directed one of the chambermaids to give me some bedding to put on the kitchen floor near the fire later that night.

The remainder of the day was a blur of work. I peeled and chopped vegetables and washed what felt like an endless stream of pots, pans, and plates.

Exhausted, I curled up into a small ball late that night, huddled in a corner by myself, trying to find some warmth by the dying fire. But as exhaustion pulled me into slumber, I soon realised there was a price to pay for "free" accommodation.

After the inn closed for the night and the last of the patrons had stumbled out, the innkeeper stepped from the shadows of the kitchen. The heavy scent of beer clung to him like a shroud, an unmistakable stench that turned my stomach. He was a figure of indulgence and excess, his silhouette imposing in the dim light.

"Well, what do we have here?" he whispered, an edge to his voice that frightened me. "A fresh face, perhaps?"

Fear gripped my heart as I tried to remain silent, shrinking back as far as the cold, hard walls would allow. His approach was relentless, and soon he was upon me, his grasp ironclad as he pulled me up off the floor and towards him, pressing me against the unyielding wall.

His huge frame towered over me, reeking of alcohol and sweat. Even though I had grown up on a farm and was familiar with what occurred between men and women, I was still naïve and unprepared for the harshness of his advances. At only twenty years old, I was inexperienced, vulnerable, and utterly alone in that moment.

"Please ... no," I whispered, my voice trembling with fear.

He chuckled darkly, his breath hot and foul against my cheek. "You'll earn your keep tonight, girl."

His beer-sodden lips forced themselves upon mine, a violation that left me trembling and trapped. His hands, rough and invasive, fumbled with my bodice, groping and squeezing my breasts with a callousness that brought tears to my eyes. I could feel the fabric of my skirt being roughly lifted, exposing my private areas to his lecherous touch as he delved into my undergarments. The fumbling of his other hand at his own clothing sent waves of terror coursing through me, a desperate realisation of his intentions.

I had lost everything—my home, belongings, and new family. However, I wasn't about to lose my virginity to some stranger in an inn in Dublin if I had any say in it. As his rough hands roamed my body, a desperate resolve surged within me. I couldn't let this happen. I had to fight. Summoning every ounce of strength, I twisted and struggled against his grip, my movements fuelled by sheer panic and determination.

Amid the chaos, I grabbed a nearby pot from the kitchen counter and swung it with all my strength. The clang of metal against his head rang out through the kitchen, and he staggered back, momentarily dazed. Seizing the chance, I scrambled away from him, my heart racing in my chest.

But escape was not easy. The innkeeper quickly regained his composure, a furious snarl on his face as he came after me.

"You little bitch," he spat, lunging for me again.

I dashed towards the door, my only thought being to get out, to run. My hands fumbled with the latch, my fingers trembling terribly. Just as he reached out to grab me again, I flung the door open and hurtled out into the chilly night air.

At this hour, the cobblestone streets of Dublin were almost deserted, a stark contrast to their usual bustling activity. My heart was racing, and adrenaline coursing through my veins as I ran, not daring to look back. The chill of the night air bit through my worn dress and pinafore, but fear drove me onward.

I didn't stop running until my legs ached and my lungs felt heavy. Finally, I stumbled upon a narrow alleyway and collapsed against the wall, gasping for breath. The surrounding silence was unsettling, amplifying my sense of isolation. I could still hear the innkeeper's lecherous words echoing in my mind, and I shuddered at the thought.

As I huddled there, feeling utterly defeated, tears spilled down my cheeks. What was I going to do now? I had almost no money, no safe place to stay, no one to turn to, and had only the clothes on my back. The harsh reality of my predicament was overwhelming.

The rough brick walls of the alley offered me little protection from the cold seeping into my very bones. Even though it wasn't winter, the fall nights in Dublin held a damp chill, and I had little protection against it. The city, which had seemed so vibrant and welcoming just hours earlier, now felt vast, unkind, and indifferent to my plight. I thought of my mother back home in Sandy Creek with my younger brothers and sobbed, yearning for her face so intensely that I could almost reach out and touch it in my mind. Her comforting embrace, her reassuring words, and even the scent of the fresh bread she used to bake filled my thoughts, intensifying the ache of separation. Each tear that fell felt like a drop of my hope slipping away, leaving me more vulnerable and desperate with every passing moment.

Chapter 14

Dublin, Ireland, 1806

"What's this then, ducks?" a gruff voice interrupted my thoughts, startling me. The face of an older woman appeared through the dim light. A kind expression softened her weathered features, and her eyes regarded me gently. Her grey hair was pulled back into a loose bun, with messy strands escaping its confines, and she pulled an old, tattered cloak tighter around her shoulders as she assessed my dishevelled state. I looked up at her, tears streaming down my cheeks.

"What kind of trouble have you landed yourself in?" she asked, her tone a blend of curiosity and concern.

My voice trembled as I spoke. "I have nowhere to go. The family I came to Ireland with has abandoned me, and I had to leave my bed in a hurry last night, so I have nowhere to sleep. I don't know what to do." I choked back a sob.

"And you're not from these parts, if I hear that accent right, are you?" the older woman said.

"No," I replied, "I'm actually from America, from North Carolina. I trusted people that I shouldn't have, and this is where I've ended up. I feel so lost and alone. I miss my mother."

"Well, lovey, I can lend a hand with that," the older woman said. "We've got to look out for each other on the streets. And it's safer for us ladies to stick together, if you catch my drift?" I definitely knew what she was getting at.

She settled down beside me and snuggled up. "Better get close, dear. You look cold, and I surely am. We can help each other out. My name's Hester, by the way."

I hesitated, unsure whether I should trust her. She seemed friendly enough, but trust didn't come easily after all that had happened to me over the past few days. She must have noticed the hesitation on my face because she gave me a sly grin.

"Don't worry, sweetheart. I don't bite—unless you've got biscuits hidden somewhere. Then we might have to fight for them."

Despite my best efforts, a small laugh slipped out, and Hester's grin grew even wider. "See? That's better. A smile does wonders, even in this miserable cold."

I moved closer to her, surrendering to the comforting feeling. Hester spread her cloak wide and wrapped it around us both. We huddled together for warmth, our breaths mingling in the chilly night air. As we sat there, she muttered, "And if anyone tries to bother us tonight, we'll just tell them we're long-lost princesses waiting for our royal rescue. That'll send them running."

The absurdity of her words made me chuckle again, a sound both unfamiliar and welcome. By the time the morning light broke through the grey clouds, I felt a small sliver of safety for the first time in what felt like ages.

The soft, early light made the world seem a bit less harsh. I stirred, trying not to wake the older woman, but she was already awake, her eyes gleaming with a blend of alertness and fatigue. She offered me a small, reassuring smile as she stretched her stiff limbs. "We made it through the night," she said, her voice a mix of relief and resolve. Now, we need to find something to eat and work out what to do with you."

She shared her story with me as we walked through the waking city. "I was born in a little village called Dundrum, just south of Dublin. My father was a miller and worked long hours to provide for us. Both of my parents passed away when I was young, leaving me alone in the world. My father had arranged for me to be apprenticed to a seamstress, and I loved the work I did at that time. When I was sixteen, I married a boy from our village, Thomas Carr, who took me to Dublin, believing we would have a better life there. Thomas was a shoemaker, and we lived in a small room above his shop. I found work doing laundry for some wealthy families in the area, and gradually, they recognised I could be relied upon to repair their clothes if needed, which brought us a little extra money. Life was tough but not unbearable, and we found happiness there. We had a roof over our heads, a fire in the hearth, and food on the table." She paused and sniffed, tears welling in her eyes.

"But that's the thing about life—it doesn't ask your permission to take everything away. Just after Christmas last year, Thomas fell ill with consumption, and a few weeks later, he passed away. When the landlady realised that I couldn't pay the rent anymore, she threw me out of our room, leaving me with nowhere to go. I've been living on the streets ever since. I tried to find sewing work, and I did manage to get some at the start, but as I've spent more time on the streets, it's become harder. No one wants to hire someone dressed in dirty rags. I've had to beg more than once, but with so many beggars around now, it's difficult."

I felt a connection with her struggles and shared my own story—my life on the farm, the sea voyage here, and the gut-wrenching abandonment by the family that brought me here. I told her how lost, alone, and scared I felt. Hester clucked in sympathy and hugged me tight. "You reckon you've got no one now, love, but you've got yourself and now me. I was you once, crying in a doorway, lost and alone with no idea how to carry on. But here we are—breathing, living. That's what counts."

"And what do I call you, dear? I can't keep calling you ducks, now can I?"

I hesitated before saying, "Elizabeth ... Church." Why didn't I tell her my real name? I'm not sure. Elizabeth Welborn felt like someone from another life, and Elizabeth Cody was as unfamiliar to me as any other name. At that moment, Elizabeth Church just seemed to fit.

Hunger gnawed relentlessly at my stomach, a constant reminder of how dire our situation had become. We came across a small bakery, its shutters just beginning to creak open. The scent of freshly baked bread teased my senses, but I knew we couldn't afford such luxuries.

With Hester beside me, I approached the shopkeeper, a burly man with strong arms dusted in flour. My heart raced as I fished out one of the few coins remaining in my neck purse, the metallic clinks of the others echoing like a mournful lament. "Please, mate," I started, my voice steady despite the desperation clawing at its edges, "would you be willing to sell me two loaves for this coin? My friend and I have got nothing to eat and not much money left."

The shopkeeper eyed the coin, his eyebrows lifting as his gaze shifted from me to Hester, who clutched my arm with a faint glimmer of hope in her eyes. Clearly, we looked like we needed his charity, and he let out a deep sigh, as if weighing the value of compassion against his daily business. After what felt like an eternity, he nodded curtly and disappeared into the dim recesses of the bakery.

When he re-emerged, he held two loaves of bread that looked like they had spent most of a week on the shelf. The crusts were rough and hard, their edges chipped like ancient stone. He handed the loaves to us with a fierce, reluctant kindness, as if we were taking a piece of his soul along with his bread.

"Thank you," I murmured, clutching the loaf tightly as my stomach growled in anticipation.

Hester picked up her loaf and examined it closely, turning it over with a discerning eye. "Well, I've seen worse," she remarked, breaking off a piece to scrutinise it further. "Not much worse, mind you. This would give a soldier's boot a run for its money." She tapped it against the counter for emphasis, the thudding sound prompting a glare from the shopkeeper.

Despite myself, I smiled faintly as I bit into the stale bread, its toughness testing my teeth. "At least it's something," I said. I thought back to those years on the farm when a loaf like this would have been crumbled up and fed to the chickens. Fresh loaves were baked daily, and even during tough times, there was always enough food to fill our bellies.

Hester grinned, her sharp humour shining through. "Oh, it's something, all right. Something you could bludgeon a thief with, should the need arise. Multi-purpose bread. That's ingenuity for you."

I couldn't help it—I laughed. Even the shopkeeper's muttered curses as he shooed us out the door couldn't dull the moment. The bread was stale, but it filled the gnawing emptiness in my belly, and for the first time in days, I felt a flicker of lightness, small but real.

As we walked back onto the street, Hester tucked her loaf under her arm like a prize. "There. Dinner and a weapon. What more could two fine ladies ask for?"

She winked, and I shook my head, smiling despite the hardness of our situation. Hester's tongue was as sharp as the crust of that bread, and at that moment, it was exactly what I needed. But we needed more—we needed to find work, any work, to find shelter and food to sustain us.

My daily routine of searching for work continued, but now I had company. Hester and I spent our days trudging through the markets, offering our services to shopkeepers, stallholders, and anyone who would give us money or food to get by. At the same time, we kept an eye open for the police—Hester said she had seen them take girls in for being on the streets before now.

At night, we sought refuge in alleyways, doorways, under bridges, and even in graveyards—anywhere that would keep us safe from street gangs and night watchmen. We managed to survive, but it was a constant struggle, and we couldn't earn enough to afford a place to sleep. My coins had run out; I'd spent the last on a warm shawl to wrap myself in at night. From then on, if we couldn't get any money, we'd have to resort to begging or stealing. Neither of us wanted to steal from the people we lived amongst—the stall keepers were poor folks struggling to get by as it was—but they were a level above us on the ladder, and we were getting desperate.

One night, as the gas lamps cast flickering shadows on the cobblestones, we stumbled upon trouble in our search for places to sleep. The alleyways were often crowded with people who had left their villages in search of work, and they could be dangerous places for two women alone. Hester was aware of a few places that were off the beaten track and not often visited by too many people. We walked closely together, our eyes darting at every unexpected sound. Despite the chill in the air, my skin prickled with unease. As we rounded a corner, a group of women stepped out from the shadows, their voices a mix of rough laughter and biting remarks.

"Look what we've got here!" one of them called out, her voice laced with sarcasm. She was a striking redhead, her fiery curls catching the dim light and setting her apart. With her arms crossed, she stepped forward, her companions flanking her like a pack of wolves ready to pounce.

"You think you can just wander onto our turf?" she demanded, her green eyes narrowing with suspicion. "We don't take kindly to new faces muscling in on our business."

I froze, puzzled by her hostility. I didn't really know what their "business" was. Hester, standing beside me, clearly caught the confusion on my face. Leaning close, she whispered, "They're prostitutes, Lizzie. They ... sell their bodies to men for, you know ... intimate things."

My stomach dropped as understanding dawned. These women thought we were here to compete with them.

I glanced at Hester, my expression reflecting my concern. Her jaw was clenched, but I could see the hint of a smirk beneath the tension. Hester, naturally, would find something to laugh about, even in this situation.

"We're not here to cause any trouble," I said quickly, my voice unsteady. "We're just—"

"No trouble?" the redhead interrupted with a harsh laugh. "You're on our patch, love. That makes it our trouble."

Her companions murmured in agreement, their expressions shifting between mistrust and mild amusement. A slender woman with dark, piercing eyes stepped closer, her movements quick and sharp like a striking snake. "You'd best keep moving if you know what's good for you. We don't want any competition."

My cheeks burned as I stumbled over my words. "We're not competition. We're … decent women, just trying to find a safe place for the night." My voice cracked slightly, revealing my nerves.

The redhead's expression shifted, her lips curling into a menacing smile. "Decent women," she repeated, her tone dripping with sarcasm. "As if we're not decent women? Let me tell you something, sweetheart—we're decent women just like you. The only difference is, we've run out of options."

Her words stung, guilt and shame knotting in my stomach. She turned to her companions with a sharp glance, and they nodded silently.

"All right," the redhead said after a long, tense pause. "But listen here—you mess with our business, and you'll regret it." Her tone was icy, and the warning was clear.

Without another word, the group melted back into the shadows, their cheap scent lingering in the air long after they were gone.

Hester exhaled sharply, grabbing my arm as we hurried down the street. "Well, wasn't that a warm welcome," she muttered, her voice low and dry. "And here I thought we were the picture of refinement. Clearly, they saw through us."

Despite myself, I let out a shaky laugh. "They thought we were competition, Hester! Competition!"

She chuckled softly, her grip on my arm unwavering. "Well, it's nice to know I've still got it, even after all these years. You, on the other hand …" She shot me a teasing glance, and for a brief moment, the tension lifted. We hurried on down the street, our hearts racing and fear clinging to us like a second skin.

Chapter 15

Dublin, Ireland, 1806

The months blurred into one long, grinding struggle as we navigated the perils of survival in the city. Each morning dawned with new uncertainties, but then, one day, a twist of fate led us to the worn threshold of a small, quiet pub. Its sign, "The Crooked Oar", swung lazily in the breeze as we pushed the heavy wooden door open, releasing the cacophony of laughter, clinking mugs, and the rich smell of ale and roasted meats into the chilly air.

Inside, the pub was dimly lit, the air thick with the scent of ale and the faint tang of pipe smoke. We approached the innkeeper, a wiry man with shifty eyes that darted around the room, as if constantly calculating his next move. His smile, when it came, was thin and unconvincing.

"What brings you two here?" he asked, his voice coated with just a hint of suspicion. We clearly didn't look like customers.

"We're looking for work, sir. Anything you have need of—serving, cleaning, washing, whatever it takes," I replied, my voice trembling slightly with the combination of desperation and hope.

He scrutinised us for a long moment, his eyes appraising and cold. Then, with a thin-lipped smile that didn't reach his eyes, he called out, "Rosie! Come here a minute."

Though past the prime of her youth, Rosie was a striking woman. With sharp cheekbones, long black hair, and bright blue eyes that seemed to see right through to your soul, she approached us with a cool expression.

"These 'ladies' are looking for work," the innkeeper said to her, his tone casual but carrying an undercurrent of something I couldn't quite understand. "I thought maybe they could start here in the pub. See if they're up to it."

Rosie's eyes flicked over us, the wheels visibly turning in her head. "Well, Mr Flynn," she said in her lilting Irish accent, "you are getting soft in your old age, taking in women off the streets."

Mr Flynn replied, "It just seems a good opportunity, after those other two … err … left yesterday."

"All right," Rosie said after considering this for a few minutes, her voice as sharp as a blade. "They can start tomorrow, cleaning and serving. We'll see if they're worth their salt."

"We'll provide you with a place to sleep and meals in exchange for your work. There's a tiny room in the attic—cramped, but it's dry and has a bed." She paused, eyeing our tattered clothing with a barely concealed grimace. "You'll need proper clothes to work in. I've got some you can use, but these,"—she gestured to our worn, dirty garments—"these need to be tossed out."

I clutched my once-beautiful blue dress, a tear rolling down my cheek. I hadn't cried all this time, not since that first awful night when I sobbed for my mother, but now I cried over my dress. It seemed like that was the last time I was really happy. Rosie's eyes sharpened. "I know it's hard," she said, "but you need to look presentable, at the very least."

She led us to our room, up a narrow, creaking staircase to a tiny space beneath the eaves of the pub. There was barely enough room for the bed, but it felt like a sanctuary compared to the streets, and we were used to huddling together for warmth. The roof felt like a protective shield overhead.

As we settled in, Rosie came back with two sets of clean, practical clothes. "These are some old ones of mine," she said, handing us the garments. "You two are skin and bone, just like I used to be." She chuckled as she placed her hands on her hips. "A bit more meat on the old bones now, hey?"

As the weeks slipped by, Hester and I focused on our work, thankful for the shelter and meals, however modest they were. Yet, we felt uneasy. It seemed as if a shadow loomed over our every move. Mr Flynn often had his eyes on me, and occasionally he licked his thick lips in a rather exaggerated manner. After the incident at the inn not long ago, this made me feel even more anxious. One night, Hester and I spoke about the two of them in our little room in the attic.

"You keep your eyes peeled and your wits about you, Lizzie. There's men come into this pub that'd sell their own mothers for a half-penny, and Flynn is one of them. Rosie is no better," Hester warned, her voice low but sharp as a knife.

I shuddered at the mention of Flynn's name, his image vivid in my mind. "Rosie watches us like she's sizing up a joint of meat."

Hester smirked, trying to lighten the mood. "Aye, well, if she's weighing me up, she'll be needing bigger scales." She patted her hips, and I couldn't help but laugh.

Her grin grew wider. "Flynn's likely thinking the same—though I'd wager he's envisioning me as a Christmas roast. Fat, juicy, and with an apple in my gob."

I burst into laughter despite myself, the absurdity of her imagery cutting through the tension. Hester had a way of turning fear into humour, a skill I was learning to appreciate more each day.

She leaned in closer, her voice low and conspiratorial. "And don't you worry about those drunks making their little comments. They're all talk, Lizzie. Half of them couldn't find their way out of their own breeches, let alone into yours."

"Hester!" I gasped, scandalised, but giggling all the same.

"What?" she said with mock innocence. "A bit of bawdy talk never hurt anyone. Besides, it's true. They talk big, but most of them couldn't lift a sack of flour without falling flat on their faces."

Despite the laughter, the unease lingered beneath the surface. Rosie, with her piercing eyes, seemed to watch us with a mixture of assessment and something more predatory.

Our routine turned into a blur of cleaning tables, serving drinks, and scrubbing floors. Once we finished, there was always laundry to tackle. The tasks were demanding, the hours long, but they provided a break from the harsh reality of the streets. Even amidst the lewd comments and lingering glances, I found solace in Hester's humour; her sharp wit served as a balm for the strain of our daily lives.

One night, as the pub buzzed with the rowdy din of patrons, a small group of men sat huddled in the back, their conversation hushed and intense. When I approached their table to collect the empty mugs, one of them leered at me with a smirk. "How much for a little extra?" he asked with a cheeky grin.

Accustomed to such propositions, I laughed it off, replying, "No extras here, love."

But he persisted, his grey eyes locking onto mine. "Are you sure?" he said softly, his hand brushing mine. "It could be good for both of us. A man gets lonely, and the nights are getting cold."

At his touch, a shiver went down my spine, but I quickly pulled away and walked off, forcing myself to remain composed. Many men made comments like this, and usually, I just felt a little sorry for them and brushed it off. This, however, was a whole different feeling. I looked back at him, and parts of my body felt like they had woken. I was lonely.

As time went on, I noticed Rosie keeping a closer eye on my interactions with the male customers. Her gaze felt calculating, as though she was weighing the potential for something more sinister. In hushed conversations with Mr Flynn, I caught snippets that confirmed my suspicions—they were considering us for something much darker than honest work at the pub.

One quiet evening, Rosie approached us, her presence disrupting the mundane rhythm of our tasks. Her expression was intense, and I could feel the weight of her eyes on me.

"You two work very hard," she began, her tone laced with something I couldn't quite define. "But you both should know there are easier ways to earn your keep."

Hester and I exchanged a quick, uneasy glance. The implication was clear, but we needed to hear it from her. "What exactly do you mean?" Hester probed, her voice steady but wary.

Rosie's eyes gleamed as she leaned in, her voice dropping to a hushed whisper.

"We have another business on the side," she revealed, her smile thin and knowing.

"Men round here, especially the ones from the docks, are keen to shell out for ... special companionship. Even you, Hester. Men are men, and loneliness can cost a pretty penny. You could make a lot more than you ever would scrubbing floors and clearing tables."

My heart pounded, but I kept my voice as steady as I could. "We're not interested."

Rosie maintained her smile, but a hint of exasperation coloured it.

"Think about it," she urged. "A comfy bed, heaps of food, and extra coin in your pockets. Life doesn't need to be this tough. The extra dosh could change everything, you know that."

Hester took a bold step forward, her chin raised defiantly. "We won't be doing that," she declared, her voice resolute.

Rosie's expression didn't change, but I caught a fleeting look of anger before she put on a wintry smile.

"Suit yourselves," she said, turning away. "Just remember the offer stands if you ever change your minds."

As Rosie slipped into the shadows of the dimly lit pub, Hester and I shared a look of mutual resolve and determination. We had made it this far by holding onto our dignity, and we weren't about to let it go now, regardless of the temptation or how easy the alternative seemed.

One night as the pub was closing, I was coming up out of the basement when I heard whispering between Mr Flynn and Rosie as they stood near the bar.

"Young Lizzie scrubs up all right, don't she?" Mr Flynn muttered. His words dripped with a greediness that sent a shiver down my spine.

Rosie gave a slow, calculating nod. "Aye. They both do. More than we expected. And she's still a maiden, I'd wager."

Mr Flynn's thick lips twisted into a smirk. "Think it's time we brought them into the fold?"

"Not yet," Rosie replied, her eyes narrowing. "Let's give it a bit more time. See how they handle themselves. Once there's a bit more meat on their bones and we've sized them up proper, we'll start tarting them up. We're always needing fresh faces."

I felt my blood run cold, my grip tightening on the tray in my hands. The realisation that we had always been on trial for something far darker than just pub work hit me like a punch to the gut. They had been biding their time, watching and waiting to see if we would fit into their broader, more sordid plans.

Later that evening, as Hester and I climbed the narrow stairs to our attic room, I shared with her the conversation I had overheard. Her face paled, but her eyes hardened with resolve.

"Well, isn't that just charming," she said, her tone cutting like a blade. "Tarting us up, is it? Flynn and Rosie can stick that plan where the sun doesn't shine."

I managed a small smile despite my nerves. "We'll have to be careful, Hester. They're watching us, waiting for the right moment."

Hester nodded and then smirked. "You've got the right idea, Lizzie. But if Rosie thinks she's going to get me dolled up like some doxy, she's got another thing coming. I'm no one's 'fresh face'. If anything, I'm a fine vintage—and one that bites back."

Her humour, though dark, eased the tension in the air. "I wouldn't put it past Flynn to try to talk me into it himself," she added, crossing her arms. "And I'll tell you what I'll say to him—'Flynn, love, I'd rather kiss a snake than let you within a mile of me in rouge.'"

I couldn't help but laugh, and Hester grinned at her small victory. "You've got to keep your spirits up, Lizzie. Don't let them see you afraid. Fear's just an invitation to men like Flynn."

Her face sobered then, her sharp humour giving way to steely determination. "We'll play their game for now. But the second I get a chance, I'm out that door, and you'd better be right behind me."

The resolve in her voice steadied me. "Let's see what happens," I said, trying to match her strength.

We knew we had to tread carefully, continue our work, and keep our ears open for any more whispered conspiracies.

Days turned into weeks, and we went about our duties with the same diligence, though the undercurrent of tension remained. Rosie's gaze was often upon us, sizing us up, but we made sure to give her no reason to doubt our work ethic.

Chapter 16

Dublin, Ireland, 1806

In early December, Dublin began preparing for Christmas. Christmas in Ireland was so different from Christmas in our small farming community in Sandy Creek. At home, the day focused on prayer, community, and family. According to Baptist traditions, there were no decorations and no real celebration. Here in Dublin, the day's focus remained the same, but the city was adorned on such a grand scale! Evergreen boughs and bunches of holly hung everywhere, churches gleamed with a thousand candles, and we hoped for a dusting of snow on the day itself. We wouldn't be required to work on Christmas Day or St Stephen's Day the following day—Rosie seemed to be mellowing.

After a particularly rowdy night in the pub, Rosie called us over to the bar with an unusual gleam in her eye.

"You girls worked hard tonight, and it's nearly Christmas. I want you to have a drink on me," she said, pushing two tankards of ale towards us.

Exhausted from the night's work, we welcomed the unexpected gesture without hesitation. The events of the past few months had drained us, and we let our guard down. I reminisced about that night in the inn in Wilmington, seeming like many years ago, but in reality, it wasn't that long ago, when I had wondered what cider tasted like. We drank deeply, and the warmth from the ale quickly spread through our weary bodies. Unused to it, it didn't take long for the alcohol to dull our senses.

Another pint of ale went down easily, and the world around us soon blurred. Laughter echoed all around, mingling with the clinking of mugs and the murmur of conversation. I felt a warm buzz easing the tension that had knotted my muscles for weeks. Hester's eyes sparkled with a newfound gleam, a fleeting escape from our harsh reality. Time became hazy, with each moment swirling into a surreal dream where the lines between past and present, reality and illusion, seemed to fade. Rosie's booming, infectious laughter punctuated the night, amplified by the dim glow of the lanterns, casting playful shadows that danced around us. I felt happier than I had since I was home with my family, before Father died, before I knew the truth about myself.

The last thing I remembered clearly was Rosie's wide grin as she handed us another drink. The room spun, and then darkness enveloped me.

When I awoke, the first thing I felt was the bone-chilling cold seeping into my very core. Quickly after, I realised I was naked, the rough, unfamiliar sheets scraping against my skin, and I felt the panic rising. I clutched at my neck but knew even before I touched my throat that my little purse was not there. My stomach dropped even further at the thought that my precious locket was gone, but I could see so little in the room that it could be anywhere. I did not know where I was—the room was unfamiliar, and the only light was from the pale moon shining through a high window. It cast eerie shadows that heightened my terror. My body felt bruised and sore, my nipples ached, and I knew that my virginity was gone, torn from me in the night.

Sitting up abruptly, my heart was pounding in my chest like a war drum. I felt completely disoriented, and my brain struggled to make sense of my surroundings. Beside me lay a man, his face obscured by shadows. A surge of dread washed over me, mingling with the cold that penetrated deeper with each passing second.

The full weight of the situation crashed down on me like a tidal wave. The realisation struck me like a dagger to the heart, filling me with a potent mix of anger and despair. My mind raced to piece together the fragmented memories of the night, but they eluded me, slipping through my grasp like sand running through my fingers. The man beside me stirred slightly and flung his arm out towards me, his movement yanking me brutally back to the present. Fear tightened its grip on me as I scrambled to gather my clothes, urgency overpowering my shock and confusion.

"Hester?" I called out with a trembling voice, praying she was unharmed.

A rustling sound from the other side of the room confirmed my fears. Hester lay dishevelled in another bed, a man sprawled next to her. Our eyes met, and we were both filled with horror.

"Elizabeth, what happened?"

"I'm not sure, to be honest," I whispered, my voice barely rising above the pounding of my heart. "I remember Rosie handing us drinks, everyone laughing, and ... that's all."

Frantically, we began to cover ourselves, panic rising with every passing second. "We need to get out of here," Hester said, her voice shaking.

At that moment, the men stirred. One of them groaned and opened his eyes, taking in the scene with groggy confusion. Their expressions quickly shifted from bemusement to alarm as they realised the seriousness of the situation.

"Get up," one of the men hissed to the other, urgency creeping into his voice. "We need to bail before that crazy bitch Rosie shows up. She told us to be gone after we finished these two, and instead, we ended up dozing off." They fumbled for their gear, their movements frantic and awkward. They knew they had to clear out, as things were bound to get messy. Silently, they slipped out of the room, vanishing into the shadows of the inn, hoping to dodge any run-in with Rosie or anyone else.

We gathered our scattered, torn clothes from where they had been flung the night before and frantically pulled them on, our fingers trembling with urgency. In the chaos, I hoped for even a moment's delay, anything that would buy us enough time to cover ourselves and salvage a shred of dignity. As we fumbled with buttons, the door burst open with a force that made it shudder on its hinges.

Rosie stormed in, her expression dark and furious. "Where do you think you're going?" she demanded, her voice dripping with anger.

The men's quick exit had bought us only a moment's reprieve. Now, standing face to face with Rosie, the reality of our situation hit harder than ever.

"Rosie, what have you done?" I demanded, stepping forward despite the tremor in my voice. "How could you do this to us?"

Rosie's eyes narrowed with a predatory glint. "You thought you could take advantage of my kindness and just walk away? You owe me now, and it's time to pay up. We've got plenty more customers for you two, or you'll be out on the street with nothing again."

Hester, who had been quiet until now, stepped forward, her hands resting on her hips. "Kindness?" she scoffed, her voice slicing through the tension like a knife. "You call this kindness? Let me tell you, Rosie, I've seen more generosity from a stray dog."

Rosie's eyes flashed with anger, but Hester didn't flinch. "You reckon we owe you just because you gave us a roof over our heads and a bit of food? We worked our fingers to the bone for you, and this is how you repay us? You've taken Lizzie's pride and innocence for what? A pint of ale and a few greasy coins? What more do you want to take from us?"

"Hester," I whispered, shocked by the night's events and now this shouting match between the two women.

"No, Lizzie, I've had enough of this snake and her games. I'd rather rot on the street than stay here and become a common whore."

Desperation clawed at my throat, but Hester's defiance lit a small spark of courage within me. "Please, Rosie, you can't do this. We trusted you."

A dark smile twisted Rosie's lips. "Trust? In this world? You're more naïve than I thought." At that, she raised the alarm.

"Night watch! Thieves! They're trying to rob us!"

Her accusation crashed down like a gavel, instantly branding us as criminals. My heart raced as the realisation of Rosie's treachery fully sank in. The heavy footsteps of the night watch echoed down the hallway, drawing closer by the second. Panic surged through me, but there was no time to think. There was no chance the night watch would take the word of poor women like us over someone like Rosie, even if she didn't have them in her pocket, anyway.

The heavy footsteps of the night watch echoed down the hallway, drawing closer by the second. Panic surged through me, but there was no time to think. Instinct kicked in.

"Hester, quick!" I hissed. Just as I was fastening the last button on my dress, something glimmering in my boot caught my eye. My heart leapt with a mix of relief and disbelief as I realised what it was—the neck purse! Even in my drunken haze the night before, I somehow had the presence of mind to tuck it safely in my boot. The precious locket it contained was still with me.

We hardly had a moment to prepare ourselves when the door swung open, admitting the night watchmen. Their rough hands grabbed us, dragging us out of the room with a force that left us breathless. Our desperate pleas of innocence echoed down the corridor but went unheard. Mr Flynn and Rosie claimed they had caught us red-handed, stealing silverware and coins. Our dishevelled appearance and the events of the previous night only made it worse.

As we were dragged through the inn's hallways, I found a small, secret comfort in the neck purse pressing against my ankle. It reminded me of who I was, where I came from, and the strength I carried within me. The city's bustling nightlife drowned out our cries as we were thrust into the cold, unforgiving street. People passed by, indifferent to our plight, as if we were ghosts in their fast-moving lives.

Thrown into a dank, musty cell, Hester and I clung to each other, feeling the weight of our situation pressing down on us. The fear of what lay ahead loomed large.

Hester was the first to break the silence, her voice low yet steady. "Well, Lizzie," she said, her lips twitching into the faintest hint of a bitter smile, "you can say one thing about Rosie—she certainly doesn't do things by halves. Sold us out good and proper, didn't she?"

I managed a hollow laugh, shaking my head. "She didn't even hesitate. All that talk about shelter and work—she never meant a word of it."

Hester squeezed my hand tighter. "No, she didn't. But mark my words, Lizzie, she'll get what's coming to her. People like Rosie always do. You can't be that mean without it catching up to you eventually."

The thought offered little comfort. "What's going to happen to us, Hester?" I whispered, my voice barely audible in the dim light of the cell. "They think we're thieves."

Hester sighed, leaning her head back against the damp wall. "I won't lie to you, love. This won't be easy. They'll probably drag us in front of some pompous judge who'll barely glance at us before deciding our fate. We're poor women, without a man to stand up for us. We'll most likely end up in gaol."

I looked at her; her face was pale in the gloom, but her eyes were sharp and unwavering. "I don't know how you do it, Hester. Stay strong like this."

She snorted softly. "Strong? Don't mistake my big mouth for bravery, Lizzie. I'm terrified, same as you. But I've learned this much—fear's like a storm. If you let it blow through you, it'll tear you apart. You stand firm, even if you're shaking inside, and you hold on to whatever you've got left."

After that, silence hung between us, the only sound the distant drip of water echoing somewhere in the darkness. Despite her words, Hester grasped my hand again, her grip strong and steady.

"Whatever happens," she murmured after a long pause, "we'll face it together. I'm not letting that witch Rosie be the last thing I see before I shuffle off this mortal coil."

Her attempt at humour brought a faint smile to my lips. "Together," I agreed softly, holding on to her words like a lifeline in the growing dark.

Chapter 17

Dublin, Ireland, January 1807

Hester and I languished in the Dublin Bridewell for about a month, awaiting our trial. The legal system faced immense pressure as poverty pushed many to desperate measures for survival, with some unfortunate souls opting for arrest over starvation.

The Bridewell was a prison, used mainly as a holding place for those poor sods like us awaiting trial. It was a place where hope was said to come to die. The air was thick with the stench of unwashed bodies, damp stone, and desperation. Our cell was a dark, cramped space packed with women whose faces told tales of hardship and despair.

The walls were slick with moisture, the straw bedding crawling with vermin, and the single bucket in the corner served both as a toilet and a grim reminder of how far I had fallen. The noise was relentless—babies crying, women arguing, the scrape of footsteps echoing through the stone halls. Each day began with the same thin gruel, tasteless and barely enough to keep hunger at bay, and ended with the same aching exhaustion, my body sore from the endless, mind-numbing labour.

The work in the Bridewell was as punishing as the conditions, and none more so than picking oakum. Each morning, we were marched to the workroom and handed piles of old, tarred ropes, their sticky, foul-smelling fibres clinging to our skin before we even began. The task was simple enough in theory: unravel the tightly bound strands of the rope, separating the fibres to be reused for sealing the seams of ships. But the reality was far from simple.

The ropes were thick and unyielding, and the tar that coated them seeped into every crease of my fingers, leaving them sticky and raw. I used a small iron spike to pry the strands apart, but even with the tool, my hands ached from the constant tension. The tar burned and cracked my skin, and the fibres dug into the open wounds, leaving my fingertips bleeding and throbbing by the end of the day.

The repetitive motion of pulling and twisting the rope made my shoulders and back scream in protest. The hunched position we were forced to sit in left my spine feeling as if it had been locked into place. The smell of the tar was nauseating, clinging to my clothes and hair and so strong that it seemed to seep into my pores.

We had to work in near silence, the room echoing with the sound of rope being pried apart and the occasional curse from someone who had stabbed themselves or snapped a fingernail. My stomach churned as I sat there, my body screaming for rest while my mind struggled to stay focused on the task to avoid attracting the guards' attention.

It was mindless, gruelling labour designed to strip us of our humanity. By the end of the day, my hands were too sore to do much else, my joints stiff and swollen, and my arms shaking from the strain. Yet, it was what we had to endure, day in and day out, with no end in sight.

The worst part wasn't even the pain—it was the sheer monotony of it, the endlessness of the task. It felt as though the ropes themselves were a metaphor for my life in the Bridewell: tangled, sticky, and impossible to fully unravel. Picking oakum wasn't just labour—it was punishment, reminding me with every aching movement that I was at the mercy of a world that viewed me as little more than a tool to be used and discarded.

There was no privacy, no peace, and no sense of self left in this place. At night, when the others finally quietened, I lay awake staring into the darkness, haunted by thoughts of what might come next and clinging to the faintest memory of sunlight and freedom, as if those fragments could keep me from breaking completely. Days went by in a blur, indistinguishable and locked up alongside prostitutes, thieves, a few unfortunate lunatics, and those who were simply there for the crime of being poor.

When our trial day finally arrived, we stood in the courtroom, our fate hanging in the balance. Ever the actress, Rosie wailed dramatically, claiming she had treated us like daughters. With false tears glistening in her eyes, she spun her tale of betrayal, insisting we had tried to rob her. Mr Flynn swore on oath that we had stolen from them, describing us as "thieving whores who took advantage of my kindness."

The magistrate barely took a moment to deliberate.

The sound of the gavel striking echoed through the room, signalling our doom.

I stood motionless in the dock, a ringing buzz in my ears. The magistrate's lips moved, but I heard no sound. Slowly, my hearing cleared, and the words came crashing through with cruel clarity.

"Elizabeth Church and Hester Carr, you have been convicted of offences against the Laws of Ireland. As such, you are each ordered to be transported to His Majesty's Colony of New South Wales for a period of seven years."

My knees buckled; I gripped the handrail tightly to avoid collapsing. Beside me, Hester's tears streamed down her face as the weight of our sentence bore down on us.

Transported ... to New South Wales. I had no idea where it was, only that it felt like the end of the earth.

Seven years—an eternity.

I wanted to go home. I longed for my mother's comforting embrace.

Would I ever see North Carolina again?

Chapter 18

Kilmainham Gaol, Dublin, 1807

As soon as the court's heavy doors closed behind us, the last few months felt like an unbearable weight pressing down on me. In a daze, I followed Hester and the others who had been sentenced that day, flanked by stone-faced constables who showed no signs of pity or remorse. My mind buzzed with shock, a cacophony of regret and fear that drowned out any trace of rational thought.

We were shoved into wooden carts, which were nothing more than cages on wheels. Their iron bars were cold and unforgiving against our skin. Every bump and rattle of the cart sent jolts of shuddering through me, yet the whole experience felt surreal, as though I were trapped in a nightmarish dream from which I could not awaken.

Through the gaps in the bars, I caught fleeting glimpses of the bustling streets of Dublin—so vibrant and full of life, yet entirely indifferent to our grim procession.

Onlookers gathered, their eyes filled with curiosity and scorn. Whispered judgments followed us, but their words barely registered. My world had shrunk down to the confines of that cart, the cold starkness of the journey to Kilmainham Gaol.

Guards strode alongside us, their muskets and batons ready to quash any attempt to escape. They did not regard us as human beings but as cargo to be delivered. The cobblestones jarred beneath the wooden wheels, adding to the sense of disorientation that clouded my thoughts.

Drawing of Kilmainham Gaol, Dublin, Illustrated London News, 30 July 1881

As we approached the gaol, its forbidding silhouette grew larger on the horizon. A numbing clutch of fear tightened around my insides, twisting my stomach into excruciating knots. The massive stone walls soared higher than I'd imagined. The gaol's entrance loomed before us like the mouth of a great beast, ready to swallow us whole. Above the vast stone doorway, grotesque carvings of five monstrous demons emerged, their stone faces contorted in eternal malice. One of the guards told us that these demons symbolised the five most horrendous crimes: murder, rape, theft, treason, and piracy.

The cart came to a grinding halt, and we were hauled out, our chains clinking. My heart hammered in my chest in a rhythm of panic and disbelief, but my body moved on autopilot, propelled by the orders shouted at us by the guards.

We stumbled into the gaol's courtyard, and the great iron doors slammed shut behind us with a resounding finality. The noise echoed through my very bones. Now, inside Kilmainham's oppressive grip, reality settled in with a weight that threatened to crush me. We stood there, an unwilling procession of the damned, awaiting whatever fate this fortress of misery had in store. I'd heard countless horror stories about this place while waiting for trial. Now I was here and had to face my fears.

My mind was still spinning, and I tried to grasp at the remnants of my old life. I clutched at Hester for support, but she looked as dazed as I felt. Every step I took into this pit of despair seemed to take me further away from my past, further away from the person who was Elizabeth Welborn.

We were led to the cells, men one way and women the other. They shoved Hester and me into a cell that already held four women, although I could barely make them out in the dim light. The tiny, dank room was probably intended for two prisoners, but Kilmainham was vastly overcrowded. Much like the Bridewell, it had rough, wet stone walls and a small, barred window that let in a sliver of grey, watery light. There were no beds, only straw on the floor for us to sleep on and a bucket in the corner for our ablutions.

I could feel the walls closing in on me, and I had to fight the urge to scream and rage against the fates that had led me to this place. As the heavy door clanged shut behind us, my knees went weak again, and I pressed my back against the wall, sliding down to the floor. From the floor, it was a bit easier to see our cellmates. I instantly recognised one of these women. Standing under the barred window was the redheaded prostitute who had once warned us away from her patch with a fiery glance and fierce words. Her red curls were filthy and unkempt, but it was her. Hester and I exchanged glances that communicated what we couldn't voice aloud: *Of all people, her?* Surely, though, she wouldn't recognise us?

The redhead looked at us through narrowed eyes, and I knew in that split second that she had placed us. Her expression turned sour, and a look of amusement flickered in her eyes.

"Well, look who's here," she said with contempt in her voice. "I guess you're not so much better than us, after all."

"We are innocent," I began, before snorts from several other women cut my words short.

"Ahh, yes," said another woman, who I could barely make out in the shadows. Another innocent person—the gaols are full of them!"

I could see that pleading my case to them was useless, and I was already bone tired. So, I decided to be civil, and Hester and I introduced ourselves to the group.

"Hannah Murphy," the redhead announced, "and don't you dare think that sharing a cell means I have to like you or be nice to you. I remember you and your mate here, acting all superior like you're better than the rest of us. Well, now you know you're not." The other women in the cell introduced themselves: Bridget Quinn, Maggie Byrne, and the one who had mocked our innocence was Matty Kirk.

The superintendent of the gaol, Dr Trevor, known by all as the "Master of Kilmainham", was an evil man, and his menacing presence stained every aspect of our lives. He was recognised for his harshness and cruelty, showing no care for the inmates. As petty criminals, we were greeted with the utmost contempt, significantly lower than the political prisoners and debtors who shared these walls and could sometimes bribe their way to a bit of comfort. We, the common offenders, were not granted such luxuries.

In winter, the gaol became a place of biting cold and relentless wind. I arrived in the icy grip of January, with snow blanketing the ground in a silent testament to the harshness of this season. The cells offered no sanctuary from the chill, as the windows allowed the howling wind to invade at times. There was no heating of any sort to fend off the freezing temperatures. Each night, we huddled together for warmth, our breath visible in the dim glow of a solitary candle provided for each cell. The bucket had to be emptied every morning, but it was unfortunate if it filled during the day and overflowed. A very basic level of cleaning took place in the rooms every morning before we were sent to work.

The rest of our days were consumed by the drudgery of whatever work we were assigned to that week. I dreaded the laundry—washing blankets especially. In winter, our hands were raw and numb from the merciless cold, and when immersed in cold water, the pain was almost unbearable. I had learned to sew at home, patching and mending as well as making clothes, which was a skill that many others did not have, and so I was often assigned to the sewing room, making shirts and mending the clothing of both prisoners and guards.

The food was beyond the worst I had ever seen, even worse than in the Bridewell, a feat I didn't think was possible. Our mornings began with a now-familiar gruel made of rice and water—milk was a luxury rarely afforded us—to break our fast. It was watery, flavourless, and often laced with grit. Meat was served once daily, but it was frequently rancid, the foul odour curling in my nostrils and threatening to turn my already weak stomach. Potatoes and cabbage were mushy at best and rotten at worst, and bread was so hard it nearly broke my teeth.

Each mealtime became a grim struggle, a battle between hunger and revulsion. Hester, always one to find humour in the bleakest of circumstances, once joked, "This bread could outlast the gaol itself. When they finally let us out, we'll still be chewing the same crusts."

I had laughed then, but the truth was, every bite felt like a small defeat. Hunger won out most days, forcing us to choke down whatever was on offer. Yet even the worst of it couldn't entirely snuff out the faint spark of defiance within us.

"Just remember, Lizzie," Hester would say, poking at her slab of meat with a grimace, "every mouthful gets us one step closer to leaving this godforsaken place. And if this is the best they've got to punish us with, I'd say we've already won."

We were granted one hour a day to walk in the exercise yard, but I was so drained by the cold, the relentless work, and the meagre food that I could scarcely move during these moments. Many women became sick— dysentery, typhus, or anything that resulted from being in overcrowded, unsanitary conditions. The only bright side, if it could be called that, is that for most of the women, their monthly cycles stopped. It was not uncommon for warders to use the women prisoners most disgracefully; the horrors they inflicted on us left scars deeper than any illness. But few of those encounters, or even the consensual ones, resulted in pregnancies, which was fortunate.

This, then, was our existence: a relentless, daily fight for survival in a place devoid of hope, where the spectre of Botany Bay loomed ever more prominent in our thoughts. I wondered if it could be worse than this living hell.

Hester was my lifeline in the gaol, someone who cared about me and gave me solace amidst the cold and despair. Many nights, she would tell us stories—old tales passed down from her grandmother's knee.

"I remember Granny so clearly," she said, "even though she died when I was quite young."

"'*Mo ghráin,*' she'd call me, which means little love in Gaelic. She'd settle me in with her before bed and tell me stories from the olden days about banshees, leprechauns, and other strange beings. Some of those stories would make the hairs on the back of your neck stand up, mind you, and it's a wonder I even slept after some of 'em!"

We all clung to these tales, especially those about clever, courageous women who triumphed over evil. They felt the complete opposite of our lives, offering a glimpse of strength and possibility.

Chapter 19

Kilmainham Gaol, Dublin, 1807

As winter reluctantly yielded to the muted promise of spring and then to the stifling heat of summer, the stench in our cells became almost unbearable. Rats overran the gaol in swarms, and I knew of hungry women who caught and ate them in sheer desperation. Lice and fleas thrived in our unwashed hair and on our filthy bodies, compounding our endless misery.

The days blurred into a monotonous cycle of suffering, with months drifting by and no word of when the next transport ship would arrive to take us away from this hellish place. We merely existed within the oppressive, dank walls of the gaol. Others sought solace in religion and clung to their faith, hoping for divine intervention. But I found no comfort in such thoughts and could not convince myself that any god would punish us like this.

My thoughts often drifted to my mother and family back in Sandy Creek. Their faces and voices grew fainter with each passing day, like distant dreams slipping from my grasp. Kindness seemed a foreign concept here, replaced only by harshness and cruelty. I still had the tiny silver locket tucked in my boot in the little purse Mother had sewn. I hid it in my clothes on the rare occasion we could wash. No one knew about it other than me, not even Hester.

Contact with male prisoners was limited. They had a larger exercise yard than we women did, as there were many more of them than us. I found relief in this segregation; the men frightened me. Well, most of them did.

One day, as I trudged through the dark corridors on laundry duty, a quiet voice behind me said, "How much for a little extra, love?" I turned, my heart jolting in fear that I was about to be attacked, and saw a face I vaguely remembered. It was the man I had seen that night in the pub, before everything went wrong—the man whose touch had sent a shock through me, his face a memory from another life. I managed a wan smile and responded, "No extras here, love," just as I had back then. He grinned, a rare light in the gloom, and touched my waist. There was that shock again!

"I'm sorry to have startled you," he said. "I was just so surprised to see a face I recognised in here." His grin widened into something warmer.

"Fancy that, you're here too," I replied. "What brought you here?" My voice trembled between caution and the strange thrill his presence sparked. His hands lingered a moment too long before he pulled back, his eyes searching mine. "Bad luck and worse decisions," he replied, "and my name is John."

"Elizabeth," I responded, putting my hand in his. "So pleased to meet you, sir!" He took my hand in his, bowed, and kissed it. "Wonderful to make your acquaintance, Elizabeth," he said. I looked at him: fair skin, slightly flushed at the moment and scarred somewhat from the cursed pox, brown hair with a few silvery grey threads at the temples, and those grey eyes. He was not handsome, but certainly attractive, and although I didn't know him from a bar of soap, I felt comfort in his presence.

I also felt something else. I was twenty-one, and John's presence was stirring parts of me into life. After the events of the night we were arrested, my deflowering, so to speak, the idea of lying with a man had repulsed me, but now, it was all I could think about.

We had to part ways that morning, but somehow, John ensured that we met up every day, and our bond grew stronger every day. At first, we just talked, standing in the corridor, with the occasional inmate passing by us. There were a few very salty comments from other men, and John knew we needed to find somewhere to hide. I needed to find somewhere that we could hide so that I could explore these feelings I was having. I had no idea how it could happen here in this hellhole.

However, John was much older and more experienced than I, and he knew his way around the prison better. He knew when the turnkeys would be busy elsewhere, where the overcrowding would benefit us, and where we would have the chance for privacy.

There was a small shed in the yard near the workshop that I could also access while working in the sewing room. Male and female prisoners were not supposed to be in the area at the same time, but during the day, it got very busy, and as we weren't the prisoners that demanded the most attention, the eyes on us were distracted. It was here that John and I arranged to meet. There was a sense of urgency between us, as we knew our time was limited. Sooner or later, a ship would come and take one of us to the other side of the world.

The first time, I walked casually to the shed and slipped inside, where John awaited me. He moved closer to me, putting his hands on my shoulders.

"No turning back now, Lizzie," he whispered, his lips grazing my ear.

My breath caught in my throat. I tilted my head back, meeting his gaze. "I wasn't planning to."

And with that, we gave in to the temptation that had been simmering between us all those weeks. The walls of the rough shed held our secrets, the long kisses, the whispered words, and the heat of a passion neither of us could deny or quench. Every meeting and touch drew us deeper into each other, the rest of that awful world fading away in that small, hidden space.

These meetings were like a moment of peace in the madness of Kilmainham, but they were just brief snippets of time when we could both escape the eyes of the turnkeys. Most of the time, we worked or were locked in our cells. At night, after our "dinner", the women in our cell played cards, talked to each other about their lives, reminisced, told stories, and generally passed the time. We were all lonely, tired, and hungry.

Maggie ended up in prison for stealing lace collars. She had two children and needed the money to buy food for them. Most nights, she cried herself to sleep, worrying about the children and what would have happened to them with her gone. She had applied for them to be transported with her, but the application had been refused, and she could only think that they would have been taken into a workhouse.

Matty had been arrested for stealing a silver watch, although she said she had been set up and was innocent. Bridget had been found guilty of stealing two yards of cloth and a yard of ribbon, which she had planned to sell. Like many others, she had been homeless, living on her wits and trying to stay out of trouble. I had assumed that Hannah had been imprisoned for prostitution. But actually, she had gone down for theft after being accused by one of her customers of stealing money from his wallet. She vehemently denied doing so. As Matty had said, there were many innocent people in gaol.

Hannah was a complex woman. Her sharp tongue made her seem unapproachable at times, but there was a softer side to her—one she revealed in small moments. She was fond of Matty, saying the girl reminded her of her younger sister. In those rare moments when her walls came down, she shared pieces of her story.

"I was born and grew up in Dingle," she began one evening, her voice low but steady. "A little village on the west coast of Ireland. My father was a fisherman, and my mother tended a small garden to help support our family of seven. We didn't have much, but we got by."

She paused, her eyes distant, as if looking back through the years. "When I was fourteen, everything changed. My father and two older brothers went out in a fierce storm. They never came back. Overnight, we went from making do to the brink of ruin. With no men to bring in the catch, there was nothing to sell, nothing to eat, and nothing to pay the rent."

Her voice tightened, but she pressed on. "My mother couldn't keep us all together. We were scattered—some to the few relatives we had who'd take us in, and the youngest two went with my mother to the workhouse. I was old enough to work, so I found a position as a scullery maid in a nearby manor."

Hannah's expression darkened, her hands twisting in her lap. "The family I worked for were English. They hated us Irish and made no secret of it. The mistress of the house was demanding and cruel, but the master ..." She trailed off, her jaw tightening. "The master took liberties. When I resisted, he dismissed me without a reference."

She let out a bitter laugh, the sound harsh in the quiet. "And that, in service, is the kiss of death. No reference, no job. No job, no food."

Her story continued, taking us to Dublin, where she'd tried to find a foothold. "I ended up in a pub, like so many others," she said. "The owner seemed kind at first, but he was just as bad as the master I'd left. He wanted me to 'entertain' some of the wealthier patrons. I resisted, of course, but when it came down to it, it was that or starve on the streets."

Hannah met my gaze, her eyes fierce, as if daring me to judge her. "So I did what I had to. And, God help me, I was good at it. I used the pub as my base, gathered some like-minded girls around me, and built something out of nothing. It wasn't pretty, but it kept us alive."

There was no self-pity in her voice, only a grim acceptance of what her life had become. For all her sharpness, Hannah carried herself with a kind of strength that was hard to ignore. She might not have been an enigma, but she was a survivor through and through. And as she finished her story, I found myself understanding her in a way I hadn't before. Her life had been shaped by choices no one should have to make, and yet she had carved out her own kind of resilience, however imperfect it might have been.

She nodded at me. "And that's when I met you two near my pub, drumming up some business for the night."

The question sprung from my lips before I could even think. "But don't you feel dirty, having strange men do all those things to you?"

Her eyebrows arched as she fixed me with a stare. "Truthfully, at first, yes. After a while, though, you sort of step out of your body and just let them do what they want, as long as they don't hurt you too badly."

Hester had been listening quietly. She tilted her head and gave a low whistle. "Well, Hannah," she said, with a tone of grudging admiration, "you've lived about five lifetimes' worth of trouble, haven't you?"

Hannah smirked, a glimmer in her eyes. "You could say that."

Hester leaned back, arms crossed, her gaze steady. "Can't say I'd have done much different in your shoes. Survival doesn't come with a rulebook, does it?"

"No, it doesn't," Hannah replied, her voice firm but low. "You do what you have to. Not what you want to."

Hester nodded slowly, her lips quirking into a half-smile. "Well, here's to the lot of us then—scraped-up women who've somehow managed to keep our heads above water. You've got plenty of grit in you, Hannah. I dips me lid to you." She doffed a pretend hat in Hannah's direction.

For a moment, the tension eased, and Hannah's smirk softened into something almost resembling gratitude. "Well Hester, coming from you, I'll take that as a compliment."

"Take it how you like," Hester shot back, her eyes gleaming. "But don't let it go to your head!"

Hannah's words stayed with me, and for a moment, I felt I understood her better. Life had dealt her one misfortune after another, and she'd been forced to adapt in ways I couldn't fathom. I still wouldn't trust her as far as I could throw her, though.

The others in the cell were fascinated when I spoke of my life in America. They'd all heard of it, of course, though likely not of my small corner of North Carolina. To them, I might as well have come from the moon. All of them had been born in this southern part of Ireland, and the idea of someone coming from so far away was almost beyond imagining.

I told them about my home, about the forests filled with wild cats and bears, and the alligators I'd seen basking on the banks of the river as we sailed out of Wilmington. Their eyes widened in disbelief. The largest animal they'd ever seen in Ireland was probably a deer, and even that was rare. Bears and wild cats were creatures from stories, not reality, and as for alligators, I'm not sure they even believed me.

"You're making that up," Maggie said with a laugh, though her eyes showed a glimmer of doubt.

"I swear to you, they're real," I replied, holding my hands out to show the size of one we'd seen. "Teeth as long as your fingers and a mouth big enough to swallow you whole."

Hannah rolled her eyes. "If they were that big, you wouldn't have lived to tell the tale."

The others laughed, but I didn't mind. Their disbelief was a welcome distraction from the grim reality of our cell, and for a little while, it felt as though the walls around us weren't so close.

After what seemed like a lifetime in gaol, rumours started circulating through the prison that a ship was being readied for the journey, but it wouldn't be for us women. The *Boyd* would be reserved for men, seeing as there were so many of them crowding Irish prisons at the time. John and I knew that we needed to make the most of the time left to us.

Chapter 20

Kilmainham Gaol, Dublin, 1808

During our times in the shed, John and I shared our stories. John's story was a patchwork of misadventures, scrapes with the law, and a hard-bitten life that mirrored the struggles of so many within Kilmainham's walls.

"My whole name is John Barefoot. It's not my real name, but it'll do for now. Names are strange things, aren't they? They stick to you like burrs, defining you in ways you never asked for. John Barefoot, though ... it feels right for now. It's a name that says I've walked miles without shoes, that I've felt the earth directly beneath me, raw and unfiltered. It's a name that's seen things, been places, survived. And right now, that's exactly who I am. A survivor."

He paused, his grey eyes meeting mine with an intensity that spoke volumes about the life he had lived.

"Things have been better for me than they are now; there is truth to that. I don't always make the right decisions or take the easiest path. I had to leave my home in England after getting into a bit of trouble with the constabulary for helping myself to one of the sheep in a field near my home. Yes, the sheep did belong to someone else, but my family was hungry, and we needed to eat. I escaped in the dead of night and ended up in Dublin, working on a boat on the Liffey."

"In the pub one night after work, I got to chatting with a couple of the others from the boats—Michael Whitethorn and James Smith. I probably shouldn't have; I knew they were rogues and always looked like they were planning something shifty. But loneliness and a need for companionship can make a man overlook many things."

"One night, Michael leaned in close to me—God, he stank of stale beer—and asked me whether I fancied earning a bit of extra coin. I was cautious but greedy and asked him what the catch was. We all know nothing comes for free, especially for those like us. 'No catch, just a little job. Easy work for a man like yourself,'" he mimicked James' accent.

"Ah, Elizabeth, I should have known better. I really should have. But the promise of extra money was too tempting. We arranged to meet later that night by the docks, where they filled me in on the plan. They assured me it would be a bit of smuggling, nothing too dangerous. Just moving some contraband under the cover of darkness."

"The job went smoothly enough. We loaded the haul of whiskey and tobacco into a small boat and set off down the river. The night was cold and clear, the water reflecting the stars above. It was so peaceful out there on the water that I almost forgot my uneasiness, lulled by the rhythmic splash of the oars and the mateship of my new companions. We delivered the goods and collected our money, then split up and went off in different directions, just in case someone was watching."

"We met at the pub that night, toasting our success with pints of ale. That is, of course, where you and I first met. I remember asking you how much it would be for a little extra—but you laughed and said there were no extras here. Maybe if my line had worked, and we'd ended up in bed that night, things would have been different for both of us."

John chuckled softly, and I couldn't help but feel a pang of something—the regret of missed chances, perhaps. He continued, his voice growing more serious.

"Anyway, I took my share of the money and thought I might turn my luck around further. You see, the pubs weren't just for drinking and chatting; they were also for gambling. Dice games, card games, betting on cockfights or ratting contests—you name it, we gambled on it. And I thought I could turn that coin into even more with a bit of extra coin in my pocket."

"At first, it seemed like Lady Luck was smiling at me. I won a few games and got excited when people looked at me like I was something special. But gambling's a game that turns on a halfpenny, Elizabeth. Win or lose, there are always those waiting to take advantage. Before long, I found myself deep in the hole, owing more than I had ever imagined. When you're losing, you keep throwing money at it, thinking your luck will change, and you'll win it all back."

"It wasn't just the locals I owed. No, there were some nasty people involved—men who wouldn't hesitate to break bones or, worse, to get their money back. My winnings turned to losses faster than I could see, and suddenly, I was in debt up to my ears."

John's eyes darkened as he spoke, the pain of those memories clear. "I knew I couldn't pay them back with honest work, but the debts—and the threats—kept mounting. Michael and James approached me again, this time with a bigger scheme. A more dangerous one. Breaking into a merchant's warehouse for silver and spices. The promise of enough money to clear my debts and start anew was too tempting to pass up. Desperation has a way of clouding your judgment."

"First job went off without a hitch. The air was crackling with tension as we crept through the darkened warehouse, but we managed to get what we came for and slipped away into the night. The constables were none the wiser. That time."

John's gaze drifted away, lost in the dark recesses of the shed.

"The pile of money we got from that job bought me some time, but it was a temporary fix. Once you start gambling, it's hard to stop. Michael and James had got more and more cocky as we got away with the smaller jobs and began planning even bigger ones. Each one carried more risk, but the thrill and the need to pay off my debts drove me to join in."

John leaned closer, the urgency in his voice palpable. "Truth is, Elizabeth, I'd been dabbling in petty theft long before the smuggling and gambling. Nicking bread and trinkets from market stalls, distracting shopkeepers while lifting a coin or two. It gave me a taste for it, a confidence that maybe I was a bit slicker than most. That's probably what gave me the courage to try my hand at what they were planning next."

"Michael had bigger plans brewing, involving another gang of men planning a much larger job. I listened to them, but it made me nervous—this was a big step up from what we'd been doing. The stakes were higher, and so were the risks. But in a world where survival is the name of the game, sometimes you have to gamble. And I knew if I wanted to stay alive and pay my debts, I would have to go along with their plans."

Chapter 21

Kilmainham Gaol, Dublin, 1808

"So, Michael had a plan. The new Theatre Royale was opening in Dublin, bringing in a flood of money. According to his informant, this money would be taken to the manager's house in Fortick's Grove, guarded by just one man until it was moved to the bank the next morning."

"Michael rounded up a few others for this job—'a bit of muscle' he called them. The plan was simple: knock on the front door, burst in, overpower the homeowner, Mr Frederick Jones, and rush the upstairs guard to steal the money. He told me they had been watching the house and knew their comings and goings pretty well. There wasn't supposed to be a lot of risk, just an old bloke downstairs and one soldier upstairs. The plan was for five or six of us to do the break-in, so it should have been easy pickings."

"Famous last words. It sounded solid enough, but I've never been known for making the best decisions ... The night of the job arrived, and there was a silence in the air that put my bloody teeth on edge. We hid ourselves in the thick bushes near this enormous house, our hearts pounding in unison as we waited for the perfect moment. Suddenly, a couple of night watchmen appeared, strolling without a care down the street. Panic gripped us like a vice, and we scattered, our plan unravelling in the moonlight. We reconvened later at the pub, where Michael slammed his fist on the table. "Damn," he cursed. "I think they were just on their normal patrol; we should have just waited!" Drunk with excitement and fear, we went over the plan again and resolved to try again the following night."

"This time, fortune seemed to favour us. No night watchmen appeared to thwart our efforts. Just before seven o'clock, Michael approached the grand, black front door, his steps echoing in the foggy night air. James, Patrick Murphy, Gilbert Smith, and I hid in the shadows between the towering columns on the front porch. My god, Elizabeth, you could have cut the air with a knife! Michael knocked, and a voice called out from within. The door creaked open, and Michael lunged forward, striking the man who answered with a sword. A sword! Where the hell had that come from? Nobody ever said anything about a sword in our plans!"

"Anyway, it was too late to go back; so much adrenaline was surging through our veins. Then it was just chaos, and sometimes it's hard for me to even remember what happened next. I saw Michael brandishing the bloodied sword, which set off a chain reaction of bedlam. The sword wasn't sharp, a small mercy in the grand scheme. We had never discussed using weapons in our countless pub sessions. Shouts and screams filled the air as people seemed to materialise from every corner, far more than we had expected."

"Suddenly, there were soldiers there—many more than the one we had planned for, and they moved quickly into the fight. Blood rushed to Michael's face, and he yelled, 'Hurrah, boys!' and struck a tall man repeatedly on the head. Blood spattered everywhere, painting a gruesome scene. Amid the pandemonium, I saw a soldier grappling fiercely with Gilbert. Michael's voice cut through the noise, 'Cut away, boys, kill the soldier!' James, Patrick, and I hesitated; this was never part of the plan. The initial victim, now drenched in his own blood, grabbed a gun and began firing into the room. Luckily for us, it shot pellets, but the soldiers' guns were far more lethal."

John continued to describe the room—Gilbert had collapsed, fatally injured, while Patrick lay lifeless in a pool of blood. The room was a bloody tableau of shattered plans and broken bodies. One of the soldiers then struck Michael over the head with his rifle. Michael crumpled to the floor, motionless. It was over.

He paused for a moment, remembering the chaos, the fear, and the failure. "We hadn't even glimpsed the money, let alone laid hands on it. We were dragged out by the police, as sorry a bunch of no-hopers as you would ever see. I caught a fleeting glimpse of James, his silhouette melting into the darkness. He had either never entered or had managed to slip away amidst the turmoil. In that moment, I wished to hell that I were him."

"The constables pushed and shoved us into a wagon, the cold iron shackles cutting into my wrists. We had taken a gamble and lost, and now we were paying the price. The journey to Kilmainham Gaol seemed never-ending, each jolt of the wagon a cruel reminder of our failure. Finally, we were thrown into a damp cell, and the reality of our situation began to sink in. Gilbert and Patrick had met their end."

"We did have some form of legal representation, but it was pretty sketchy, and we were fighting for our lives. Not only were we facing charges of assault, which would have resulted in a long prison sentence, but we had also injured a police officer. Under the 'Chalking Act', this was punishable by execution. But it was not me, it was Michael, you understand, Elizabeth? He was the one who had brought the sword, hit the officer and plunged us into this nightmare. Our planning had never included using any weapons, so the sword was what lost Gilbert and Patrick their lives and put me here facing death. The more I thought about it, the more resentful I got, so I decided to talk to the authorities."

"I approached the magistrate, my heart pounding like a drum. I laid bare everything I knew. I spoke of Michael's broader gang, his smuggling operations, and every dark secret that might aid them. My confession flowed like a dam finally bursting. I even revealed James' involvement, even though I knew it would lead to his arrest."

The tears poured down John's face as he recounted his tale of betrayal.

"Each word I spoke felt like a knife twisting in the bonds of friendship we once shared. But it was a matter of survival, survival in the treacherous waters that Michael had plunged us into. When I had finished, I felt sick, as though I'd been sucker-punched, but I knew if I was going to salvage something out of this, I had to be alive to do it, and this was the only way I could see to live."

"Our trial was quick, with the evidence against us painting a picture of ruthless criminals who wreaked havoc and violence. Judge Day summed up the proceedings, instructing the jury that "if you have found no evidence to incriminate the defendant Smith, you shall acquit him. As for the other two, if you have any reasonable doubt, you should acquit them. However, if you are completely convinced by the testimony of the witnesses, you must find them guilty." The jury was completely convinced—they returned a guilty verdict for Michael and me. James got off."

In his most resounding voice, John mimicked the pronouncement of the judge: "John Barefoot, Michael Whitethorn, you have been found guilty of armed robbery and attempted murder. You are hereby sentenced to death. Take them down."

"So once again, we found ourselves dragged back to Kilmainham to await our fate. The waiting gnawed at our souls. On the bleak morning of the 24th of December, the heavy door to our cell creaked open, and Michael was taken away. I sat trembling, consumed by a nauseating mix of relief and guilt, as the news was delivered: because of the evidence I had provided to the courts, my sentence had been commuted to transportation to New South Wales for the term of my natural life."

"Elizabeth, the feeling I had then was like nothing I'd ever felt. I had a second chance at living after almost feeling that bloody noose around my neck. I remember dropping onto my knees on that hard, cold floor, with tears streaming down my cheeks. At the same time, the guilt that I would live, and Michael would die hit me so hard in the guts. As if to rub it in, the gaoler told me that Michael had been taken to be hanged that very day. And so, he was. The gallows were set up above the main gate; we could see them silhouetted against the grey sky. As the sleet came pouring down in relentless sheets, Michael was hanged."

As John finished his story, we both felt tears pour down our faces—tears for those who had been lost and for the broken bonds that could never be mended. Our fingers entwined, and we fell into each other's arms for comfort.

COMMISSION INTELLIGENCE.

DUBLIN, WEDNESDAY, DEC. 10.

Michael Whitethorn, *John Barefoot*, and *James Smith*, were put to the bar, who stood indicted for assaulting Edmund O'Reilly, Esq. at Fortick's Grove, in the county of Dublin, against Lord Ellenborough's Act; there were five other counts laid in the indictment.

An application was made to the Court on behalf of the prisoner, Barefoot, that he had given full information to the Magistrates, under the hope of pardon; that they had been received and acted upon, and, therefore, it was hoped that he would be admitted an approver.

Judge Day said, he must have regular documents verified by affidavit to act upon, and gave permission to have such made, if they could be done.

Shortly after, the affidavit of Barefoot was read, the purport of which stated, that having undergone examinations, and given informations before Edward Trevor, Esq. a Magistrate of the county of Dublin, by which indictments have been found against persons now to be tried; that he did so in the hope of pardon, and now prayed to have his trial postponed, or to be admitted an evidence.

Judge Day desired to have the facts ascertained, whether such compacts had been entered into by the Magistracy, and if so, the Court will hold it and pay attention to it.

The affidavit of Edward Trevor, Esq. was then produced, and stated in substance, that previous to the information of prisoner being taken, he was told, that he was not to expect hope, nor was he required to give such under the impression of fear; but that any thing disclosed by him should not be made use of against him; and that if his information should be deemed useful, he would be admitted an approver, but that they were not deemed to be such.

Judge Day said, he would take care that any disclosure of that nature should not be made use of against him.

The trial of those persons was then proceeded upon.

Mr. Greene stated the case on the part of the prosecution. The first witness called was

Edmund O'Reilly, Esq. who deposed, that on the 4th of November last, he was at the house of Mr. Jones, at Fortick's Grove, about seven o'clock in the evening—he was sitting in the front parlour with Lieutenant Hammersley and Dr. Kiernan—Mr. Godfrey was in the hall, and said he heard a noise, and he desired the witness to open the hall-door—witness did so, and went out—he saw nothing, but heard the noise of feet, and retreated into the house—some men immediately rushed in after him—and Whitethorn, one of the prisoners at the bar, cried out, hurra, boys—Whitethorn struck at Dr. Kiernan, and they closed, and Murphy struck at the witness—Whitethorn cried out, cut away, boys, kill the soldier, meaning Lieutenant Hammersley, who was at this time wounded—witness received cuts in two places in the head—witness got a fowling piece, and when presenting it, Kiernan cried out, take care, and witness fired wide—the officer and Kiernan, and Whitethorn and Murphy, continued engaged—witness being then very bloody and weak, with loss of blood, went down stairs for cloths to wipe himself—on coming up stairs, he saw one man dead, and another dying (the names of these two were Murphy and Smith), and two in custody, whom he identified to be the prisoners, Whitethorn and Barefoot.

On his cross-examination, he said he never saw the prisoner Smith until this day; he did not see Barefoot in the parlour, but saw him in the house afterwards in custody; Whitethorn was armed.

Frederick E. Jones, Esq. Manager of the Theatre Royal, was next called, who being sworn, said he supposed he came there to tell the truth, the whole truth, and nothing but the truth—which being acquiesced in, he was proceeding to state a long story, but was told he must confine himself to relevant facts. Witness then stated that he received information from Mr. Justice Godfrey in the month of October last, that his house was to be attacked by a desperate gang who infested that neighbourhood, and who were to attack other houses; witness told Godfrey he wished they would give him the preference, that it might be over, as the Theatre was to open on the 3d of November. Godfrey mentioned to him the day the attack was to be made, and witness brought soldiers to the house in coaches on the evening of the 3d of November, however no attack was made that night, but it was fixed for the next evening, and in consequence of which, about two o'clock on the 4th of November, Godfrey called upon witness at the Theatre where arrangements were made by Godfrey and the witness. The plan proposed by the witness was, that soldiers should be placed in out-houses, and when the robbers entered the house that they should be secured; but Godfrey stated that two gangs were to join in the attack, and as he did not know what numbers they might amount to, he arranged it otherwise. The Guard arrived at Fortick's Grove about half past six o'clock, on the evening of the 4th of November. Godfrey had information that they intended to attack a particular room up stairs, where they conceived there was a quantity of dollars, and as this was supposed to be the place of the greatest danger, and there being a young woman and children to be protected, Godfrey and the witness had some remonstrances, each being extremely desirous of having that station; witness went up stairs with some soldiers; witness had a blunderbuss charged with about 20 slugs, he stood in front, the soldiers behind him, he heard them charging as they stood behind him, and he desired them to desist; at about ten minutes before seven o'clock, he heard the hall-door open, heard O'Reilly exclaim, heard persons rush in, heard a shot fired, came down, saw soldiers firing through the door into the room, the firing ceased, and Mr. O'Reilly came out; one man dropped down and died immediately after. Whitethorn, Barefoot were taken prisoners below stairs;—as a Magistrate witness said he thought it but right to state that Barefoot gave much useful information.

On his cross-examination, he could not say whether or not Barefoot's information went to the Grand Jury.

Patrick Leggat one of Justice Godfrey's Constables, was in the parlour—witness took the prisoner at the bar, Whitethorn, into custody below stairs first—and Barefoot afterwards, both in the house.

Peter Hargan, a Surgeon, knows Mr. O'Reilly, attended him from the 4th of November last—he had three cuts in his head, given by a sword or some instrument not quite sharp.

The Learned Judge charged the Jury with his usual precision, he recapitulated the evidence, and laid down the law—the Indictment was laid under a particular statute, commonly called Lord Ellenborough's Act, which comprehended what was provided against by the statute which was formerly known in this country called the Chalking Act, and which makes the crime with which the prisoners at the bar stand charged a capital Felony—the Jury, his Lordship observed, had no evidence to criminate the prisoner Smith; they would therefore acquit him—of the other two, if they had any reasonable doubt which should weigh in their minds, they would acquit them; if, on the contrary, they were perfectly satisfied as to the testimony of the witnesses, it was his duty to tell them they ought to find them guilty.

Verdict—James Smith, *Not Guilty*. Michael Whitethorn, and John Barefoot, *Guilty*.

Report of John's court case, Belfast Commercial Chronicle, 10 December 1806

Chapter 22

Kilmainham Gaol, Dublin, 1809

Twelve more agonising months dragged by before *Boyd* was ready, and the men in Kilmainham were loaded into wagons to make their way to Cork. There, they would board the ship that would take them to an uncertain fate.

During that time, John and I grew close. We whispered promises to find one another on the other side of this ordeal—whatever that may look like. The thought that someone might be waiting for me at the end of this nightmare provided some comfort during the long days and nights after he left.

John left a hole in my heart as though he had taken it with him. Each passing day without the distraction, or even the possibility, of being with him felt like a lifetime, and without him, I gave in to despair. There were days when I simply sat in the cell and stared at the wall, so black was the fog of sorrow that shrouded me. Hester and Matty tried to comfort me, but they couldn't understand the depth of my bond with John.

Hannah—well, I think Hannah knew exactly what had been going on. She had seen me disappear into the shed and had probably seen John either going in or coming out, but for her own reasons, she had kept quiet.

Maybe it was an unspoken solidarity, or perhaps she had her reasons for maintaining the delicate balance of secrets within these grim walls. By keeping our clandestine meetings to herself, Hannah likely saw a way to hold on to her influence and control, realising that a shared secret could be a valuable currency in a place where trust and power were hard to come by.

Another endless year passed before news finally came for us. *Providence* was waiting in Cork harbour, and the women from Kilmainham would join it tomorrow, bound for exile in a land far from anything we'd ever known.

Being taken from the gaol in Dublin to the docks at Cork was a gruelling ordeal, a final insult added to our already harsh existence. Standing on the precipice of an uncertain fate, I absorbed my last moments on Irish soil with a mixture of dread and resignation.

The guards descended upon us as dawn broke, their voices harsh and unyielding. "Up! Move along!" they barked, yanking us out of our fleeting moments of sleep. The chilly morning air was merciless, biting at our exposed skin as we were herded together, our shackles producing an eerie symphony of clinks and clatters. Many of us were shadows of our former selves—pale, emaciated, and weakened by the relentless grind of imprisonment. The heavy chains seemed unnecessary and an additional layer of cruelty.

The march through Kilmainham's imposing gates was a silent procession of despair. Each step felt weighted with memories of our suffering, and the stone walls bore silent witness to our despair. As we trudged out, the grim guardians of our misery prodded us along, indifferent to our pain, treating us more like livestock than human beings.

Packed tightly into wooden wagons, we set off on our journey to Cork. The rough, bumpy roads jostled us mercilessly, each jolt sending fresh waves of agony through our already aching bodies. Conversations were scarce, our voices little more than murmurs against the backdrop of our shared dread. The beauty of the rolling Irish countryside only served to remind us of all we were leaving behind. The greens and greys of the landscape blurred as tears welled in my eyes. This was the second land that had been snatched away from me.

Upon arriving in Cork, the fresh, salty tang of the sea hit us, mixing with the ever-present stench of unwashed bodies and decay. The docks were alive with the chaotic hustle and bustle, but our eyes were glued to the hulking vessel that awaited us. This was *Providence*, the ship that would take us to an unknown land on the other side of the world.

When we arrived at a makeshift camp near the dock, they stripped us of our ragged gaol clothes and burned them. We were given soap and instructed to wash using the barrels of water provided. A ragged cheer rose from the women at the thought of being clean again. It was like a tiny piece of our humanity was restored.

However, restoring our humanity wasn't a priority for the English authorities. Even amidst the chaos of loading the ship and the last-minute preparations for our voyage, we faced what felt like a final indignity: we were to have our heads shaved. News had spread quickly among us that the authorities intended this to rid us of lice before the long journey to New South Wales. But for many of us, losing our hair felt like a final, unbearable assault on the little dignity we had left.

When the guards approached, brandishing their scissors and razors, a wave of resistance rippled through our ranks. We stood our ground, our shackles producing a collective clink of defiance. The thought of having our already fragile sense of self stripped even further spurred a fierce resolve within us.

"No! This we won't accept!" declared one of the older women, her voice trembling yet resolute. The sentiment was reflected in the determined faces around me—this was a boundary we wouldn't allow them to cross.

The guards were taken aback by the unexpected show of solidarity, and they hesitated. We could see their uncertainty, their glance shifting uneasily between us and their superiors. It was a moment of rebellion that they did not expect, even from what I overheard them call us—"stroppy Irish bitches".

Somehow, our stand against head shaving succeeded. Perhaps it was the sheer intensity of our refusal, or maybe the guards figured it was more hassle than it was worth. Whatever the reason, they backed down and allowed us to wash it instead. While it was a small victory, it was still a victory. It reminded us that even in the bleakest circumstances, we could cling to fragments of our dignity and humanity.

I plunged my hands into the water. It was shockingly cold, and my breath caught in my throat as I sluiced off the worst of the grime on my skin. I worked the soap into a lather, its sharp, medicinal scent cutting through the stale stench that clung to me. After months of filth and despair, the sensation of it slipping between my fingers felt foreign, almost luxurious.

I scrubbed furiously, trying to remove not just the dirt but also the memories of where I had been. The water darkened quickly, carrying away layers of filth that had become a second skin. My scalp tingled as I massaged soap through my hair, the act both soothing and strangely intimate, like reclaiming a part of myself I had forgotten existed.

The other women around me laughed and chatted as they scrubbed, their spirits lifted momentarily by the simple act of being clean again. It was as if the water washed away more than just dirt; it stripped us of the despair we had worn like cloaks. I ran the cloth over my arms, savouring the cool smoothness of my skin beneath the suds. For the first time in what felt like an eternity, I felt lighter and less burdened by the past.

When I finished, I stood back, my skin raw and pink from the scrubbing. The air against my damp skin was cool but invigorating. A clean shift was handed to me, rough but blissfully clean. As I pulled it over my head, I felt almost human again. The smell of soap lingered faintly on my skin, a small but powerful reminder of what it meant to feel whole, even if only for a moment.

Looking around at the other women, their faces scrubbed clean and hair damp, I saw something I hadn't seen in months: a glimmer of hope. It wasn't much, but it was something—a flicker of light amidst the darkness of exile. We had been stripped down to nothing, but we had this small victory for now. And for now, it was enough.

When told to strip off, I carefully hid the little pouch from my mother in a boot. When it became clear that our boots would be destroyed, I had to remove and palm it quickly. As I did this, I met Hannah's eyes, and she slowly raised an eyebrow.

"Well, well, Elizabeth," she said slowly, "what do you have there?"

"Nothing," I said and locked my eyes with hers. "Absolutely nothing."

"We'll see," she said. Another secret she could tuck into her bodice.

Impression of the ship *Providence*. Painting by Thomas Whitcombe (1850), National Maritime Museum, Greenwich.

As we were finally herded onto the ship, the incident at the docks lingered in my mind. I knew that dignity could endure. But just beneath the surface, fear churned like the waters below. The voyage ahead was a journey into the unknown with no guarantees. The thought of what awaited us on the other side gnawed at me, yet there was a glimmer of hope too—the hope that I'd find John, that somehow, against all odds, everything would be all right, and we'd have a future together.

Chapter 23

Cork, Ireland, 1810–1811

Providence set sail from Cork in December 1810 and sailed to Falmouth to load supplies and more soldiers heading to New South Wales. The weather turned foul during the Christmas week, delaying our sailing until the sky cleared and the winds calmed down a little.

We sailed from Falmouth on the 21st of January 1811, under a sky that spat freezing rain and a wind that, while less than it had been, cut straight through to the bone. We watched out the small portholes as England faded from sight, knowing we would likely never set foot on those shores again. Sandy Creek felt as distant as the moon as the ship pulled away. I was twenty-four, and the weight of my fate felt heavy on my shoulders. There were 140 male and 41 female convicts on board, all Irish—or like me, convicted in Ireland, crammed in with 45 guards from the 73rd Regiment and about 55 crewmen, most of whom were Spanish or Indian.

They crammed us into dark cells below deck. We could hear the men—especially the snoring and groaning at night—but we were well separated from them. It seemed like a herd of wild animals were next to us! It was not uncommon for a couple of the women to disappear into the soldier's quarters from time to time, and I couldn't begrudge anyone a little companionship.

With only roughly forty women, we all got to know each other pretty well and heard each other's stories, sometimes several times! Many of us were being sent across the world for simple crimes like stealing cloth. As one of the other women explained, it was pretty easy to steal and easy to sell onwards. Everyone needed it to make clothing. Some of the women, like Hester, had found themselves widowed or orphaned or otherwise homeless and been swept up by the night watchmen for vagrancy—and for some of these women, being exiled was probably the best thing that could have happened to them. There were quite a few women who had been arrested for selling their bodies—all of them talked about how they'd had no other options; it was that or starve or for their children to starve. All of them seemed to hope that they would not have to do such work in the future. While we all formed a bond, being shut up with each other for so long, some were closer than others. Catherine Buckley became a particularly close friend. She was from Cork and just a couple of years older than me. Like me, she'd been convicted for stealing—though her crime was taking a scarlet cloth, and she freely admitted stealing it.

However, the cramped living conditions made it unavoidable for arguments and fights to erupt among the women, and Hannah often found herself at the heart of these disputes. Even when she wasn't actually throwing punches, she'd prod and irritate until tempers flared. To be honest, I reckon she did it for her own amusement. I made a point of keeping my distance from her.

The atmosphere among the women was a strange mix of relief and anxiety. We were glad to be out of the prisons, but the future ahead remained a mystery. Some viewed it as a chance to start anew, to build a better life, and I supposed it could hardly be worse than what we had just left behind. I spent those first few days on the ship, lost in thought and questioning everything. Given the last few years of my life, I'd probably made a terrible mistake leaving Sandy Creek. By now, I would've been married and maybe even had children. I thought about my mother, the secrets she kept, and my father—both of them. When no one was watching, I opened the silver locket and looked again at the picture of my grandmother. She appeared strong; she seemed like she could handle anything.

My life had taken turns I never saw coming, and now I was being hauled off to the ends of the Earth. But one thing kept me going: the thought of seeing John again. In my dreams, he was always there, waiting for me, and I clung to that hope with everything I had. Yet, deep down, I knew I barely knew the man. There was a physical attraction, to be sure, but that may have been due to loneliness and fear.

We'd shared bits and pieces of our lives in Kilmainham, but it wasn't much time at all. Did I really know him well enough to want to spend the rest of my life with him? Or was it just the safest choice I had? In a land full of men, it made sense to have the protection of someone I at least knew a little bit about, even if my feelings weren't clear.

Our close quarters on the ship made it unavoidable that we'd chat with the redcoats, and the uncertainties of Botany Bay filled our conversations. None of them had ever set foot there, and the tales they'd heard from other regiments—about strange creatures and fierce, warrior-like black people—made them uneasy. It brought back memories of my childhood experiences with black people back home. Though my father never owned slaves, several of my uncles did, and I'd seen plenty of them toiling in the cotton and tobacco fields. I couldn't help but wonder if they were the same in this new land.

After that harrowing voyage to Ireland just a few years earlier—though it felt like a lifetime—I dreaded the prospect of facing the open ocean once more. The thought of being confined to the ship's cramped, dimly lit quarters for such a long journey filled me with unease. Memories of that earlier crossing, with its relentless waves and ceaseless motion, haunted me. It wasn't just the physical discomfort I remembered, but the sense of isolation, of being cut off from the world, adrift in a vast, indifferent sea.

We were promised brief respites—we were allowed on deck a couple of times a day, weather permitting—but those moments of freedom felt far too short. The journey ahead was daunting, stretching across some of the largest, most unforgiving oceans on Earth. I knew we would be at the mercy of the elements, with nothing but endless water and sky in every direction, and the thought of it filled me with a deep, gnawing dread.

Yet, there was no choice. I steeled myself for the long months ahead, trying to find solace in the little things—the feel of the wind on my face during those precious moments on deck, the occasional glimpse of a distant coastline, or the sight of a bird soaring high above us, reminding me that land still existed somewhere beyond the horizon. But the ocean was vast, and the voyage seemed endless, each day blending into the next as we sailed ever farther from everything I had ever known.

The journey was as gruelling as I had feared. After parting ways with HMS *Narcissus* at Tenerife—likely there to guard against Spanish attacks—we pressed on across the North Atlantic toward Rio de Janeiro, Brazil. The crossing took nearly nine weeks, and I was seasick the whole time. Fortunately, the weather turned warm during the last four weeks, and the seas calmed. Time spent outside the cabin became my lifeline. On deck, the sun kissed my face, the breeze tangled in my hair, and for a brief moment, I could fill my lungs with fresh air instead of the suffocating stench below decks—where the foul odour of filthy bodies, overflowing buckets, and seasick souls clung to everything. Those moments of respite, as brief as they were, felt like a taste of heaven amid our floating prison.

We lingered for three weeks in the harbour at Rio before setting off on the final leg of our journey—around the southern tip of Africa and on to New South Wales. The last twelve weeks at sea were brutal. The ocean raged for ten of those weeks, and I spent most of my days retching until there was nothing left in me. We lost two of the women about a month out of Rio—Mary Driscoll succumbed to consumption, and poor Matty Kirk passed away from dropsy. I know that four of the men also died earlier in the voyage, including Daniel Kelly, who was quite young but had to have his leg amputated before we set off on the journey. His leg went bad, and he suffered from a fever so high that he ultimately succumbed to it.

We finally arrived at Port Jackson in early July, after a journey of nearly seven months since leaving Ireland. A cool breeze swept across the harbour as we blinked in the bright sunlight, our first glimpse of this new land. Even though we were told it was winter here, it felt more like the mild winters of Sandy Creek than the harsh ones in Ireland.

The ship sailed between sandstone cliffs towering on either side of the entrance to the harbour, a breathtaking expanse of calm, sparkling blue water. Its sheer size was quite astonishing, with little coves and inlets everywhere surrounded by thick bush. The blues and greys of the trees were unlike anything I had seen before and seemed to shimmer in the golden sunlight.

I gripped the railing tightly, my eyes scanning the landscape. Nothing like Dublin, nothing like Wilmington, the settlement at Sydney Cove came into view. The town comprised a small cluster of wooden buildings, a handful of more substantial stone structures, and scattered tents. Smoke from cooking fires curled into the sky, and we could hear faint sounds of life from the tiny figures amongst the buildings.

Longboats and smaller vessels moved across the harbour, going about their business, their occupants pausing to glance up at the newly arrived convict ship. Soldiers stood watch on the docks, their red coats striking against the landscape, while settlers and convicts in chains worked on the shoreline, unloading goods and repairing boats.

Hester stood beside me. Her expression was hard to read—there was anticipation there as well as wariness. "Doesn't look like much, does it?" she muttered, eyes scanning the settlement.

"It's rough," I admitted. "But it's better than staying on the ship."

Catherine nodded quickly, her shawl pulled tightly around her shoulders. "Aye, anything's better than that ship. Even this."

Hester snorted, though there was no malice in it. "We'll see about that soon enough. It's one thing to look at it from up here and another to live it."

Catherine leaned closer, her voice low. "We'll stick together, won't we? You and me, Lizzie—and you too, Hester."

Her words warmed me more than I expected. I hadn't known Catherine long, but her kindness had been steady, a balm in the chaos of the voyage.

Hester grinned. "Of course, we'll stick together. Can't have you two wandering off and getting into trouble."

As the anchor dropped and the ship creaked to a halt, I felt a knot tighten in my stomach. We had arrived, and the next chapter of my life was about to begin, and I had no idea what it would hold.

Before anyone could leave the ship, we were examined to check our health. This was like the final straw in making us feel less than human, especially when they ordered us to open our mouths to inspect our teeth. The doctor barked instructions, poking and prodding us to see who was fit for work straight away and who might need immediate attention.

Afterwards, we were questioned about the voyage—whether we'd been beaten, mistreated, or denied food or water. Hester nudged me and muttered under her breath, "Like they care about us now. They just don't want the captain to be in any trouble." I stood silently on the deck, the sun beating down on my face, waiting for my turn.

Finally, it was time to disembark. The men were the first to leave the ship and rowed to shore in longboats; then, we women were loaded on and headed for dry land. The dock bustled with activity. Soldiers and overseers shouted orders, workers unloaded crates, and convicts shuffled along, their chains clanking as they moved. A small group of women in coarse clothing watched us with a mixture of curiosity and pity.

Once on the dock, they lined us up like livestock for selection. The wealthier settlers, government officials, and soldiers—those who had been assigned a servant—moved down the line, scrutinising us as if we were cattle at a market. Their sharp eyes darted over every face and frame, assessing who might suit their needs. Many of the women, including Hannah, were selected quickly.

She tossed her red curls over her shoulder and shot me a spiteful look, her smug expression a silent declaration that she had triumphed over me yet again. Even in our shared misery, there was clearly still a place for minor rivalries and petty victories.

As Hannah adjusted her bonnet and prepared to leave with her new master, she leaned in close to me, her green eyes gleaming with malice.

"Well, Lizzie," she drawled, imitating my accent, "I reckon we'll bump into each other again soon enough. This colony isn't big enough to keep us apart for too long."

She paused for a moment, her gaze narrowing as if to savour what came next. "And good luck finding your precious John. I'll bet he's found someone else to share his bed by now. But cheer up love, there are plenty of other men out there that I'm sure will be glad of someone to warm their bed." She waved expansively at the men in the nearest chain gang. "Otherwise, you know the quickest way to make some coin." At that, she gave me a lewd wink and cackled as though it was the funniest joke ever.

I felt my heart lurch at her words, even though I knew she was as much in the dark as I was about John's whereabouts.

My heart raced as I stood there, watching names being called and men and women led away, one by one. Each selection felt like a heavy stone, adding to the weight of uncertainty in my chest. I didn't want to be tied to just anyone. I wanted to be tied to John. My gaze flicked to the faces of those making their choices, but no one stopped before Hester or me. No one called either of our names. It seemed we would stay together for now at least, and for this, I was grateful.

We women were bound for a place called Parramatta, to the Female Factory. Standing on that dock, I couldn't stop thinking of John. Would he know I was here? Would we find each other again?

With the shackles off, we staggered down a gangplank from the dock to a small boat. The new world around me overwhelmed my senses. The sights, sounds, and smells of this strange place flooded my mind, leaving me feeling both lost and curiously alive.

Chapter 24

Parramatta, New South Wales, 1811

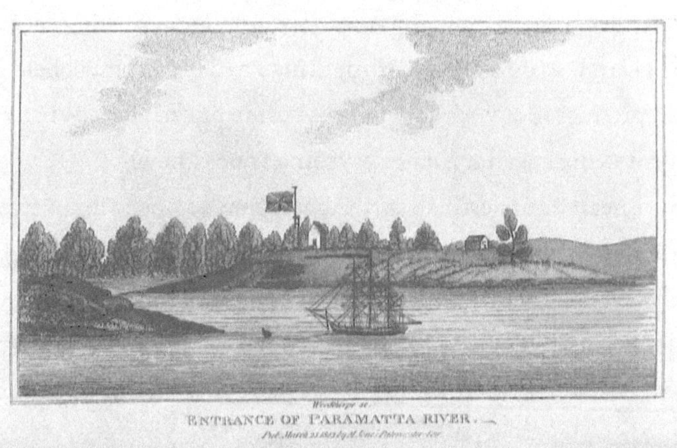

Entrance of the Parramatta River, New South Wales from George Barrington,
The History of New South Wales (London, 1802). British Library shelfmark 9781.c.12.

Gliding steadily along the Parramatta River, the small boat advanced with each pull of the oars, leading us deeper into this unfamiliar land. The sky above was a rich, intense blue, and the sun bathed the river in light, making the surface shimmer as if it were dotted with diamonds. The air was crisp, carrying a coolness far gentler than the biting winters I had endured in Ireland. The landscape felt so alien compared to what I had grown up with, and my heart sank at the thought of how far away from my family I was now.

The landscape unfolded around us as we rowed upstream, revealing a foreign and mesmerising world. Fingers of land jutted into the river, dotted with clusters of strange, twisted trees and patches of wild, untamed grass. Occasionally, we passed by small coves and inlets where the water lapped softly against the shoreline. The scent of wood smoke drifted towards us, mingling with the briny smell of the river—a combination that overwhelmed my senses. The smoke wafted from small fires along the banks, tended by unseen hands. I wondered who they were—other convicts? Free settlers? Perhaps the native people I had heard whispers of but hadn't yet seen.

It was beautiful in a raw, untamed way, stirring something deep inside me. This land, so different from anything I had ever known, held a kind of wild promise. But with that promise came uncertainty. What kind of life awaited me here, far from everything I once knew?

As we neared our destination, the boat rounded a bend in the river, and there it was—the Parramatta Gaol, rising from the water's edge. Above it was the Female Factory. This would be our new home, where we would work, spinning and weaving wool. The sight of it made my stomach clench with anxiety, but I swallowed my fear. I had survived the voyage and the trials before that—I would survive this, too.

View of Parramatta – with Parramatta Gaol and the Female Factory on the far right. Painting by J. Lycett (c.1820), Mitchell Library, State Library of New South Wales.

We arrived late in the day, just as the sun began its slow descent towards the horizon, casting a golden light over the landscape, the strange trees almost grey. As the boat gently bumped against the shore, they herded us off, our legs unsteady after so long at sea. As we made our way to the factory, the sandstone walls loomed above us, cold and imposing. Yet there was a strange comfort in being on solid ground, away from the endless rocking of the ship, safe from the elements and whatever wild beasts might lurk beyond the riverbanks.

Stepping through the doors of the Female Factory, I forced myself to stay calm. The building was dark and crowded, filled with the hum of women's voices and the clatter of work. It was far from welcoming, but it was much better than being locked up on the ship. I could almost taste the fresh air, and the sunshine felt wonderful when we could get out of the building; it would be a place to gather my strength. As I took in my surroundings, one thought, one hope, kept me moving forward: John.

Somewhere in this strange land, he was here, and he would find me. That hope was all I had, and I clung to it with everything I had left. Using my mother's locket as a talisman, every night I would take it out from its safe hiding place and touch it, thinking of my mother and family, and hoping that John would find me.

I hadn't seen John in what felt like a lifetime, but I knew he was out there somewhere, hopefully as desperate to find me as I was to be found. Of course, he may have already found someone and been married—his ship, *Boyd*, had landed here almost two years ago—two years for him to have started a new life here, a new life that might not have included the young American woman he met in gaol in Ireland. But I clung to the hope that he would walk through the door and pull me into his arms. The days were long and tiring, a blur of relentless work and restless nights. But it was not all work, and we were not in a gaol, and for that, I whispered my thanks to the stars that I could see through my window. The factory was overcrowded—far too many women were sleeping and living together in too small a space, but it was nothing like the hell holes of the Bridewell or Kilmainham Gaol.

Every week, people came from the surrounding farms to claim women to take with them as domestic servants, or sometimes soldiers would choose wives from amongst us. Just days after our arrival, a farmer named James Ware claimed Hester to work on his farm in Windsor.

The night before she left, we sat together on the rough wooden floor of the dormitory, speaking in low voices while the other women slept.

She reached out and took my hand in hers. "It feels like so many years have gone by since I first found you sobbing, alone in that alleyway in Dublin. We've shared some good times and a lot more tough ones, Lizzie," she continued, her voice low and steady, "and it looks like this is where we go our separate ways. But don't you dare think I'm leaving you behind for good. You're like the daughter I never had, *mo ghráin*, and I'll do my best to see you whenever I can."

I nodded, my throat tight with emotion. "You've been my lifeline, Hester. I don't know what I'd have done without you."

She reached out and patted my hand, her grip warm and firm. "You'll manage, love. You've got more fight in you than you realise. Keep your wits about you, and don't let anyone take that fire away."

"Hester ..." I hesitated, unsure of how to voice the fear that had been gnawing at me. "What if John doesn't come? What if ... what if he's already moved on?"

Her eyes softened, and for a moment, the tough exterior she always wore seemed to crack. "Then you make your own way, Lizzie. But if he's half the man you believe him to be, he'll come for you. And if he doesn't, well ... there's more to life than pinning it all on one man."

After that, we sat in silence, listening to the muffled sounds of the night outside.

The following day, I watched as she was led away, her back straight and her head high, ready to face whatever lay ahead.

I was terrified that someone would choose me before John could find me, that I'd be assigned to a stranger, and our chance would be gone forever. But just two weeks after arriving in Parramatta, I heard a voice call my name.

The sound stopped me cold. It was so unexpected, so out of place amidst the drudgery of the factory, that I froze. My heart pounded as I turned toward the door, barely daring to hope. And there he was—John. Solid and real, standing there as though he'd stepped straight out of my dreams. His eyes were wide with disbelief, and then, as a wave of relief washed over him, his whole face softened.

The wool I had been holding slipped from my hands, and before I even realised it, my legs were moving. Tears blurred my vision as I ran to him, and when I reached him, I threw myself into his arms. I clung to him as though I could root myself there and never let go. For that moment, everything else faded—the factory, the strange new land, all the hardships we had endured. There was only John, his arms around me, holding me as if he never wanted to let go.

"We have to get married," he whispered, his voice rough with urgency and emotion. "We must do it right away before anything else can tear us apart."

I pulled back just enough to look into his eyes, my tears spilling over as I nodded. He was right. We had both lost too much, suffered too much, and I couldn't bear the thought of losing him again.

"How did you find me?" I asked, my voice trembling.

He smiled faintly. "Well," he began, "I've been something of a pest around here ever since I landed. Every ship that's come in, I've been asking questions—who's on it, where they're from, and whether there were any women from Ireland."

He paused, taking a deep breath before continuing. "*Indispensable* came just after *Boyd*, but I knew all the women on board had been tried in England. Then *Ann* arrived the following year, but that was all men.

Same with *Canada*. *Indian* brought more men, but then I heard from some soldiers on board that the next ship would have women prisoners from Ireland. When *Providence* arrived, I knew you had to be on it. I tried to get to the docks to see for myself, but they wouldn't give me leave. So, I've been haunting this place, hoping, praying you hadn't been chosen or sent elsewhere, that somehow, you'd end up here."

His words caught in his throat, and I could see how much the search had weighed on him. He'd carried that hope and fear every day since we were torn apart, never letting go, never giving up.

That very day, John applied for permission for us to marry, and it was granted almost immediately. Governor Lachlan Macquarie encouraged convicts like us to marry, and this would mean I'd be assigned to John until I finished my sentence.

The banns were read at St John's Church in Parramatta under the stern gaze of the Reverend Samuel Marsden, and for three long Sundays, we waited. But this time, we weren't waiting in uncertainty or fear.

That night, as I lay on the straw that was my bed, listening to the gentle murmur of the river through the open window, I felt a glimmer of hope that I hadn't dared to feel in what seemed like years. The fear and uncertainty that had weighed me down for so long seemed to lift just a little. I was in a new world, facing challenges I couldn't imagine, but I would have John by my side. Together, we would face whatever came our way.

Chapter 25

Parramatta, New South Wales, 1811

The Reverend Samuel Marsden thundered from his pulpit every Sunday, and as convicts in the Female Factory, we were required to attend. I sat there as I had sat in the Primitive Baptist Church at Sandy Creek and listened to another angry male voice go on and on about sin, primarily women's sins. The air in the chapel was thick with the smell of sweat and unwashed bodies. During summer, after it rained, the humidity became almost unbearable, and being inside in such close quarters with so many others was a trial in itself. Listening to the Reverend Marsden's booming voice haranguing us was a further trial. His words rang out from the pulpit, as unyielding as the wooden benches on which we squirmed uncomfortably, and his sermons were always variations on his favourite themes: obedience, morality, hard work, the role of women and civil order. We convicts were to be left in no doubt of our place in this society.

"Let no man or woman here believe they are beyond the reach of God's judgment!" he thundered, his piercing eyes scanning the room. "Drunkenness, immorality, idleness—these are the tools of the devil, and those who wield them will burn in eternal fire unless they repent!"

I sat stiffly in the pew, my hands clenched in my lap, my lips pursed. The reverend's words felt like stones pelting my skin, each one sharper than the last. My thoughts drifted to John. In a few weeks, we would stand in this very chapel to be married, and the thought filled me with nervous thoughts. Was I worthy of such a fresh start? Marsden's words planted a seed of doubt in my heart.

As he turned to the subject of women's virtue, I felt my chest tighten.

"A virtuous woman," Marsden continued, his voice rising to a near roar, "is the foundation of a godly home. But women who stray into sin—who allow their virtue to be corrupted—are no better than the serpent in Eden, leading men to ruin and their families to destruction."

I felt my cheeks flush, heat rising to my face. I cast a furtive glance around the room, my shame twisting into discomfort. Did they all know that I was not virtuous? Did they see me and think of me as one of the fallen women Marsden spoke of? While I had managed to throw off many of the church's teachings from my childhood, it was hard to ignore the weight of Marsden's fiery words. The morality instilled in me during long Baptist sermons back in North Carolina still clung stubbornly, like burrs on my skin. The warnings of hellfire and the insistence on virtue as a woman's greatest currency had been drilled into me from the time I could first walk. Even now, with years and oceans between me and those teachings, their shadow loomed large.

While I had learned to question them, to see the cracks in the harsh rules that had shaped my early years, some part of me—profound and inescapable—still felt the sting of shame when I fell short of those ideals. Marsden's words stirred up memories I thought I had buried: the clatter of hymnals, my mother's whispered prayers for me to be "good", and the stern words from the pastor whenever a girl in the congregation was thought to have strayed.

In this harsh colony, survival often left little room for morality, but that did not silence the voice in my head that whispered accusations when I tried to sleep. Marsden's booming sermon had only amplified it, making me wonder if I could ever truly escape the judgment—of others, of myself, or a God I wasn't even sure I still believed in.

My gaze flicked to John, standing tall near the back of the chapel. His face was steady, his expression unreadable as he listened to Marsden's sermon. I envied his calm; he seemed unaffected by the heavy judgments pouring down from the pulpit. I wondered if he ever had doubts about marrying me.

When the service finally ended, the congregation began to shuffle out, the silence heavy after the force of the clergyman's words.

I sat on the low stone wall outside the chapel, staring at my hands. The congregation had dispersed, and the quiet buzz of conversation had faded into the distance. My chest felt tight, as if Marsden's words were still ringing inside me, bouncing off every corner of my mind.

"Lizzie?"

I looked up to see John standing nearby, his head tilted as he studied me. I nodded slightly but didn't say a word. He hesitated momentarily before stepping closer and easing himself down beside me.

"You're quiet," he said softly.

I nodded again, my gaze dropping back to my lap. "His words ... they stay with you, don't they? Like they're carved into stone."

John leaned forward, resting his elbows on his knees. "He does have a way of making you feel like you've already been sentenced before the judge even arrives."

I let out a shaky breath. "It's not just his words, John. It's what they bring back. Back home, in the Baptist Church, it was the same thing. Over and over, week after week—women's virtue, sin, judgment. My mother used to pray over me, beg God to keep me 'pure.'" My throat tightened, but I pushed on. "And now look at me. I wonder what she'd think if she knew."

John turned to me, his brow knitted in concern. "Elizabeth, what happened to you wasn't your fault. You did what you had to do to survive. If your mother knew the whole truth, she'd get it. I get it."

I shook my head, my voice trembling. "But do you? Do you really? Because sometimes I don't even understand myself. Those sermons—they carved something deep into me, John. That no matter how hard you try, if you fall, you're broken forever. And Marsden ... he made me feel it all over again."

John reached out and covered my hands with his own, the warmth of his touch steadying me. "You're not broken, Lizzie. You're here. You've made it through things most people couldn't even imagine. And you're starting over, with me. That's what matters now."

I looked at him, my chest aching with doubt. "But what if those words never leave me, John? What if I can't shake them? What if I can't shake the shame?"

He held my gaze, his voice low and sure. "Then I'll remind you, every day if I have to, that you're worth more than Marsden's sermons or the judgment of men who've never lived your life. You're strong, Lizzie. You've proven it over and over. And together, we'll make something better than anything those preachers ever dreamed of."

I felt a tear slip down my cheek before I could stop it, but it didn't feel like sadness—it felt like hope, fragile and flickering. I squeezed his hand, my voice barely a whisper. "You're good to me."

John smiled, faint but warm. "You're worth it. Remember, I haven't exactly lived a blameless life myself."

A laugh escaped my lips, soft but genuine, breaking through the tightness in my chest. The weight of Marsden's words was still there, but sitting beside John, his hand in mine, I felt like I could breathe again.

Reverend Marsden and Governor Macquarie didn't always see eye to eye, but they marched in lockstep when it came to marriage. Marriage, to them, was not about love or companionship; it was about control, about maintaining order in a colony they were desperate to civilise.

I'd heard Marsden read Governor Macquarie's proclamation enough times to recite it myself. It was clear and uncompromising: couples living together without the sanctity of marriage were deemed immoral, a stain on the society Macquarie envisioned. Children born out of wedlock were seen as a mark of shame, and the proclamation made it plain that this wouldn't be tolerated in the new world they were trying to build.

Macquarie and Marsden wanted us bound by vows, claiming it was for our own good. But we all knew what it was really about—control. Marriage, in their eyes, was a tool to tame the unruly and impose the "proper" British sense of decency on a colony filled with convicts, emancipated prisoners, and the poor. It didn't matter that many of us came from lives where marriage had been an impossible luxury. Here, it was a requirement, not a choice.

Marriage offered certain protections, of course. A married couple might be granted land or find favour with the authorities. It legitimised children and kept the church and the law off your back. But for most of us, it wasn't a matter of romance. It was survival.

I wasn't naive enough to think my wedding day would be some fairytale. On the 17th of August 1811, just six weeks after I first set foot in this strange and beautiful land, John and I stood before Reverend Samuel Marsden in St John's Church in Parramatta.

I looked at John as we said our vows, his face steady and sure. For a moment, I let myself hope. Maybe this wasn't just about survival. Maybe, somehow, we could make something good out of this. Marsden's booming voice echoed in the church, binding us together in words I barely remembered. The weight of his judgment pressed on my shoulders, but John's hand in mine was warm and steady.

For all their proclamations and sermons, Macquarie and Marsden didn't understand what marriage meant to people like us. It wasn't about upholding some moral standard or creating a perfect society. It was about holding on to each other in a world that didn't give second chances.

At home, Mother would have spent weeks making a new dress for this occasion, but there was no Mother here, and I had no coin to buy cloth. I thought wistfully about the pretty blue dress that had been made for me all those years ago in Wilmington. How lovely it would have been to have something like that now. However, from the factory, we managed to procure a few little ribbons and bows to decorate my dress, and I picked native flowers from the bush as a bouquet. The vibrant colours of the bottlebrushes did much to make the day cheerful and bright.

John gave me a small silver chain, which meant that the little silver locket that my mother gave me could finally come out of safekeeping and be shown off. To be able to wear it on my wedding day was a tiny reminder of her. As I fastened the delicate chain around my neck, the locket rested warmly against my skin, a tangible link to the past and the loved ones who had once surrounded me.

My heart pounded with happiness and nervous excitement as I walked down the aisle, my hand trembling slightly in Catherine's steady grip. My joy grew when I spied Hester's familiar face in the front of the church. Her gaze softened as it met mine, and a broad smile lit her face. She had been given leave to come to my wedding.

John stood at the end of the aisle, slightly taller than me. His face was slightly flushed with anticipation, and his dark brown hair was combed down into an orderly style—different from his usual wind-tousled look! I walked quickly to meet him in front of the Reverend.

I couldn't help but smile, remembering how I teased my sisters for marrying "old men". How naïve I had been! Now, here I was at twenty-five, standing beside John, who, at thirty-seven, didn't seem old at all. When our eyes met, I felt a warmth that melted away any lingering doubts. We had waited so long for this moment. While it wasn't the fiery love my mother had described with Jacob Cody, it was steady and comforting. There was passion there, for sure, and maybe that would grow into love when we knew each other a bit better, but for now, it was enough. It was safety and protection in a place where women had little of either. This colony was harsh, with far too many men and far too few women, and I didn't want to find myself at the mercy of a stranger or, worse, forced into servitude.

"Ready, Lizzie?" John's voice was a whisper, his rough hand squeezing mine.

"More than ever," I whispered back, my smile widening.

Catherine stood by my side, her presence a comforting reminder of the friendship that had carried me through so many dark days. At John's side was Benjamin Jacobs, who had come out on *Royal Admiral* years ago and had worked alongside John as a gardener in Windsor.

Reverend Marsden began the ceremony in stern tones that commanded respect. "Dearly beloved," he intoned, his voice resonating within the wooden walls of the church. "We gather here today to witness the union of John and Elizabeth as they pledge their commitment and duty to one another in this new home."

As we exchanged vows, I could feel the weight of each promise settle into place, binding us together in a way that was both profoundly new and strangely comforting. "I, Elizabeth, take you, John, to be my wedded husband," I said, my voice steady despite the tears threatening to fall. "To have and to hold, from this day forward, for better or worse, for richer or poorer, in sickness and health, till death do us part."

John's response mirrored my commitment, his eyes never leaving mine. "I, John, take you, Elizabeth, to be my wedded wife," he declared, his voice rich with emotion. "To have and to hold from this day forward, for better or worse, for richer or poorer, in sickness and health, till death do us part."

Reverend Marsden's eyes, sharp and unyielding, surveyed us both as if to gauge the sincerity of our vows. His presence lent gravity to the occasion, making every word we spoke feel etched in stone.

"These vows are not to be taken lightly," he admonished, his voice a stern reminder of our commitment. "In this land, fraught with trials and tribulations, you will need the strength of these promises to sustain you."

As he pronounced us husband and wife, a ragged cheer rose from the small group of other convicts who had become an unlikely family in this new world. The happiness on their faces brought warmth to the chilly room, and I felt a surge of gratitude for their support.

After the ceremony, as the small group of us gathered outside St John's, Hester's eyes fell on the locket resting against my dress. Her brows arched, and a wry smile tugged at her lips.

"Well, well," she said, stepping closer. "Would you look at that? I thought I'd never see that locket again. You had it tucked away all this time, didn't you?"

I nodded, my fingers brushing the delicate silver. "I didn't dare wear it before. It was the one thing I had left from my mother. I couldn't risk losing it. I didn't realise that you knew I had it."

Hester let out a soft chuckle, shaking her head. "I used to see you take it out sometimes in our room above the pub, when you thought I wasn't watching. I knew it was special, and that you would tell me about it if you needed to. And here it is, and on your wedding day, no less."

Her voice turned gentler as her fingers brushed the locket lightly. "Your mother would've been proud to see you wearing this today. She'd know you haven't forgotten her, even in this strange land."

I swallowed hard, her words stirring something deep in my chest. "It's the only piece of her I've got," I said softly. "And now, it feels like she's here, just a little."

Hester gave a short nod, her gaze steady. "She's here, all right. She's in you, Lizzie. That locket's just a reminder."

Her words settled into me, warm and sure, as the locket rested against my skin. For a moment, I saw my mother's face clearly in my mind, felt her presence as though she were standing beside me. It wasn't much, but it was enough to hold onto.

Hester patted my shoulder, her touch firm but kind. "She'd be proud of you, Lizzie. Don't ever doubt it."

Catherine emerged from the shadows of the chapel and gave me a hug of congratulations. She looked a little flushed, and the words tripped out of her mouth. "There's someone I want you to meet."

I frowned slightly, my curiosity prickling as she beckoned me to follow her a few paces away from the others. Hester trailed behind us; her brow arched in silent interest.

Catherine turned and gestured toward a man who had also just emerged from the chapel. He was tall, with a steady, confident stance, his dark hair swept back from his face. He had the look of someone who had worked hard but carried himself with quiet assurance.

"This is John Connor," Catherine said, her voice soft but filled with something that made my heart pause. "He works at the Lumber Yard. We ... well, we've been seeing each other for a little while now."

"It's good to meet you, John," I said, offering him a smile. "Catherine's been a rock for me. I hope you know how lucky you are."

He grinned, a flash of humour in his eyes. "Oh, I do. Don't let her fool you into thinking otherwise."

Hester, standing slightly behind me, let out a low chuckle. "Well, this is a turn, isn't it? Catherine's gone and found herself a man. You sure you know what you're getting into, Connor?"

John laughed, glancing at Catherine with a fondness that was impossible to miss. "I think I've got a fair idea."

Catherine glanced at me, her eyes shining. "We're hoping to marry as soon as we can get permission."

I reached out my hand and squeezed hers. "I'm so very happy for you, Catherine; he seems like a good man."

That evening, as darkness settled over Parramatta, we huddled around a small fire outside our new home, John's arm wrapped securely around my shoulders. The vibrant flames danced against the backdrop of the vast, open sky, casting flickering shadows on the ground. The native wildlife seemed to join in our celebration, their calls and movements adding a symphony of life to the night.

"What a day it's been," John murmured, his voice filled with wonder and exhaustion.

"Yes," I agreed, leaning into him. "It feels like a dream, one that's just beginning."

His hand found mine, rough but comforting, and we sat in companionable silence, watching the stars emerge one by one. This land, so different from everything we had ever known, was beginning to feel like a place where we could truly start anew. There were many challenges, but together, we believed we could face them.

Nº 369 } John Bedford ______ of the Parish St John Parramatta & Elizabeth Church of P. ______, — were Married in this Church by Banns ______ this Seventeenth Day of August in the Year One Thousand eighty Hundred and eleven. By me Samuel Marsden ______ This Marriage was solemnized between Us { John Bedford x his mark / Eliz.th Church her x mark in the Presence of { Benjamin Jacobs his mark x / Catherine Buckley her mark x

John and Elizabeth's marriage entry in the St John's Parish Register, Sydney, 1811

Our first home as a married couple was a humble slab-and-bark hut, and I couldn't help but reminisce about the log cabin Father had built in Sandy Creek. This hut was much smaller, yet it had an undeniable charm that quickly grew on me. There were two rooms—a bedroom and a living area—but its simplicity felt like a fresh beginning, a clean slate after all we had been through. Our bed might have been government-issue but nonetheless came with a genuine mattress!

"Oh, John," I sighed as I sank into it that first night. "I'd almost forgotten what sleeping in a proper bed felt like."

John chuckled as he stretched out beside me, the creak of the bed a comforting sound. "Better than that dirty straw, eh? I reckon we've earned this bit of comfort."

After months of sleeping on filthy straw in gaol, swaying in hammocks on the ship, and then back to the straw on the cold, hard floor in the Female Factory, this bed felt like pure luxury. I could hardly believe it was real. As I lay there, feeling the softness beneath me, I hoped this small comfort was the beginning of something better. Yet even as I closed my eyes, exhaustion pulling me under, I couldn't shake the nagging thought that it might not last. Comfort had become a fleeting thing in my world, often snatched away just as quickly as it was given.

· · · · · ·

Chapter 26

Parramatta, New South Wales, 1811

We were issued new clothing—simple but sturdy and clean. For me, it was a shift, a linen jacket, new shoes, and a very appealing straw bonnet. John received a shirt, trousers, a heavy and durable blue woollen jacket, shoes, and a leather cap. We felt so smart in our new outfits, like we'd been given a fresh start in this new world.

"Look at us," I teased. "We clean up well, don't we?"

John grinned, tipping his leather cap. "Aye, almost respectable."

Life in the colony was hard, but it had a rhythm that I found oddly satisfying. Work started at sunrise each day. John would head off with Benjamin to the farmland nearby, where they cleared trees with other convicts in the government gangs. The sound of axes biting into wood echoed through the mornings, a constant reminder that this land was still being tamed. They worked until about three in the afternoon, when the drums signalled the end of government work.

But the day wasn't over for John. Like many men, he found other jobs to fill his hours, jobs that paid extra money or provided us goods for his services. He spent many afternoons labouring, either continuing to fell trees or helping to build houses for friends.

While John was off working, I spent my days at the factory, learning the craft of spinning and weaving fabric. It was all new to me—Mother had never done anything like it back in Sandy Creek. At first, my hands fumbled with the rough tufts of wool, the spinning wheel spinning too fast or too slow, but with time, I found a rhythm, and I started producing a fine, even yarn. As a bonus, the lanoline in the wool made my hands quite luxuriously soft.

"Look at you, Lizzie," one of the other women said, nodding at the fine yarn I had spun. "You've got a knack for it."

I smiled, proud of the compliment. "It's not so bad once you get the hang of it." The fabric I wove from the yarn was soft, almost luxurious, and the dressmakers in Sydney Town snapped it up as soon as it was ready.

Our food was provided mainly by the government, and rations were delivered every couple of weeks. We got salt beef or pork, depending on what the ships had brought, maize or corn, and bread from the government bakers. Sometimes, the meat was rotten if it hadn't been stored properly on the ships, but mostly, it was just tough and chewy. We usually cooked up a big stew with the meat, corn, and whatever vegetables we could get. It wasn't fancy, but it was enough to keep us going.

Saturdays and Sundays were our respite from the hard work of the week, and we made the most of them. Most days, we'd gather with a small group of friends—fellow convicts from England and Ireland. We'd sit around drinking and playing cards or just gossiping about the goings-on in the colony.

I had never really spent time with friends before—my life back home had been all about family and survival—but here, I found a new kind of friendship.

"Come on, Elizabeth, have a drink," Catherine urged one Sunday afternoon, handing me a cup of what they called grog.

I hesitated, memories of Ireland flashing through my mind. The only time I had tasted alcohol before had been a night best forgotten. But here, everyone drank. It was part of the culture of survival in this harsh land.

"Just a sip," I said, taking the cup from her. It was intense, and I wrinkled my nose at the taste. "What is this?"

"Grog," John answered with a laugh. "Sometimes beer, sometimes rum, most often watered down with whatever's at hand. The governor wants us to drink beer, though. Says it's better than the illegal rum, which is what you've got there."

"Aah," I said, "the lure of the good beer! Is that why you spend time down at that pub at Kissing Point?"

John laughed. "It's important to try the local brew, you know. The feller that owns that pub, James Squire, he was a convict, a First Fleeter. He was the first one to grow hops in this country to make the beer. I could learn a lot from a man like him."

As we sat there, sharing stories and laughter, I realised that this was what made life bearable—the friendships we had formed, the small joys we found in each other's company, and the hope that, with time, things would get better. Life was hard, and the bush behind our hut was a constant reminder of the wildness that surrounded us, but we had each other, and that was enough—for now.

As night fell, the sounds of the bush encroached on our little community of huts. The calls of nocturnal animals, the rustling of leaves, and the low hum of insects reminded us of the untamed wilderness that lay just beyond our newfound home. The bonfire in the centre of our circle crackled, its flames dancing and casting flickering shadows that seemed to merge with the surrounding darkness.

"Do you miss home, Lizzie?" Sarah, one of the younger convicts, asked quietly, her eyes reflecting the firelight. I looked around at the faces of my friends and then at John, feeling the weight of my past settling on my shoulders. "Sometimes," I admitted, my voice soft. "But my real home is so far away from this place. My real home is in America, not Ireland, or even England. I've moved countries twice now, uprooted from the life I knew in North Carolina and then again from Ireland to here. It's not just about missing a place; it's about missing the sense of belonging that came with it."

"It still feels strange here," I continued, my gaze drifting to the open sky above. "In North Carolina, my family's farm was in among the thick woods, and the air smelled of pine and earth. I used to wake up to the sound of birds that sang differently from those here, and the landscape was green and familiar. And all I knew in Ireland, really, was Dublin and the docks, so seagulls and sparrows. Now, here, it's all so different. Even the stars are so different to either America or Ireland, and they are so bright! It's starting to feel like home, though. It's different, but it's ours. We're all making something new here."

The following months were a whirlwind of weddings, each a small celebration in our lives. In April, Maggie Byrne asked John and me to stand as witnesses at her wedding to Silvanus Williams. The ceremony was simple, yet there was a warmth to it that filled my heart with joy. I couldn't help but smile as I watched Maggie and Silvanus exchange vows, their hands trembling slightly as he slid the plain band onto her finger.

Then, in June, Maurice Hickey, who had come out on *Boyd* with John, married little Bridget Quinn, who had been there in Kilmainham Gaol, and then, of course, transported with me on *Providence*. John Connor stood beside them as a witness, with a very pregnant Catherine by his side. I couldn't help but feel a pang of concern for her, knowing the strain she was under, but she smiled through it all, holding her head high. Even though they had applied for permission to marry as soon as she found she was with child, John had been of "bad character", according to the authorities, and permission had been denied. We all found this very strange, given the governor's push for us all to marry, but they had to wait.

Finally, in August, Catherine and John received permission to marry and did so as soon as they could get the banns read. They had a double wedding with a new babe in arms, and standing beside them was John's sister Mary, who married Michael Dowling on the same day. The joy in the air was palpable as we all celebrated together, knowing the hardships they had overcome to reach this moment.

Hester came to Catherine's wedding accompanied by Jim Ware, the man she had been assigned to. Ware had come out in early 1804 on

Coromandel and had done well for himself over the years, gaining a land grant at Windsor to farm. He seemed to be a kind man and looked at Hester with what seemed to me like real fondness.

Hester and I sat outside sometime later, the faint smell of eucalyptus mingling with the warmth of the fading sun. She was unusually quiet, and her face softened into something contemplative as she gazed out at the horizon.

I broke the silence, curious. "You've got something on your mind, Hester. What is it?"

She sighed, running a hand through her hair, then looked at me with an expression I'd never quite seen on her before—vulnerable, almost shy.

"I do," she admitted, her voice low. "It's about Jim."

I blinked, caught off guard. "Jim Ware?"

She nodded, her gaze dropping to her hands. "He's a good man, Lizzie. Better than most I've ever known."

I tilted my head, studying her. Hester didn't often talk about feelings, and seeing her like this tugged at something in me. "I've seen how he looks at you," I said softly, "and how you look at him when you think no one's watching."

Her gaze flicked to mine, her lips curving into a tentative smile. "He asked me to marry him," she said finally, her voice barely above a whisper.

"And?"

"I told him I'd think about it," she said, the faintest glimmer of hope in her eyes. I laughed, nudging her shoulder. "So what's stopping you? He's kind, steady, and clearly smitten with you."

Hester let out a long breath, shaking her head. "It's not that simple, is it? After everything I've done, everything I've been ... What if he deserves better than me?"

"Hester," I said firmly, turning to face her fully. "You've survived things most people couldn't even imagine. You've fought for every bit of dignity you have, and you've kept going when others would have given up. That's worth something. Jim sees that in you, or he wouldn't be asking."

She was quiet for a moment, staring out into the distance. "Since Thomas died, I thought that part of my life was over," she murmured, her voice thick with emotion. "I thought I'd never feel this way again. But Jim ... he makes me feel happy, Lizzie. Truly happy. More so than I've been in years." She paused, her eyes shimmering. "It scares me."

I reached out and placed a hand on hers. "It's not a bad thing to feel happy again, Hester. It doesn't mean you're forgetting Thomas or the life you had. It means you're living."

I smiled, squeezing her hand. "You shouldn't think about it too long. A good man like that doesn't come around every day."

She let out a soft laugh, shaking her head. "All right, Lizzie, don't get too sentimental on me." Then, her voice softened again. "But thank you. I didn't think I'd ever feel this again ... like I deserve it."

"You do," I said, my voice steady. "More than you know."

For a moment, we sat in silence, the warmth of the setting sun wrapping around us. And for the first time, I saw a lightness in Hester's eyes, a glimpse of the happiness she had thought she'd lost forever.

So, in October, my dear friend Hester married Jim. I watched her walk down the aisle, her face glowing with the happiness I had longed to see. As they exchanged their vows, I felt a swell of emotion. Hester had been my rock during the darkest times, and now she was stepping into a new life with a man who truly cared for her.

Chapter 27

Parramatta, New South Wales, 1811

Life in Parramatta was both strange and wonderful. Our little slab-and-bark hut, with its rough-hewn walls and a roof that let in more rain than it kept out, was nestled near the edge of the bush, not far from the winding Parramatta River. The bush, as they called the vast stretches of untamed forest, was a place of mystery, full of strange sounds and smells.

The gum trees surrounding our small hut reached up towards the sky. I was amazed by the intricate patterns under the bark, by the way that it curled and flaked off in long, rough strips, revealing the smooth, pale wood underneath. On some trees, it was pure white; on others, various colours lay awaiting the kiss of sunlight. The air was thick with the scent of eucalyptus, sharp and clean, mingling with the earthy smell of damp soil after the rain. The yellow flower I had noticed on the first day was called wattle. It was everywhere, the bushes all different sizes and producing huge bunches in shades of yellow.

And oh my! The animals! The animals drove home to us that we were in a very foreign land. I didn't know much about the wildlife in Ireland, but in North Carolina, we frequently saw deer and squirrels and heard the black bears and sometimes wolves in the forests. There were rabbits and foxes, of course, and opossums and occasionally, we would see or hear a bobcat. There were no rabbits or foxes here, and the possums were very different, great bush-tailed ones and tiny little ones with a tail curling around a tree's branch. We would hear them scurrying through the trees at night, their enormous eyes glowing in the firelight. They were curious little creatures, often coming close to camp, drawn by the scent of our food. But they were quick to dart back into the safety of the branches if anyone got too close. Their calls—sharp, guttural sounds—would echo through the night, adding to the chorus of unfamiliar noises surrounding us.

I could hardly believe my eyes the first time I saw a kangaroo. Soon after we moved into the hut, early on a crisp spring morning, I was out gathering firewood near the edge of the bush when I caught sight of a creature that seemed to be a cross between a giant rabbit and a deer. It stood on its hind legs, taller than a man, towering over the scrub, with a long tail stretched out behind it for balance. Its ears twitched, and its dark eyes stared right at me, unblinking and curious. I stood frozen, not sure whether to approach or back away.

"John, come quickly!" I called out, my voice tinged with both excitement and fear. "There's something out here, something I've never seen before!"

John came running, and when he saw the kangaroo, he laughed. "That, my love, is a kangaroo, and there'll be plenty more of them around." And sure enough, dozens of them would come down to the water and drink, and we grew used to seeing them almost every day.

We watched in amazement as the kangaroo bounded away with incredible speed, covering the ground with each leap as if flying. Despite its size, its movement was graceful. I had never imagined an animal could move like that, and for days afterwards, I couldn't stop thinking about it.

One night, I heard an animal crashing through the undergrowth. I thought it was some kind of wild pig, perhaps even something more dangerous. The noise was so loud and sudden, like a boulder tumbling through the dense brush. But when I finally caught sight of the creature, I was struck by how different it was from anything I had seen before — short and stout, with a lumbering run and a very sweet little face. At first I thought it was some sort of badger, but John told me they were called wombats.

Then there were the echidnas. While fetching water from the nearby creek one morning, I spotted what looked like a spiky rock moving slowly through the grass. As I approached, I saw the small, shy creature snuffling around for food, its long snout probing the ground. I was fascinated by its quills, which glistened in the sunlight like a halo of tiny spears.

The birds were the most startling of all. They were like nothing I had ever known. The colours were brighter and more vivid, as if someone had dipped them in a painter's palette. With their brilliant reds, blues, green and yellow, the Rosellas looked like flying jewels, flashing through the trees in a blur of colour. Their calls were sharp and piercing, nothing like the gentle trills of the birds I had grown up with. The white cockatoos were just as striking, with their stark white feathers and yellow crests. Their loud, raucous screeches could be heard from a great distance, and they seemed to enjoy causing a ruckus, swooping down in noisy flocks that made the entire sky seem alive with movement. Sometimes, flocks of magnificent black and red cockatoos flew over, occasionally landing in the trees around our hut. The laughing kookaburras often came by late in the afternoon, and we could hear the babies learning to laugh deep in the bush. And there were so many others.

Not all the encounters were so peaceful, though. There were snakes, too—long, sinuous creatures that moved through the grass with a quiet menace. I had been warned about them, told to constantly watch my step and never reach into tall grass without looking. The first time I saw one, it was coiled up on a sunny rock, its scales gleaming in the light. I felt a shiver run down my spine, knowing that some snakes were deadly.

Even the insects here were different—giant spiders with thick legs that spun enormous webs and strange, buzzing beetles that seemed to fill the air with their noise. I quickly learned to be cautious, shaking out my shoes, clothes and bedding each morning to make sure nothing had crawled inside during the night.

In many ways, the native animals of Australia seemed as wild and untamed as the land itself. They were a constant reminder that I was a long way from home, in a place where the rules I had grown up with didn't always apply.

The magpies were my favourite birds. Their song was unlike any birdcall I had ever heard: a rich, warbling melody that echoed through the early morning air. It was haunting and beautiful, a sound that made me feel a strange mix of joy and sorrow. I often stopped whatever I was doing just to listen, letting the song wash over me as I tried to memorise its notes.

"Listen to that, John," I said one morning as we sat outside our hut, the sun just beginning to warm the earth. I was perched on a log, a mug of freshly brewed tea in my hand, while John was busy mending a pair of old boots. "Have you ever heard anything so beautiful?"

John paused, looking up from his work to listen. He smiled a slow, thoughtful smile that made the corners of his eyes crinkle. "Aye, it's something, all right. Almost makes you forget where we came from, doesn't it? Almost makes you forget that we are still convicts."

I nodded, my gaze drifting across the landscape. The land was so different from anything I had ever known. Back in North Carolina, the fields were green, and the air was often damp and heavy, but here, the earth was a rich, reddish-brown, and the trees seemed to stretch up forever, their leaves a silvery green against the endless blue sky. Even the light was different, sharper somehow, casting long, transparent shadows in the early morning.

The weather here was another marvel—unpredictable and extreme. One moment, the sun would blaze down, baking the ground beneath your feet until it felt like it would crack open. Next, a sudden downpour of rain would drench everything in sight. The rain came in fierce bursts, hammering on our roof and turning the dirt outside our hut into a muddy mess. Then, just as quickly, the clouds would part, and the sun would return, drying the land like the rain had never happened.

I quickly learned to keep a close eye on the sky, watching for the dark clouds that signalled an approaching storm. "Looks like we're in for it," John would say, glancing up at the heavy, brooding clouds that rolled in from the west, carrying the scent of rain on the wind. We would scramble to bring in anything that might get soaked, the two of us laughing as we raced the storm, our clothes clinging to us as the first fat drops fell.

And then, just as suddenly as it started, it would be over. The air would be cool and fresh, the ground steaming as the sun came out again. Everything felt renewed, as though the rain had washed away the dust and heat of the day. I loved those moments after the storm when the world seemed to hold its breath, and the only sounds were the dripping of water from the leaves and the calls of birds as they shook off the rain.

Chapter 28

Parramatta, New South Wales, 1812–1813

Our first task as a married couple had been to plant a small garden in front of the house. We'd cleared a little patch of land, turning over the soil with our hands and rudimentary tools, and planted corn seeds. It took me back to life on our farm in Sandy Creek, and I wished I had paid more attention to my parents and what they were doing. Every morning, I would step outside and check on the tiny sprouts pushing their way through the earth, whispering encouragement to them as though they were children. I tried to remember my childhood, following my father around the corn, as those little plants were our hope for something more than just surviving.

"Think we'll have enough to last us through the winter?" I asked John, squinting at the young plants as I leaned down to touch their delicate leaves.

"If the animals don't get to it first," he replied with a grin, standing up and stretching his back. His hands were calloused from work, rough but gentle as he reached out to brush a stray lock of hair from my face. "But we'll make do, one way or another."

The work was hard, but it felt good to be doing something with my hands, to be building a life for ourselves, no matter how humble. While the government provided us with rations, they were basic, and we had to grow or barter for anything fresh. That little patch of corn was more than just food; it symbolised our independence and determination to make a life here.

We did everything possible to avoid attracting the authorities' attention. John had previously worked on the chain gangs building roads before I arrived, witnessing first-hand the brutal consequences of defying the redcoats or any authority figure. The man who married us, the Reverend Samuel Marsden, was known for his ruthlessness, earning him the grim nickname "the Flogging Parson". He was a sight to behold and to fear, strutting around in that long black robe, like a crow. He always appeared so severe, as if he was judging everyone he passed, and you could feel the weight of his gaze upon you, as if he knew all your sins.

He and Governor Macquarie didn't see eye to eye, not at all. I think the Reverend thought Macquarie was too soft, what with all his ideas about giving convicts a second chance and helping them make a fresh start. Marsden believed in strict punishment—no mercy for people like us. Macquarie, on the other hand, wanted to see people improve; I think he thought a bit of kindness might go a long way. Marsden stuck to his guns, letting us convicts that he believed we needed hard work and even harder discipline.

And the redcoats themselves were everywhere, of course. Macquarie's 73rd Regiment had largely replaced the soldiers who had run the settlement by managing the rum trade—we heard all about this from convicts who'd been here longer than us.

As we settled into our new life, we had more contact with the local Aboriginal people, who were from the *Burramattagal* clan. They were not at all like the black people who worked in the fields of North Carolina.

At first, they were a distant presence—shadowy figures glimpsed at the edge of the bush, watching us with wary eyes. Gradually, as the days passed, they approached us, curious about the newcomers who had moved onto their land.

"They're showing us they mean no harm," John explained later when he came inside, wiping the sweat from his brow. "They're curious about us, just like we're curious about them."

I had seen a group of Aboriginal people standing at the edge of the bush near our hut one day, their eyes watching us as we went about our daily chores. Their presence had startled me at first, but John's calmness reassured me. He had taken the time to watch and speak to them, to understand some of their gestures and movements. He knew that their cautious and deliberate approach was a sign that they meant no harm.

John continued, his voice thoughtful. "They've lived here for generations, and now we've come and started clearing their land, cutting down trees, planting crops. It's no wonder they're wary of us."

I nodded, feeling a pang of guilt. The land we now called home had been theirs long before we arrived, and our presence disrupted their way of life. But while John and I were happy to extend a hand of friendship, we knew that not everyone felt the same way.

A deep tension existed between the Aboriginal people and the white settlers, simmering just beneath the surface. The settlers, eager to carve out their own stake in this new world, often viewed the Aboriginal people as obstacles, standing in the way of progress. When the Aboriginals fought back to defend their land, the settlers reacted with anger and violence, and, unfortunately, they had weapons.

"There's been some trouble down by the river," John mentioned one evening as we sat by the fire. "A group of settlers clashed with some Aboriginal men. It didn't end well."

I shuddered at the thought of the brutality that could erupt when fear and resentment took hold. We tried to keep out of it as much as possible, sticking to our little hut and tending to our small patch of land. However, it was impossible to ignore the growing unrest. Every now and then, we would hear tales of skirmishes and land disputes that turned deadly. It served as a reminder that beneath the beauty of this land, an undercurrent of conflict simmered, one that wouldn't be easily resolved.

In August of 1812, with the cool winter air settled over Windsor, I noticed something that sent a flutter of both excitement and apprehension through me—I had missed my monthly flow. At first, I brushed it off. It had stopped before, when I was in prison, and had only started again here in Parramatta, when things were more settled, I suppose. But as the weeks passed and still nothing, I began to wonder. Could it be?

One evening, as John and I sat by the modest fire in our little hut, the soft glow illuminating his weathered but kind face, I mustered the courage to speak.

"John," I began, my voice barely above a whisper, "I think … I think I might be with child."

He looked up from the wooden carving he was working on, his eyes widening. "Are you sure, Elizabeth?"

I nodded slowly, biting my lower lip. "I've missed my monthly flow twice now, and I've been feeling … different."

A slow smile spread across his face, reaching his eyes and making them sparkle. He set aside his carving and moved closer, taking my hands in his.

"That's wonderful news," he whispered, pulling me into a gentle embrace. "A child, our child."

Relief washed over me. We hadn't discussed children before, the chaos of our lives leaving little room for such conversations, but hearing the joy in his voice settled any lingering doubts I had.

The months that followed were a whirlwind of emotions. My belly grew rounder with each passing week, and with it, so did our excitement. Hester and Catherine fussed over me endlessly, offering advice and remedies passed down from their mothers. Despite her sharp tongue, Hester seemed to take a particular happiness in the whole process, almost as if it were her own.

"You're lucky to have me," she teased one evening, handing me another cup of her strange herbal tea. "I've had years of watching women waddle around like ducks. Not that I've ever been in their shoes, mind you." She said it lightly, but I saw the flicker of something deeper in her eyes.

There were moments of fear, of course. The uncertainty of childbirth in this distant land weighed heavily on me. But with John by my side, Catherine's calm steadiness, and Hester's humour cutting through the tension, I felt ready to face whatever came.

The time finally arrived as the hot summer gave way to the cooler days of autumn. On the 8th of April 1813, the pains began, building slowly before crashing down like waves. Hours stretched on, testing the very limits of my strength. Catherine held my hand, her voice soft and steady.

"Breathe, Lizzie," she murmured, wiping the sweat from my brow.

Hester, pacing like a restless cat, chimed in from the corner. "Come on now, Lizzie. You're made of sterner stuff than this. And don't think you're getting out of my tea once the baby's here—it'll get you back on your feet in no time."

Despite the pain, I managed a weak laugh. "You and your teas, Hester. I think they've done their job."

When the cry of a newborn finally filled the hut, a wave of relief and overwhelming joy washed over me. Catherine placed the tiny, squirming bundle into my arms, her own face lit with wonder.

"She's beautiful," Catherine whispered, her voice trembling.

I looked down at my daughter, her delicate features scrunched up, her tiny fists waving in the air. A mop of dark hair covered her head. Standing beside me, John reached out a trembling hand to stroke her cheek.

"Rosetta," I murmured, the name rolling off my tongue like a cherished secret. "Welcome to the world, little one."

Hester, who had been uncharacteristically quiet, stepped forward, her sharp eyes softening as she gazed down at the baby. "Well, Lizzie," she said, her voice steady but quieter than usual, "you've done yourself proud." She reached out, hesitantly, before gently brushing a finger against Rosetta's tiny hand.

"She's got a grip, this one," Hester added, a small, wistful smile crossing her face. "Strong already. Just like her mother."

Something in her tone caught my breath—a mixture of pride, longing, and the faintest shadow of sadness. Hester, who had never had her own children, seemed to fall in love with Rosetta.

"Strong like her Auntie Hester, too," I said softly, meeting her eyes.

Hester blinked quickly and laughed, brushing off the emotion as she always did. "Aye, she'd better be. She's got me to keep her in line."

John chuckled, pressing a soft kiss to my forehead. Despite my exhaustion, a deep sense of peace filled the room. In that moment, surrounded by love and the promise of new beginnings, I felt the threads of family tighten around us—not just blood, but the bonds we'd forged through struggle and survival. Rosetta's first cry marked the start of something new, something exciting.

Chapter 29

Parramatta, New South Wales, 1813–1814

John and I settled down for supper one evening in our modest little hut. The fire crackled cheerfully in the hearth, casting warm, flickering shadows across the rough-hewn walls. I'd just served a hearty stew, its aroma mingling with the earthy scent of burning wood. John sat opposite me, his face lit by the firelight, but tonight, a seriousness in his eyes made me pause.

"Lizzie," John began, breaking the comfortable silence that usually accompanied our meals, "I've been thinking about something."

I looked up from my bowl, intrigued by the tone of his voice. "What's on your mind, John?"

He took a deep breath as though gathering his thoughts before speaking. "Tim Daley has been talking about going to Van Diemen's Land once he gets his ticket of leave. They're offering land grants to those willing to settle and work the land. We could have our own farm."

The notion of starting fresh in a new place was enticing but scary. And what did we know about farming? I didn't think our little veggie patch really counted as a farm, and I couldn't remember much from my childhood. I suspected that John was a city boy—he had never mentioned being on a farm, but this also underscored how little I knew about this man I called husband.

I leaned in closer, feeling the warmth of the fire on my face. "Land grants? That sounds interesting. But we can't just leave Sydney without certificates of freedom. We're bound here."

While it was sometimes hard to remember, we were still prisoners here. And while I would be free soon by dint of serving my sentence, John was here for life, which meant never moving away from this area and constantly having to report to the constables.

John nodded, his brow furrowed in deep concern. "I know. But Tim mentioned something else. There's a way I might be able to get that certificate sooner."

I could sense the gravity of his words, the weight of a tough decision about to be revealed. "What do you mean?" I asked gently.

He hesitated, then leaned closer, lowering his voice. "There are two men I know who've been running an illegal still. The magistrate's begun a crackdown on this sort of thing. If I were to inform the authorities, it might be enough to expedite my freedom."

The enormity of his suggestion hit me like an icy wave. "John, if you do that ..."

"I know," he interrupted, his voice laden with worry. "It's a risk. If word got out that I was the one who snitched on them, the others would turn on us. We'd be shunned, maybe worse."

A knot of dread twisted in my stomach. "But you'd have a chance at your freedom ..."

John's eyes locked onto mine, a mix of determination and nervousness flickering within them. "Exactly. It's a chance to do something for our future, something that otherwise we'll have to wait years for. And that will mean years more of me working for someone else. This is a chance for us, Lizzie. A chance to escape this endless cycle."

I reached across the table, placing my hand over his. "John, I trust you. I know you're trying to do what's best for us. But this ... it's dangerous. We have to think it through carefully. There are lives at stake here, not just ours."

He sighed, rubbing his hand over his face, the firelight casting shadows that seemed to underscore the gravity of our situation. "I know, Lizzie. It's a gamble. But the thought of us being stuck here with no hope of change … I can't live with that too much longer. I want a future where we can have our own land, build a real home. We'll never do that here."

I glanced around our humble hut, feeling the weight of the decision hanging over us. The thought of abandoning everything we'd built, everything familiar, filled me with dread. "What's the next step if you decide to go through with it?"

John leaned back, his expression thoughtful. "I need to gather some evidence and then report it to the magistrate. But I need to weigh the risks carefully. Make absolutely certain it's worth it. I don't want to destroy everything we've fought for. As I said, if word gets out that it was me that provided the information …" He left the sentence hanging, but we both knew what it would mean if others knew that we had been the ones to turn in a fellow convict.

The flickering flames of the fire continued to cast their warm glow, but the atmosphere between us was tense. John's shoulders bore the weight of the decision, and I could feel the anxiety gnawing at my insides.

"John, are you sure this is the only way?" I asked, trying to steady my voice.

He nodded slowly. "I've thought it through, Lizzie. The odds of getting that certificate any other way are slim to none. This might be our only shot. But we need to tread carefully, as I said, and gather more information before making any moves."

I took a deep breath, trying to calm the racing thoughts in my mind. "We need to be prepared for any fallout. How would we handle it if things go wrong?"

John's eyes met mine, a mix of fear and fierce determination. "We'll stay close to each other, remain vigilant, and trust no one else. If I move forward with this, I'll do everything I can to protect us. But Lizzie, if there's any doubt in your mind, tell me now. I won't do it if we're not in total agreement."

For a moment, silence enveloped us, the crackling fire the only sound. I searched my heart, weighing my desperate hope for a better future against the very real dangers.

"John," I said softly but firmly, "I trust you. But we need to be absolutely sure. Let's gather more information, listen carefully for any whispers or signs, and then decide."

He nodded, relief mingling with the worry in his eyes. "All right, Lizzie. We'll take it slow, be cautious."

In the days that followed, we moved through our routines with a heightened sense of awareness. John took every opportunity to gather information, listening for any signs of unrest or suspicion among the settlers and convicts. I noticed a subtle change in him—a carefulness in his interactions, a watchfulness in his eyes—as though he were constantly calculating the next move.

One evening, as we sat by the fire after a long day, John shared another piece of the puzzle. "I spoke with Tim today," he said, keeping his voice low. "He heard some rumours about the magistrate's crackdown. It's more intense than we thought. If the authorities catch wind of the still, they'll come down hard on anyone involved."

I swallowed hard, the gravity of his words settling like a stone in my gut. "But that could work in our favour, couldn't it? The harsher the crackdown, the more eager they'll be to reward any information."

John watched and waited for the right time, carefully weighing his options as if the decision before him was a delicate balance. The tension of his contemplation was palpable, but I admired his resolve. I could see it in the way he furrowed his brow when lost in thought.

A couple of weeks later, as the sun dipped low in the sky and the twilight colours painted the world in soft hues, John came to me with a serious look. "Lizzie," he said, his voice steady, "I've made up my mind. I'm going to speak to the magistrate."

My heart skipped a beat. "Are you absolutely sure?" I asked, holding

Rosetta close to me as she gurgled softly.

John nodded. "Yes. I've decided to report them. It's the only way I can see getting my certificate of freedom, and we can make a different future."

We sat together in the quiet of our small home, the sounds of the bush settling around us as nightfall enveloped the land. I reached out and took his hand, squeezing it gently. "I trust you, John. But remember, this is risky. The consequences could be severe."

"I know," he said, his eyes meeting mine. "But I've done it before in Ireland, and it's the reason we're here, the reason I am still alive. It's not a great thing to do, and especially to men who I've known and worked with for years. It makes me feel sick to my stomach, if the truth be known, but I just can't see any way that we will ever be able to live our own lives without having the redcoats' foot on our neck."

John prepared for his meeting with the magistrate in September of 1813. He gathered his thoughts, made sure he had all the necessary information, and steeled himself for the conversation that could change everything.

Finally, the day arrived. John dressed in his best clothes, the ones he had received from the government—a clean shirt, trousers, and his blue woollen jacket. I watched him leave with a mix of hope and anxiety, clutching Rosetta close to my chest as I prayed silently for his success.

When John returned later that day, his expression was one of cautious relief. "Lizzie," he said, his voice trembling slightly with the weight of his emotions, "I did it. I spoke to the magistrate and reported the men for their illegal still. They're following up on it, and we'll know soon."

I let out a breath I hadn't realised I was holding and hugged him tightly. "Let's wait and see what happens then."

Several weeks later, the news reached us. The two men had been arrested, their illegal still confiscated. The story spread quickly through the settlement, whispered from one mouth to another like a flame catching on dry grass.

"They've been flogged," Hester said, her voice low as she leaned against the doorway, watching me hang out the washing. "One hundred lashes each, and they've been sent to Norfolk Island." I shuddered at the thought.

I froze, the damp sheet slipping from my fingers. One hundred lashes. Norfolk Island. The words hung in the air, heavy and suffocating. My stomach twisted as I tried to picture it—those men, backs torn to ribbons, loaded onto a ship bound for that godforsaken place.

I shuddered, the guilt settling deep in my chest. We'd done this. We'd played a part in their punishment. The washing in my hands suddenly felt too heavy, the weight of what we'd set in motion pressing down on me like lead. Norfolk Island. It wasn't just a punishment—it was a sentence to something worse than death.

Hester glanced at me, her sharp eyes narrowing. "You knew, didn't you?"

I paused, my hands gripping the wet linen. I couldn't lie to Hester; she knew me too well. "John ... he told the magistrate," I said quietly.

Hester straightened, her arms crossing over her chest. "John?"

"He thought it was the only way," I said, my voice trembling slightly. "He wanted his certificate of freedom, Hester. He thought if he did something to help the authorities, they might grant it."

Hester let out a low whistle, shaking her head. "Well, he's got guts, I'll give him that. But this isn't going to sit well if the others find out, Lizzie. You know how people talk. And John—he's going to feel this, whether he admits it or not."

She wasn't wrong. That night, as we sat by the fire, the weight of John's silence pressed down on me. He stared into the flames, his jaw tight, his hands resting on his knees.

"You did what you thought was right," I said softly, breaking the silence.

His head turned slowly toward me, his eyes dark with something I couldn't quite name. "Did I?" he asked, his voice low and rough. "Two men whipped within an inch of their lives, locked away like animals. All because of me. I've already got the blood of Michael Whitethorn on my hands, now these two."

I moved closer, placing a hand on his arm. "You didn't force them to run that still, John. They knew the risks. And Michael ... well, you know that if you hadn't told the magistrate about him that, you wouldn't be here either."

He shook his head, pulling away slightly. "That doesn't change the fact that I'm the one who sold these men out. I wanted my life, my freedom, Lizzie, but at what cost? I know these men, have worked with them. I know they have families. They've got children who'll go hungry now."

The guilt was like a shadow clinging to him, and no matter what I said, I could see it wouldn't be easily shaken.

Hester visited again the next day, her usual sharpness softened. "You've got a good man, Lizzie," she said as we sat outside, shelling peas. "But he's carrying a heavy weight. You'll need to keep an eye on him."

"I know," I said, glancing toward John, who was chopping wood with a ferocity that seemed more punishment than necessity.

"He's not the first to make a hard choice in this colony," Hester continued, her tone thoughtful. "And he won't be the last. But people have long memories. If word gets out ..." She trailed off, letting the implication hang in the air.

I nodded, my stomach twisting. "I'll look after him," I said firmly. "We'll get through this. Together."

But as the days passed, the tension in John's shoulders didn't ease, and the whispers in the settlement grew louder. It was clear that even in this new land, freedom came at a price—and sometimes, that price was heavier than you could ever anticipate.

In November, John's certificate of freedom was granted, and we received the small piece of paper that meant so much for our future.

John just looked relieved. His desperate gamble had paid off. "Now we can think about our future beyond here. I need to be away from here, away from the memories of what I've done. As soon as your freedom comes through, we can leave Sydney, explore new opportunities, and build a life somewhere else."

The enormity of the moment sank in, and I could hardly believe how far we had come. From the harsh realities of prison to the humble beginnings of our new life, and now, a chance at a better future—it was almost too much to take in. And there was something else. We had obviously celebrated well in September, and now another baby was on the way.

We began to make plans for what lay ahead. John's certificate of freedom was more than just a piece of paper; it symbolised hope and possibility. Now, all we had to do was for me to get my freedom, which would happen soon. We talked about the prospects in Van Diemen's Land, dreamed of a land grant, and imagined the life we could build for Rosetta and a new baby.

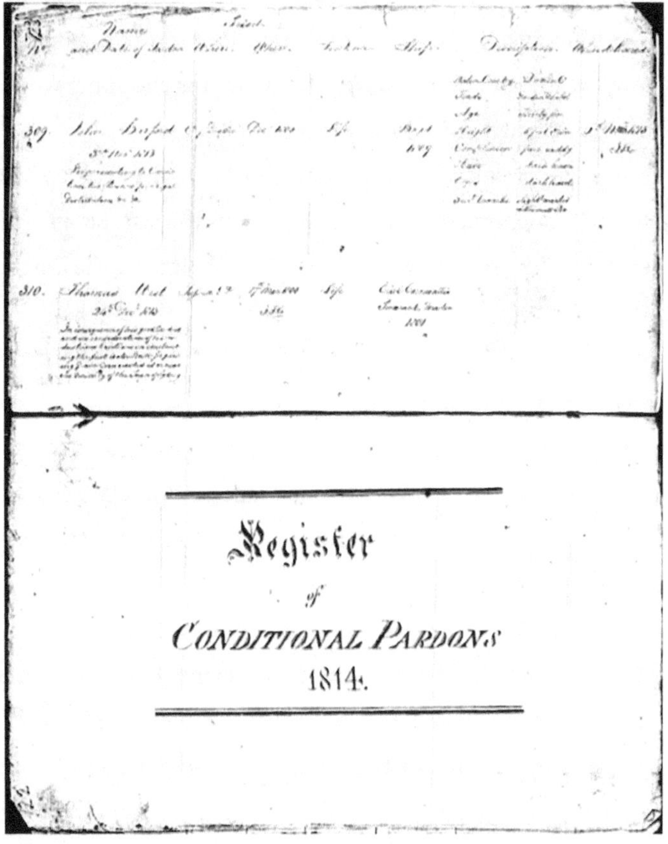

John's record of Conditional Pardon, NSW State Archives Collection, 1814

Chapter 30

Parramatta, New South Wales, 1814–1817

In January 1814, the day I awaited had arrived—I became free by servitude. I had fulfilled my seven-year sentence for a crime I had not committed, a milestone that should have felt like a triumphant conclusion to a long chapter. But life had a way of complicating even the most straightforward of victories.

John and I continued discussing the possibility of moving to Launceston. It seemed like a beacon of hope, a new start where we could seize the opportunities that Van Diemen's Land promised. Yet, every time we talked about it, the time felt wrong.

My health was not good, and the arrival of our second daughter, Elizabeth, whom we called Betsy, in June was met with a mix of joy and anxiety. She was so small and quiet, and the cold winter made our draughty hut feel even more inhospitable. We worried incessantly about her survival. John did everything he could to patch up the gaps in our home, while Catherine and Hester came over to help whenever they could.

As the days grew colder, my milk dried up. I couldn't feed Betsy, and the thought of her going hungry broke my heart. Thankfully, our small community rallied around us, and we were gifted a goat for milk. Despite this small blessing, the days seemed endless. John worked tirelessly, spending his mornings in the government gangs, clearing land, and his afternoons working for extra money. We saved every penny we could. Our first crop of corn was somewhat successful, though the kangaroos found the tender green shoots most appetising. The cabbages and potatoes we planted in winter fared better, and we managed to trade our surplus with others for wheat to make bread.

In December, just as life was starting to feel steady again, I found out I was pregnant again. The news left me with mixed emotions. Of course, another baby was a blessing, but with two little ones already demanding my every moment, exhaustion was a constant shadow.

When I told Hester, she let out a hearty laugh that startled the magpies perched on the fence outside. "Lizzie," she said, grinning from ear to ear, "you're a regular rabbit, aren't you? At this rate, we'll have to rename the colony Barefoot Bay!"

I rolled my eyes but couldn't help laughing. "It's not like I planned this, Hester."

"Oh, I know, love," she replied with mock solemnity. "But you might want to let John know that you're not running a nursery for the entire colony. Maybe he'll give you a bit of a break." She patted my shoulder, her grin turning wicked. "Though knowing him, I wouldn't count on it."

Her humour, as always, was a balm. Even when my body ached, and my patience wore thin, Hester's laughter reminded me to see the joy in what I had.

The months passed in a blur of hard work, a growing belly, and Hester's endless commentary. "You'd better hope this one's not a crier," she said one day while helping me hang laundry. "Otherwise, between the three of them, you'll never sleep again. Not that you look like you've been sleeping much anyway."

In September 1815, after hours of labour and with Hester at my side, our son was born. The cry of a healthy baby filled the room, and as John strode into the room, I saw his face light up with pride.

"A fine boy," Hester said, peering over John's shoulder at the tiny bundle.

"We'll call him John," I said, my voice soft but firm. "Johnny, to keep it clear."

John grinned so wide I thought his face might split. The next day, he took Johnny around Parramatta, introducing him to everyone we passed. "This is my boy," he told them all, his voice brimming with pride.

When Hester came by again, she leaned over the cradle, arms crossed. "Well, Lizzie, you've done it again. A fine-looking little lad. Though I'd suggest giving it a rest for a bit, unless you're planning to populate the whole colony yourself."

I laughed, swatting at her. "I'll let John know he's on notice."

But life, as it often does, had its own plans. In March 1816, I found myself pregnant once more. The fatigue was overwhelming, and it felt like I was perpetually either expecting or nursing a baby. The sickness that accompanied this pregnancy was far worse than with Betsy. By early November, I was exhausted and worried.

The day I went into labour was unseasonably hot. I struggled through the pain, but something was wrong. As I pushed, I felt a tearing, agonising pain, unlike anything I had experienced before. The baby was stillborn, never having taken a breath of life. My grief was profound, and as I lay in our bed, sobbing uncontrollably, John took our daughter's tiny body and buried her by the creek, his face set in sorrow.

After this, I told John we needed to take a break from having children. I could not bear the thought of becoming pregnant again so soon. His reaction was a shock to me. For the first time in our life together, I saw a side of him that I did not recognise—a side that I did not like.

He stood at the foot of the bed, his arms crossed tightly over his chest, his jaw set in a way that made him look like stone. For a moment, I thought he hadn't heard me, but then his eyes narrowed, and he spoke, his voice low and clipped.

"A break from children?" he repeated, as if the very idea were foreign to him. "That's not how this works, Elizabeth. A man expects his wife to bear him children. That's the way of things."

I stared at him, stunned. My grief was still raw, my body aching from the ordeal, and here he was, speaking as if the loss of our daughter were nothing more than a brief inconvenience. The tenderness I had always seen in him, the warmth that had drawn me to him, seemed to vanish, replaced by something colder, harder.

"I'm telling you, John," I said, my voice trembling with emotion, "I can't. Not after this. Not now. Please, try to understand."

His expression darkened further, his brows knitting together. "Understand? What I understand is that a family doesn't grow without children, Elizabeth. And this—" he gestured vaguely toward me, lying in the bed, still weak from labour—"this isn't just about you. I have needs, and you, as my wife, are expected to attend to those needs. You'll be better soon, you're young and you'll heal. And I want more sons. I want to leave a legacy."

His words struck me like a blow. I had expected comfort, understanding, and maybe even a glimmer of the man I thought I knew. Instead, I saw someone driven by pride, by expectations I hadn't known he held so deeply.

"I've just lost a child," I said, my voice breaking. "Our child."

For a moment, his face flickered with something—guilt, perhaps, or regret—but it was gone as quickly as it appeared. "We'll talk about this when you've had time to think," he said, his tone softer but dismissive. "You'll see reason."

He turned and left the room, his boots heavy against the floorboards. I lay there, stunned, the weight of his words crushing me as much as my grief.

John returned home that night very drunk. When he climbed into bed, his actions were unlike those of the gentle, caring man I knew. He pressed himself against me, his hands roaming under my shift, squeezing my breasts. I pushed him away, my voice sharp and clear with a "No." For a terrifying moment, I thought he might force himself on me, as his eyes, clouded with drink, looked different—hard, unseeing. He stumbled away, collapsing into the armchair by the fire.

In the morning, John seemed regretful, though his apology was wrapped in words that left a sour taste in my mouth. He spoke of a wife's duty, his tone gentle but laced with an expectation that unsettled me. There was a quiet but unmistakable sense of ownership in his words that made my chest tighten.

I had never thought of us as equals—how could I, in a world where men ruled home and colony? But I had believed John was better than this. He had always treated me with a kind of care, a respect that made me feel safe, even when the world outside was cruel. Now, that illusion was slipping, and I didn't know how to stop it.

I remained silent, struggling to reconcile the man I thought I knew with the one standing before me. Perhaps he didn't even realise what he was saying, but to me, his words cut deeper than he could imagine. I had given him my trust, my love, my body, and now it seemed they were no longer gifts but something he believed he was entitled to. My grief swelled, not just for our daughter but for the quiet loss of something between us that I wasn't sure we'd ever get back.

As the months went by, it would have looked like John and I were managing, but the truth was that we were both deeply unhappy people. I was overwhelmed, drowning in the demands of caring for our three young children—Rosetta, just four; Betsy, three; and little Johnny, not yet two—while still carrying the heavy grief of losing our baby daughter.

I couldn't seem to shake the heaviness that hung over me, pressing down on my chest like a weight I couldn't lift. Every morning felt the same—another day stretching ahead, filled with tasks I could barely bring myself to face. The children's laughter, once a balm to my soul, now grated against me when my nerves felt too raw to bear.

I loved them; I knew that much. But the joy I used to feel when I held them, the warmth that spread through me when Rosetta ran into my arms, or Betsy reached for my hand, felt like a distant memory. Now, I moved through the days in a kind of haze, going through the motions without really feeling present.

I should have been happy. I told myself that every day. We had a roof over our heads and food on the table. But this didn't seem to touch the emptiness inside me.

At night, when the children were finally asleep, I would sit by the fire and stare into the flames, feeling a hollowness I couldn't explain. Sometimes, I would cry, though I didn't know why, and when John asked what was wrong, I couldn't find the words to tell him.

The worst part was the guilt. I felt it constantly, gnawing at me like a hungry rat. What kind of mother felt like this? What kind of wife? Women all around me managed so much more, with so much less, and yet here I was, barely holding on.

Some days, I wanted nothing more than to stay in bed, pull the sheet over my head, and shut out the world. But the children needed me, and the housework needed doing, so I forced myself up and forced myself forward. Every step felt like trudging through mud, but I kept moving because I had no choice.

I didn't speak of it to anyone. Who would understand? Who could? This wasn't a sickness people saw, like a fever or a wound. It was invisible, silent, and so I bore it alone, praying that one day it might loosen its grip on me.

Months passed, and John's persistence in resuming our intimate relations only added to the strain. Each time he reached for me, I pulled away, the fear of becoming pregnant again seizing me with an icy grip. I couldn't bear the thought of another loss, another tiny grave beside the creek. My body, already worn thin, felt like it could not endure another trial.

At first, John tried to be patient, but he clearly didn't understand. I could see his frustration growing each time I rejected him. Finally, he seemed to relent, withdrawing his advances, but his unhappiness hung in the air like a storm cloud.

The reprieve came with a cost. His silence turned sharp, punctuated by snide remarks that stung more than I let on. "Not much of a wife if you can't even warm your husband's bed," he muttered one night, the words cutting through the stillness like a blade.

I didn't respond, biting back the retort that rose to my lips. I knew he was angry, and perhaps he had a right to be, but his bitterness only widened the growing chasm between us. I once thought John was better than this: kinder and more understanding. Now, I wasn't so sure.

Each day, I carried on, hoping the heaviness between us would somehow lift, but with every snide comment and every lingering silence, the weight only seemed to grow.

One afternoon, Hester took the children on an adventure down to the creek, allowing me to catch up on some much-needed sleep. When they returned, we sat together, preparing the evening meal. She looked at me carefully, her eyes narrowed. "What's happening, love? I can feel something's wrong. Whenever John is mentioned, you wince like you're in pain."

I told her about what had been happening, and the way that it made me feel. She listened, her expression unreadable at first. Then she let out a low sigh and shook her head.

"Well, Lizzie, men are simple creatures in the end, aren't they?" she said, her tone cutting but not unkind. "They think a bit of affection and a meal on the table entitles them to everything else. But you've been through hell, love, and if John can't see that, then he needs a good shake—or a good slap."

I couldn't help but smile, though it was faint. Hester had a way of saying exactly what she thought; sometimes, that bluntness was what I needed most.

She leaned in closer, her voice softening. "You're doing the best you can, Lizzie. And if he can't see that, well, that's his failing, not yours. A man's pride is a stubborn thing, but it doesn't mean you have to break yourself just to keep it intact."

I let out a shaky breath, the weight of her words settling over me. "I just wish he'd understand," I murmured. "I don't know how to explain to him how I feel, but I feel ... heavy. Like I'm wading through a swamp. No matter how much I do, it never seems to be enough. I feel as though my life is overwhelming, and I am never going to get on top of things ever again. Sometimes I just sit in a chair and cry, for no particular reason."

Hester's expression softened, and she put her hand over mine, giving me a gentle squeeze. "You're worn out, love, and still grieving over your lost little girl. You've had the stuffing knocked out of you, and you have to give yourself time to get better. As for John ... men don't always understand what they don't feel themselves. It's going to take time, Lizzie, but you will heal, and hopefully, you will want John in your bed again."

Hester's words stayed with me long after she left. Her blunt advice and her fierce loyalty were like a light cutting through the fog of doubt that had settled over me. She was right, of course. I couldn't keep shrinking under the weight of John's frustration or my own grief. But knowing that and acting on it were two different things.

For a long time after, John and I simply got along. The spark of passion we'd had when we first met, the fire that carried us through the worst of our trials, felt as distant as the moon. Our lives were consumed by the relentless demands of raising children and the grind of survival in this unforgiving land. One day blurred into the next, the connection we'd once shared fading into the background of our daily struggles.

But I missed it. I missed the warmth of John's touch, the comfort of his presence beside me. I missed being close to the man who had once been my refuge in a world that seemed determined to break me. Yet fear held me back—the fear of another pregnancy, another loss, and the pain that would come with it.

As the months passed, though, time worked its quiet magic. My body began to heal, and the sharp edge of my grief dulled to a more bearable ache. I found myself thinking more about the life we had built together, the family we were raising, and the love that was starting to grow between us.

Memories of our early days together crept back to me—the moments of laughter, of hope, of desire. They initially felt like distant whispers, but gradually, they grew louder, reminding me of what we had shared. I realised that if we were going to find our way back to each other, I needed to let go of the fear that had kept me at arm's length.

It wasn't easy. Fear had a way of planting deep roots, twisting itself into every quiet moment. But I knew that John and I couldn't keep living like this—coexisting in a fragile truce, any love between us buried beneath layers of exhaustion and pain. I needed to take the first step, to meet him halfway, if we were ever going to reclaim what we had lost.

One evening, after the children were fast asleep in their beds, I turned towards John in our bed and opened my arms. It was a simple gesture, but it felt like the most challenging thing I had ever done. I didn't know if he would welcome me or turn away if the distance between us had grown too great.

But he didn't need a second invitation. He moved closer, his arms wrapping around me with a tenderness that I had feared was lost. At that moment, the tension that had hung between us for so long seemed to melt away. The warmth of his touch and familiar smell brought back the feelings we had once shared.

We held each other in the quiet of the night, reconnecting in a way that went beyond words. It wasn't about passion or desire, though those feelings were there. It was about finding each other again and healing the wounds left open for too long.

In the days that followed, things didn't magically become easier. We still had our struggles, our worries, and the weight of our responsibilities. But there was a new understanding between us, a renewed sense of closeness. We began to talk again, to share our thoughts and fears like we hadn't in what felt like a long time.

The feeling of ownership that had recently laced John's words seemed to fade, and the snide comments stopped. We started working together as a team again, facing the challenges of our life in the colony with a shared purpose. I knew the road ahead would still be difficult, but I also knew we were stronger together.

Chapter 31

Parramatta, New South Wales, 1818–1820

In August of 1818, I began to suspect that I was pregnant again. The realisation came with a mix of joy, fear, and a resigned acceptance of what lay ahead. Rosetta, now a sturdy five-year-old, had grown into a confident little girl, able to look after herself to some extent. Betsy, almost four, had her own independent streak, and little Johnny, at two and a half, was full of energy and mischief.

I knew adding another baby to our already bustling household wouldn't be easy. But this is what women do, isn't it? We bear children, care for them, and keep our families together through thick and thin. I reminded myself of this as the months passed, and my belly grew heavy with the life inside me.

By early April of 1819, the weather had softened into a perfect balance—sunny days without the harsh bite of the summer sun or the suffocating humidity of summer. Yet, despite the pleasant weather, a heavy weight pressed down on me, both from the baby growing inside me and the nagging worry that something wasn't quite right. Each movement of the baby brought a sharp twinge of discomfort, a constant reminder that the time was near. But unlike my previous pregnancies, this one felt different.

The midwife visited regularly, her hands firm and experienced as she felt the baby's position. "It's not turned yet," she said one day, her voice tinged with concern. "We'll need to be ready, Lizzie. This could be a hard labour."

Her words settled like a stone in my stomach. Hard labour. Here, in this godforsaken country, in a bark hut with a dirt floor. The thought of it sent a shiver down my spine. But what could I do? All I could do was wait and hope for the best, even as fear gnawed at me with every passing day.

The discomfort grew into a dull, constant ache as the days passed. The midwife's visits became more frequent, her brow furrowing deeper each time she checked on me. But she didn't say much, and I tried to take comfort in that—if something were truly wrong, she would tell me, wouldn't she?

Then, one night, the pains started in earnest. They came on fast and strong, leaving me breathless and clutching at the sheets. Pale and wide-eyed, John ran for the midwife, but Hester arrived first, bursting through the door like a whirlwind of calm determination.

"Move aside, John," she barked, waving him toward the corner. "Let me see to her until the midwife gets here."

She was at my side in an instant, her hands firm but steady as she pushed my hair back from my sweat-soaked face. "Breathe, Lizzie," she said, her voice low and steady. "You've got this."

The midwife arrived moments later, her face set in a grim expression as she quickly assessed the situation. "This one's coming feet first," she muttered, her hands already working. "It's going to be a tough one, Lizzie, but you're tougher."

Hester's eyes widened briefly, but she recovered quickly, grabbing my hand and holding it tightly. "You hear that?" she said, her voice steady but with an edge of fierce encouragement. "Tougher than this baby, tougher than anything. You've got it in you, Lizzie."

The hours dragged on, with each contraction more intense than the last. I felt like I was being ripped apart, the pain sharp and unrelenting. Through it all, Hester stayed at my side, her grip grounding me, her sharp voice cutting through the haze of agony whenever I faltered.

"Come on, Lizzie," she said fiercely, her face inches from mine. "You've been through too much to let this beat you. You push when she says, and we'll get this baby out together."

I held on, gritting my teeth as the midwife guided the baby's legs free. It felt like an eternity, every second stretching into what felt like hours. The midwife's hands moved deftly, her expression unreadable as she worked.

Finally, with one last, searing contraction, I felt the baby slip free. The room seemed to hold its breath as the midwife turned the tiny, squirming body upright. A strong, lusty wail filled the air, and I let out a shuddering sob of relief.

Hester let out a triumphant laugh, squeezing my hand tightly. "That's it, Lizzie! You did it! Tough as nails, just like I said."

The midwife handed the baby to me, his small, perfect body warm and wriggling in my arms. Tears blurred my vision as I gazed down at his tiny face, his delicate features scrunched up in protest at the world he'd just entered.

He was small but strong, his cries loud and insistent. As I looked down at him, a wave of relief washed over me, the fear and pain of the past hours fading into the background.

We named him Michael, in memory of Michael Whitethorn. From the moment he took his first breath, he was a lusty, loud baby, his cries filling our small hut with noise. A shock of dark hair crowned his head, and he clenched his tiny fists as if ready to take on whatever the world threw at him. As I held him close, feeling his warmth against my chest, I couldn't help but smile through the exhaustion.

The months that followed Michael's birth were a blur of sleepless nights and endless days, the rhythm of caring for a newborn consuming our lives once again. Every moment seemed to blend into the next, a haze of feeding, rocking and trying to catch whatever sleep I could manage.

John seemed content with our growing family, but I noticed he was spending more and more time away from home. He often disappeared for hours, sometimes well into the night, drinking at the pub or spending time at a mate's house. I tried not to let it bother me, convincing myself he deserved a break after working so hard. But as the days dragged on, his absence became a weight I carried alone.

As the weeks turned into months, Michael grew rapidly, his loud cries giving way to giggles and coos that filled our tiny home. The other children adored him, their little hands always reaching out to touch his soft cheeks or make him laugh. But even as his laughter echoed through the walls, I felt as though a shadow was creeping in, growing darker every day.

The days stretched endlessly, a relentless cycle of feeding, cleaning, and tending to the children's needs. Though Michael's sweet laughter brought fleeting moments of joy, they never seemed to linger. Instead, an unease settled over me, heavy and suffocating. I grew more tired, my patience fraying at the edges. Every small task felt insurmountable, and everyday things like the chatter of the children sometimes drove me to the point of screaming.

John was no comfort. He seemed distant, his eyes clouded with thoughts he kept to himself. I sensed a restlessness in him, a growing discontent that made him less present, even when he was home. I tried to speak with him about it, but the words felt heavy in my mouth, and his answers were vague and unsatisfying.

At night, when the children were finally asleep, and the house was still, I sat by the fire, feeling the weight of the day press down on me. My thoughts raced, a jumble of worries and fears that I couldn't seem to quiet. The bottle of rum we kept for special occasions caught my eye one evening, and I poured myself a small measure. Just a sip, I thought, to calm my nerves, to help me sleep.

At first, it worked. The warmth of the liquor dulled the edges of my anxiety, quieting the restless thoughts that plagued me. But soon, it became more than that—a crutch to lean on when the nights felt too long, a way to numb the creeping dread I couldn't quite put into words.

I told myself it was temporary, and I'd stop when things got better. But deep down, I knew something was shifting inside me, a darkness I couldn't shake. Even surrounded by the life we'd built, I felt untethered, as though I were drifting further from myself with each passing day.

John, too, seemed to be wrestling with his own demons. He spoke more frequently of Van Diemen's Land and the fresh start that awaited us there. But his tone was different, darker, as if he were trying to convince himself as much as me. The idea of starting over, of leaving everything behind, seemed less like a hopeful dream and more like an escape—a way to outrun whatever was chasing us.

In May 1820, it felt like it was now or never. The thought of a fresh start in Launceston called us. The opportunities, the land, the chance to build something lasting for our family—it all seemed within reach if we were brave enough to seize it. It was time.

Even though we were both now free, this was still, after all, a penal colony, and there were hoops to jump through before we could leave. We needed to put a notice in the Sydney Gazette to show that we were leaving the colony, to make sure we didn't leave any debts, and in case we were owed money. John did this, making our intentions known to the world. It felt so final, seeing it in print, but a sense of excitement was also bubbling beneath the surface. We then had to get Governor Macquarie's permission to leave, which we got from the judge advocate's office. We would need that pass to show to the government officials in Launceston that we had permission to leave New South Wales and settle there. John then booked our passage; from that moment, our lives were set on a new course.

The days leading up to our departure were a whirlwind of activity. We sold what we couldn't take with us and packed the rest, ensuring we had enough provisions for the journey and setting up a new home once we arrived. The older children were abuzz with excitement, their youthful energy bringing some lightness to the heavy task of uprooting our lives.

As much as we tried to focus on the practicalities of life, there was an undercurrent we couldn't shake. The laughter in our home still echoed, but it was tinged with a tension neither of us dared to name. We were moving forward, yes, but underneath it all, there was an unspoken understanding that things were not as they should be.

CLAIMS AND DEMANDS.

MR. JOSEPH JAMES proceeding to Port Dalrymple, requests all Claims to be immediately presented for Payment.

CAPTAIN MACKEY, of the Ship Acteon, proceeding in said Vessel, requests Claims to be presented.

MR. JOHN GORDON leaving the Colony in the Ship Acteon, desires Claims to be presented.

MR. ALEXANDER M'FARLAN leaving the Colony in the Ship Acteon, all Claims to be presented.

ANN INNIS and HENRY TALBOT (a Child) leaving the Colony in the Ship Claudine, request Claims to be presented at No. 18, O'Connell-street.

JANE GOSLING proceeding to Port Dalrymple, requests Claims to be presented.

ANN SHEA proceeding to Port Dalrymple, requests Claims to be presented.

SUSAN PAWLEY leaving the Colony for Port Dalrymple, all Claims to be presented.

ANN OGLE proceeding to Port Dalrymple, requests Claims to be presented.

O. TARNI leaving the Colony in the Schooner Little Mary, all Claims to be presented.

JOHN BAREFOOT and Family leaving the Colony in the Schooner Little Mary, all Claims to be presented.

'Claims and demands' page, Sydney Gazette 6 May 1820 (http://nla.gov.au/nla.news-page494610), and the muster of the schooner Little Mary, of Sydney (AO Reel 1255 (4/1235.8, 4/1235.11). John is number 16 in the list of convicts and Elizabeth is number 5, free by certificate No. 10/1583.

John's late nights grew more frequent; his excuses grew thinner. He spoke of extra work or meeting with neighbours, but I knew better. There was a distance in him, a restlessness I couldn't quite reach. At first, I thought it was the burden of providing for a growing family, the weight of making ends meet in this harsh land. But deep down, I began to suspect it was something more.

The shadows in his eyes hinted at a guilt he wouldn't speak of. I knew him too well to miss it. He carried the weight of those two men—the ones he'd betrayed to the magistrate, whose lives had been destroyed, along with their families. He had tried to justify it to himself, to me, but the truth lingered between us like a spectre.

Some nights, when he thought I was asleep, I heard him pacing outside, his boots crunching against the dry ground. Other times, he'd sit by the fire, staring into the flames with a look that made my chest ache. He was running, not from me, but from the guilt that gnawed at him.

I wanted to confront him, to tell him that we couldn't keep living like this, with a divide growing between us that neither of us would acknowledge. But fear kept me silent—fear of what he might say, or worse, of what he wouldn't.

Instead, I turned inward, trying to carry the weight alone. But the cracks in our lives were becoming harder to ignore, the tension stretching thinner with each passing day. Even as Michael's laughter filled the house, even as we made plans for the future, I couldn't shake the feeling that we were teetering on the edge of something that could break us both.

As the day of our departure approached, the sense of foreboding grew stronger, casting a long shadow over the excitement of the journey ahead. The prospect of Van Diemen's Land, once so full of promise, now felt like the brink of something darker. We were leaving behind the familiar, stepping into the unknown, and whatever awaited us there felt as uncertain as the storm clouds gathering on the horizon.

One of the hardest parts of leaving was saying goodbye to the friends who had become my lifeline in this strange new world. Catherine, Maggie, and Hester had seen me through some of the darkest moments, sharing in the joys and sorrows of this life of exile. The thought of leaving them behind added a weight to my heart that I could scarcely bear.

The day before we were to leave, Catherine came to visit. She held me tight, her eyes glistening with unshed tears. "I can't believe you're really going, Lizzie," she said, her voice thick with emotion. "I don't know what I'll do without you."

I forced a smile, trying to be strong for both of us. "You'll be fine, Catherine. You have quite the family with John and the little one on the way. You'll be all right."

"But what about you?" she pressed. "Are you sure about this? It's not too late to change your mind."

I shook my head, though doubt gnawed at me. "We've made our decision. John thinks it's for the best, and maybe he's right. Maybe this is what we need—a fresh start, away from everything here."

Maggie and Hester came by later that afternoon, their presence a small comfort amidst the turmoil. Maggie, ever the practical one, handed me a bundle of clothes she had sewn for the children. "For the journey," she said, her voice brisk but kind. "And for your new life. I expect it'll be cold down there, colder than you're used to."

"Thank you, Maggie," I said, hugging her. "You've always been so good to us."

Hester lingered near the doorway, her expression shadowed with something heavier than her usual demeanour. When it was time to say goodbye, she pulled me aside, her hands gripping my arms tightly as her dark eyes searched mine.

"Lizzie," she said, her voice low and trembling slightly, "I don't like this. I don't like any of it." She paused, her gaze softening but her grip firm. "I'm worried about you. You've been ... different, love. Since your poor wee babe died ..." She trailed off, but her unspoken words hung heavy in the air.

I tried to pull away, brushing her off with a weak smile. "I'll be fine, Hester. Really. We just need a fresh start. That's all this is."

"Don't lie to me, Lizzie," she snapped, her voice sharper now. "I've seen it in your eyes—the sadness, the way you drift off when you think no one's looking. And I know you've been drinking ..." She hesitated, her jaw tightening. "You think I haven't noticed, but I have. A sip here, a sip there. It's not you, Lizzie. You're carrying too much, and I'm scared you'll break if you keep going like this."

Her words hit me like a blow, and I couldn't stop the tears that welled in my eyes. "I'm just tired, Hester," I whispered, my voice cracking. "Tired of everything."

Her grip on me tightened. "I know, love. I know. But you've got to promise me something—promise me you won't let it swallow you whole. You're stronger than this, Lizzie, but even the strongest of us need help sometimes. If it gets too much, you send a message to me. I'll find a way to get to you."

I nodded, my throat too tight to speak, and she pulled me into a fierce hug.

"You're like a daughter to me, you know that," she murmured against my shoulder, her voice thick with emotion. "And I'm not about to lose you to some dark corner of your mind or the bottom of a bottle. You hear me?"

I nodded again, clinging to her like a lifeline, her words cutting through the haze of my guilt and despair.

When she pulled back, her eyes were red, but her voice regained some of its usual edge. "Now, don't think this lets you off the hook. If I don't hear from you, I'll show up in Barefoot Bay or wherever you end up and knock some sense into that thick head of yours."

I laughed softly through my tears, grateful for her humour even in this moment of heartbreak. "I promise."

As she walked away, her shoulders squared but her steps slow, I felt the weight of her words settle over me. Hester saw the cracks I tried so hard to hide, and her worry felt like both a burden and a gift. Leaving her behind felt like losing the last person who truly understood me, and for a moment, I wasn't sure how I'd manage without her.

For the first time, I noticed how much she had aged. Her movements had slowed, her back not quite as straight as it once had been. Her face, weathered by years of struggle, bore the lines of a hard life, and her dark hair was streaked heavily with grey.

Hester turned briefly at the end of the path, her gaze meeting mine one last time. She raised a hand in a small, almost reluctant wave, and then she was gone, disappearing with Maggie around the corner. The sight of her fading into the distance left an ache in my chest. It finally hit me that I would likely never see her again, and the sense of loss was almost overwhelming.

For the past twelve years, Hester had been like a mother to me, and watching her walk away now stirred emotions I had long buried. It reminded me all over again of the goodbye I had never said to my mother. When she left me with the Church family, we thought we would see each other again, that it was only a temporary parting. But life had taken a different turn.

She wouldn't have known what happened to me, wouldn't have known that I'd been taken to Ireland, or abandoned or how far I'd fallen. The next time my uncle had come to Wilmington and come to check on me, I would have simply disappeared. Had she searched for me? Had she mourned, wondering if I were dead or lost to the world? The thought was unbearable, yet it clung to me, heavy and inescapable.

And now, as Hester walked away, the weight of those unanswered questions pressed down on me. This felt like another kind of goodbye, one I wasn't ready for, though I could see the inevitability of it in the slow, deliberate steps of the woman who had filled the space my mother once occupied. It was a reminder of the loss I had never fully reckoned with, a grief that lingered just beneath the surface, as raw as it had ever been.

As John and I sat by the fire that night, I couldn't keep the unease from creeping into my voice. "John," I began hesitantly, "are you sure about this? Leaving everyone we know behind, starting over in a place like Van Diemen's Land?"

He looked at me, his face hardening. "We've been through this, Lizzie. This is what we need. The opportunities there ... they're worth the risk."

I wanted to believe him, to trust that he knew what he was doing. But as the firelight flickered across his face, casting shadows in the hollows of his cheeks, I saw something in his eyes that gave me pause. A determination, yes, but also a desperation I hadn't noticed before. What demons was he running from?

Chapter 32

Parramatta, New South Wales to Van Diemen's Land, 1820

The day we set sail for Van Diemen's Land, the sky was a perfect shade of blue, with only a few clouds lazily drifting across it. Our schooner, *Little Mary*, a 60-ton vessel that seemed both sturdy and fragile at the same time, was anchored at the docks, ready to take us to our new life. I clasped Michael tightly, his tiny body warm against mine, while Rosetta and Betsy clung to John's legs, their eyes wide with excitement and a little fear. Little Johnny, too young to understand the gravity of our departure, babbled happily as we boarded. As we sailed away, I glanced back at the shoreline, the now familiar sights of Sydney fading into the distance, replaced by the vast, open sea ahead.

As we sailed down the south coast of the colony, the coastline stretched out like a rugged spine, the land rising and falling in jagged cliffs and sandy coves. The water was a deep, endless blue, and the wind caught in the sails, pushing us steadily onward. We saw seals sunning themselves on the rocks, their sleek bodies glistening in the sun, and dolphins leaped playfully alongside the ship, their movements graceful and free. Even Rosetta, usually so talkative, was quiet, her eyes wide with wonder as she watched the dolphins.

"Look, Ma!" she finally exclaimed, pointing at the water. "They're so close!"

I smiled down at her. "Aren't they beautiful, love? They're saying goodbye to us, wishing us luck on our journey."

John stood beside me, his gaze fixed on the horizon. "I wonder if we'll see any whales," he murmured, more to himself than to me.

"Maybe," I replied, trying to keep the mood light. "Wouldn't that be something?"

The first few days passed in a blur of ocean and sky, the ship creaking and groaning as it cut through the waves. We kept to our small quarters most of the time, the children playing quietly while John and I talked about the future that awaited us in Van Diemen's Land.

There was a strange sense of peace in those conversations, as if we were both trying to hold on to the good things, the dreams we still shared, even as the reality of our situation lingered in the background.

One evening, as the sun dipped below the horizon, painting the sky in shades of pink and orange, we spotted whales gliding gracefully alongside the ship. Their massive bodies broke through the water's surface, their movements both powerful and mesmerising. Several seemed to delight in the ship's presence, flipping themselves out of the water, slapping their fins, and putting on a show that left us all speechless.

The children crowded eagerly around the railing, their laughter and shouts of delight rising above the creak of the ship. "Look at that one!" Johnny cried, pointing at a particularly playful whale as it breached with a splash that sent excitement through the group.

"Look at them," I murmured to John, my voice filled with awe. "Aren't they the most amazing creatures you've ever seen?" He nodded, a rare smile tugging at the corners of his mouth. "A good omen," he said softly. "Maybe this journey will bring us the fresh start we need."

But as we rounded the southern tip of land, the weather turned for the worse. The skies darkened, heavy clouds rolling in as the wind picked up, howling through the rigging with a ferocity that made the schooner shudder. The groaning of the timbers was soon joined by the relentless crashing of waves against the hull, each impact rattling the very bones of the ship. As we crossed Bass Strait, the schooner pitched and rolled violently, the sea seeming intent on swallowing us whole.

My stomach churned in protest, and each lurch of the ship made the sickness worse. Below deck, the air was thick with salt, fear, and the stifling stench of vomit. The children clung to each other, their wide eyes glinting in the dim, swaying lantern light. I cradled Michael to my chest, his cries drowned out by the unrelenting roar of the storm. Every creak of timber and every shudder of the ship set my heart racing, each moment feeling like it might be our last.

After what felt like an eternity—a night and day of misery—the storm began to relent. The winds softened, the waves eased, and the schooner stopped its relentless thrashing. When the rugged coastline of Van Diemen's Land finally came into view, the sight filled me with a strange mix of hope and fear.

This was a new beginning, a fresh chapter, but it also marked the end of everything familiar. As the schooner sailed into the harbour, the air damp with the smell of sea and earth, I held my children close, feeling the weight of our journey and the choices we'd made settle over me. The future was unknown and uncertain, and I could only pray we were strong enough to face it.

"Welcome to Van Diemen's Land," John said quietly, his arm around my shoulders as we stood on the deck, watching the land approach. "Our new home."

Chapter 33

Launceston, Van Diemen's Land, 1820

Launceston, nestled at the mouth of the Tamar River in the north of Van Diemen's Land, was a curious settlement caught between two towns. Governor Macquarie had envisioned George Town as the heart of the colony, but most settlers gravitated toward Launceston, where the water was clearer and the land more suitable for farming. We chose to make our home in Launceston, even though the region remained quite wild and untamed.

Tim Daley, who had gained his freedom just before John, had settled in Launceston a few months before we arrived. Seeing his familiar face amidst the unfamiliar landscape was a comfort. He was living with another ex-convict whom he had met in Sydney and brought with him, though she didn't join him when he came to greet us. Tim had arranged a small wattle and daub hut for us—simple, but it felt like a refuge after the journey. It was on Brisbane Street, near the corner of Charles Street, close to the market on Paterson Street.

The bush surrounding the settlement was beautiful, so different from home and distinct from Sydney—towering gum trees and plenty of grassland. Just like in the bush at Parramatta, there were lots of furry grey kangaroos and smaller ones called wallabies. But by far the strangest animals we had ever seen were the Devil and the Tiger. The screeches of the Devils at night were spine-chilling! And then the Tiger ... not a tiger like the ones I've seen in pictures, but a bizarre-looking creature that resembled a dog, though with large dark stripes along its back, unlike any dog I've ever come across.

Actual dogs were everywhere—throughout the township, in the bush, hunting alongside both whites and blacks. There were also wild pigs, which had escaped from farms—they made for delicious eating when you could come across one and kill it. Of course, it was forbidden. Such animals were to be reported to the constables (who I suspect went out and shot them themselves!), but there was a thriving black market for fresh meat of any kind.

We were off government stores now, so we had to fend for ourselves. I learned to make do with what was available, often cooking up the local "kangaroo steamer"—a hearty stew of kangaroo meat and a small slab of salty pork, cooked until the gravy was rich and the meat tender. The children took to it well, and it became a staple on our table, stretched out with a few potatoes when we had them. Muttonbird was plentiful in the right season and made for quite a feast when we could get one. But many days, we just had soup made with whatever leftover meat we could use, barley or oats to fill it out, and some damper, preferably with the weevils picked out of the flour first.

This was truly a new land, with different ways of doing things compared to Sydney or Parramatta. The town of Hobart, down on the south coast, was the colony's main settlement, but it had only been established around fifteen years before we arrived. Launceston, featuring a mix of convicts, freed convicts like us, soldiers, and a few free settlers, was still small—a cluster of about one hundred huts. Redcoats were everywhere—supposedly to protect the local citizens from convicts, but, as in Sydney, they tended to get on the grog and cause havoc in town.

However, while we were now free, and so were many others, Van Diemen's Land was still mainly a place where the English dumped their convicts. The division between those who came free and those of us with the convict stain ran deep, a reminder that freedom didn't erase history.

Even among the settlers, there was a quiet but unmistakable hierarchy. Those born in the colony — like our children — were often referred to as currency brats, a term derived from the makeshift money that circulated in the early years of New South Wales. Like that unofficial currency, they were regarded as inferior—of dubious value compared to the British-born sterling.

It was a distinction that overshadowed everything, a mark of subordination that no amount of hard work or good behaviour could entirely erase. Those without the convict stain looked down their noses at us, regardless of how far we'd come or what we'd built in this new land.

A few months after we arrived at Launceston, a muster was held. We registered ourselves—John and I, now both with a certificate of freedom—and our children, who were listed as children of free people. Rosetta, more often Rose now that she was growing up, was now eight, Betsy six, Johnny three, and Michael one.

The older children loved Launceston and were quite wild, running around the town and playing with new friends. There was some talk around the traps about setting up a school so that the children could learn to read and write, but nothing much came of it. The middle-class and wealthy folk had tutors for their children, who didn't mix with ours anyway. After all, who wanted to educate the currency brats, and for what purpose? Our children were destined to be labourers or to do the unwanted tasks of those better off than them.

The Macquarie Harbour prison colony was newly established on the western side of the island, serving as a place where the most unruly convicts were sent—a site of brutal punishment that locals whispered about as "Hell on earth". Only about 200 miles away, its presence served as a constant reminder of how close we were to the edge of civilisation. Tales circulated through the town of breakouts, bushrangers, and even cannibals. Everything felt much closer, more immediate than it ever had in Parramatta.

Then, there was also the ongoing conflict between the white settlers and the blacks, the *Mairremmener*. While there was some friendly interaction between the two groups, I heard too many stories in town to believe that a comfortable coexistence was ever possible. As the colony expanded, I knew we and our sheep took over much of their traditional land, destroying the breeding grounds and living spaces for the kangaroos they hunted, which provided most of their food. This led to the blacks often hunting settlers' cattle and killing their sheep, earning fierce reprisals from the colonists. How could such conflict ever be resolved peacefully?

The tendrils of darkness continued to creep into our marriage. One evening, as we sat by the fire, John turned to me with an expression I hadn't seen before. The flickering flames cast shadows on his face, and his voice was low, almost hesitant. "Elizabeth, there's something I've never told you. Something I should've told you ages ago."

My heart skipped a beat. "What is it, John?"

He took a deep breath, gazing into the fire. "When I told you I stole that sheep to feed my starving family, I left something out. I had a family back in England—a wife and a couple of children."

The words hit me like a blow. "You were married?"

"Yeah, so when I headed off to Ireland, I left them behind. I've got no clue what happened to them. When I met you, I wasn't thinking clearly. I needed a fresh start, and I ... well, I kept it all from you."

I felt something inside me snap. All these years, all the struggles and sacrifices, and it had all been built on a lie. I wanted to scream, to cry, to hit him, but all I could do was sit there, numb. "So, our marriage isn't even real?"

He nodded, shame clouding his eyes. "In the eyes of the law, no. But I've always been fond of you, Elizabeth. I've come to love you, you know that. It doesn't have to change anything, does it?" he asked. His words felt hollow. The man I thought I knew had deceived me, and it gnawed at me, festering like an open wound.

Of course, no one else had to know about his previous marriage—his first wife wasn't likely to ever come to Van Diemen's Land and find him—but I knew. And that knowledge, that betrayal, started to poison everything. It made me question not just him but also myself. What sort of man could abandon a wife and children as if they were nothing more than an inconvenient chapter of his past? And what sort of fool was I to think I was any different? If he'd done it once, what was to stop him from doing it again?

John looked up from the fire, his face lined with the weight of his confession, but there was something else in his expression—fear, perhaps, or maybe just shame.

"So why tell me now?" I asked, my voice cold and steady despite the storm rising inside me. "Why after all this time, after a wedding, after all these children? Why now?"

He licked his lips, avoiding my gaze, his eyes drifting toward the corner of the room as if he were searching for an escape. "Well ..." he began, his hesitation revealing more than his words ever could.

"Does this have anything to do with why we left Parramatta?" I pressed. The vague unease I'd felt during those final weeks before we sailed suddenly sharpened into focus. At the time, I'd chalked it up to John's restless nature, his constant chatter about new opportunities. But now ... now it felt like more.

John shifted uncomfortably on his stool, his hands fidgeting with the edge of his coat. "Ah ... actually, yes. If we're being completely honest," he admitted, his tone heavy with reluctance.

"Please," I said, my voice cutting like a blade. "That would be a good start, wouldn't it?"

He flinched but didn't argue. "I'd been talking with Tim about moving here. And I really needed to go somewhere that I wasn't always reminded of those two men on Norfolk Island, away from their families. So that much was true. But the timing ... the timing wasn't exactly my choice."

"Why?" I demanded, unwilling to let him sidestep the truth any longer.

"I heard a name," he said finally, his voice barely above a whisper. "At the pub one night. A name I'd hoped never to hear again. Thomas Bennett."

I frowned, the name unfamiliar. "And who, pray tell, is Thomas Bennett?"

John swallowed hard. "He's my wife's brother. My first wife. And he's here ... in the colony. I heard he'd been transported for something or other back in the old country. And ... well, I knew it wouldn't end well if he found me."

My stomach turned, the pieces clicking into place with sickening clarity. "So, what, you thought you could just run away? Drag me and the children to this godforsaken place to avoid your past catching up with you?"

"I thought it was the only way," he said, his voice rising defensively. "Thomas would've told you everything—probably in the harshest way possible. And he could've done worse than that. I don't know what he would've done to me for abandoning his sister like that. I don't know what happened to her; I suppose she could have ended up in the workhouse. And the man's not exactly known for his forgiveness. I figured we'd be out of his reach if we came here. But ..." He trailed off, running a hand through his hair. "It's been eating at me ever since."

I stared at him, my heart racing. Part of me wanted to scream, to lash out at him. I bet it hadn't been eating away at him; I was pretty sure that his fear of being discovered spurred him on. But another part of me, the part that had learned to cope in this harsh, unforgiving land, knew that anger wouldn't change a thing.

"So, what now?" I asked finally, my voice weary but firm. "Do you expect me just to forget this? To go on pretending like nothing's happened?"

John met my gaze, his eyes shadowed with regret. "I don't know," he admitted. "I just ... I didn't want you to hear it from him. And I didn't want to lose you."

I stood, the firelight casting my shadow long against the wall. "You already have, John. Maybe not entirely. Maybe not yet. But this ... this has changed things."

The silence between us was thick, almost suffocating. I had no idea how to even process the betrayal that had just been laid bare. Yet even as the truth settled like a stone in my chest, I felt another burden pressing down on me—one I hadn't voiced yet.

I hesitated, my hand unconsciously resting on my stomach. The words were caught in my throat, and I almost couldn't bring myself to say them. Finally, I took a deep breath, steeling myself for what I had to do.

"I guess now isn't the time to tell you that I'm with child again, is it?" My voice came out quieter than I intended, a mixture of sadness and bitterness.

John's head snapped up. For a moment, the severity in his expression softened, replaced by something that almost looked like regret. He opened his mouth to speak, but no words came out. I could see the conflict in him, the guilt and the uncertainty, and it only made the ache in my heart grow stronger.

"How long have you known?" he finally asked, his voice barely above a whisper.

"A few weeks," I admitted, wrapping my arms around myself as if to shield myself from the cold reality of it all. "I didn't want to say anything until I was sure. But now ... now I don't know what to think, what to feel."

John reached out as if to comfort me, but I took a step back, the distance between us widening not just physically but emotionally as well. His hand hovered in the air before he slowly let it drop, his shoulders slumping with the weight of our shared burden.

"I'm sorry, Elizabeth," he said, his voice thick with emotion. "I didn't mean for any of this to happen."

I shook my head, tears welling up in my eyes. "But it has, John. And now ... now we have another child on the way, and I don't even know who you are anymore."

The room fell into silence once more, the only sound being the crackling of the fire. I felt lost, adrift in a sea of confusion and pain. How could I bring another child into this world, into this broken family? How could I trust John when the fundamental truth I believed I knew about him had been completely turned upside down?

In that moment, I realised that the pain of his betrayal wasn't something I could simply brush aside or forget. It was a wound that would fester, eating away at what we had once shared. I felt as though we had come to love each other in our different ways, and this felt like a betrayal of that bond. As much as I wanted to believe we could move past it, the truth was I wasn't sure if we really could.

Sensing the turmoil within me, John tried to close the gap between us. "Elizabeth, we'll get through this. We've faced worse before, haven't we?"

But his words rang hollow in my ears. I wasn't sure if we could survive this. And as I looked at him, I felt a wave of sorrow and disappointment wash over me—so deep, so consuming that I knew I would need something more substantial to numb it.

I turned away from him, retreating into the shadows of the room. "I need to be alone, John. Please ... just give me some time."

He nodded, though I could see the hurt in his eyes. Without another word, he left the room, the door closing softly behind him. And as the silence enveloped me once more, I knew things would never be the same between us.

I reached for the bottle I'd hidden away, the one I'd sworn I wouldn't touch again. But tonight, it was the only thing that could drown out the pain, the only thing that could quiet the storm raging inside me. And as I took that first, bitter sip, I knew I was stepping onto a path from which there might be no return. I took my mother's locket from around my neck and wrapped it in a piece of fabric I'd saved many years ago. I felt ashamed of how my life was turning out, and I didn't want my mother to be present in any way to witness it.

Chapter 34

In May of 1821, the atmosphere in Launceston crackled with anticipation as the visit of Governor Macquarie and his wife, Elizabeth, drew near. The town had buzzed with preparations; government buildings received a fresh coat of whitewash, while every street underwent a thorough cleaning to present our little corner of the world in its best light. As evening approached, a different kind of transformation began to unfold—a transformation that would etch this day into my memory forever.

Torches and lanterns were lit throughout the town, casting a warm, golden glow that seemed to breathe life into the air itself. The overcast greyness of my daily struggles melted away beneath the brilliant lights that adorned the streets. Even the simplest homes, often overlooked in the rush of daily life, appeared resplendent under the soft flicker of candlelight shining from every window.

As night enveloped Launceston, the entire town sparkled like a sea of tiny stars. Children giggled and pointed, their faces lit with wonder, while adults paused to take in the beauty of our transformed surroundings. Bonfires were lit in open spaces, their flames licking the night sky and casting long shadows that danced in rhythm with the evening. The warmth of the fires drew people together, creating little pockets of community. I stood on the street with my children; Michael was fixed to my hip, while Rose, Betsy, and John danced around a bonfire alongside the other children.

Mrs Macquarie moved through this enchanting scene with grace.

Her face was serene yet curious, lending an air of warmth and genuine care. Her presence felt almost luminescent, as if she were both a part of the spectacle and its very source. She stopped and spoke to me, her eyes twinkling in the lantern light, and I felt a connection that went beyond our different stations in life. I was very clearly with child, and she stopped and touched my belly wistfully.

Governor Macquarie was nearby, speaking with another group, his figure exuding authority and the quiet confidence of a man who believed in himself and his vision. From the corner of my eye, I saw him glance toward his wife, a faint smile softening his features before he returned to his conversation.

What's your name, dear?" she asked.

"Elizabeth, ma'am, same as you," I answered. She smiled and nodded.

"How far along are you?" she asked, her voice soft and filled with genuine interest.

"Seven months, ma'am," I replied, feeling both honoured and slightly nervous under her attentive gaze.

Mrs Macquarie's eyes softened even more as she looked down at my growing belly and Michael on my hip. "And this will be your ...?"

"My fifth, ma'am," I answered. "I have this one," gesturing to a squirming Michael, "and three others over there dancing around the fire."

Her expression shifted subtly, a mix of warmth and sadness. "You are very fortunate to have such a large family," she said, almost to herself. "I only have one child, my dear Lachlan Junior, but we lost many before him. It's a grief that never truly leaves you."

I nodded, fighting back tears. "Yes, ma'am. I also know the pain of losing a child. It is always there, but the love for the ones we have keeps us going. But it is tough to provide for all of them, and I am always fearful that I won't be able to do what I must for them."

Mrs Macquarie's eyes filled with deep empathy as she squeezed my hand gently. "I am so sorry to hear that, my dear. The pain of loss and the weight of responsibility can indeed be overwhelming. Your resilience, your love, that is your greatest gift to them," she continued, her voice steady. "Many women of means may never know the strength you exhibit every day."

"Thank you, ma'am," I said, my voice trembling. "Your words have given me more strength than you know."

She nodded, a gentle smile gracing her lips. "And I will keep you in my thoughts and prayers, my dear. Remember, every act of love and every small victory is a testament to your strength."

After this meeting, I felt a sense of comfort, a warmth that seemed to stay with me even as I watched her move on to greet others. The slightly manic laughter of my children playing by the fire blended with the mellow cracks of the bonfire and the faint hum of the town's celebration.

As the months passed, our lives continued with the usual challenges, but Mrs Macquarie's words stayed with me and gave me strength and courage for what was ahead of me.

Annie was born in August 1821. She was a small but strong-willed child who quickly made her presence known with loud cries and fierce determination. As I held her for the first time, I felt a fleeting moment of peace, a connection to this new life that had come into our world. But that peace was short-lived.

John barely glanced at his new daughter. Almost mechanically, he kissed her on the forehead and muttered something about needing some air. Within an hour, he was off, out with a bunch of mates, drinking and celebrating like the way men did—without a thought for the wife he'd left behind. Days passed before I saw him again, and when he finally staggered back, the stench of alcohol clung to him like a second skin. He mumbled an apology, but his words felt empty, and his presence only widened the growing chasm between us.

In his absence, I had to deal with the never-ending demands of a newborn and four other children. Rose, at eight, and Betsy, at seven, tried to help where they could—fetching water, sweeping the floor, or soothing Michael when he cried—but their little hands could only manage so much. Little Johnny, at four, was a whirlwind of mischief and boundless energy, making him more of a handful than a help. I'd send him to collect firewood, only to catch him chasing frogs or climbing trees instead. His questions came in a steady stream—"Why does the fire crackle? Where does the sun go? Can I ride the cow?"—and while his energy was unending, his attention span was fleeting. And Michael, still a baby himself, was always at my feet, tugging at my skirts and crying for attention.

I understood this was a woman's lot in life—to bear the children, to care for them, to keep the household running while the men did as they pleased. But understanding didn't make it any easier. Each day stretched out endlessly, the weight of it all pressing down on me. I felt a slow burn of anger deep in my belly, a resentment simmering just below the surface. How could John be so thoughtless? How could he leave me to shoulder this burden alone while he chased his plans and ignored the chaos at home?

But the anger quickly turned inwards. I began to see myself as weak, a failure. Other women managed, didn't they? I told myself I should be stronger and more capable, but the truth was, I felt consumed once more by the dark, suffocating fog that clouded my thoughts and dulled my senses.

Some days, it was all I could do to get out of bed. The children's cries became a constant, grating noise that drilled into my skull, and the weight of Annie in my arms felt like an anchor dragging me down. The daily grind of cooking, cleaning, washing, and caring for the children became unbearable, an endless cycle that I couldn't escape.

Even the simplest tasks felt insurmountable. Getting laundry done became a never-ending ordeal. Rose and Betsy tried to help hang the clothes up, their little hands struggling to pin the wet fabric on the line. Johnny, meanwhile, turned it into a game, running through the drying sheets and making them muddy chaos. Michael, always underfoot, trailed behind me, crying if I dared put him down for even a moment.

I knew I was neglecting them. I could see it in the way Rose hesitated before asking for help or in the tear-streaked cheeks of Betsy when I snapped at her over something minor. Yet the fog wrapped around me, pulling me deeper into despair, and I felt like I was drowning. No matter how hard I tried, I couldn't break free.

The revelation about John's past still gnawed at me, a relentless ache I couldn't shake. Months had passed, yet the wound it left felt fresh, compounding my already fragile state. And so, the days slipped by in a blur of exhaustion and darkness, the children's laughter merely a faint echo of what should have been a happy home. I felt trapped, battling the shadows in my mind, unable to find my way back to the light. John found work felling trees, helping clear land, earning money for the household and food for the table. But I could never seem to get on top of anything.

I reflected on my mother, who raised ten children while managing a farm and maintaining a household. How did she do it all? The comparison only heightened my feelings of failure. I was neglecting my children—I was aware of it, and so were they. There were days when we didn't have enough food, and I could see the hunger in their eyes. They ran wild around town, barefoot even in winter, dressed in clothes that resembled rags. Sometimes, I attempted to clean them up, but they fought me tooth and nail, and eventually, I just gave up.

One evening, as I stared at the meagre meal I'd managed to scrape together, I felt something inside me snap. The weight of my own inadequacy pressed down like a heavy fog. I poured myself a drink and then another, and soon, the fog began to lift, replaced by a warm numbness. It was easier to drown my sorrows than to face them, easier to numb the pain than confront the reality of what my life had become.

Then, in June 1823, it felt like John's plans for our future finally came together. He was granted fifty acres of land in the Gordon Plains area, a stretch of fertile soil bordered on one side by the South Esk River. The river's steady flow promised a good water supply, and the land was rich and full of potential. It was the kind of land a man could build a future on, the type of land that could provide for a growing family. John started building a house on it in his spare time, and we set up a tent on the property and moved into it. It was rough, but it was ours.

It was a mild yet sunny afternoon in late spring that year, the sun casting long shadows as Tim approached with the woman that I assumed to be the mysterious wife. I was in the middle of tending to the children, trying to keep the chaos to a minimum. Little Annie was crying incessantly, Michael was tugging at my skirt for attention, and Rose and Betsy were bickering over a ragged doll. Johnny, at least, was occupied, though with what I had no idea. He was likely up to some kind of mischief.

"Elizabeth, is that really you?" Hannah called out, her tone dripping with false sweetness as she approached. I could hardly believe what was in front of me—Hannah Murphy, of all people. Tim stood back quietly, looking somewhat nonplussed.

I swear she did not look a day older than I had last seen her in Sydney when we first disembarked *Providence*. Her curly red hair did not seem to have changed at all, and she still had the same slim figure she had had back then. I felt saggy and droopy just looking at her, and I knew that my once dark red-brown hair was liberally streaked with grey. My head was cloudy from drinking the night before, and I felt like an old hag in comparison.

But I straightened up, wiping sweat from my brow and plastering what I hoped passed for a smile on my face. "Hannah Murphy," I said, forcing a smile. "What a surprise."

Tim was somewhat taken aback by our exchange. "You two know each other then?" he asked.

Hannah smirked, "Oh yes, we go way back, don't we, Lizzie dear?"

Her eyes scanned our small settlement, taking in the state of disarray. "My, my, you certainly have your hands full, don't you?" she remarked, her smirk widening as her gaze fell on the children. "How ever do you manage?"

I felt a sting of resentment but swallowed it down. "We do our best," I replied, trying to keep my voice even. "And what brings you here today?"

Hannah glanced at her husband and then back at me, her expression smug. "Tim and I thought we'd come by and see how our new neighbours are settling in. It seems like you've got quite a bit on your plate." She arched an eyebrow. "Is John not helping out?"

I could feel the tension tightening in my chest. "John's been busy with the farm," I said, my voice betraying none of the turmoil inside. "It's a lot of work."

"Yes, well, men can be like that," she said with a sigh that sounded more like a performance than genuine. "Tim is just the same. But I always make sure he knows what's expected of him." She leaned in closer, a gleam in her eye. "And at least it's only fifty acres, not like a big grant."

I forced a laugh, though it came out more strained than I intended. "I'm sure John will find his way, and it's plenty big enough for us, for now."

She regarded me with false sympathy. "Oh, Elizabeth, you look absolutely knackered. How many children do you have now? Five? Six?" She chuckled, and I could sense the scorn beneath it. Tim shuffled from foot to foot, clearly wishing he were anywhere but here.

"Yes, five," I said, trying to keep my composure as Michael tugged at my skirts again. "And you, Hannah?"

"Just two, but I have a woman to help me with them," she said, as if rubbing salt into a wound. "We've been very fortunate. Tim has done well with the farm, and we get convicts allocated to us now to help out." She gave Tim a sugary glance, which he acknowledged with a meek smile.

I felt my temper rising but kept it under control. "That's good to hear. We're managing as best we can."

Hannah's eyes flickered with a mix of amusement and pity. "Oh, I'm sure you are, Elizabeth. It must be quite a challenge, especially with John being so ... preoccupied," she said, raising an eyebrow for emphasis.

A tear pricked the corner of my eye, but I refused to let it fall. "John is working very hard for our family."

Tim, perhaps sensing the tension, cleared his throat. "Right then, shall we go? We don't want to overstay our welcome."

Hannah smirked again. "Of course, Tim. We'll leave Elizabeth to her … responsibilities."

As they turned to leave, she glanced back over her shoulder. "Do let me know if you need anything, Elizabeth? I'm always happy to lend a hand … or give you some advice …"

I stood there, watching them walk away, my heart heavy with frustration and sadness. It took all my strength not to crumble in front of my children. I forced a smile and turned back to them. But in the pit of my stomach, a knot of anxiety twisted tighter, as the weight of Hannah's words settled in.

Chapter 35

Gordon Plains, Van Diemen's Land, 1823–1825

Later that year, we received a visit from the Chief Constable of Launceston, who asked John to become a district constable at in the local area. The job had a pretty high turnover—it wasn't all that great. The hours were long, late nights were usual, and the pubs and streets of Launceston were rowdy. People like us, ex-convicts, were often treated like lepers, while others were regarded as slightly better than convicts, but not by much. Yet, John puffed up with pride, as if he'd been selected for a prestigious role, and accepted it.

I thought it would be a step in the right direction, but he became rather arrogant, as if he was above some of his old friends. And I suspected right from the start that, at the very least, he accepted bribes to turn a blind eye. He was unnecessarily rough with some of the people he dealt with, mainly the drunks, and bragged to me about it. It was as if being in a position of authority brought out the bully in him. I'd caught glimpses of this—when he tried to force himself on me, he seemed like a different person, a meaner, nastier version of the man I knew.

John had completed the basic house for our family to live in. It was just two rooms with sturdy walls made from thick slabs of timber sourced from the nearby forest, and the roof consisted of strips of stringy bark. At one end of the house, there was a fireplace, and the wall dividing the rooms was fashioned from sheets of stringy bark nailed to beams on the ceiling and floor. The floor was dirt, compacted as hard as we could make it, and we had several kangaroo skins laid out as rugs.

> **Government and General Orders.**
> *Government House, Hobart Town,*
> *Friday, September 12th, 1823.*
> JOHN BAREFOOT is appointed a District Constable at Gordon's Plains, Port Dalrymple, *vice* Railton, resigned.
> By Command of His Honor
> The Lieutenant Governor,
> H. E. ROBINSON, *Secretary.*

Notice of John's appointment as a district constable, Hobart Town Gazette and Van Diemen's Land Advertiser, 13 September 1823 (http://nla.gov.au/nla.news-article1089966)

We had made beds from timber and mattresses from stout calico stuffed with straw. John constructed shutters for the windows, allowing us to prop them open on sunny days and air the house out—it did get smoky inside, but that was not unusual. Unfortunately, spiders loved the stringy bark ... big, hairy spiders that scared the living daylights out of me.

And then, of course, I discovered I was pregnant again. I had genuinely hoped that my days of childbearing were nearing their end, but it seemed that this was not the case just yet. I had a smooth pregnancy, which was a blessing, as John was hardly around.

Helen was born in mid-June 1824, a bright and cheerful baby who lifted my spirits for a short while. However, that happiness was fleeting, disappearing just a few weeks later, and I fell back into the melancholy I had experienced after Annie's birth.

I was alone most evenings, with John either out working or out drinking. I continued to drink at home, rum I had managed to get hold of from one of the many sly grog shops. One particularly dark evening, I found myself alone in the corner of our small home, a half-empty bottle in my hand. The flickering lantern cast distorted shadows on the walls, mirroring the chaos in my mind. As I took another swig, I thought of Elizabeth Macquarie and her words of encouragement, now feeling like a distant, unreachable memory. I remembered my mother's words … you are more resilient than you know. Yet, I didn't feel resilient at all. I felt defeated.

The change in John's behaviour was reflected in how he approached our intimacy. In the past, aside from the stillbirth of our little girl all those years ago, he had been caring and gentle, mostly considerate of my needs and moods. Now, there was none of that. When he was home, he demanded his conjugal rights, sometimes forcefully, if I wasn't immediately compliant. Several times, he slapped me hard across the face when I tried to refuse him. I suspected he was seeing other women, perhaps even prostitutes, and just hoped he wouldn't bring back some horrible disease.

Unfortunately, I fell pregnant again almost as soon as Helen weaned herself, and in September of 1825, another daughter arrived—Bridget. It was exhausting, both physically and emotionally. I felt as though I was barely catching my breath between pregnancies, and this new child only added to the strain. My older girls, Rose and Betsy, were twelve and eleven now, but they seemed determined to run wild instead of offering any real help. They came and went as they pleased, ignoring my pleas for help, staying out late, and answering back with sharp tongues whenever I dared ask where they'd been. Some days, it felt like I was juggling everything—new baby, household chores, and the endless clamour of younger children—alone. The weight of it all sank me deeper into melancholy, and I found myself wishing—though I hated to admit it—that Rose and Betsy would either be the dutiful daughters I needed or else vanish entirely so I wouldn't keep hoping in vain for their help.

Fear finally snapped me out of this melancholy. Our family was somewhat isolated on our little farm, and the threat of being robbed or attacked by bushrangers was always in the back of my mind. Although we were dirt poor, we still had things that these men wanted—even if just flour, salt, and sugar. We also had two young girls and myself, and I shuddered to think of what might become of us should we be attacked.

In early December, John came home with alarming news. A violent prisoner named Thomas Jeffries had escaped from the gaol at Launceston, along with two others—John Perry and Edward Russell. The air seemed to grow heavier with each passing day, filled with the weight of unspoken worries and dread.

Late one night, John confided in me about this man, Jeffries. His face, usually so stern and impassive, was etched with genuine fear as he spoke. "You need to understand, Elizabeth, this man Jeffries … he is not just a criminal; he is a monster," he began, his voice barely above a whisper.

John explained that Jeffries was a convict and had been appointed the flagellator at Launceston gaol, a role that marked a man as the most despised and reviled in the convict world. The flagellator's job was to administer brutal punishments, typically assigned to inmates with a cruel streak—those whose ability to inflict severe pain and injury made them valuable to the authorities. In many ways, they were seen as traitors to their fellow convicts, having aligned themselves with the oppressors to break and brutalise their peers.

"He took pleasure in it," John murmured, a shiver running through his body. "Many convicts viewed the flagellator as a traitor, someone who had sold his soul to gain favour with the authorities. But Jeffries … he was more than that. He drank heavily, and there were whispers—rumours among the constables—that he would rape the women in his custody, often with unspeakable brutality."

As John continued, I felt a cold knot of fear tighten in my stomach. "And now he's on the run. He and his gang have raided several huts along the South Esk, so he's out there somewhere."

The weight of John's words settled heavily upon me. Knowing that such a man was at large, potentially anywhere near our isolated farm, was terrifying. I tightened my hold on Bridget, who lay peacefully asleep in my arms, oblivious to the terror that now gripped me.

Despite the recent strains and conflicts between us, John's presence seemed more necessary than ever. "What should we do, John?" I asked, my voice tense with worry.

"We stay vigilant," he said, jaw tight. "I'll do what I can do to make sure the house is secure, but you need to keep the children close. Do not let them wander, even during the day. This man is dangerous, and you must be prepared for anything."

He paused, giving me a sharp look before continuing, "That particularly goes for Rose and Betsy. They've been running pretty wild lately, and we can't let them do whatever they want when there's genuine danger about. You've got to keep them in check, Lizzie, or someone else will — and I doubt they'll be kind about it."

Nights became more restless than ever as the dread of Jeffries' possible approach hung over us like a dark cloud. The children could sense the tension, and even the slightest sounds in the night would cause my heart to race. John never let his musket leave his side, and I held Helen tighter, her innocent breaths providing a small measure of comfort amid our fear.

Days turned into a routine of constant watchfulness and heightened anxiety. For once, Rose and Betsy seemed to understand the gravity of the situation. They stayed close to home, helping with chores and minding the younger ones without complaint. Their sombre expressions and lack of usual sharpness were a stark reminder of the threat that hung over us.

In mid-January of the new year, John received grim news about Jeffries. We sat outside our home, and the children safely sat inside, where they could not hear what was said.

John began his story. "Just after Christmas, the gang raided John Tibbs' farm near Launceston. Several people were bailed up, including Mrs Tibbs and her baby son, as the bushrangers robbed the house. They bundled their stolen goods up and took their prisoners and the plunder into the dense bushland around the property." He drew a breath and continued.

"The group had then split up, with two of the bushrangers taking one lot of captives and Jeffries the remainder. As they marched through the bush with their prisoners, tensions grew, and two of the hostages, including Mr Tibbs, were shot. Despite being badly wounded, Mr Tibbs escaped and made his way to Launceston, raising the alarm."

"The two groups of bushrangers then reunited and continued their journey. It was during this trek that the most sickening act occurred. Mrs Tibbs had slowed down to attend to her crying baby. Jeffries had snatched the child from her and took it into the bush, where one of them smashed the child's head against a tree, killing the innocent life in an instant. Returning to the distraught mother, Jeffries lied, telling her they had sent the child to a man named Barnard. For some reason, the bushrangers decided to release their prisoners the next morning, leaving the survivors to make their way back to safety, although with memories I would not wish on anyone. Mrs Tibbs, in particular, was in a terrible way—her dress was torn to shreds, and she had been raped more than once."

He halted, nervously looking around and avoiding my gaze. I felt sick, bile rising in my throat at the thought of what this man had done to those innocent people. He continued, "I've got to join the search parties, Lizzie. You know I have to. I'll try not to go too far from home, but I need you to put as much as you can behind the door and not open it for anyone you don't know." Although the idea of him leaving was terrifying, and even with how strained things were between us, I knew he was right.

"We'll be all right, John. You go and do what you need to do and catch this monster," I replied, with more confidence than I felt.

That afternoon, John left to join the search parties, which were hunting for Jeffries and his gang. The days blurred into one another as I stayed close to the house, ensuring the door was barred securely each night. The children and I hunkered down, enduring the long nights fearfully.

In mid-January, John returned briefly with grim news. A friend of his, Magnus Bakie, a constable in George Town, had been brutally murdered by Jeffries. The bushrangers were thought to be somewhere north of George Town, offering a bit of relief, but not enough to quell the anxiety that gnawed at me.

John's time at home was brief; the urgency of the hunt called him away again. Each departure filled me with dread, but also a resolute determination to protect our family. Despite the harrowing circumstances, I had to stay strong for my children.

Our days unfolded in a tense routine. I relied heavily on Rose and Betsy, who kept the younger ones occupied and safe. Each night, I ensured the door was fortified, praying silently for John's safe return and the capture of Jeffries. As I awaited news, the weight of protecting my family rested heavily on my shoulders. I yearned for the sweet embrace of the bottle, for the numbness I knew it would bring, but I realised I couldn't tread this path, not right now.

Weeks passed with little news, and I clung to the routines of daily life: cooking, cleaning, and caring for the children, all while keeping a vigilant eye on the horizon. Every shadow and every sound became a potential threat, and sleep came fitfully at best.

One hot evening at the end of January, a knock came at the door. My heart leapt into my throat. Keeping my voice steady, I called out, "Who's there?"

"It's John," came the weary reply, and relief washed over me as I hurried to open the door.

He entered, looking more worn and haggard than I'd ever seen him. His clothes were mud-stained, and his face bore the marks of endless days spent searching. "They caught him, Lizzie," he said, his voice heavy with exhaustion. "Jeffries and his gang have been captured. It's over."

A sob of relief escaped my lips, and I hugged him tightly, tears of joy mingling with the remnants of fear and exhaustion. For a brief moment, nothing else mattered except that he was home, that we were safe, and that Jeffries was no longer a threat.

Later, I heard the rest of the grisly story. We sat with a mug of rum each in the evening light, the children happy to be playing outside without fear again. "So, what happened?" I asked quietly.

"Oh, Lizzie, I really shouldn't tell you. It's worse than anything I have ever heard before." He started, making sure that no children were in earshot. "They'd run out of food and got lost in the bush. Jeffries shot a cockatoo, and they cooked it, dividing it between them, but there's not much meat on a cockatoo. So, they were still starving. Three or four days later, Jeffries suggested to the others that the first one to fall asleep would be shot and become food for the others."

I shuddered, already horrified, but John continued.

"Russell and Perry agreed. Could you imagine? Then, two days after that, they were climbing a rocky, scrubby hill. They all sat down to rest around eleven in the morning, and Russell fell asleep. Perry, sitting close to him, took a pistol from his knapsack—it was loaded with three balls—and shot Russell in the forehead. He said Russell died without a groan."

My hands tightened around my mug, the idea of such cold-blooded murder almost too much to bear.

"Perry took out his knife," John continued, his eyes dark with the weight of what he had to recount, "and cut off about seven or eight pounds of flesh from Russell's thighs. They made a fire and broiled some of it, eating about a pound each. Perry put the rest into his knapsack, and they travelled on, leaving Russell's musket by his body. Jeffries also left his musket there. Perry had a fowling piece and three pistols, and Jeffries had two."

His voice faltered for a moment, then steadied. "Five days later, they reached a shepherd's hut. The shepherd was a bloke I know; he's called 'Yorkshire Jack'. He's only a young feller, not even twenty. They made him kill two sheep, and when they left, they took the remains of the two sheep, about four pounds of flour, and a musket. And, not wanting to waste anything, Jeffries and Perry ate the remaining 'steaks' made from Edward Russell, along with fried mutton."

I felt nauseous, the bile rising again in my throat as I grappled with the horror John was recounting—the unimaginable cruelty and desperation of these men, driven to such extreme and savage acts.

"John," I managed to whisper, my voice trembling. "How could anyone do such things?"

John sighed deeply, his face etched with exhaustion and sorrow.

"Desperation, Lizzie. It's what turns men into monsters. Hunger and fear drove them beyond the boundaries of humanity. But make no mistake, Jeffries enjoyed it. He's a different breed entirely—cruelty is in his nature."

We sat in silence for a moment, the evening light casting long shadows across our little homestead. The sounds of the children's laughter in the distance were a stark contrast to the dark tale that had just been shared. I clutched my mug of rum, trying to steady my nerves.

John's expression hardened. "They've taken Jeffries back into custody. The authorities will make sure he hangs for his crimes. But what I've seen and heard will haunt me for a long time."

I nodded, the weight of his words settling like a lead weight between us. As John turned away from me, his shoulders tense, I knew we were still miles apart, that this horrible time had not brought us closer together at all.

Chapter 36

Gordon Plains, Van Diemen's Land, 1826

In March, I realised I was once again with child. My breasts ached, and I felt exhausted all the time, though that wasn't much different from the usual. The relationship between John and me remained strained, although the events of the last few months had brought us somewhat closer. I told John about the pregnancy, and his face went pale.

"Not another one, Lizzie," he said, "please, not another one."

I looked at him squarely. "John, you know what causes babies as much as I do. You know I get pregnant easily. If you don't want more children … you know what we must do. Or not do." He hung his head. As I expected, he had no answer to this.

The months passed slowly, each day blending into the next with a relentless monotony. My body grew heavier with the weight of the pregnancy, and the strain seemed to magnify the tension in our household. John and I rarely spoke of anything beyond the mundane necessities of daily survival. Our brief moments of connection were overshadowed by our unspoken fears and grievances.

When William was born in September, he came into the world with a cry that pierced through the haze of our existence. Holding him in my arms, I felt a surge of love so profound it was almost paralysing. Yet, this new life also added another layer of responsibility to our already burdened lives. The demands of a baby stretched my endurance to its breaking point.

John was distant again, both physically and emotionally. His brief, tired smiles at William did little to mask the exhaustion etched into his features. Work consumed him, and when he was home, he often retreated into a silence I couldn't penetrate. It was as if we were both drowning in our own ways, unable to reach out to each other for rescue.

As the weeks turned into months, my sense of despair deepened. The household jobs piled up, the children's demands were almost overwhelming, and the weight of our strained relationship grew virtually unbearable. In the rare quiet moments, I found myself staring blindly at the walls, feeling the dark cloud within me grow thicker. I was drinking more frequently, not just in secret at home, but also in the company of a group of women who understood this all-encompassing struggle. The gatherings at the pub in Launceston became a temporary escape, a place where the cheap grog flowed as freely as our shared laments.

But the respite was fleeting. No matter how much I drank, the harsh reality awaited me at home: the endless cycle of care, the invisible wall between John and me, and the small, demanding cries of a baby whose future seemed as uncertain as my own.

One night at the pub, as the laughter and clinking of glasses filled the dimly lit room, a hushed conversation caught my attention when I overheard my husband's name. I strained to listen as one bloke leaned in and whispered to another, his words slicing through the haze of smoke and booze. "I heard John Barefoot's been offering his two oldest girls to anyone who can shell out a few coins for them—both virgins—for now," he smirked, and the two chuckled maliciously.

I couldn't believe what I was hearing—couldn't believe that John could have stooped so low. These girls were thirteen and twelve. However, it sort of fit with the way that he had been behaving lately, even when he was at home. I sat there, drowning in a sea of alcohol and self-destructive tendencies, and I knew deep down that I was too far gone to muster the strength and courage to confront John. The darkness that had consumed me for so long had taken root too deeply, clouding my judgment and making me blind to the harsh realities of my daughters' lives.

I pushed the damning information to the recesses of my mind and buried it beneath the numbness of drunkenness. The thought of facing the truth, of unravelling the web of deceit and cruelty that John had woven, was a task too daunting for me to bear. I kept drinking.

The constables raided us now and then, and a few of us ended up arrested. Maybe this time it was my turn—I don't reckon I was the loudest or drunkest in the group, and I suppose I should be grateful it wasn't John who arrested me. Rose was at home looking after the rest of the children, and I knew I'd have to get back soon to feed William, who'd be squawking by now. Anyway, I headed to court that morning, feeling pretty sheepish and embarrassed, and the magistrate fined me five shillings and gave me a right old lecture about being a good mother and blah blah blah. Just another man telling me what to do. He reminded me a bit of the pastor from our church in Sandy Creek.

This was repeated a couple of months later, with another fine of five bloody shillings we didn't have to spare. On the way home from the magistrate's office, I ran into an old friend, Judith Quinlan, and I'm afraid to say she convinced me to have a few drinks right then and there. I'd like to say that I was hard to persuade, but honestly, I'm not entirely sure I was even sober from the night before, so I doubt I needed much convincing.

When the magistrate saw me again that afternoon, he was not happy. He decided I hadn't learned my lesson and should be placed in the stocks for a few hours. From there, I was to be sent to the Female Factory at George Town for a month.

I sat in the town square of Launceston, the weight of the stocks pressing down on my ankles, reminding me of my place in society. As I looked out at the crowd gathered around me, their eyes filled with a mix of curiosity and judgment, I could feel a dull ache in my head from the remnants of the night before.

Suddenly, a wave of nausea washed over me, a reminder of the excesses of the previous evening. I felt a surge of bitterness and frustration rise within me, but it was quickly overshadowed by my throbbing headache and the foggy haze that clouded my thoughts.

I attempted to speak out against the onlookers' judgment, but my words came out slurred and disjointed. "Go ... look after ... your own families," I mumbled, my voice trailing off weakly as I struggled to maintain my focus.

And who was looking after my family? Rose and Betsy stood nearby, their faces a mix of concern and embarrassment. I could see their disappointment, a reflection of the turmoil my actions had caused our family.

William, my baby boy, was with them. Because he was still breastfeeding, he would have to come to the factory with me. Rose gave him to me, then turned on her heel and ran, tears pouring down her face. There was no sign of John.

Upon arriving at the Female Factory in George Town, we were led into a room where the matron's assistant recorded our details. The matron, Mrs Graves, looked at me sternly and read out a lengthy list of rules and regulations, along with the punishments for any breaches. We had to obey orders, refrain from using profane, abusive or obscene language, avoid disobedience, work hard, and so forth. Breaking any of their ridiculous rules would result in confinement to a cell. Except there were no cells, only four large rooms, and the place was in disrepair. There were gaps in the fence; evidently, it was common for people to throw items over it—things like grog.

We were meant to work sewing clothes, like in Parramatta, but there wasn't much work, so we mostly sat around doing nothing. One of the other prisoners in the Female Factory, Ann King, was a ribbon maker back in Dublin—she had been transported for stealing two pound notes and four ten-penny coins from a man in a public house. She was also a skilled seamstress and taught me how to "pretty up" the basic clothes we could piece together from the cheap fabric available. I ended up with "new" clothes—clean clothes at least, and a weekly change of them while in the factory, for which I was grateful. My own rags were washed and bundled up for me to take when I left.

William was allowed to stay with me the entire time in the factory, and for that, I was grateful. At first, the novelty of having just one child to care for was nearly exhilarating. I didn't have to juggle a dozen demands at once or mediate endless squabbles. For the first time in what felt like years, I could give my undivided attention to one small, precious life. It felt like a reprieve, a fleeting moment of peace amidst the chaos of my life.

But the novelty wore off quickly. By the third or fourth day, the silence began to creep in, curling around me like a heavy fog. I desperately missed the other children—the sound of Rose's bright laugh, the way Johnny tugged at my skirts, his little voice calling "Mama" with such urgency. I even missed the chaos—the chatter, the mess, the mischief that made my home a home. Without them, the emptiness gnawed at me, sharp and relentless, a reminder of everything I had left behind.

And then the fear set in. It started as a whisper at the back of my mind but soon grew into a constant, crushing weight. What was happening to my children while I was here? Were they being fed? Were they safe? Or worse, had the authorities come for them?

Other women told me their stories in hushed voices—their children taken and placed in orphanages, the eldest apprenticed out as farm labourers or servants, often never to be seen again. One woman wept as she recounted how her fourteen-year-old son had been sent to a distant property as a farmhand.

I could feel the dread settling in my stomach like a stone. What if the same fate awaited mine? What if the magistrate decided I was unfit, that I could no longer provide for my children? The thought of them being scattered, torn from each other, from me, was unbearable. I imagined Betsy, her defiance hiding her fear as she was handed over to strangers. I pictured little Johnny, his wide eyes searching for me, crying when he realised that I wasn't coming to get him. And my youngest—how would they survive without me to care for them?

At night, as William lay curled against me, his warm little body a fragile anchor, I prayed—desperate, pleading prayers—that I would find them all still there when I returned. The waiting was agony, each day dragging on endlessly, every moment filling me with more doubt and despair.

William seemed to sense my distress. He clung to me more than usual, his small hands gripping my dress whenever I tried to put him down. His cries at night were softer, almost plaintive, as though he missed the presence of his siblings as much as I did. I held him close, whispering promises I wasn't sure I could keep: that we would be together again soon, that everything would be better when we got home.

After a few weeks, they must have decided I had dried out enough and sent me home. When the gates finally opened, they handed me my belongings and pushed me out without ceremony. I adjusted William on my hip, his small body feeling heavier than ever, though I knew it wasn't just his weight—it was the exhaustion, the dread, and the unrelenting worry that weighed heavily on me. His head rested against my shoulder, his warm breath uneven, a small comfort that only deepened my fear. As I began the long walk home, the rhythm of my footsteps seemed to echo the same desperate plea over and over in my mind: Please be there. Please be there.

The path stretched endlessly before me, each step heavier than the last. The sun hung low in the sky, casting long shadows that seemed to mock me with every stride. The familiar sights of the road—the twisted gums, the dusty tracks—blurred into the backdrop of my racing thoughts. I pictured arriving to find an empty house, the children gone, their laughter silenced forever. Rose apprenticed out to strangers, while Betsy and Johnny taken away to fend for themselves. My little ones, too young to grasp it, left in someone else's care. The stories the other women had shared haunted me, each one carving deeper into my dread. Please be there, I repeated silently, as if those words alone could conjure them back.

By the time the hut came into view, my arms ached from carrying William, and I felt every painful step in my legs and back. But it wasn't the physical pain that made me pause. It was the sight of the door—so close now, yet holding the answer to my greatest fear. I swallowed hard, my breath catching in my throat as I imagined what might be waiting inside. The fury on John's face was inevitable, but it was the thought of the children that truly froze me in place. If they were gone, if they had been taken while I was locked away, I wasn't sure I could bear it.

I steeled myself and pushed the door open. There they were. Every last one of them. Little Johnny looked up from where he was crouched on the floor, his face lighting up when he saw me. Rose shot me an angry, hurt look, and Betsy leaned against the wall, her arms crossed as always, her expression unreadable. The littlest ones clung to each other in the corner, but when they saw me, they toddled forward, their small cries filling the room. My heart felt like it might burst at the sight of them, the relief overwhelming. They were here. They were all here.

John stood in the middle of the room, his arms crossed and his face dark with anger. His eyes landed on me, then shifted to William, who stirred in my arms. His silence was sharp, cutting through the noise of the children as they clambered around me. I braced myself, knowing the storm was coming, but in that moment, I was just grateful. Grateful for their little faces, for their voices, for the chance to hold them again.

"You're back, then," he said sharply.

"I am," I replied, my voice small.

He let out a bitter laugh and shook his head. "Do you even care what you've left behind? Do you have any idea what you've done to them?"

I shifted William in my arms, his weight pulling on my tired muscles, and looked away. "I—"

"You what?" he snapped, his voice rising. "You didn't mean to? You didn't think about it? Rose's been doing her best, but it hasn't been easy. A few of the wives of other constables have taken pity on us and brought stew for us to eat—we've managed to stretch that out while you've been gone, but it's not much. Little Bridget has been coughing herself sick every night, with no one to comfort her. She's just a baby, and she needs her mother. And you—where were you? Locked up in the factory with your bottle! We came so close to them being taken away from us—it was only because of my job that we've managed to still be here. There was talk—the minister in town informed the magistrate that because we were so poor and you were in the factory, the children would be better off in the orphanage—and you know what that's like?

Tears welled in my eyes, and I picked up Bridget to comfort her. She whimpered softly, her little hands curling around my neck, and I pressed my lips to her forehead. "I'm sorry," I whispered, though the words felt hollow even as I said them.

"Sorry?" John barked. "Do you think that fixes anything?"

The room fell into silence, the tension between us thick and suffocating. I sat on the edge of the bed, the tears finally spilling over.

The other children peeked out from behind Rose, their eyes wide and wary. She stood protectively in front of them, her small frame stiff with the weight of responsibility she should never have had to bear.

The air in the hut felt heavy, as if it bore the weight of every hardship we had faced. Yet outside, the world continued on, as unforgiving as ever. It wasn't just our family that was at odds. The colony itself seemed to be on the brink of collapse, tensions spilling over into every aspect of our lives. That year, the conflicts with the black people escalated significantly. What had once been distant skirmishes had crept closer to home, that uneasy coexistence often breaking into outright violence.

There were frequent attacks on colonists—killings, theft, and the burning of buildings. We were constantly on edge, always watching for signs of either the blacks or the bushrangers, unsure which we feared more.

Colonel Arthur, now our Lieutenant Governor, issued orders that sent a shiver down everyone's spine. He authorised colonists to treat hostile black people as enemies. It was to be war, although openly calling it that was avoided. Stories spread through the town, told in hushed whispers—of ambushes, killings, and brutal reprisals. Some claimed to have seen entire groups of the native people wiped out, while others said they heard cries echoing through the bush in the dead of night.

We knew things were bad, but as the months went by, the lines between defence and outright cruelty became increasingly blurred. Fear drove many to commit unspeakable acts, leaving the rest of us wondering how close we were to being next.

In February 1827, the law that John had been proud to enforce came back to bite him. He was charged with accepting a bribe and neglecting his duties as a constable. They dismissed the charges, but the stain remained. It felt as if the world was turning against us, stripping away the last remnants of the life we had tried to build. With the knowledge I held close, I felt as though John was walking a tightrope. He was almost certainly guilty of taking bribes—there just wasn't enough evidence to convict him. I sensed he was on the verge of something crashing down around him, and by this time, I didn't care.

As a family, we were in a relentless struggle for survival on multiple fronts. Putting food on the table was a ceaseless battle, a daily exercise in stretching resources to their limits. However, providing our children with even the most basic clothing posed an insurmountable challenge. Each garment they wore resembled little more than tattered rags, frayed threads clinging desperately to their fragile frames.

In the midst of our dire circumstances, a small beacon of light appeared in the form of the local minister, Reverend Youll. Recognising our poverty and the desperate state of our children's clothing, he took it upon himself to intervene on our behalf, recommending that we be considered for assistance by issuing slops clothing. This clothing was humble in its construction and quality, made from basic, rough materials and cut to fit a broad section of the community. Still, these clothes provided a semblance of dignity and decency to our children's appearance.

Though the slops clothing may have given them a veneer of respectability, the fabric bore the unmistakable mark of its origin—government stores. Despite their semblance of presentability, the clothes served as a tangible reminder of our family's reliance on charity and the stark reality of our circumstances.

As the suffocating weight of despair settled on my shoulders once again, I found myself teetering on the edge of the abyss. The constant struggle to resist the allure of the grog dens had proven futile, the darkness beckoning me back into its unforgiving embrace. Despite my best efforts to break free from the grip of addiction, the insidious pull of alcohol remained a formidable adversary.

One fateful day, as I lay in the grip of my demons, Judith appeared at my doorstep like a harbinger of chaos. With a knowing look in her eyes and an unspoken invitation hanging between us, she beckoned me into town, her presence a bittersweet promise of both respite and recklessness. I forgot all about the misery of my last stint in the Female Factory, the fear of losing my children, about the anguish on their faces, and John's anger. All was swept away as we embarked on a bender that unfolded in a blur of swirling emotions and numbing intoxication. Each drink was a fleeting escape, a temporary reprieve from the harsh realities that plagued my existence. We laughed and sang, drowning our sorrows in the sea of alcohol that consumed us, heedless of the consequences lurking on the horizon.

As the sun dipped below the horizon and the moon cast its pale light upon us, things got wilder and wilder, and I thrust to the back of my mind the inevitable reckoning that awaited. But the morning brought with it a harsh awakening; the consequences of our actions laid bare before us in stark relief.

The magistrate's gavel fell with a resounding finality, the sentence reverberating through the room like a death knell. Another month in George Town—a symbolic exile from the familiar streets of Launceston and a harsh reminder of the price I paid for succumbing to the bottle. The words of the sentence echoed in my mind, intertwining with the relentless fear that my children might be taken from me and the suffocating guilt of having failed them yet again.

With a heavy heart and a soul burdened by shame, I picked up the pen. My hand trembled as I signed the surety with a shaky cross, a silent witness to my fragile promise to change. The words on the page blurred before my tear-stained eyes, the ink spreading like an accusation, stark against the paper. It served as a grim reminder of the tenuous hold I had on my resolve and the seemingly bottomless depths of my despair.

Chapter 37

Gordon Plains, Van Diemen's Land, 1827

After successfully walking the straight and narrow for three months, I couldn't help but feel a glimmer of pride in my newfound resolve. I had managed to keep the demons at bay, steering clear of the bottle and the troublesome influence of Judith. However, my companions were limited to those who had once joined me in raucous drinking sprees. If I wanted to maintain my newfound sobriety, I knew I had to distance myself from their tempting company. I remembered my chance encounter with Elizabeth Macquarie, where she spoke about my strength. I needed to tap into that inner strength now more than ever.

Memories of my dear friends from Sydney—Hester, Catherine, and Bridget Quinn—flooded my mind, a bittersweet reminder of the past. Years had passed since I last had contact with them, and the echoes of our shared laughter and friendship had long faded. As I longed for their presence and wondered about what had happened to them, a sense of wistful nostalgia washed over me, mingling with the lingering shadows of a tumultuous past. I thought about my mother, wondered if she was still alive, and wondered how the lives of all my brothers and sisters had turned out. How many nieces and nephews did I have that I would never know? I had missed out on all that family that had been so important to me. And my own children were growing up, some faster than I would wish.

Rose had been such a sweet child, but her life since we came to Launceston had been difficult. Things had started to go wrong with her when she first saw me in the stocks, roaring drunk. She'd turned away from me and run home and had been distant ever since.

She'd become wild and reckless, forever disappearing into the night with her head full of secrets. She'd stumble home at odd hours; cheeks flushed, the smell of rum clinging to her clothes. I'd ask her where she'd been, but she'd just shrug off the question or glare at me like I was the one out of line. I suppose, in a way, I'd lost the right to question her, what with all my own failings. But still, it stung to see her spinning out of control at such a young age.

As I was sweeping the floor one morning, Rose drifted in like a ghost. She had this quiet resolve about her, an odd calm that didn't match the fire I usually saw in her eyes. Truth be told, it unnerved me. She was only fourteen, yet she carried herself like she'd seen a lifetime of trouble. And maybe she had, thanks to John's intentions and my inability to shield her from them.

"I know what Father's been planning," she began, her tone clipped and cold. She wouldn't meet my gaze at first, just stood there, fiddling with the hem of her dress. "He wants to sell me off, doesn't he? Make me ... some man's property."

My heart lurched. She'd never said it out loud before, and hearing those words fall from her lips made me want to sink to the floor. "Rose, I—" I started, but she cut me off.

"I'm not gonna let him do it," she said flatly, and there it was—her steel. "I've been working on that farm, you know. Milking cows, hauling water. I met someone there."

I felt the blood drain from my face. "Someone? Who?"

She lifted her head, finally looking me in the eye. "William Graves," she said. "He's been in London, Sydney, and then here. He's ... older."

"How much older?" I asked, though I could already guess that it was a fair bit.

She shrugged, a harsh laugh escaping her. "He's thirty-six, Ma." She spat the number like it was no big deal, though the corners of her mouth trembled. "But at least with him, I'm not some piece of meat to be sold. I get to decide. I want to marry him."

The words hit me like a hammer. My fourteen-year-old daughter was asking for my blessing to wed a man more than twice her age. A convicted man, at that. Her eyes were clear, though—no slur of drink or that usual rebellious flame. This was determination, pure and simple.

"I won't be Father's whore," she pressed on, voice ragged. "I'm sick of his schemes, sick of him treating me like ... like currency. William's not perfect, but he treats me better than that."

She was trembling, anger or maybe fear coursing through her. For a moment, I stood there, stunned, trying to figure out which was worse: letting her marry an ex-convict nearly old enough to be her father, or watching John carry out his vile plans. Shame churned in my gut—shame that I'd never been strong enough to protect her from any of this.

I reached out, resting a hand on her arm. "Rose," I whispered, but I couldn't find the words I needed. How was I to explain the ugliness of this world to someone who'd already seen it?

She swallowed, tears hovering on her lashes, but she blinked them away. "I know you're disappointed in me, but I'm not changing my mind. I'm done letting other people run my life." I felt like crying. She was just a child, already half-drowned in booze and wild living. Yet, one look at her face told me it was pointless to argue with her. The bitterness in her eyes indicated she'd outgrown childhood long ago.

Finally, I nodded. It wasn't approval so much as acknowledgment. "All right," I said, though it tasted like sand in my mouth. "I can't stop you. Just ... be careful."

She scoffed, wiping at her eyes. "Careful," she repeated, like it was a foreign concept. Then she turned on her heel and left me there, standing in the half-swept room with a broom clutched in my hands.

The wedding was a small affair—nothing grand, just a brief respite from our daily grind. Rose wore her best dress, which I'd brightened with some leftover ribbons and lace. It was still plain, but those small touches and a few tips from Ann King gave it just enough to pass for a wedding garment.

Before we left for the church, I handed Rose my mother's silver locket. I'd often told the children how it had been passed down from my grandmother to my mother, and then to me, so she understood its significance. Her fingers curled around it, and for a moment, she was my little girl again, her face full of a vulnerability I hadn't seen in years.

"Are you sure you want me to have it?" she asked quietly. "I'm not sure my grandmother would be very proud of me."

"You just do your best, Rose, my love," I said softly. "All I want is for you to be happy and safe."

William arrived in his best clothes—threadbare but clean. Despite their worn condition, he was serious as he prepared to marry Rose. We walked through the church doors with more nerves than smiles. The ceremony itself was quick—just a few words and blessings, enough to make it binding in the eyes of the law and the Lord. The plain wooden benches, the unadorned walls, the dusty air—all of it felt fitting for the occasion.

As I signed a simple cross to bear witness to their marriage, a silent prayer of hope and apprehension lingered on my lips. Meanwhile, John remained absent, his whereabouts and motives shrouded in mystery. When he returned home at the end of the week, I told him about Rose; he shrugged his shoulders and muttered something like, "He'll be sorry".

Just two months later, the relative peace of our lives was shattered. John was dismissed from his post as constable. While this wasn't an uncommon occurrence, considering that most district constables were convicts on a ticket of leave, John's explanation left me puzzled.

When he came loping home at lunchtime, John explained, "Lizzie, I know it may seem like there's more to this than meets the eye, but trust me, it's just a matter of disobedience of orders. That's all there is to it."

I looked at John, my heart heavy with suspicion. His explanation seemed like a flimsy veil covering a deeper truth, and I couldn't shake the feeling that there was more to the story he wasn't telling me.

"John, something doesn't add up. The way you're explaining it, there's something you're not telling me. I need to know the whole truth," I insisted, my voice tinged with anger.

He let out a heavy sigh, the weight of guilt and uncertainty evident in his posture. "All right, fine. Disobedience of orders, and ..." He paused, hesitating to address the more troubling matter. "Well, this is a bit difficult. The other charge was grossly immoral conduct."

GOVERNMENT NOTICE.

COLONIAL SECRETARY's OFFICE, Nov. 27, 1827. HIS Excellency The LIEUTENANT GOVERNOR has been pleased to approve of the following alterations in the Police of this Colony :—

Mr. Jesse Pullen, to be District Constable at the Green Ponds, *vice* Whitfield deceased.

Shadrach Williams, 696, Woodman, to the Field Police at Campbell-town.

John Barfoot, Conditional Pardon, dismissed from the Office of Constable at Launceston, for disobedience of orders, and grossly immoral conduct.

Mr. T. D Toosey, resigning the Office of Chief District Constable and Pound keeper, on the West Bank of the Tamar.

John Winslaw, free, Lady Ridley, dismissed from his Office of Constable for improper conduct.

By Command of His Excellency.

J. BURNETT.

Notice of John's dismissal, Hobart Town Courier, 8 December 1827 (http://nla.gov.au/nla.news-article4225610)

"What?" I gasped, my disbelief written all over my face. "What the hell have you been up to?"

John's response was unsettling. With a slight grin, he said, "Ahh, well, cohabiting with a woman with whom I have had children while I have a wife in Ireland."

My first feeling was of anger and betrayal. Then the penny dropped, the revelation hitting me like a thunderbolt. I stared at him in astonishment. "*Me*? I'm the woman you're cohabiting with?"

I was genuinely shocked. Many men and women had been married in their homeland only to start new relationships or remarry once in

Australia. It was highly unlikely they would ever see their partners again, and so their previous marriages were treated as if they had not happened, although bigamy was illegal. John and I exchanged vows in Sydney under the watchful eyes of Reverend Samuel Marsden, a strict guardian of the sanctity of marriage, if ever there was one.

"And how the hell did the police magistrate know about your other family?" I spat at him.

"Ummm … well … years ago, when we were first transported, I confided in Tim about my family back in England. It seems he shared that information with Hannah," John revealed, his words hanging heavily in the air between us.

It all made sense now. With her penchant for trouble and gossip, Hannah Murphy had been waiting for the chance to use this information against me—against us. And now she had, and it had cost John his job—money our family needed to put food on the table.

"Hannah Murphy." I said, "Always looking for an opportunity to cause trouble, and she seized it with both hands."

I didn't know what to do or where to turn. Rage bubbled up inside me—rage against John for betraying me like this; rage against Hannah for using that information; rage against the world in general for me even being in this godforsaken country. The anger boiled over until it demanded release.

Overwhelmed by the weight of it all and teetering on the brink of despair, my resolve to stay sober faltered. The lure of oblivion called to me, pulling me back into the clutches of my past. Indulging in the familiar escapism of old habits, I succumbed once more to the temptations that had long plagued me. Back in town, back to the grog dens, back to my old mates, back to the bottle. Who could honestly blame me?

It seemed that the magistrate could. With an unforgiving hand, the consequences of my actions quickly caught up with me. The verdict was immediate and unyielding—back to the factory for a month.

During that month, my thoughts and emotions circled endlessly. The guilt of leaving my children, especially after John's confession, gnawed at me, relentless and sharp. This time, at least, I was allowed to bring William and Bridget with me, but I was always scared that the other children might be taken away by the authorities and sent to the orphanage. Constantly in my mind was a picture of their little faces, confused and frightened, wondering why their mother had disappeared yet again. But it wasn't just guilt that consumed me. Anger at John made me want to scream with rage, my fists clenching as I replayed his betrayal in my mind. How could he have done this to us? To me?

Then there was the worry about how we'd manage now that John had lost his job as constable. The farm wasn't enough to keep us afloat, especially with so many mouths to feed and debts piling up faster than we could ever hope to pay them off.

Rose was married and living her own life now, but what about the others? Betsy, restless and rebellious, was already showing signs of heading down a dangerous path. And the little ones, who was taking care of them? Would John do it, or would he leave them in Betsy's unreliable care? Would Rose come back home to look after them? The thought of the children being taken into care, ripped away from what little family they had left, haunted my every waking moment.

This time, there were over forty women in the factory, along with about ten children, making it uncomfortably crowded. These women shared stories that mirrored my own, each of us connected by mistakes, loss, and a society that viewed us as little more than expendable labour. Some were hardened by years of survival, their faces etched with tales they would never share. Others were young, barely more than girls, clutching infants to their chests, desperate to hold on to the only family they had left.

After four weeks, the gates opened, and we were thrust back out again to return home. With William on my hip and little Bridget clutching my hand, I returned home, dreading what I might find. John was outside, chopping wood with a steady, deliberate rhythm, his face set like stone. He didn't look up as I approached, and his silence felt like a cold, heavy weight. Inside, the house was in disarray—evidence of the chaos my absence had caused. Betsy greeted me with a sharp glance, her arms crossed in defiance. "You're back, then," she said, her tone dripping with judgment.

The room felt stifling, and the tension thickened as my eyes searched for the other children. Relief swept over me when Betsy carelessly added, "Johnny and Michael are down at the river fishing. Annie and Ellen are at Mrs O'Malley's. She took them in when you left."

John said little that evening; his few words were clipped and curt. He busied himself with farm tasks, leaving me to confront the mess I'd created. The younger children eventually settled down, but Betsy's behaviour took a turn for the worse. She slipped out of the house that night without a word, returning late with the smell of smoke and trouble clinging to her. I wanted to scold her, to demand an explanation, but what right did I have?

That night, as I lay awake in the stillness, I couldn't shake the thoughts that swarmed my mind. Had John's other family endured this pain? Had his children tossed and turned, wondering why their father had deserted them? Had his wife been left to piece it all together, bearing the heavy burden of keeping everything intact? And would John do the same to us one day?

In the days that followed, I tried to piece my life back together and mend the rift between Betsy and me. However, her behaviour became increasingly reckless. Her anger toward me simmered just beneath the surface, and her sharp tongue was quick to lash out whenever I attempted to talk to her. The older boys were initially reticent, but they seemed to get past that, and soon our relationship returned to what it had always been.

Gradually, life began to resemble something like normal. The small, steady routines of daily life—cooking, cleaning, and looking after the children—provided me with something to focus on, something to cling to, and something to develop. Each day brought a sense of stability, even if it was delicate and uncertain. John and I spoke very little, our words carefully chosen to sidestep the weight of the past. His confession about his other family lingered between us like a shadow, unspoken yet always present.

We found purpose in the land and the need to put food on the table for our family. Our property, rich and fertile, became our anchor. John planted most of it in wheat, which was always in demand, while I tended a small home garden, coaxing potatoes, turnips, pumpkins, and cabbages from the soil. John built a yard with rail fences for the few cattle we had, hoping to grow the herd for meat, milk, and profit. With our chickens and a couple of sheep, things began to feel more secure. I just needed to leave the past behind and look to the future.

But first, I wanted a few words with Hannah Murphy.

The dusty trail stretched out before me, each step carrying me closer to the inevitable showdown with Hannah Murphy. The sun beat down upon the parched earth, mirroring the intensity of the anger burning within me.

When I arrived at Tim's farm, I squared my shoulders, determined to confront her for once and make her understand how destructive her words had been. "Hannah," I called, my voice steady despite the whirlwind of emotions swirling inside me.

Hannah stepped out from the farmstead, her gaze cool and calculating. "What brings you here, Elizabeth?" she asked, a smirk tugging at the corners of her lips.

I met her gaze squarely, the burden of years of resentment and animosity weighing heavily between us. "You know exactly why I'm here, Hannah," I declared, my voice icy with anger. "That little stunt you pulled—telling the magistrate that John had another family—what the hell did you think you were doing?"

"Well," she replied, "I must admit I didn't think that it would explode in quite such a spectacular way, but it was quite exciting, you know!"

I looked at her in astonishment. "You lost John his job—we have almost no coin to buy food. Is that what you wanted?"

She glared at me. "That's not my fault; it's John's. They were going to sack him anyway. I've heard stories about him—disobedient, taking bribes; you name it—if it's dodgy in Gordon Plains, John's got a hand in it. I also heard he was trying to trade the girls as well. I didn't even need to use that little nugget, but I'm sure the chief constable would still be interested."

I stared at her in disbelief. "How do you know all these things about John?" I demanded, my voice laced with a blend of curiosity and suspicion. The air crackled with tension as I awaited her response, my gaze fixed on her with a fresh intensity.

Hannah replied. "Oh, I have my ways, Elizabeth," she replied cryptically, her tone dripping with insinuation. "Let's just say that some secrets have a way of finding their way to the surface."

As much as I wanted to slap her face, I kept my cool. I wouldn't let her get any more pleasure from my situation, and I'm certain that if I did slap her, she'd have the constables on me in the blink of an eye. I clenched my jaw, stifling the urge to confront her further.

"I don't have time for your games, Hannah," I said, my voice icy. "Leave my family alone from now on, or you'll regret starting this."

With a final glare, I turned on my heels and walked away, leaving the conflict behind me.

I returned home, feeling lighter now that I had finally confronted Hannah. I didn't reckon it would halt her meddling, but I hoped she wouldn't cause any more strife for our family.

About a week later, word reached me that I wasn't the only one who had had enough of Hannah. I was in Launceston, picking up supplies, when I overheard two women gossiping near the market.

"Did you hear?" one of them whispered. "Tim Daley's been arrested! Apparently, he beat his missus, Hannah Murphy."

My heart sank. Tim? I pulled my bonnet down and stepped closer, pretending to browse the vegetables, catching more of their conversation.

"She'd been stirring up trouble again, running her mouth about him and others. Apparently, she was the one who dobbed in John Barefoot. Tim finally snapped and gave her a good hiding. Now he's had to sign a surety to stay out of strife for three months."

I stood there, the weight of the news pressing down on me. Tim's frustration was evident, as Hannah had a knack for provoking others until they snapped. I knew it wasn't right. I'd been on the receiving end of a beating a couple of times, though not enough to warrant involving the constables, but it was hard to feel sorry for her.

On my way home, I stopped at their farm and saw Tim stomp out from the barn, his face as dark as storm clouds. He spotted me and paused, wiping his hands on his trousers, clearly still simmering with anger.

"I heard Hannah and you the other day," he muttered, his eyes narrowing as if the memory alone could set him off again. "I caught wind of what she said about John ... allegedly pimping out the girls. Even if he did say something like that—and if he did, I'll have a word with him myself. She's got no right spreading filth like that. It's bad enough without her stirring the pot and making things worse for all of us."

I nodded, biting the inside of my cheek, fully aware of how toxic Hannah's gossip could be. "I agree, Tim," I said gently, observing as his shoulders slumped slightly, the tension in his face easing but not completely vanishing.

He looked down at the ground, kicking a bit of dirt with his boot. "I'm sorry I beat her; I truly am," he muttered. "But God ... sometimes she's like a dog with a bloody bone. She won't let anything go, just keeps gnawing at it until she's ruined everything around her." His voice cracked with frustration, and for a moment, I could see the weight he carried—his guilt, his anger, and his helplessness.

"Tim," I said, careful with my words, "we've all had enough of her, but you've got to be careful. You've signed that surety now. If anything happens again ... you'll land yourself in gaol."

He nodded grimly, his eyes hardening. "I know. I'll be careful." I walked away, unsure if he meant careful about not beating her again or careful in some other way.

Chapter 38

Gordon Plains, Van Diemen's Land, 1828

A year later, in November, I was back before the magistrate. The sour taste of last night's grog still lingered in my mouth. My hands trembled, though I tried to hide it by clenching them at my sides.

Magistrate Lyttleton looked down at me from his bench, his expression stern yet weary. He shuffled through the papers before glancing up, fixing me with a sharp gaze. "Mrs Barefoot," he said, his voice heavy with disappointment. "It's been nearly a year since you last stood before me in this state. I had hoped ... perhaps foolishly, that we wouldn't meet like this again."

I stared down at my feet, unable to meet his eyes. I could feel the judgment of the whole room weighing on me—men who had no clue what it was like to live my life, to have your body turn into a prison, to feel the crushing weight of responsibility with no way out.

"Eight children, and now ... another on the way, I hear," the magistrate continued, his tone softer now. "And yet here you are again, drunk and causing a ruckus in the streets. I'm disappointed, Elizabeth."

I wanted to shout at him and tell him he didn't understand. I was also disappointed—with this pregnancy, my husband, and my life. But what good would it do? My heart pounded in my chest as the words stuck in my throat. All I could manage was a quiet, "I don't ask for this, Your Worship."

He sighed heavily, shaking his head. "Maybe not, but your actions have consequences. You've received warnings before, yet you choose to keep going down this path." He paused, flipping through the papers again, his eyes scanning them with resigned frustration. "I could send you back to the Female Factory," he continued, his voice stern yet tinged with disappointment. "But this isn't the first time you've stood here, Elizabeth. The Female Factory is for women who need a place to work or live, not for those who repeatedly break the law and disrupt the peace."

I swallowed hard, the weight of his words pressing down on me.

"No," he said, his voice firm now. We need to stamp down on this behaviour to keep the peace here. This is about discipline, about sending a message. One month in Launceston Gaol."

The room seemed to close in around me, the cold finality of his sentence echoing in my ears. Gaol. Not the Female Factory with the other women, but the unforgiving stone walls of Launceston Gaol, where the air hung heavy with punishment. My mind raced back to the horrors of my time in Kilmainham Gaol. Is this to be my future now? In and out of gaol?

My heart sank, but I didn't object. What would it matter? I'd be locked away, and John would still be free. Free to keep putting me in this state, free from the mess he'd made of our lives.

The cell was cold, damp, and reeked of urine. I leaned against the rough stone wall, head pounding from last night's drink. My throat felt dry, and my stomach churned—not just from the baby growing inside me, but from the harsh reality of where I was. I wanted to scream, but all I could manage was a hoarse whisper.

"Why, John? Why couldn't you just leave me alone?" I rubbed my hands over my face, feeling the grime of days without a wash. The anger that had burned so hot the night before was now a cold, bitter resentment. He'd done this to me again, only thinking about what he wanted in that moment. Another child. Another mouth to feed. Another burden when we were barely getting by as it was. He wouldn't be happy about this, even though it was his fault that I was in this state.

At home, I pictured him standing in the doorway, seething with anger that I was gone again for a month, and he'd have to deal with day-to-day things like feeding the children. Someone from the pub would have filled him in on where I was after I'd been arrested; I could be sure of that. At least this time, I knew the younger children would be all right with Mrs O'Malley looking after them – even though she'd only agreed to look after them that night when I realised that I was pregnant yet again and broke down in a fit of tears in her arms. Ah damn it, John would just have to sort it out himself.

"I didn't ask for this!" I cried out, to no one but the empty cell walls. "I didn't ask for any of it! I want to go home."

When the guard came to throw me a crust of bread, he didn't bother with pleasantries. "You'll get out when your time's up, Lizzie. Maybe try to stay sober this time, eh?"

I glared at him. "Easy for you to say. You don't have nine mouths to feed."

"Not my problem," he grunted, walking off.

I stared at the bread but couldn't bring myself to eat. Another child, a month in this pit, and John still out there—free. How is it always me who pays the price?

A loud groan came from the other side of the cell. I peered through the gloom and could just make out the shape of another person on the other cot in the cell. I'd thought I was alone in here, but I wasn't.

The groan startled me, cutting through the fog of my thoughts. I squinted into the dim light, trying to make out the figure lying on the other cot. My head still pounded from last night's drink, and my stomach twisted, but curiosity got the better of me.

"Who's there?" I croaked, my voice rough from thirst and despair.

The figure shifted, a shadowy lump of rags and limbs. Slowly, she sat up, her face barely visible in the gloom. "Just another poor soul stuck in this hellhole," she muttered, her voice hoarse and weary yet still rich with a thick Scottish burr. "What's it to you?"

I leaned back against the cold wall, trying to make sense of her. "Thought I was alone in here."

She gave a bitter laugh, though it was more of a cough. "No one's ever alone in places like this. Just trapped, same as you. What'd they get you for?"

I sighed, rubbing my temples. "Drunk again. My husband ... he's the reason I'm in this mess. Pregnant again, and I couldn't handle it. Found a bottle, dumped my children on a neighbour, and here I am."

She snorted, her laughter devoid of any real joy. "Men. They take what they want, and we're left to deal with the wreckage."

I didn't argue with her. She wasn't wrong. The anger I'd been nursing swelled back up inside me, bitter as bile. "I've got eight at home already. Another one ... I don't know if I can do it."

She turned slightly toward me, her face still obscured in the shadows, but I could feel her eyes on me. "It's not about whether you can. It's about what they expect. They want us to break. They want us to do what we're told to do without question. But you hold on to that anger, you don't let it kill you. That's what they really fear—women like us who won't lie down and give up."

Her words were cold comfort, but there was truth in them. My fists clenched, and I felt the rough skin of my palms scrape against the stone. I thought back to when I was a child, stubborn and opinionated, according to my father. I had refused to attend church, refused to marry the person they wanted me to. I had stood up for myself more. What had happened to me?

"I'm not giving up," I muttered, more to myself than to her.

"No," she agreed. "You survive, and you make sure they never forget it."

I closed my eyes, letting her words sink in. One month in this pit, then back to John, back to the children, back to the burden. But something had changed. I wasn't going to just take it anymore. I'd survive—out of spite, if nothing else.

"What is your name?" I whispered, suddenly aware of our strange solidarity, even in this miserable place.

She was silent for a moment, then spoke in a low voice. "Does it matter?" she said softly. "We're all the same in here." She shifted, and in the dim light, I caught a glimpse of her features—sharp cheekbones and hard-won lines of experience.

"My name's Helen, Helen Wood. I'm in here for being a loud-mouthed trollop ... or so my master says." She gave a cackling laugh.

"He likes his women silent, he does. And I was never very good at that. The first time I talked back to him, I got a warning. The second time, they locked me in a cell with bread and water for three days. This time – ahh well ... I was tired of being treated like a dog, wearing these convict rags we have to wear, so I slipped into the mistress's bedroom one day when they were not home and pulled one of her dresses on over my shift. I didn't hurt anyone, didn't even dirty the bloody clothes, but when she came home, she caught me by surprise. She was not impressed by what she saw, shrieking and yelling like I'd committed a real crime. And here I am. In the gaol for a week because of that. Locked up with other women like me; thieves, whores and troublemakers, and drunks, by the sound of it! Well, I'd rather be with that sort than women like my bloody mistress."

In the following days, Helen and I spoke about our lives, filling the long hours with tales of what we'd lost and what little we had remaining. I shared with her this latest pregnancy, about how exhausted I felt— exhausted from the endless cycle of survival, of bringing children into a world that showed no kindness for them, of bearing burdens that never seemed to lighten. She sighed, the sound heavy with comprehension.

"I understand," she murmured. "I do. But I'd give anything to hold my bairns once more. And I never will."

Her voice cracked, just a little, before she swallowed it down. She had two boys and a girl, all taken from her when she was arrested, their fates lost to time and distance. She didn't even know if they were alive, if they'd been left with her father as she'd hoped, or if they'd been scattered like so many others. It was a familiar tale in this godforsaken colony—women torn from their children, their families shattered, their names reduced to prison records and tally marks.

A couple of weeks later, they released me for good behaviour—which really meant I'd followed their rules, swallowed my pride, and pretended to be the meek, obedient mother of eight they expected me to be.

This time, my homecoming felt different. There were no grand reunions, no heated arguments or tearful embraces. Just another day. It seemed as if my absence had been nothing more than a small disruption, a temporary inconvenience. A hiccup, soon forgotten. And perhaps, in the end, that was what stung the most.

The first wave of pain took my breath away, sharp and sudden. I dropped the pot I was scrubbing, clutching my belly as another contraction rolled through me. It was too soon—this wasn't meant to happen for a few more weeks, if I'd worked out the timing right.

I stood there for a moment, my mind racing. The children were out, most of them busy, but Bridget was nearby, playing with Willie. I steadied myself, leaning against the table. "Bridget!" I called out, my voice strained.

She came rushing in, wide-eyed and worried. "Mama? What's wrong?"

"Go," I managed to say between breaths, "fetch Mrs O'Malley, quick as you can. The baby's coming."

Bridget's eyes widened, but she nodded and dashed out the door before I could say anything more. The midwife wasn't far—just down the road— and I hoped she was home and would arrive in time. The pains were so sharp, unlike anything I had experienced before.

The labour was harder than I ever imagined. Pain ripped through me like fire, and I could barely breathe through the contractions. I gripped the sheets, my body drenched in sweat, every muscle screaming. It felt like hours—no, days—had passed, yet still, the baby wouldn't come. Something was wrong. I could feel it deep in my bones.

Mrs O'Malley's face grew tight with worry as she checked me. "Something is wrong," she muttered, her voice low but urgent. "We've got to get him out, Lizzie, or he won't make it."

Fear gripped me then. I didn't care about the pain—I just wanted the baby out, wanted it to take a breath. But no matter how hard I pushed, it wasn't enough. My vision blurred, and everything around me seemed to slow down. I felt as if I might die.

"Come on, love," Mrs O'Malley urged, her hands working quickly. "One more big push. You've got to try, or we'll lose you both."

I felt weak, but I pushed with everything I had left. A scream tore from my throat, and at last, I felt the baby slide free. But there was no cry. Nothing. The room was silent except for the sound of Mrs O'Malley moving frantically.

I could see it was a boy, but the cord was wrapped around his neck, choking the life out of him. His still, blue body was the last thing I saw before the world went dark.

When I came to, the first thing I heard was a cry—a faint, gasping sound. My heart lurched. Mrs O'Malley had done it. She had somehow brought him back. The baby was breathing. Barely, but he was alive.

"You did it, Lizzie," Mrs O'Malley said, her voice thick with relief as she placed the fragile body in my arms. "He's a fighter, this one."

But I felt as if I'd been broken. My entire body ached, and I was still bleeding. Too much, I realised, as the edges of my vision blurred once more. Mrs O'Malley's voice was calm yet firm as she worked to stop it. I could hear Bridget sobbing in the corner of the room, terrified.

"Bridget…" I tried to speak, but the words wouldn't come. I could feel the life draining out of me, as if all my strength had gone into bringing this baby into the world.

"Stay with me, Lizzie," Mrs O'Malley commanded, her hands pressing down hard. "I'm not losing you."

The pain was unbearable, and I felt myself slipping. But somehow, against everything, I held on. Hours passed in a blur of pain and blood, but eventually, the bleeding slowed. I didn't die. I nearly had, but I survived.

The baby was alive, and so was I, but I knew I'd never forget how close it had come. When John finally arrived, hours later, I could barely speak.

"Another boy?" he asked, glancing at the baby. "What have you called him?"

"How about George, after the King?" I replied, half-expecting him to scoff.

John gave a short laugh. "Sort of fitting, seeing as it was George who sent us both out here in the first place, eh? Different George now, but yes, George is fitting."

"And that's the end, John," I said, my voice barely more than a whisper, but firm. "There'll be no more babies. I'll die next time; I know it."

John's face darkened as he crossed his arms and looked away, his jaw tightening. "You know you'll be right in a month or so, Lizzie. But no more babies means no more …" His voice trailed off when he caught sight of Bridget, who sat beside the bed holding little George.

I saw the sulkiness in his eyes and the frustration in his voice, which filled me with a cold rage. Here I was, barely hanging onto life, and all he could think about was himself. "You listen here," I said, forcing myself to sit up a bit. "I'm over it. If you can't accept that, then bloody bad luck."

Bridget looked up, wide-eyed, sensing the tension but saying nothing. John opened his mouth, then closed it, staring at the floor.

"Right," he muttered finally, scratching the back of his neck. "We'll talk later."

But we both knew there was nothing left to say.

Chapter 39

Gordon Plains, Van Diemen's Land, 1829

By the time George was six months old, exhaustion had seeped deeply into me. I hadn't slept through a single night since his birth, his cries piercing the darkness like clockwork. When Betsy and Johnny were home, they lent a hand, but neither was often around. Betsy ... well, I wasn't quite sure what she was up to, but whatever it was, it kept her away for most of the day. She wasn't at home much at night either. I suspected she was seeing someone, but she was secretive, and no amount of gentle probing could coax her into opening up.

Johnny was a different story altogether. Everything was an adventure for him—exciting, challenging, and worth sharing. When he was home, he chattered endlessly about his day: who he had seen, how the interactions had gone, and what mischief he'd gotten up to. It was a constant stream of words, and while it could be exhausting, I loved how he shared his world with me, his excitement being a small bright spot in the chaos of my days.

The younger children, however, seemed to pick up on the tension in the house. They ran wild and out of control, their energy unrestrained and impossible to keep up with. Their noise and mischief left me more frazzled than ever; my nerves stretched thin. Each day felt like a battle just to get through to the evening, only to collapse into bed and wake up to the same chaos again the next day. I felt as though a black cloud was wrapping around me, and I was unable to fight it.

But it wasn't just the fatigue and the children. It was John. He had been even more distant and cold since I had put my foot down about no more children. He hadn't touched me since that day and barely even spoke to me unless it was to bark orders or grumble about money. His silence weighed heavily on me, a constant reminder of the growing chasm between us.

One evening, after George had screamed for what felt like hours, I'd had enough. I left the children with my neighbour, promising I wouldn't be too long—a promise I reckon she knew wasn't worth a tuppence. I headed to the pub, desperate for some relief, some momentary peace. I just wanted to forget it all—John's sulking, the endless work, the sleepless nights.

I didn't remember stumbling into the street, but the next thing I knew, I was weaving between houses, shouting into the night. "Where's my life?" I bellowed into the dark, staggering as I went.

I stumbled home late the next day, after yet another night in the cells and another fine. As I approached along the dusty road, I spotted a woman standing outside the door, hand shielding her eyes, seemingly waiting for someone. She was an older woman, somewhat stooped, with grey hair. Something about her silhouette triggered a memory buried beneath the weight of the years.

It wasn't until I drew closer that recognition flared. "Hester?" I called, my voice cracking. Was I imagining this? How could Hester be here?

The woman turned sharply, a broad smile breaking across her weathered face. "Elizabeth, *mo ghráin!* It is you."

Before I could respond, she shuffled towards me, her arms outstretched. I stood frozen, the past colliding with the present in a wave of confusion. Hester's embrace was strong despite her frail appearance, and for a moment, I felt the years melt away.

"I knew I'd find Barefoot Bay somewhere around here," she laughed, stepping back to gaze at me. Her eyes softened, her voice laced with both warmth and concern. "I've been trying to track you down. Thought you might've been swallowed up."

I gave a hollow laugh. "Not yet."

She didn't press me, but her gaze lingered, taking in my state—the dirt-streaked clothes and the haggard lines on my face. "Well, let's get you inside," she said gently. "I reckon we could both do with a proper cup of tea."

The house was dirty and cluttered inside, reflecting my chaotic life. I shoved a chair free of a pile of laundry and gestured for Hester to sit. She waved her hand dismissively and began bustling about, locating the kettle and setting it on the hearth.

"Not much of a homecoming, I know," I muttered, sinking into a chair at the rough-hewn table.

Hester shot me one of her sharp looks, the kind that could cut through any excuse. "Stop that nonsense," she said briskly. "I've seen worse, believe me. Tell me how many children you have now —and where they are?"

Her words hit me like a punch to the gut, and I looked away, embarrassed. "There are nine of them, but Rose's married, and Betsy … I have no idea what Betsy is up to anymore. Johnny is working, and … and baby George is just six months old. I left them with Mrs Hughes, a neighbour, last night. Couldn't—couldn't cope," I admitted, my voice barely above a whisper. "George wouldn't stop screaming. The younger ones were tearing through the house like wild animals. I just … needed a break." Hester's eyes didn't leave my face, her sharp gaze cutting through my feeble excuses. "And where have you been all night, Elizabeth? Don't tell me you've been hiding under that pile of laundry."

I flinched at her tone, the weight of her disappointment settling over me. "I … I went to the pub," I admitted quietly, the words tasting bitter in my mouth. "I just needed to forget, Hester. Forget the screaming, the chaos, John's sulking—everything."

Her eyebrows rose, but she didn't interrupt. I felt compelled to keep going. "I had too much, as usual. Ended up shouting in the street like a madwoman. The constables dragged me off to the cells, slapped me with another fine, and left me to stew until this morning."

Hester let out a long breath, her expression a blend of disapproval and concern. "You've got yourself in a right mess, haven't you?" she said, her voice low yet steady. "Do you reckon drowning yourself at the bottom of a bottle is going to fix anything?"

"No," I whispered, shame burning my cheeks. "But sometimes it's the only way to quiet the noise in my head."

Her face softened, the sharp edges of her expression giving way to something gentler. "Elizabeth, love," she said, her voice quieter now, "I understand what it's like to feel as though the world's against you. But you've got nine children relying on you, and even if John's no help, you've got to find strength for their sake."

I nodded, my throat tight with unshed tears. "I know, Hester. I know I've let them down."

She reached across the table and placed her hand over mine, the warmth of her touch grounding me. "You've made mistakes, sure, but you're here, and you're trying. That's more than some would do. But you can't keep doing this by yourself. Let me help."

I squeezed her hand, a flicker of hope cutting through the fog of despair. "Thank you, Hester. I don't deserve it, but thank you."

When the tea was ready, she set a steaming mug in front of me and sat down across the table, her sharp eyes locked onto mine. "Now then, Elizabeth. Spill it. I didn't travel all this way to see you wallow. What on earth has been going on?"

The words spilled out before I could stop them, like a dam bursting after years of restraint. I shared everything with her—the state of my marriage to John, the fleeting hope that Launceston might offer a fresh start, the relentless grind of the bush, the children, the poverty, the betrayal. I admitted my descent into drinking, my neglect of the children, my shame. The words felt jagged and raw, ripping out of me until there was nothing left.

Hester sat silently, her hands wrapped around her mug, her expression unreadable. When I finally fell silent, I braced myself for her sharp tongue.

"Well," she said at last, her voice low and steady, "you've certainly made a bloody mess of things, haven't you?"

I flinched.

"But" she continued, leaning forward, "you're still here. Still standing, even if you're swaying like a sapling in a storm."

Her words hit me like a balm and a slap all at once. "I don't know if I can fix it, Hester," I whispered. "I don't know where to start."

She reached out, her roughened hand covering mine. "You start by standing up, love. By taking one step, then another. And the first might be to get rid of that bottle of rum. You've got those little ones to think of. They need their mother, not a ghost of one."

I nodded, the lump in my throat threatening to choke me. "And what about John?" I asked bitterly. "What if I can't forgive him?"

Hester's eyes sparkled with sharp humour. "Then you don't. But you also don't let him drag you down. Men like him will stumble over their own boots soon enough, mark my words. Keep your chin up, do what you need to do for yourself and those children, and let him stew in his own juices."

A weak laugh escaped me, and for the first time in years, I felt a flicker of something lighter, something almost resembling peace.

"I've missed you, Hester," I murmured.

She gave my hand a squeeze. "And I you, Elizabeth. But I'm here now, and that's a start."

"How are you here?" I asked, as it seemed like nothing short of a miracle.

"Well, Jim has done quite well for himself over the years. We had a decent bit of land in Parramatta, enough to keep us comfortable. But as time has passed, my health has started to decline. Those years on the streets and in gaol didn't help, you know. And, to be honest, I couldn't stop thinking about you. You were always like the daughter I never had,

Elizabeth." Her words caught me off guard, and I felt a tightening in my chest. She looked at me with the same sharp yet compassionate eyes I remembered, as if she could see right through the mess I'd become. "So, Jim suggested we come here. He reckoned the air might do me good, and that it would give us a chance to find you—if you were still here, that is. So we bought a little farm just nearby, and here we are. We've only been here a few days, and I've been trying to find you since we arrived. I obviously asked the wrong people—should have just asked the constables!"

I stared at her, stunned. "You came all this way ... for me?"

"Of course," she said simply. "You didn't think I'd let you vanish into the wilds of Van Diemen's Land forever, did you? You're still my girl, Elizabeth, even if life's tried its damnedest to pull us apart. And I'm here now, for as long as I can be."

Tears welled in my eyes, and I struggled to find the words. Instead, I reached across the table, taking her hand in mine. The years hadn't dulled her strength—her grip was as firm as ever.

"I don't deserve you, Hester," I whispered, my voice breaking.

"Nonsense," she replied sharply, although her own eyes shimmered. "We all need someone, and I've never ceased to believe in you, even when you stopped believing in yourself."

Chapter 40

Gordon Plains, Van Diemen's Land, 1829

A few weeks later, I bumped into Hannah Murphy at the market. As usual, she was wagging her tongue and gossiping with a small group of her cronies.

"Heard your man's been looking elsewhere, Lizzie," she sneered, not even bothering to lower her voice. "Maybe if you weren't such a drunk, he'd still find his way to your bed."

Something inside me snapped. I stormed towards her, fists clenched, and snarled, "Keep that mouth of yours shut, Hannah, or I'll shut it for you."

The other women in the market hooted, pulling back as if anticipating a fight to erupt. Hannah's smug grin wavered, but she didn't back down. "Go on then," she taunted. "Give it a go. See where it gets you."

I stepped closer, but a constable was already marching over. He grabbed my arm before I could do anything else, hauling me away while Hannah stood there smirking. "Dear God, what are you women up to now?" he said, shaking his head.

The charge of assault and threatening to beat her never stuck—Hannah's reputation wasn't any better than mine—but the anger at her lingered long after the constable let me go. I stomped over to Hester's place to vent my frustrations to a friendly ear.

"I've had it up to here with Hannah Murphy," I spat, pacing in her kitchen. "She knows too many of the family's so-called secrets. I wish Tim would just get rid of her." Hester looked up from where she was mending a shirt. Her sharp eyes met mine, and a slight smirk danced on her lips.

"She hasn't changed a bit, has she?" she said, her voice calm but knowing. "Hannah Murphy was always trouble, even back in Dublin."

I stopped mid-step and turned to her. "You remember how she was, don't you? Always wagging her tongue, always stirring the pot. Well, she hasn't changed, not one bit."

Hester let out a dry chuckle, threading her needle with steady hands. "Oh, I remember. Loud as a brass bell and twice as annoying. She used to rile up the guards just for the fun of it. You and I would sit back in that damp cell, counting the minutes until she got herself dragged off again."

I couldn't help but smile at the memory, even though it was bittersweet. Those were tough times, but somehow, Hester always managed to make them bearable. "She never could keep that mouth of hers shut," I said. "And now, here she is, doing the same thing all these years on. Except now, she's got a whole market full of people to listen to her lies."

Hester raised an eyebrow. "And you? Still letting her get under your skin?"

I sighed, slumping into the chair across from her. "It's hard not to, Hester. She's making a mockery of me, of John, of our whole family. And worse, she's right about some of it."

Hester set down her mending and leaned forward, her expression softening. "Elizabeth, love, listen to me. Hannah's always been the same. She thrives on stirring trouble; the more you react, the more power you give her. Don't let her have it."

I shook my head, feeling my frustration boil over. "That's easy for you to say. She's not airing your dirty laundry all around town."

"Oh, I know," Hester said, her voice now sharp. "But I've felt the sting of that tongue, and, no doubt, if I cross her, I'll feel it again. But you know how to handle her sort, don't you?"

I blinked at her. "So you're saying that I should just ignore her?"

Hester's smirk returned. "What I mean is, you need to rise above her. She's looking for a fight, and you're giving her exactly what she wants. Let her prattle on. The people who matter will see her for what she is—a bitter woman with nothing better to do."

Her words settled over me, quieting some of the anger swirling inside. "You always know what to say, Hester," I murmured.

She reached out and gave my hand a gentle pat. "That's because I've been where you are, love. I won't let you be dragged down by someone like Hannah Murphy. Now, let's put the kettle on. I need a cuppa to get through the afternoon."

Two days later, I was having an afternoon nap with George, who had settled down since the early hectic months, when a raucous din erupted from the nearby fields. I went to find out what was causing the ruckus.

Three massive bullocks had wandered into our wheat fields, their voracious appetites leading them to graze contentedly on the tall, golden stalks. Amidst the chaos, John and Michael desperately tried to herd the unwelcome intruders out of the wheat, their voices raised in a cacophony of frustration. Yet, the bullocks remained utterly unfazed, their placid munching sharply contrasting with the frantic attempts to drive them away.

"Are they Tim's?" I called out to John, who was scrambling through the fields in a valiant effort to corral them.

"Yeah," he replied with a hint of frustration, "that's the third time this week. I've had a gutful of this. If Tim wants them back, he can bloody well sort it out himself."

With a determined air, John finally managed to herd the trespassing bullocks and swiftly hitched them to the back of the wagon, his actions reflecting a resolve not to tolerate further incursions onto his land. He took them down to the local constable, where they were impounded.

Just after sunset, John noticed movement near the cattle yard. His eyes narrowed as he peered out the window. "That bloody Hannah Murphy is down there," he growled, his voice low and sharp. "She's just taken a rail off the fence. We've got about twenty-five head of cows and calves in that yard. What the hell is she up to?"

We stood in silence, watching the dark shapes move in the distance. The full moon, just beginning to rise, cast an eerie glow over the scene. An hour passed, and then she returned, lingering at the fence like a shadow, watching. She vanished again, only to come back a while later, and then again, until she seemed to be making rounds through the night.

"What's she up to?" I whispered, the tension in the room thick enough to choke on.

"I don't know," John muttered, his jaw clenched. "But it's nothing good, that's for certain. I need to keep an eye on her—and the cattle."

At one in the morning, we finally discovered what she'd been planning. John hissed under his breath, "She's back, and she's not alone. There's someone with her, probably one of the men assigned to them—John Baptiste."

The children, who had been nervously whispering and shifting all night, suddenly buzzed with excitement. "Right," John snapped, "that's it. She's taken down the other three rails. They're in with the cattle."

He bolted out the door, with Betsy, young Johnny, and Michael sprinting after him. I grabbed young Willie before he could slip out. My heart hammered as I followed close behind, hearing the chaos erupt outside. Hannah's voice rang out, shrill and wild, "Drive them all out!"

The dogs barked madly, cattle bellowed in confusion, the children shrieked, and over it all, John and Hannah's furious yells clashed in the air. I froze, staring at the madness unfolding in front of me. Hannah was dressed in a man's coat and hat, but her white petticoat gleamed in the moonlight, like a ghost in the night. Was she drunk?

John scrambled up onto the fence, his voice cutting through the din. "Stop, or I'll shoot you!"

But Hannah and the men with her just laughed. They hurled stones and sticks at John and the children, laughing as if it was all a joke. It was pure, unrestrained pandemonium—the dogs snapping at the air, the cattle stampeding, children yelling, and Hannah, wild-eyed and taunting, daring us to stop her.

John's face was a mask of fury, yet there was something else in his eyes—a sharp, cold edge. He reported it to the constables the following morning, and Hannah and John Baptiste were duly charged with breaking into our stockyards and stealing four head of cattle. It went before Police Magistrate, James Gordon. John Baptiste's roommate lied and provided him with a false alibi, and both he and Hannah Murphy claimed that nothing had happened. So, despite our statements, the magistrate acquitted Baptiste of the charges. While he didn't convict Hannah, he did reprimand her.

She didn't like that one bit, and I overheard her snapping to Tim, "It is ridiculous that I have been bound over to keep the peace when the charges weren't even bloody proven." I hoped that would keep her out of our hair and off our property for a while, at least.

And for the most part, it did. I managed to avoid Hannah Murphy and her poisonous gossip. I mostly stayed off the grog. Although I still allowed myself the occasional tipple, I only had a small taste to take the edge off, rather than indulging in excess. I'd like to say things between John and me had improved, but they hadn't. If anything, since George's birth and my saying there would be no more children, his mood had only darkened. The man I once thought could protect me turned cold, even spiteful. He seemed to find pleasure in humiliating me, making me feel small and useless.

Over that time, Hester and Jim were a true blessing. As Hester and I rekindled our friendship, we spent countless hours catching up on what had happened with the others we'd known in Parramatta. Their home, warm and welcoming, became a haven for me and the younger children. Hester and Jim quickly embraced the role of grandparents, and I could see how much the little ones, in particular, adored him and his stories. Watching them with my children often reminded me of my own mother and what she would have said had she seen me now.

Despite the comfort I found in their home, there was an undercurrent of unease in Hester and Jim's relationship, a feeling I couldn't quite place. At first, I thought it was just my imagination, a side effect of the upheaval in my own life. But the signs were evident: the way Jim would glance at Hester with worry etched on his face when he thought no one was watching, or how Hester sometimes winced when she stood up too quickly, brushing it off as nothing.

One evening, as we sat by the fire after the children had gone to bed, I finally mustered the courage to press Hester about it. "You've been quiet tonight," I remarked, watching her intently. "What's going on, Hester? And don't say it's nothing. I know you too well."

She sighed, setting down her knitting and meeting my gaze. "It's just old age, Lizzie," she said lightly, though her tone lacked its usual sharpness. "These bones aren't what they used to be, but I'm fine."

But I wasn't convinced. "It's more than that, isn't it? You've never been one to shy away from the truth, Hester. If something's wrong, I need to know."

She hesitated, her hands resting in her lap. I thought she might tell me for a moment, but then she shook her head. "There's no use worrying yourself over things that can't be changed," she said softly. "We've all got our burdens to bear."

Her words hung in the air, heavy with unspoken meaning. I wanted to push further, to demand the truth, but the look in her eyes stopped me. She wasn't ready to share whatever was weighing on her.

So I let it go, though the unease lingered.

Further unease arose when it came to John. He rarely spent time at home anymore, which, while a blessing, made me wonder what on earth he was up to. I would soon find out.

One evening, he stumbled through the door late, mumbling something about working late on the farm, though God knows what he was truly up to. His clothes reeked like he'd been anywhere but the fields. He hardly glanced at me as he flung his jacket over the chair.

I don't even know what set me off. Maybe it was the exhaustion. Maybe it was how he refused to meet my eyes, like I didn't even exist. But I snapped.

"So what is it now, John?" I demanded. "Out working or off drinking with your mates? Or is there something else? Someone else?"

He glared at me, his face twisted in anger, but he said nothing. Just that cold, hard stare that said everything.

A week later, I discovered the full extent of John's betrayal. Jim Ware stood in the doorway, his expression serious. "Elizabeth," he said, taking off his hat, "I'm sorry to deliver bad news. I thought you should hear it from me."

My stomach churned as he explained. John, drowning in debt from gambling, had sold the farm to James Cox, a neighbouring landowner and magistrate. Our home, our livelihood, was gone, swallowed up to cover John's recklessness.

The weight of the betrayal was suffocating. Stunned, I sat at the table while Jim rested a comforting hand on my shoulder. "You'll have a place with us if you need it," he offered. Hester stood by the hearth, her lips pressed tight with fury, but she said nothing.

When I confronted him later, John simply shrugged in response. "What else was I meant to do?" he asked, his voice flat. "It was either that or debtors' prison."

"So, you've left us with nothing, have you?" I spat, tears rolling down my cheeks. "We're supposed to pack up and leave our home, the one we built here, all because of your foolishness?"

John leaned back in his chair, a hardened expression on his face as his lips curled into a sneer. "Our home?" he said, his tone saturated with disdain. "Don't flatter yourself, Elizabeth. It was never yours. The land, the house, the cattle—it's mine to do with as I please. Just like you."

The words landed like a slap, leaving me breathless. "What did you just say?" I whispered, barely able to find my voice.

"You heard me," he said coldly. "You're mine. You were assigned to me back in Parramatta, and you're my property. Mine to marry, mine to control, and mine to discard whenever I like. Don't think you're any different from the rest of them."

I stared at him, my vision blurring with tears of disbelief and rage. "After all we've gone through, after all I've been through, you stand there and tell me I'm just another piece of property to you?"

He stood up suddenly, the chair scraping noisily across the floor as he grabbed his jacket. "Spare me the theatrics," he said, his tone sharp and dismissive. "Pack our stuff. We've got to be out by the end of the month."

He didn't wait for a reply, slamming the door behind him as he left. The silence that followed was deafening, shattered only by the faint creak of the house settling around me. My hands shook as I gripped the table's edge, trying to steady myself against the storm of emotions tearing through me. Anger, despair, humiliation—all battled for dominance, leaving me feeling hollow and raw.

I looked around the room, the home we had built together. Every corner bore the marks of my labour, the evidence of the life I'd tried to create here. And now it was all gone, taken by John's selfishness.

For a moment, I allowed myself to cry, my tears falling freely as I mourned what had been lost—not just the farm, but the hope that John could ever be the man I once thought he was.

But as the minutes ticked by, the tears dried, leaving a simmering anger that wouldn't be ignored. He might have taken away my home, my security, and my dignity, but I wasn't finished. Not yet. Somehow, I would find a way to start over. I had no choice—for myself and for the children who depended on me.

Chapter 41

Launceston, Van Diemen's Land, 1830

I left John.

"I've had enough," I said, my voice trembling but determined. "I can't do this anymore. The insults, the neglect. I'm done."

He actually laughed at that—a nasty laugh. "What, you think you can just walk out, Lizzie? Go where, exactly? With what money? You've got nothing without me."

His words stung, yet I didn't allow them to break me. I stared him down, feeling the weight of all those years—the children, the fights, the loneliness—crashing down.

"I'll figure it out," I whispered. "I'd rather have nothing than this."

The next day, I gathered the children—all except Johnny, who stubbornly refused to leave his father, and Betsy, who had her own reasons for staying put, whatever they were—and made my way to Rose's place. She and William had been married for nearly three years now, living in a modest little home in Launceston. It wasn't much, but they had two bedrooms and no babies yet, so we could squeeze in for a bit.

Rose welcomed me with open arms, sensing the burden of my decision. As I guided the younger children inside, I experienced a strange blend of relief and guilt. Relief because I was finally away from John, from the chill that had settled in our marriage like a thick fog. But guilt, because deep down, I knew I was fracturing the family.

Still, I had to do it. For myself, if no one else.

A few days later, word reached me that John had placed an announcement in the Launceston Advertiser. "The Public are hereby cautioned not to give credit to my wife Elizabeth Barefoot, otherwise Church, she having eloped from me without any just cause, and of her own free will."

> THE Public are hereby cautioned not to give Credit in any shape to my wife ELIZABETH BAREFOOT, otherwise CHURCH, she having eloped from me without any just cause, and of her own free will.
>   JOHN BAREFOOT.
> August 13th, 1830.

Public notice regarding Elizabeth, Launceston Advertiser, 13 August 1830, p. 1 (http://nla.gov.au/nla.news-article84774474)

I laughed out loud, a deep, genuine laugh that felt foreign to my own ears. The children, startled by the unfamiliar sound, stared at me wide-eyed.

"Without any just cause?" I snorted. "That's a good one, John! And yes, definitely of my own free will!"

His threat to cut off my credit was no joke; I realised it would lead to serious problems. Without the option to buy anything on credit, I had to find work. But what could I do? My skills were limited, mainly to cleaning and caring for children, and I doubted either could provide a sustainable income.

But it seemed work was available in the many pubs scattered throughout town. It wasn't the best place for me to be while I was grappling with my own addiction, but it was better than the bawdy houses. It wasn't glamorous, and it could be dangerous—especially in Launceston, where convicts, sailors, and labourers frequented the pubs, not to mention the rough sealers—but I was in urgent need. So, I started to ask around, fully aware that I couldn't afford to be picky. Fortune smiled on me; Mr John Fawkner had recently had his license for the Cornwall

Hotel reinstated after being denied the previous year for being deemed "not a proper person to keep an hotel", and he was looking for staff.

So, I found myself back in the pub scene, mostly cleaning and washing dishes, so there wasn't much difference from my daily life. Mr Fawkner was quite a character, a bit of a legend in Launceston. His father, a convict, had arrived in Van Diemen's Land during its early days. In his twenties, Mr Fawkner supplied a whaleboat and tools to help seven convicts escape, a plan that went horribly wrong, leading to a punishment of 500 lashes and three years of hard labour at Newcastle. He eventually returned to Launceston, became a baker, started a newspaper, and sold illegal alcohol before opening the Cornwall Hotel.

His wife Eliza was also an ex-convict who had just received her conditional pardon. She was an unusual-looking woman, her face pockmarked and one eye straying in a different direction than the other. She empathised with my situation and encouraged her husband to hire me. Mr Fawkner held progressive views on women and their right to work independently, which contrasted with the prevailing attitudes of the time. Given our shared backgrounds, I seemed to fit in well. The only caveat was that—unusually for a hotel owner—he was a teetotaller who couldn't tolerate drunks, a consideration I needed to remember given my past.

In the ten years we had lived in this colony, the conflict between settlers and the *Mairremmener* people had escalated, and by the end of September, Launceston was on high alert. We all heard countless stories about blacks breaking into and burning down the homes of settlers in the outer areas and of working parties being ambushed and murdered by them. Still, I heard men speaking proudly about killing black men, as well as about the kidnapping and rape of black women and children. I was relieved not to be out on the farm then, but like everyone, I feared what would happen.

Governor Arthur declared the black resistors to be "enemies of the state", which permitted soldiers to raid camps and arrest any Aboriginals they encountered. However, rather than making arrests, this resulted in many being shot on sight, including women and children, which, of course, escalated the violence in retaliation. These rising levels of violence in the district led to the deaths of around a hundred settlers, with casualties among the black community likely numbering in the hundreds as well.

To put an end to this resistance, Governor Arthur directed all settlers to help the police create a human chain across Van Diemen's Land. This line, made up of settlers, police, and military, aimed to herd the native people like animals as it progressed southward over approximately six weeks. Its ultimate goal was to push the Aboriginal people onto a small peninsula in the south, where they would be rounded up and relocated to smaller islands.

Both my husband John and our son Johnny were called to participate, along with most of the local men, especially those on the farms. They took part, but it was apparently a colossal waste of time, with Johnny telling me they never encountered a single native and only heard reports of shootings. Only two blacks, a man and a boy, were captured.

Mr Fawkner was outraged by this entire affair. In his newspaper, he vehemently criticised Governor Arthur for squandering £35,000 from the colonial treasury with no results. I felt a sense of relief that the operation had fallen through.

Meanwhile, I despaired at what was happening with the older children. John came to see me one night in a drunken rage. He stormed into the house, face flushed and eyes wild, slamming the door behind him. "Do you know what Betsy's been up to?" he spat; his voice slurred yet filled with anger. "She's been sneaking out to meet that Thomas Bird. He works in the Survey Department. He's twice her age, and she's just a child! That bastard's taking advantage of her!"

I stared at him, feeling a surge of disgust rise in my chest. The audacity of him, of all people, to act so high and mighty. I couldn't hold back. "Taking advantage of her?" I hissed, my voice low but sharp. "Given your plans to prostitute both the girls, I don't see what issue you have with Betsy's relationship. At least Thomas isn't planning to sell her off!"

John's face drained of colour, turning a sickly shade of white. He opened his mouth to respond but could only manage to splutter a few incoherent words. For the first time, he was truly speechless. His fury ebbed away, replaced by something else—shame, guilt, or perhaps just the burden of his hypocrisy. He muttered something under his breath, too low for me to catch, then turned on his heel and stormed out, slamming the door behind him. I exhaled slowly, relieved he was gone. While I didn't necessarily agree with Betsy's choice of men, if John was against it, I found myself willing to defend her.

Thomas Bird was certainly no saint. He had been convicted, along with six others, on charges of disposing of forged bank notes, and while initially sentenced to death, that had been commuted to fourteen years transportation. He was sent out on *Lord Hungerford* in 1821. The three ringleaders, those who actually forged the notes, had all been hanged outside Warwick Gaol. Plus, he was fifteen years older than Betsy.

And my worries didn't stop there. Rose, my eldest, faced her own challenges. She'd been married to William for nearly three years, and it was obvious that things weren't right. When she finally opened up to me that she was expecting a child, she broke down in my arms, sobbing uncontrollably. I was stunned to learn the truth about her husband, William. He seemed calm, respectful—even kind—on the surface. But behind closed doors, especially after a skin full of grog, he transformed into a different man: cruel and violent.

Rose pushed up her sleeves and lifted her dress just enough to reveal the marks—fresh bruises, purple and raw, alongside others fading to yellow. My heart shattered. She was only seventeen, stuck in a nightmare, trapped in a life she couldn't escape. She shared how jealous William was, how he would fly into a rage at the mere thought of her looking at another man.

How could I not have noticed this while living under the same roof as them? What could I say now that I knew about it? If she left him, we'd all end up on the streets. And with the baby on the way, her options were even more limited. I'd seen her drinking start to spiral out of control and wondered if this was at least part of the reason. She was following my path, and the realisation made my chest tighten with dread.

I tried to warn her. "Rose, be careful," I said one evening when I caught her pouring herself another drink. "Don't let it take over your life like it did mine. You're stronger than this."

But she just shrugged, her movements slow and indifferent, as if she didn't care. "What does it matter, Ma?" she muttered, not even looking at me. "There's nothing left to ruin anyway."

That worried me the most—she'd already given up, and she was so young. The light in her eyes that had once burned so brightly was now dim, replaced by a dull resignation. I wanted to shake her, to pull her back from the edge, but I knew from my own struggles that words wouldn't be enough. She had to want to fight for herself. And that, I feared, was a battle she wasn't prepared to face.

And Johnny. My son was turning into a man I barely recognised. He had a respectable job as a ploughman and a genuine love for horses, but he was easily swayed by others, and his drinking troubled me deeply. When sober, he was the son I had always known—kind, hardworking, and earnest. But when the alcohol took over, he transformed into someone much like his father—loud, rude, and spiteful. His bravado was particularly unsettling; he seemed to take on every challenge without a second thought, as if he were daring fate to test him. I worried about where this reckless path might lead him, which broke my heart.

We were all trapped in our own ways. Betsy, with her much older suitor or the future her father had planned for her. Rose was stuck with her violent husband and a baby on the way. Johnny was lost in his increasingly wild ways. And I was struggling to hold it all together, feeling that no matter how hard I tried, the pieces would always be just out of reach.

We were all just surviving, one day at a time.

Chapter 42

Launceston, Van Diemen's Land, 1831–1834

Summer in Launceston—the land lay parched beneath a relentless sun. Not a drop of rain had fallen in months, and it seemed that the drought was all people could talk about. Farmers who came into the Cornwall Hotel for a drink spoke of cracked earth, fields barren of grass, and starving cattle. Bushfires were a constant threat, and the dry undergrowth along with brittle eucalyptus trees made perfect kindling. Smoke lingered in the air most days, and we were advised to be cautious about where we smoked or struck a match, as even the slightest spark could start a blaze. These fires were unlike anything we had ever experienced, tearing through the bush with terrifying speed, the gum trees exploding like fireworks, sending the inferno racing for miles.

Late one evening at the end of February, while the heat still clung to the air, Rose went into labour. A massive thunderstorm had rolled through earlier, bringing brief relief with heavy rain, but by nightfall, the rain had disappeared, leaving only the stifling humidity behind. The air was thick, and despite my efforts to cool her down by soaking towels in water, it felt like we were battling nature itself. Rose's face was flushed, her body drenched in sweat, but she was determined, pushing through with her teeth gritted.

Just after midnight, her son was born, the labour blessedly short. I cradled the tiny boy in my arms, his skin still soft and wrinkled, his cries barely a whisper in the stillness of the night. My first grandchild. Something swelled inside me as I looked down at him—a powerful feeling, unlike anything I had experienced before. It wasn't the same as when I held my own children, though those memories remained vivid, etched deep in my mind. This was something new, a love that felt bigger, older, as if it had been waiting to be born just as much as this little boy. At his father's insistence, they named him William, after his father and his father's father.

In September, Betsy told me that Thomas had asked her to marry him. After her father's explosion, when he first learned of their relationship, she moved out of his home and into Thomas', so I was happy that he was doing what was considered to be the right thing: marrying her. She was just seventeen, but I could see in her face that she was determined, so I gave my permission.

Thomas, still a convict, needed permission from the governor to marry. He applied to the Police Magistrate, Mr Lyttleton, and permission was granted without any issues. The banns were read at St John's in Launceston, and the ceremony took place on the 31st of October. As for Rose's wedding, there were no special clothes, just the best ones we could put together. We'd all seen weddings here in Launceston with brides in elaborate gowns of silk and lace, in lovely colours, but we knew this wouldn't be for us. A few ribbons for decoration and a bunch of pretty flowers picked from the bush would have to suffice.

About six weeks later, John barged into Rose's house, furious and demanding answers about Betsy. He was livid, pacing the room as he explained how he'd gone so far as to petition Governor Arthur himself. He'd paid a writer to craft the letter, laying out a grand tale of how Thomas had carried on a clandestine relationship over the past eighteen months with Betsy, then seduced her, luring her away from The Springs and taking her to a brothel in Launceston, where John claimed they were living. He had begged the governor to intervene and return Betsy to his guardianship as if she were still his little girl. He was brandishing a letter from the governor, which he flung on the table in disgust. Its contents had been read to him, and he knew that avenue was closed to him.

"John, you're barking up the wrong tree," I said, shaking my head. "Not only did Thomas ask for permission to marry Betsy, and get it, but they're already wed. And no, they're not in some brothel in Launceston. They've got a proper house on a farm near Perth. Thomas is working there now, earning an honest living." This was a slight stretch, as I was not really sure how Thomas earned his money.

John's face fell, his bravado collapsing under the weight of the truth. He stood frozen momentarily, as if the words were too much to bear. His fists clenched at his sides, his eyes narrowing with rage and helplessness. But there was nothing he could do, and he knew it.

Without uttering a word, he spun on his heel and stormed out of the cottage, slamming the door with such force that the walls trembled. I lingered for a moment, gazing at the shut door. Rose, who had been quietly perched in the corner, finally glanced up at me, her eyes wide with concern and relief.

"Hopefully, that's the end of that," I sighed.

Later that night, Jim read the letter to us. The governor, quite rightly, had refused John's request and went so far as to record that he believed that the object of John's objection had been to extort money and noted that John "was of very bad character and had often connived at the prostitution of his children."

It was the end of it with John; whatever semblance of a partnership we'd once had was long gone, leaving nothing but resentment and silence in its wake. But more immediately, there was trouble brewing between Betsy and Thomas.

Their situation was unravelling, and it was clear they weren't doing well. Despite my bold words to John, Thomas appeared to be constantly in and out of gaol, facing various debts, defrauding people, and engaging in general dishonesty. Each time I heard his name mentioned in town, it was associated with yet another scandal—a botched land deal, unpaid rent, or allegations of fraud.

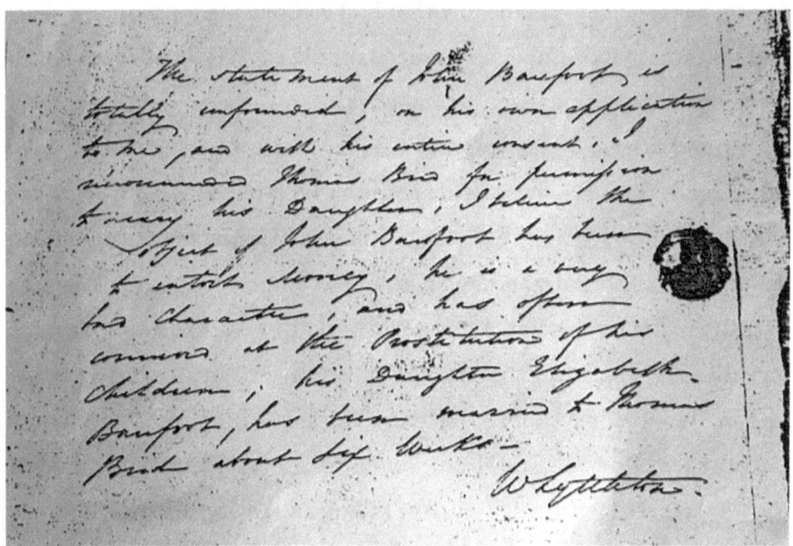

Letter from Magistrate Lyttleton to Governor Arthur, 1831, Tasmanian Archives, CSO1/12443, p. 282

Their drinking had spiralled completely out of control. Betsy seemed to no longer care who saw her staggering through the streets or what people thought of the unsavoury company she kept. Ruffians, gamblers, and drunks came and went from their house at all hours, transforming it into a den of chaos and disorder.

The house itself bore the marks of neglect and destruction. The windows were shattered, some patched haphazardly with cloth, others left open to the elements. The door hung loosely on its hinges, battered and splintered from frequent abuse. Inside, the floors were sticky with spilled drink, the walls smeared with grime, and broken furniture lay strewn about. The once modest but tidy home had become a wreck, a place where noise and trouble reigned. And I knew that Thomas owed almost a year's rent on the property, which he had no way of paying. It seemed that there was always another scheme to pay off the debts that just seemed to lead to further debt.

While I worried about my three oldest children, my life went on. I hardly felt the deep melancholy that had gripped me for so many years, and I was more mindful of how much I drank, especially since I was still working at the Cornwall for Mr Fawkner.

Among our regulars was Mr Batman, who often gathered with other men to discuss business. I couldn't help but wonder if he chose the Cornwall specifically because he knew it irritated Mr Fawkner, who despised him. Mr Batman had an air of self-importance, a man used to basking in his reputation. A few years back, he had made quite a name for himself by capturing the notorious bushranger Matthew Brady. Brady, unlike the hideous Thomas Jeffries, was something of a "gentleman bushranger". He rarely stole from women and certainly never committed the vile acts that Jeffries had, such as killing and eating his victims. Brady had been injured in a gun battle with soldiers, and Mr Batman found him limping in the bush, alone. Mr Batman convinced the outlaw to surrender, and, possibly because he was so ill, Brady did just that.

Mr Fawkner seemed to have boundless energy, channelling it into his relentless criticisms of John Batman. He often called him "vainglorious," a word I hadn't heard before. When I asked what it meant, Fawkner explained it with a disdainful snort. "A man full of his own self-importance," he said. "A braggart. And in Batman's case, a murderer."

The accusation lingered heavily in the air, and he wasted no time elaborating. Mr Fawkner often recounted the grim tale of how Mr Batman had led an attack on a group of about seventy sleeping blacks, slaughtering most—men, women, and children alike. Those who managed to flee were hunted down and shot like animals. Only a mother and her child survived. The mother was sent to Flinders Island, while Batman kept the boy, claiming he would raise him.

"Kidnapping, plain and simple," Mr Fawkner would say, his voice dripping with scorn. "Batman thinks himself some great pioneer, but he's nothing more than a land-grabber with blood on his hands."

The story haunted me, not just for its brutality but for the way Fawkner recounted it, as if he were daring anyone to challenge him. It served as a stark reminder of the world we live in—a world where men like Batman could commit atrocities and still be hailed as heroes.

Meanwhile, Hester was starting to struggle. She tried to hide it, brushing off my concerns with a sharp tongue or a forced laugh, but I could see the toll it was taking on her. Her hands, once so steady, now trembled as she worked, and her sharp wit seemed dulled by exhaustion. She spent more time sitting by the fire, a blanket wrapped tightly around her shoulders, her face pale and drawn.

"Just old age catching up with me," she'd say when I pressed her. But it was more than that, and we both knew. Jim fussed over her constantly, bringing her tea and reminding her to rest, yet even he seemed resigned to the truth. The vibrant, sharp-eyed woman who had been my rock for so long was slowly slipping away, and I wasn't ready to confront what that meant.

My Betsy gave birth to her first child in August of 1832—a daughter, and they named her Zipporah! I laughed when I heard it. Zipporah, the wife of Moses! How on earth they settled on that name, I'll never know. After all my years sitting in the pews at Sandy Creek Church, I never imagined my grandchild would have a name from such an ancient and distant story.

The baby was healthy, a little bundle with a good set of lungs, and both Betsy and Thomas appeared happy enough as new parents. I hoped this might be the moment Betsy would turn a corner. A baby was a fresh start, a reason for her to pull herself together and leave the chaos behind. I wished that becoming a mother could give her the strength to step out of the shadows and create something better in her life. But there was something in Betsy's eyes, a flicker of doubt she couldn't entirely hide. A shadow lingered over her smile, and I couldn't shake the feeling that she was already regretting her life choices.

Marrying a man nearly twice her age—maybe it seemed like a good idea back then, a means to achieve some stability. But now, with a wailing infant in her arms and Thomas more absent than present, I wondered if the reality of it all was finally starting to sink in. I could see that she loved her daughter, but there was a distinct lack of tenderness in the way she held her. It was all brisk efficiency, as if she was keeping the fragments of her life together with gritted teeth and sheer determination.

Hester, always watchful, finally chose to intervene. One afternoon, she strode over to Betsy's house, carrying a loaf of bread and a jar of jam. Hester never required an invitation when she had something to say. She found Betsy slouched in a chair, the baby crying in her arms, and Thomas nowhere to be found.

"You've got yourself a fine little girl there," Hester said, putting the bread on the table. "But babies don't raise themselves, Betsy. You need to pull your socks up and start considering what kind of life you're offering her."

Betsy scowled, her defences rising straight away. "I know what I'm doing," she snapped, her voice cutting. "I don't need anyone telling me how to be a mother."

Hester wasn't fazed. "Oh, don't you?" she replied, her tone sharp. "From where I'm standing, you've got a husband who can't be bothered and a house that's falling to bits. Do you reckon that baby deserves this? You're tough, Betsy. But toughness isn't enough. That little girl needs you to lift your game—for her sake."

Betsy opened her mouth to argue but shut it again, her glare wavering. For a moment, she glanced down at the baby in her arms, and in that instant, the shadow in her eyes seemed to darken. "I'm doing the best I can," she muttered, though her voice lacked conviction.

"Then do better," Hester said with conviction. "You have it in you. But if you keep this up, you'll lose everything that matters."

The words hung in the air, heavy with truth. Betsy said nothing, but the tension in her jaw revealed the struggle within her. Later, Hester told me about the encounter, and I felt a flicker of hope. If anyone could reach Betsy, it was Hester. Yet, even as I held onto that hope, I couldn't shake the fear that gnawed at me—that the shadow I saw in Betsy's eyes might already be too deep to lift.

Rose was expecting another baby, yet she was drinking heavily and felt utterly miserable in her marriage. She didn't want another child—she made that clear—but we both know how little say we women have in such matters. The situation between her and William hadn't improved, and then she dropped a bombshell. There was another man, and as she described him, I knew who she meant—"Yorkshire Jack" Wilcox, a familiar face in the local taverns. He'd been transported for seven years for passing counterfeit money; he was young and good-looking, and Rose was head over heels. He was also the shepherd whose hut the cannibal Jefferies had broken into all those years back. I suspected from how she spoke that this baby might not be William's.

We talked for hours, and I told her the first step was getting through this pregnancy. After the baby came, we could figure out the rest.

But sometimes, life takes a cruel turn. Not long after we spoke, Rose went into labour, two months early. The midwife rushed over but arrived just in time to deliver a tiny baby girl, born far too soon. She didn't even get the chance to take her first breath. The moment Rose realised the baby was stillborn, she let out a scream—a sound so full of pain it chilled me to the bone. In an instant, my own heart was dragged back to that dreadful day, years ago, when I lost my own child.

We sat together on her bed, holding one another, two grieving mothers drowning in our sorrow, mourning the daughters we would never hold.

And then I did what I knew I shouldn't—I turned to the bottle. I nicked a bottle of rum from the hotel and found a quiet spot beneath a tree, where I drank until the world blurred. I heard the whispers and disapproving glances from the more proper folk of Launceston as they passed by, but their judgment couldn't pierce the fog of grief I was drowning in. I sat there, wallowing, uncaring about what anyone thought.

At some point, a constable found me sitting there with tear-streaked cheeks and an empty bottle. He charged me with drunkenness, and I didn't protest. The following day, in front of the magistrate, I braced myself for a scolding. But instead of the harsh lecture I'd received before, he spoke softly. He fined me five shillings, but with an air of compassion rather than condemnation. "You're getting too old for this, Elizabeth," he said, his voice almost fatherly. "I understand your grief, but women can't be seen sitting drunk in the streets."

The words stung, but what followed cut deeper. Mr Fawkner pulled me aside the next day, his face drawn with disappointment. "I'm truly sorry for your loss," he said, his voice clipped and business-like, "but I can't have drunks working for me. It's bad for business—and worse for you."

He was right, of course. I knew it, and the regret sat heavy in my chest. But it was too late to undo what had been done.

Before he left, he softened for a moment, surprising me with a quick, firm hug. "Take care of yourself, Elizabeth," he said, winking at me as he stepped back. "And come back for a drink sometime … but just one."

Hester didn't take long to share her thoughts on the affair. When she visited me the day after Mr Fawkner let me go, her face revealed a mix of disappointment and concern. She settled into the chair opposite mine, her movements slower than usual, her frame wrapped in a shawl despite the warmth of the day. I couldn't overlook how pale she had become, how laboured her breathing was. It was no secret now—Hester was dying, and her time was limited.

"So," she began, her tone blunt but weary, "you've gone and made a proper fool of yourself, haven't you?"

I flinched at her words, though I couldn't deny their truth. "I didn't mean for it to happen," I muttered, unable to meet her gaze. "I just felt so sad, so out of control again."

"Nothing just happens, Elizabeth," she snapped, though there was a softness beneath her sharp tone. "You picked up that bottle and drank it. And now look at the mess you're in. Losing a job, being hauled before the magistrate—it's not just yourself you're dragging down. What about those young children of yours?"

Her words stung, but they were tempered with something else—an urgency that wasn't there before. Hester wasn't just worried about me; she was running out of time to set me straight, and we both knew it.

She sighed, the sound heavy with effort. When she finally spoke, her voice was softer, yet it carried the weight of someone who had weathered her own storms. "Grief is a devil, Elizabeth. If you let it, it'll wrap itself around you and squeeze the fight right out of you. But you can't let it win. Not now, not ever."

She leaned forward, her hand resting lightly on mine. Her skin felt frail, her grip weaker than I remembered, but the strength in her eyes was undiminished. "You're stronger than this, love. I've seen it. You've pulled yourself out of worse than this before, and you'll do it again. But it starts with putting down that bottle and facing what's before you."

I looked at her through tear-filled eyes. "What if I can't? What if it's too late?"

"It's never too late," she said firmly, though her voice wavered slightly. "I'm running out of time, Elizabeth, but you're not. Not yet. You've still got the chance to make things right, for yourself and for those children. Don't waste it."

Her words struck me like a blow. She was right—she had always been. But hearing her talk about her own time running out left me feeling hollow. The thought of losing her, the one person who always saw me clearly and never gave up on me, was nearly too much to bear.

Hester must have seen it in my face, because she gave me a faint smile and squeezed my hand. "I'll be gone soon, love," she said quietly. "And I won't be here to pull you back when you fall. So you've got to do it yourself. Promise me you'll try."

Tears streamed down my face as I nodded. "I promise, Hester."

She sat back, her expression softening, but I could see the exhaustion creeping over her. "Good," she said, her voice fading. "That's all I needed to hear."

Things reached a breaking point between Rose and William in June of the following year, resembling a storm that gathers strength before it finally breaks. Their arguments, which had already become a norm, had intensified, with words thrown like weapons. Rose was drinking far too much, though I couldn't discern whether the alcohol was fuelling the arguments or if the arguments were pushing her to the bottle. Likely both.

One afternoon, as we sat in the cramped kitchen, Rose leaned across the table, her voice low and trembling. "He blamed me, Ma," she said, her words slightly slurred from the drink in her hand. "Blamed me for the baby arriving early. Said it was my fault." She paused, staring at the scratched surface of the table. "And when she didn't survive, he just … shut down. Shut me out completely."

She wiped her eyes angrily, as if furious with herself for showing vulnerability. "He stormed out," she continued, her voice rising with frustration, "face white as a ghost, like I'd killed her myself. Left me to grieve alone."

I nodded, feeling the weight of her pain but unsure of what to say. I could see how that grief had consumed her, how it had drawn her closer to Yorkshire Jack. The baby's death might have been the final straw, but I knew their marriage had been unravelling long before that.

Only weeks later, William returned home to find Jack and Rose in the marital bed. The details of what followed spread through town in scandalised but amused whispers: how William, white with rage, lunged at Jack; how the younger man, quick and strong, had bested him effortlessly. I pictured the scene—the shouts, the blows, and William staggering away in defeat, his pride in tatters. That night, he departed for Hobart, his exit abrupt and final.

Jack wasted no time moving in with Rose and little William, who was nearly three now. From the outside, it might have seemed like a fresh start, but I knew better. Both Rose and Jack were heavy drinkers, their lives a blur of booze and brawls. It reminded me far too much of my own darkest days. I'd fought my way out of that pit once, and I wasn't about to fall back in—not now, not ever.

When Hester's health began to decline and Jim came to me seeking help, I didn't hesitate. Escaping Rose's chaos felt like a relief, and moving in with Hester and Jim provided me with a purpose I desperately needed. If I couldn't turn around Rose's life, at least I could be there for Hester in her final days.

Chapter 43

Launceston, Van Diemen's Land, 1835–1837

In the summer of 1835, excitement buzzed around Launceston. The news spread like wildfire—Mr Fawkner had overheard Mr Batman and his Port Phillip Association discussing their plans to sail to Port Phillip and establish a settlement there while at the Cornwall one day. Little land remained in Van Diemen's Land that was suitable for farming, and Mr Batman sought more land. Mr Fawkner, always quick to seize an opportunity, acted swiftly to get ahead. Although there had been previous attempts to settle the Port Phillip area, mainly to prevent the French from establishing a foothold, Mr Batman and Mr Fawkner were focused on a bigger prize.

Mr Batman set sail on *Rebecca* in May. Upon his arrival, he navigated up the Yarra River and signed a treaty with the Aboriginal people on behalf of his Tasmanian Association. The treaty with the *Wurundjeri* people was for the lease of thousands of acres of their land in exchange for tools, blankets, and food. Mr Batman left some of his men behind at a place they called Indented Head, where they constructed a wattle-and-daub hut, planted crops, and laid the groundwork for a settlement. He then returned to Launceston to present the land claim to Governor Arthur.

Mr Fawkner was determined to achieve more than this, convinced that a more promising site for a settlement awaited on the mainland. His resolve was steadfast, and he went about organising and provisioning a schooner, *Enterprize*, to pursue his vision. By August, with the vessel loaded and ready, he and his crew of first settlers set sail up the Tamar River, heading for the mainland territory.

However, fate intervened just as his plans seemed on the verge of success. Burdened by debts he couldn't shake, Mr Fawkner was forced off *Enterprize* before it could depart the river. It must have stung him deeply to watch his ship sail away without him, his grand aspirations slipping beyond his reach. Yet, his crew and passengers pressed on, undeterred by his absence.

Near the end of August after surveying several promising sites, they moored beside the Yarra River and set up camp, erecting tents, building a small store, and beginning to clear land for vegetable growth. There were only a few passengers, but among them and the crew were a pair of carpenters, a builder, a ploughman, and a blacksmith. The blacksmith's pregnant wife also made the journey, bringing an unusual but vital companion—a cat!

The image of that little cat padding through the undergrowth of the untamed land always stuck with me. It was such a small, humble thing, yet it carried with it a sense of home, of comfort amidst the unknown.

Though Mr Fawkner wasn't there to witness it, his vision had set the wheels in motion. Even from afar, I imagined he must have felt some satisfaction in knowing that his dreams of a new settlement had begun to take root—albeit imperfectly.

At the same time, the Governor of New South Wales declared that the treaty Mr Batman had brokered was invalid and that his party was trespassing.

When news of Mr Fawkner's venture reached Mr Batman, he was absolutely outraged. Despite threats from Mr Batman's group, Mr Fawkner's crew remained steadfast, continuing their work without hesitation. By the time Mr Batman returned to the site he had envisioned for his village, it was already October, and Mr Fawkner's settlement was firmly established. Mr Batman's earlier exploration and dubious sale deed with the *Wurundjeri* had proven inadequate to secure the land before Mr Fawkner's arrival.

I caught wind of all this and decided to stop by the Cornwall on my way to visit Rose. Mr Fawkner and Eliza were there, and Mr Fawkner was practically vibrating with excitement. "I've heard reports, Elizabeth," he said, his eyes alight with enthusiasm, "reports of the splendid country around this new settlement. And it's a place free from Governor Arthur's tyranny and this old system's constraints. A person like you, a freed convict, would thrive in this new environment." His words struck a deep chord within me, echoing the hope for a fresh start and the promise of freedom from past constraints.

I made my way to Rose's cottage, hoping for a quiet visit, but as soon as I opened the front door, I was greeted with sheer chaos. Both she and Jack had been drinking heavily, their laughter and singing ringing out through the tiny house. They were well into their cups, and I'm embarrassed to admit I joined them. It was too tempting to resist—the sight of them so carefree and full of life. It had been ages since I felt that young and lighthearted, if indeed I ever had.

I was approaching fifty, and its weight bore down on me. It felt as if my time was running out, that I had lived whatever life I was meant to and would soon be gone. So we all got quite drunk. The more we drank, the more I began to wallow in my sorrow, crying into my glass about how my life had gone off track, how nothing had turned out the way I'd imagined it would.

Jack and Rose, on the other hand, grew even louder, their laughter turning raucous, almost hysterical. It wasn't long before the constables came knocking, drawn in by the noise. Another charge of drunkenness, another fine. I felt ashamed — and while Hester gave me a telling off about it, Rose and Jack laughed it off, saying it was a small price to pay for a good night. I thought that five shillings each could have been better spent—not the least of which to make their house a bit more comfortable. Poor little

William had just gone to bed last night, probably used to hearing the raucousness from the other room.

In October, Mr Fawkner and Eliza set off once more for the fledgling settlement of Melbourne, this time with no thought of returning. Their departure stirred something in me, a longing I couldn't quite define. I wondered what it would be like to start afresh in a place where the shadow of the convict stain didn't follow my children or me like a brand seared into our backs.

They said Melbourne was still rough and raw, but it offered a promise of a better life for those willing to work hard enough. No convicts had been transported there, so I imagined the social classes of Van Diemen's Land and Sydney hadn't taken root. Perhaps it was a place where your past mattered less than your future, where the choices you made today could reshape the life you led tomorrow.

I pondered what it would be like to live without the burden of past judgments weighing on you. To enter a room without others knowing, or assuming they know, the worst aspects of your history. A fresh start.

I thought back on my life. I'd been taken from my homeland by people I had mistakenly trusted, then abandoned by them. I'd done what I had to do to survive on the streets of an unfamiliar city, and then I was convicted of a crime I did not commit and transported to this new colony. I'd served my sentence, but the stain of that sentence followed me to this raw, young part of the world. I wondered whether I could muster enough courage to start again at my age. I want to reinvent myself, if you will, in a new place. Elizabeth Welborn, Elizabeth Church, Elizabeth Barefoot ... I dreamed on.

The Hockey brothers entered our lives that year, undoubtedly drawn by my three younger girls. Annie, Ellen, and Bridget were blossoming into young women, though to me, they were still just children. At sixteen, Annie carried herself with confidence beyond her years, while fourteen-year-old Ellen was quieter and more observant. Bridget, just thirteen, still leaned more towards being a child, though she seemed determined to prove otherwise whenever the brothers were around. Samuel, at twenty-six, and his older brother James, who was four years his senior, were serving convicts who had arrived aboard *Sir Charles Forbes* in 1830. They soon became regular visitors at our supper table, and when they occasionally brought extra meat along, we didn't ask too many questions about where it came from.

James seldom spoke about the crime that resulted in his transportation, and when he did, it was with a calm, detached tone that unsettled me. "Stole a gelding worth twenty quid," he'd say, as if he were discussing a market deal gone awry.

But twenty pounds was no small sum. That gelding wasn't just a horse— it was a lifeline for the farmer who owned it. A sturdy animal, capable of hauling carts, ploughing fields, and earning its keep many times over. Its loss wasn't just a theft; it was a blow that could ruin a family. And James, along with Cornelius Loxton, had taken it without a second thought.

It wasn't their first offence, either. Before stealing the gelding, they'd been arrested on suspicion of nicking a saddle and bridle, though the charges hadn't stuck. The horse theft, however, was bold enough, brazen enough, to seal their fates.

They were caught in no time. Horses weren't exactly easy to hide, and the gelding was too well-known to simply disappear. By the time James and Cornelius stood before the court, the evidence was overwhelming. The judge's verdict came quickly: they were to hang.

James recounted this part of the story with an unsettling calm. "They commuted it to transportation," he said, a faint smile tugging at the corner of his mouth. "Fourteen years in Van Diemen's Land. Lucky, I suppose."

James also seldom spoke about the family he had left behind. From what little I knew, his wife had been pregnant and struggling when he was imprisoned. With no one to support her, she ended up in the workhouse with their two-year-old daughter in tow.

"I've got no idea what happened to her after that," he admitted once, his voice flat and unfeeling, like the barren fields after harvest. "Or the child she gave birth to. I did apply to have them sent out here to join me, but permission was refused."

His tone was as distant as his words, as though he were recounting someone else's tragedy rather than his own. That detachment and coldness were always there, lingering beneath the surface.

Even when he talked about narrowly dodging the hangman's noose, it was with the same glib indifference. "Guess they figured we'd be more useful in Van Diemen's Land than swinging from a rope," he'd said, the faintest smirk tugging at his lips.

And yet, despite his calm exterior, something about him unnerved me. A shadow. A calculation I couldn't overlook. James wasn't a man who acted out of desperation or passion. Every move he made felt measured, deliberate.

I couldn't shake the feeling that if given the chance, he'd do it all over again. The farmer's loss, his wife's suffering, and the unknown fate of his children—none of it seemed to weigh on him. He had walked away from it all, untethered and unrepentant.

But Samuel was a different story. Just a month after James had been caught stealing a horse, Samuel followed in his brother's footsteps—or perhaps his shadow—and pinched an ass from a local farmer. While the two crimes were similar, the brothers handled the weight of their actions quite differently.

Samuel appeared genuinely remorseful. "I was young and reckless," he confessed one evening, gazing into the fire. "I didn't consider the consequences—not just for the farmer, but also what it would cost me or anyone else. I only focused on getting what I needed in that moment."

The ass he'd taken was worth twenty shillings—a considerable sum, particularly for a working farmer who depended on the animal for his livelihood. Samuel understood that now, and the regret etched on his face was genuine, not something you could feign.

Since arriving in Van Diemen's Land, James and Samuel managed to avoid serious trouble—at least by the colony's standards—but they were far from model prisoners. Their records reflected an ongoing tension with authority, though how they navigated their punishments was as different as the men themselves.

James had accumulated a few minor charges: drunk and disorderly conduct, insolence, and indecent language. These misdemeanours had landed him a stint on the whipping post, where he endured his twenty-five lashes in cold, almost defiant silence. Hearing him recount it later was little more than a bother, a temporary hassle.

On the other hand, Samuel appeared to struggle more profoundly with his new life. While he seemed remorseful about the crime that had led him here, the unrelenting grind of servitude under watchful eyes seemed to shatter something within him. Disobedience, neglect of duties, and insolence surfaced repeatedly on his record.

His punishments were harsher and more frequent. On one occasion, Samuel received twenty-five lashes, and then, for neglecting his master's flock of sheep, fifty lashes—more than enough to split a man's back and leave scars that would never fade.

While listening to these stories at the supper table, I felt a prickling unease creep up my spine. I glanced at my girls—Annie, Ellen, and Bridget—who appeared to be hanging on every word.

James sighed and straightened, his tone brightening as if he was determined to shake off the moment. "But life's not about looking back, is it? We all have to make our way here. Build something new."

I thought I nodded just because it was expected of me, but I could feel a knot tighten in my stomach. Was this really what these girls needed? Rose and Betsy had made some poor choices and were suffering for them. Would either of these men be any better?

Edward Cassidy was the third member of our extended family, and he was a completely different story. At just twenty-two, he was still quite young. Edward had been born free in Sydney, much like my older children. However, his parents carried the convict stain—his father was transported for nicking a shirt and a pair of silk stockings, while his mother's reasons were ones I never fully understood. After his father passed away, Edward's mother struggled to look after her five children, and Edward spent part of his childhood in an orphan school. Maybe that's why he had a quiet steadiness, a resilience that seemed to draw people in. He'd decided to try his luck in Van Diemen's Land, hoping to secure enough land to farm there.

Hester's health continued to fail, and with each passing day, she appeared closer to the end. One night, she sat resting in the chair by the fire, her hands tightly folded over her lap as if holding onto the last of her strength. I sat beside her, my fingers idly twisting the hem of my apron, anticipating what I knew was about to happen. Hester never let a moment go by without sharing her wisdom, and tonight, I felt it was to be her final gift to me.

"I must admit," she continued, pausing to take a shaky breath, "I thought those Hockey brothers were a couple of rogues from the moment I laid eyes on them. Since arriving in the colony, they've found trouble more times than I can count—drinking, ignoring orders, neglecting their duties, and making a general ruckus wherever they go."

I nodded, but Hester wasn't finished. Her voice gained a faint edge, like a knife pressing gently against my resolve.

"There's a charm about them," she said. "But it's the sort that often leads to broken hearts and poor choices. You've seen it before, the type of man who talks a big game but brings nothing but heartache."

I swallowed hard, glancing toward the sleeping forms of the girls in the next room. Hester's words echoed my own unease, the doubts I had tried to ignore.

"They're not what you or those girls need," she said firmly. "Men like that are trouble, Elizabeth. And trouble like that doesn't just disappear."

I knew she was right, but the girls were so headstrong that they'd never listen to me. I also realised it was time to think about myself and my future.

Hester passed away in the early morning hours, just as the first light began to creep through the cracks in the shutters. The room was silent, except for the faint rustle of the wind outside; the stillness felt heavy and final. Jim and I had sat with her through the night, watching as her breaths became shallower, her grip on our hands loosening until it slipped away completely.

She was gone.

For a long time, I couldn't move. I just sat there, staring at her peaceful face, trying to reconcile the stillness of her body with the woman she had been. Hester was more than a friend; she was like a second mother to me, guiding me through the darkest times of my life with a sharp tongue and a softer heart than she ever let on. She scolded me when I needed it, encouraged me when I doubted myself, and never allowed me to wallow in self-pity.

And now she was gone.

The fire had burned low in the hearth, and the room felt colder, emptier, without her presence.

I recalled her final words, the advice she offered me with the little strength she had remaining. "You've got a chance to do better. To leave this mess behind and start fresh. After everything you've been through, you deserve that chance, *mo ghráin*."

Her voice echoed in my mind as I wept for her. For the woman who had seen me at my worst and never turned away. For the guidance I would no longer have, the warmth of her steadying presence. Hester had been the anchor I hadn't realised I relied on so heavily, and now I felt adrift, lost in a sea of uncertainty.

As I went about my day, my grief trailed behind me like a shadow. I felt her absence in every corner of the house and in every decision I made. Yet, beneath the ache, a small seed of determination was sown by her words.

As I prepared to lay her to rest, I promised her one thing: I wouldn't let her wisdom go to waste. I'd find a way to build a better life, a clean slate, just as she had urged me to. And even though I grieved for her deeply, I carried her with me, her voice a steady guide in my heart.

Chapter 44

Launceston, Van Diemen's Land, 1837

Later that year, my world tilted yet again.

My son-in-law, Thomas Bird, and my son, Johnny, were arrested, along with Thomas's assigned man, William Lancaster. Even now, I can't claim to know the full story. Rumours swirled like flies around a carcass—ugly and persistent—but the facts were damning.

Thomas had planned to travel to Hobart Town to buy tin. His own horse, worn out from countless trips, wasn't up to the journey. Rather than waiting or seeking another solution, Thomas, Johnny, and Lancaster opted to steal two horses from Charles Wilkins, a local blacksmith.

According to Wilkins, the horses were taken from his paddock one night. The men removed logs from the fence to let the animals out, ignoring the locked gate just a few feet away. One of the horses was a dark brown mare with a distinct J brand on her neck. The other was her foal, barely weeks old and still nursing. My stomach turned when I heard about the foal left behind to fend for itself. The poor creature didn't stand a chance. By the time anyone noticed, it had grown weak from hunger and passed away within days.

The men, oblivious—or perhaps indifferent—rode hard toward Hobart Town. They stopped at inns and ferry crossings along the way, leaving a trail of witnesses in their wake. Constable Henry Lark saw them at the Castle Inn on the 9th of November, sitting in the taproom while their horses stood outside, too fatigued to walk properly. "They could scarce stand," Lark later testified. Another constable, Isaac Stephen, saw them at Bridgewater Ferry the same evening. He remembered the mare well—so weak she had to be lifted from the ferryboat. "Why would you ride her in such a state?" he'd asked, but all Thomas had said was that she'd been watered too heavily at a public house, as though that excused the cruelty.

By the time they reached the outskirts of Hobart Town, the mare collapsed and died outside the Fox Inn. She was discovered the following day, her body mangled, the cost of their reckless haste. The second horse, still alive but in terrible condition, was found in a stable near the town.

When I heard the whole story, I felt sick—not just at what they'd done but at what it revealed about them. They weren't just thieves; they were cruel, indifferent, and thoughtless. How could they not see the suffering they caused? The foal starving, the mare pushed beyond her limits until her body simply gave out. How could Johnny have done this? He was a ploughman who always worked with horses, and as far as I knew, he treated them with care and respect.

The trial was swift, and there was no leniency for either of them. Johnny and Thomas were convicted of horse theft, one of the gravest offences in the colony. The sentence was harsh but not unexpected: life. Life as convicts. My son, once full of promise, would be branded a convict, just like his mother and father before him. Johnny was sent to Port Arthur penal station, while Thomas was sent to Norfolk Island. Who knew what horrors awaited them in those places? Stories about each of them sent shivers down my spine.

Tuesday December 5.
John Barefoot and William Lancaster stood charged with stealing a mare, guilty, but not sentenced.
This was a case of most atrocious character. The mare was taken away from the foal, which starved to death in consequence, and the mare was spoiled by being obliged to retain her milk.

Brief newspaper mention about the horse theft, Hobart Town Courier, 8 December 1837, p. 3 (http://nla.gov.au/nla.news-article4168212)

I was devastated; the weight of the sentence settling like a stone in my chest. I had hoped for so much more for Johnny. After all, we had endured numerous struggles to carve out a life in this new land, but this was not the future I had envisioned for him. He had been born free, with opportunities ahead of him that others' actions deprived me of. But now, all that was gone, stripped away instantly by a foolish, reckless act.

I couldn't look at Thomas the same way anymore. His choices had led them down this path, and while I knew Johnny had gone along willingly, I couldn't shake the bitterness towards Thomas. He was older and more experienced—he should have known better. A husband, a father, a man with responsibilities, and one who had achieved his freedom by serving his sentence just a few years back. He should have been the one to steer them away from this stupidity, to consider the consequences. But instead, he had dragged them both into a senseless crime that would forever change all our lives.

Yet, in the end, none of that mattered. Blame didn't change the outcome. They were both guilty in the eyes of the law and now we were the ones left to pay for it.

I was worried about how Betsy would handle Thomas's conviction and subsequent exile. When he was first arrested, her reaction was one of pure rage. She stormed into the watch house, her face flushed with anger, to confront him. She made it clear just how furious she was, demanding to know how she and their children would cope without him now that he faced an uncertain future. She could no longer afford the rent on the nearly derelict house and would soon be evicted.

However, there was a significant shift in Betsy's attitude when the verdict was finally delivered, declaring Thomas guilty and sentencing him to effective exile on Norfolk Island. The fire in her eyes faded, giving way to a contemplative silence.

We sat one afternoon, a pot of tea on the table between us. "How are you holding up, Betsy?" I asked softly. Her response was surprisingly grounded. "I'm okay, Ma," she replied, her voice steady yet betraying a deep unresolved emotion. "You know, I haven't been happy for quite a while. Thomas might as well be dead now; you know he's never coming back from Norfolk Island, so I need to look after myself." With a faint but determined smile, she added, "I reckon this might be the opportunity I need to start afresh."

Starting fresh. The thought had quietly grown in my mind for a while, but after Hester's passing, it settled there like a small but persistent flame. By my count, I was nearly fifty—half a century spent mainly living in the shadow of my conviction in Dublin for a crime I didn't commit. Half a life shaped by choices often not my own, by the relentless grind of survival, and by the sacrifices demanded of a mother in a world that never made it easy.

I couldn't stop thinking about Sandy Creek, the girl I'd been before the world turned against me. Back then, I'd envisioned a future where my life was my own, where my days were filled with the kind of quiet contentment that only freedom could bring. But that dream had been buried beneath years of hardship and compromise, left to gather dust while I focused on raising my children, keeping them fed, clothed, and out of trouble.

Now, though, that dream stirred again. My children were largely grown, carving out their own lives, with only the youngest boys still dependent on me. I loved them fiercely, but the house felt emptier now, quieter, and I heard the echo of my own desires in that silence. I wanted a life where I wasn't just surviving, where I wasn't defined by the choices made by others or the mistakes of my past.

The yearning caught me off guard at times, sharp and raw, like the sting of an old wound reopening. I longed to be in a place where no one knew my history, where no one looked at me and saw only the convict woman I used to be. I wanted to wake up each morning feeling the lightness of possibility, to know that my days were mine, not dictated by duty or survival or the ghosts of the past.

It wasn't that I wanted to abandon my children—far from it. But I couldn't shake the feeling that something was still out there waiting for me, something I hadn't yet discovered. A chance, however slight, to live the life I had dreamed of all those years ago. I want to make something of what's left of my time, not as a convict, mother, or widow, but simply as Elizabeth. And for the first time in a long while, I allowed myself to hope it might be possible.

Chapter 45

Launceston, Van Diemen's Land, 1838–1840

Helen and Edward had been busy, it seemed. They came to see me after they had been courting for several months to confess they believed Helen was with child. They were not wrong. And it seemed that Annie and Bridget had decided which of the Hockey brothers they fancied—Annie announced she was pregnant to James.

Several months had passed, and it was becoming increasingly clear that Betsy was taking steps towards moving on with her life. One morning, I caught sight of her belly, and it was undeniable that she was expecting. Given the timing, Thomas couldn't be the father of this baby. When I delicately broached the subject, her usual openness turned into an impenetrable silence.

I understood that her silence was her shield, a way to keep her counsel and protect whatever story lay behind her pregnancy. Realising that pressing her for answers would only deepen the divide, I held my tongue. Rather than seeking answers, I supported her as best I could.

Later in the year, Rose told me she was also pregnant, and Jack was over the moon about the news. However, my joy for them was overshadowed by a growing sense of fear for Rose's wellbeing. She and Jack had taken to drinking heavily, almost nonstop, it seemed. More than once, I had to bring little William home with me when they were too drunk to care for him properly. The thought of them bringing another child into that unstable environment filled me with dread.

Their living situation was equally troubling. The house had become increasingly run-down and filthy, a stark contrast to the tidiness Rose once upheld. It seemed she had relinquished any effort to make their home even remotely comfortable or clean. My visits to their place were always distressing as I witnessed the chaos that drinking had inflicted on their lives. It made me reflect on the years when I would drink heavily, pondering whether others had viewed me the way I sometimes view Rose.

On the eve of the new year, Helen and Edward welcomed little Richard James Cassidy into the world. At just fourteen, Helen still resembled a child herself, but there was a determined, even defiant glow in her eyes. Edward, while obviously proud, appeared burdened by the enormity of their new responsibilities.

Despite their youth and the difficult conditions they faced, Richard's birth gave them both a sense of purpose. Their marriage, set for February, added another layer of complexity to their young lives, but it was a step they were committed to taking.

In early January 1839, Annie and James's baby, a little girl named Matilda, was born. Then, on the 5th of February, Helen and Edward were wed in the newly established Catholic Church on Cameron Street, with the Reverend Cotham officiating. When the priest asked about her age, she confidently replied, "Eighteen," without so much as a blink, revealing the untruth. Despite my initial doubts, I had a good feeling about their relationship— unlike with the older girls. Edward seemed genuinely devoted to Helen.

Shortly after that, on the 1st of April, Annie and James were married, with babe in arms and Reverend Browne presiding at St John's Church. James had recently received his ticket of leave, and I held a quiet hope that the influence of Annie and baby Matilda would provide the stability he needed. April also saw the birth of Betsy's child. She had a healthy boy and named him Theodore. However, she still wouldn't tell me who the father was.

One chilly evening, after dinner, we gathered around the blazing fireplace. The younger children were already in bed, their soft breathing the only sound interrupting the cosy silence. The house felt oddly quiet now, with many of the older children living in their own homes. That night, it was just Betsy, Michael, Bridget, and me. We sat talking about events in the neighbourhood, the warmth of the fire casting a gentle glow on our faces.

I decided to share the thoughts that had been brewing in my mind for months. "I've been considering following Mr Fawkner to the new settlement in Melbourne. There will be plenty of opportunities there, and it feels like a chance to leave my past behind. I should never have been here as a convict, and this seems like my way to step beyond that."

Their eyes widened in astonishment, but I could see a flicker of intrigue and possibility in their gazes. The idea of a fresh start, a new adventure, was taking root in their imaginations just as it had in mine.

Bridget spoke up first, her voice brimming with excitement and uncertainty. "I'd love to go to Melbourne with you, but Samuel and I want to get married, and he isn't free yet. We'll have to wait until he receives his freedom certificate, then we can follow you." And then she dropped her little bombshell. "Actually, getting married is a bit more urgent than it may have sounded when I mentioned that. I think I'm having a baby."

I nearly dropped my cup of tea. I looked intently at Bridget. Girls seemed to grow up quickly in the colony, or perhaps it was the inherent danger of being a lone female. Whatever the reason, here she was, pregnant.

Michael's response was much more direct. With a hint of eagerness, he said, "I've got nothing tying me down here, except for Pa, of course, but I reckon it would be a great adventure."

Betsy's eyes sparkled with newfound determination. "I've been thinking that this is a good idea too, Ma. I believe I made a huge mistake marrying Thomas, and I'm keen to move somewhere and have the chance to start fresh."

Listening to their responses filled me with a sense of relief and excitement. The prospect of starting fresh in Melbourne seemed more achievable and promising. In the days that followed, I had discussions with Rose and Annie about the chance of them joining us.

Both girls were excited to hear about my plans, but, like Bridget, their husbands were still convicts, so they would have to wait until they received their conditional pardon or were freed through servitude. Helen and Edward, however, decided to stay in Launceston. While life there was not easy, they knew how to navigate it. Edward had found a good job as a coachman, and they had a network of friends who could assist them. They might consider coming in the future, but the time wasn't right for them at the moment.

I decided I really should go and talk to John about the move. Our relationship had been quite civil since we stopped living together, and we had seen each other at our children's weddings and when the babies were born.

When I arrived, he was ploughing a field and seemed grateful for the interruption. He wiped his brow with his hat and suggested we sit down for a cup of tea. John introduced me to Ann Hammond, who was busy making a fresh pot. I knew from the children that she had been living with John for a while now.

"John," I began, "I want to move away to Melbourne and live out my life there. Mr Fawkner will give me work, and Betsy deserves a fresh start." He nodded.

"Well, I guess that's fair enough, Lizzie. What about the other children?"

I told him that Annie, Bridget, Helen, and Rose were staying, while Michael, William, and George would accompany Betsy and me to Melbourne. Once Johnny had served his sentence, he could decide what to do.

John listened intently as I laid out the plans for our children. His face, weathered by years of hard work, seemed to soften with understanding.

"Well, Lizzie," he said, gazing at his hands, "I reckon it's for the best for all of you. And Melbourne, it's as good a spot as any. The boys will need to take on a lot more, especially George. But they're tough lads; they can manage."

John said softly, taking my hand, "We were good together in the early days, Lizzie, and you know I did love you in my own way, don't you?"

I looked at him, feeling a swirl of old emotions come back. "Yeah, John, I know. And I loved you, too. It's just that every time I had a baby, it felt like the world was crashing down on me. I was so overwhelmed, like I was drowning."

He nodded slowly, a look of understanding dawning in his eyes. "I never really got what you were going through back then. I should've been there more, helped out more."

I squeezed his hand gently. "We all did the best we could with what we knew. I didn't even know how to explain it myself. It felt like a dark cloud would settle over me, and no matter how hard I tried, I couldn't get out from under it. Every little thing seemed enormous, and I felt hopeless and lost."

John's eyes softened with empathy. "I wish things could have been different, Lizzie. I truly do. But I'm glad we can talk about it now and that you're finding a new path for yourself and Betsy in Melbourne."

A wave of relief washed over me as I realised he had finally grasped a part of my struggle. "Thanks, John. I reckon this move will be good for all of us."

John squeezed my hand gently, his eyes distant with memories. "You know, Lizzie, I often think about your journey from Sandy Creek to Ireland, meeting in gaol, then finding you in Paramatta. It seems like a lifetime ago."

I smiled softly, recalling that time. "It does. I remember the shock I felt when I realised we were in Ireland, and then the dreadful period after the Churches abandoned me, getting arrested and tossed in jail—it was all so overwhelming and terrifying."

He nodded, warmth in his gaze. "I've always admired your courage. You left everything behind and were thrown into the unknown. And despite everything you've faced, you never completely gave in. There were tough times when I worried you might, and I'm sorry to say that I was probably part of the reason for those times."

Listening to his words, I felt we had finally come full circle and could part as friends. "Thank you, John. It feels good to hear that. Those early days shaped us both."

John sighed, glancing at the horizon. "Life has a knack for getting in the way sometimes, but I'm grateful we shared those moments. They were real and mattered, even the tough times."

I nodded, feeling the weight of his words. "Yes, they did matter. We built a life, faced challenges, and grew from them. And now it's time for the next chapter."

"It is indeed," he said. "And I think Ann and I will be getting married. She wants to, and I can't say no. The trouble is, you and I are already married."

"Are we?" I said, raising an eyebrow. "Or were you married before me, making our marriage not entirely legal? More than seven years have passed since you last saw your wife in England, so maybe you're technically a bachelor now." Once upon a time, finding this out had devastated me; now, it was water under the bridge.

He chuckled, relief evident in his voice. "You're a clever one, Lizzie. Would you be upset?"

"No," I said, shaking my head. "You do whatever makes you happy, and I'll do the same."

So, our plans moved forward. Betsy booked tickets for herself and the three children on *Hamilton* for late June. She was set to go first to Melbourne to find us a house and look for work. I wanted to stay until Rose's new baby arrived, Bridget and Sam got married, and their child was born, which happened early in the following year.

Times were exceptionally tough in Van Diemen's Land during this period. The halt of transportation of convicts from England to Sydney meant that all convicts were now sent to this colony, resulting in a significant influx of both convicts and freed individuals. The sheer number of new arrivals quickly created an oversupply of labour. This surplus made it extremely difficult for everyone, not just newly freed convicts, to find work.

Many freed convicts were struggling, competing for resources with new settlers and other emancipists. Things were tough for most working people because of the lack of jobs and the lower wages available. We had enough food to get by from our farms and the money brought in by the older children, and occasionally, one of the Hockey boys would lend a hand by butchering a sheep or a cow. We stored as much meat as we could and swapped the rest with others for essentials like flour and sugar. But it was hard going, particularly for the younger couples. I suppose, in a way, there was an upside to still being a convict—supplies were still provided.

In July, young John Wilcox made his way into the world with as lusty a pair of lungs as I have heard for many years. As I cradled the tiny wriggling bundle, I couldn't help but feel a surge of hope. Perhaps this new baby would bring much-needed stability to Rose and Jack's somewhat turbulent life. But deep down, I knew it was a faint hope. Their behaviour was entirely set, and habits were hard to break.

In January 1840, my eighth grandchild arrived. Bridget had a baby girl, Isabella. She was a bonny, dark-haired little one, and when she looked at me right after her birth, her eyes seemed to recognise exactly who I was. It was a bit uncanny to see such awareness in a newborn.

Bridget and Samuel married a month later, officially starting their new family together. It brought a sense of joy and renewal amidst the struggles of life in the colony.

And then, the time had come for me to leave Launceston. Packing up our worldly possessions didn't take long, and within two weeks, we had bought our tickets to Port Phillip and made our way to the docks. I stood on the pier, looking back at the town and reflecting on when we first set foot on these shores and how much had happened in those twenty years. It was the longest I had ever lived in one place, longer than in my childhood home.

In Van Diemen's Land, John and I had faced and survived great challenges. We had added five children to the four we already had, and now we had eight grandchildren. The memories of our struggles and triumphs here filled my heart with a bittersweet sense of closure. Launceston had been our home, a place of change and growth, of loss and love.

I reflected on my youth, on my mother and father, and the brothers and sisters with whom I had grown up. I could still picture my mother's face, even after all these years, and I wondered what she would have thought about the events that had unfolded in my life. I could imagine my father shaking his head in bemusement! I thought about the misadventure that took me to Ireland, to gaol, and then to this new world I had come to cherish. I remembered the man with whom I had shared so many years through both the joyful moments and the dark times. I contemplated how many oceans I had stood on the brink of and then crossed—surely more than most. I wondered if my grandchildren would remember me and whether my great-great-grandchildren would ever know or think about my journey through life.

My family was there to wave us off: Rose and Jack with William and baby John, Annie and James with Matilda, Helen and Edward with Richard, and Bridget and Sam with Isabella. As I looked at them, my heart swelled with pride, and I knew I would miss them dearly until I saw them all again. Rose stepped forward.

"I know you gave this to me, ma, but I think you should take it with you. It's travelled all over the world, and I reckon it needs to go with you now." She handed me the silver locket, wrapped in a delicate piece of lace. I smiled and slipped it around my neck, fastening the catch carefully. Yes, it felt right.

Hugs and kisses all around, and then it was time.

As I turned to face the ship set to take me to my new life, I felt a mix of sadness and excitement. At my age, I realised time was running out, but I was determined to embrace my future and everything it had to offer. And at least the boat ride was short this time!

Epilogue and genealogical notes

Elizabeth Welborn (Cody, Church, Barefoot): who was she?

Family history researchers have known for the last thirty years or so that our ancestors transported to Australia were convicts—Elizabeth Church and John Barefoot (or Bedford). All we knew of them was that they had been transported from Ireland—we didn't know what Elizabeth had been convicted of, and on their muster documents in Australia it just said that they were "from Ireland". We searched for years in the Irish record to find any trace of them, but nothing was found until the Catholic records were released to Ancestry and only one Elizabeth Church born at about the right time was found. However, none of us have ever had any matches to anyone with this name, or from this area of Ireland. Neither Church nor Barefoot are Irish names.

Then DNA testing became available through Ancestry, and descendants of John and Elizabeth started testing. There were no DNA matches to anyone in Ireland. Instead, Karen King-Cain and I started noticing that all of these tests were coming back with common matches in America. The more data that we gathered, the clearer the matches became, and we narrowed the potential parents down to Sarah York and Jacob Archdeacon Cody.

Problem was, they were not married, in fact Sarah was married to John Welborn, and already had five children with him. Undaunted, we continued looking at matches. There were no matches, among all those we had tested, to John Welborn's family—his parents or his siblings. Nothing. But we had many, many matches to Sarah's parents, Semore York and Sylvania Aldridge, and to many of their children. We also had multiple matches to Jacob Cody's parents, James Archdeacon Cody and Sarah Womack, and, critically, to many of Jacob's children.

The evidence from DNA is overwhelming and incontrovertible, although many cannot accept it. The more of Elizabeth's descendants do DNA testing, the stronger the evidence is. Every single one of them carries DNA from the York and Cody families. There are no common matches to anyone in Ireland, for either Elizabeth or John.

Insofar as what we know for certain about Elizabeth—we know she was transported to Sydney from Ireland on *Providence*. We know she married John in 1811 and that the marriage was officiated by Samuel Marsden. We know she sailed to Van Diemen's Land with John, Rosetta, Elizabeth, John, and Michael. We know of her charges for drunk and disorderly, the last being in 1833. After that, nothing. No death records, no shipping records, just a blank.

John Barefoot

Nothing is known of John before his appearance in court on 10 December 1806. Even DNA has not shown any strong evidence for his antecedents, although he was most likely English.

John's first land acquisition in Launceston is on a site that is now in the Brisbane Street Mall. The land grant he received is now a shotgun firing range for the Tasmanian Gun Club, at 200 Nile Road, Evandale.

Many thanks to the Tasmanian Family History Society (Launceston Branch) for their assistance in finding information about John Barefoot in particular.

In May 1840, John married Ann Hammond, a forty-eight-year-old widow with four children, in the Catholic Church, by Banns. He states he is a farmer but doesn't mention that he is still married. However, this marriage did not last long.

In the Launceston newspapers for 24 May, 3 June, 10 June and 16 July[1] there were variations on this notice:

---

1   http://nla.gov.au/nla.news-article84752474

NOTICE.

I Hereby give Notice that I will not be answerable for any debt or debts contracted by Hannah Barefoot, otherwise Hannah Hammond, she having absconded from her home without any provocation.

All persons are therefore cautioned not to harbour the said Hannah Barefoot, otherwise they will be dealt with according to law.

his
JOHN x BAREFOOT,
mark.

John seems to have become a bit of a wheeler and dealer in land around Launceston, and then died there 21 July 1846.

Outline Descendant Report for Elizabeth Welborn

..... 1 Elizabeth Welborn b: 22 Apr 1786 in Randolph County, North Carolina, United States
..... +John Barfoot b: Abt. 1774 in England ?, d: 31 Jul 1846 in Launceston, Van Diemen's Land, m: 17 Aug 1811 in Parramatta, New South Wales, m: 21 May 1840 in Launceston, Van Diemen's Land
.... 2 Rosetta Barefoot (Rosie) b: 08 Apr 1813 in Parramatta, New South Wales, d: 06 Dec 1846 in Longford, Van Diemen's Land, Australia
.... +John (aka Yorkshire Jack) Wilcox b: 1804 in Yorkshire, England, d: 1879 in Hobart, Tasmania, Australia.
.... +William Graves b: 1791, d: 29 Mar 1876 in Depot, Tasmania, Australia, m: 24 Sep 1827 in Launceston, Van Diemen's Land
.... 2 Elizabeth Barefoot b: 1814 in Paramatta, New South Wales, d: 11 Oct 1886 in Geelong, Victoria
.... +Thomas Bird b: 1799 in Birmingham, Warwickshire, England, d: unkn in Norfolk Island, m: 31 Oct 1831 in Launceston, Van Diemen's Land
.... +William Black Smith b: 14 Mar 1814 in Edinburgh, City of Edinburgh, Scotland, d: 19 Feb 1881, m: 25 Feb 1843 in St James, Melbourne
.... 2 John Barefoot b: 1815 in Paramatta, New South Wales, d: 29 Jan 1905 in Bendigo Benevolent Asylum, Victoria
.... +Ellen Mc Anally b: 1825 in County Armagh, Northern Ireland, d: 1860 in Melbourne, Victoria, Australia, m: 29 May 1848 in St. Josephs, Launceston, Van Diemen's Land
.... +Priscilla Wilde
.... 2 Michael Barefoot b: 1819 in Paramatta, New South Wales, d: 13 Jan 1853 in Geelong, Victoria
.... +Hannah Cronin b: 1818 in County Cork, Ireland, d: 24 Oct 1874 in Geelong, Victoria; Age: 56
.... 2 Ann Barefoot b: 1821 in Pt.Dalrymple, Van Diemen's Land, d: 09 Oct 1896 in Kyneton, Victoria
.... +James Hockey b: 20 May 1806 in Evercreech, Somerset, England, d: 29 Nov 1870 in Elphinstone, Vic, Aus, m: 1826 in Ashwick, Somerset, Eng, m: 01 Apr 1839 in Launceston, Van Diemen's Land
.... 2 Ellen (Helen) Barefoot b: 18 Jun 1824 in Port Dalrymple, Van Diemen's Land, d: 30 Oct 1897 in Launceston, Tasmania
.... +Edward Cassidy b: Abt. 1814 in New South Wales, d: 20 Jun 1891 in Launceston, Tasmania, m: 05 Feb 1839 in Launceston, Van Diemen's Land
.... 2 Bridget Barefoot b: 1825 in Port Dalrymple, Van Diemen's Land, d: 09 Dec 1880 in Mooroopna, Victoria
.... +James Gladwin Clover b: 23 Aug 1818 in Writtle, England, United Kingdom, d: 20 Jun 1881 in Mooroopna, Victoria, Australia, m: 1850 in Kilmore Presbytian Church, Victoria
.... +Samuel Hockey b: 23 Jan 1811 in Shepton Mallet, Somerset, England, d: 02 Mar 1886 in Geelong, Victoria; Age: 75, m: Jan 1840, m: 1871 in Victoria
.... 2 William Barefoot b: 1826 in Lodden Vale, Van Diemen's Land, d: 22 Sep 1856 in Melbourne, Victoria
.... +Mary Ann Steele b: 1839, d: 06 May 1911, m: 1857 in Victoria
.... 2 George Barefoot b: 1829 in Launceston, Van Diemen's Land, d: 02 Dec 1897 in Tasmania
.... +Louisa Soden b: 14 Apr 1850 in Launceston, Tasmania, Australia, d: 04 Dec 1914 in Emu Bay, Tasmania, Australia, m: 28 Mar 1866 in Torquay, Tasmania

Note: All descendant reports have been generated from the Ancestry tree of the author.

Rose (Rosetta, Rosilla) Barefoot

Rosetta Barefoot born 8 April 1813 Paramatta, New South Wales. Baptised 8 April 1813 at St John's Church in Paramatta by Reverend Samuel Marsden.

Rose married William Graves on 24 September 1827 at Launceston, then lived with John ('Yorkshire Jack') Wilcox. No marriage to John Wilcox has been found.

William Graves was tried at the Old Bailey, found guilty of stealing, on the 22 May 1816, two shirts (value 5s.), two pairs of shoes (value 4s.), the property of James Goldsmith; two trunks (value 15s.), three gowns (value 2 pounds), two petticoats (value 10s.), two shifts (value 15s.), four aprons (value 8s.), one pair of shoes (value 5s.), three yards of ribbon (value 2s.), two bonnets (value 1 pound. 8s.), three one-pound bank notes, the property of Sarah Herbert. Transported for seven years.

John Wilcox was tried at the Old Bailey on 17 February 1831, found guilty of selling three counterfeit half-crowns. Found guilty and transported for seven years on *William Glen Anderson* in 1831.

"Yorkshire Jack" was indeed the shepherd whose hut it was that the cannibal escapee Thomas Jeffries broke into and demanded that he provided him with sheep.

Sadly, Rose died at the age of just thirty-three in Longford, Tasmania. She left behind four children. William is an invention—there is no evidence for a child born to her and William Graves, but they were together for many years before Yorkshire Jack Wilcox seemed to come on the scene. The newspaper article mentions four children, so I added in one and a stillbirth as it would be unlikely for her to not fall pregnant during those years.

This is the newspaper article[2] about her death:

CORONER'S INQUEST.—An inquest was held on Tuesday last at the house of Mr. William Saltmarsh the Longford Hotel, before Charles Arthur, Esquire, Coroner, on view of the body of Rosetta Graves who had been found dead in bed, about four o'clock on the morning of that day. It appeared that the woman, who had been living with a well-known character named Yorkshire Jack, had been so constantly in the habit of getting drunk that a few days previous to her death Jack beat her with a rope, and she left his house, and was staying with a man named John Martin. They had slept together, and during the night, she had said she was dying for a *drain*, she did not then, however, have any liquor, but was not quite sober from the effects of what she had drunk on the previous day; and when Martin awoke he found her quite dead. Dr. Paton, who had made a *post mortem* examination of the body, stated that there were no external marks of violence, and that the cause of death was apoplexy. The Jury returned a verdict accordingly.

The effects produced upon this woman by continual hard drinking, have been to keep herself and her four children in the most miserable, dirty, and ragged condition, in a house as dirty as herself, and which might have been made a comfortable house had she been a sober woman. The man she lived with always supplied her with sufficient of every thing necessary for herself and children; but, for drink she disposed of every thing that she could turn into money.

---

2   *The Cornwall Chronicle* (12 December 1846), p. 660. (http://nla.gov.au/nla.news-article65942716)

Descendant Report for Rosetta Barefoot (Rosie)

..... 1   Rosetta Barefoot (Rosie) b: 08 Apr 1813 in Parramatta, New South Wales, d: 06 Dec 1846 in Longford, Van Diemen's Land, Australia

.....   +John (aka Yorkshire Jack) Wilcox b: 1804 in Yorkshire, England, d: 1879 in Hobart, Tasmania, Australia.

.... 2   John Wilcox b: 17 Jul 1839 in Longford, Van Diemen's Land, Australia, d: 1912 in Hobart, Tasmania

....   +Sarah Rosier b: 24 Nov 1842 in Ormley, Tasmania, Australia, d: 27 Dec 1917 in Launceston, Launceston City, Tasmania, Australia, m: 07 Feb 1859 in Longford, Van Diemen's Land, Australia, m: Abt. 1865 in Port Sorell, Tasmania, Australia

.... 3   John Wilcox b: 1869, d: 14 Aug 1957 in Launceston, Tasmania, Australia

.... 2   Sarah Elizabeth (Mary Ann) Wilcox b: 17 Jul 1841 in Longford, Van Diemen's Land, Australia, d: 25 Oct 1915 in Launceston, Tasmania, Australia

....   +Richard Henry Lowe b: 02 Dec 1811 in Hobart, Tasmania, d: Australia, m: Abt. 1874 in Port Sorell, Tasmania, Australia

.... 3   Gertrude Amanda Lowe b: Dec 1864 in Sheffield, Tasmania, Australia, d: 14 Oct 1953 in Launceston, Tasmania, Australia

....   +James Henry Ryan b: 24 Jun 1855 in Bothwell, Tasmania, Australia, d: 13 Feb 1924 in Launceston, Tasmania, Australia, m: 26 Dec 1884 in St. Patrick's, Latrobe, Tasmania

.... 3   Sarah Ann Lowe b: 1866 in Tasmania, Australia, d: 26 Nov 1910 in Gormiston, Tasmania, Australia

....   +Alfred Gillard b: 1862 in Tasmania, Australia, d: 20 Dec 1936 in Ulverstone, Tasmania, Australia, m: 30 Apr 1884 in Ulverstone, Tasmania, Australia

.... 3   Joseph Barrington Lowe b: 1868 in Barrington, Tasmania, Australia, d: 22 Feb 1873 in Sheffield, Tasmania, Australia

.... 3   Arthur Albert Lowe b: 22 Oct 1872 in Sheffield, Tasmania, Australia, d: NSW

.... 3   Edward Augustus Lowe b: 06 May 1874 in Port Sorell Tasmania Australia, d: 27 Mar 1955 in Warragul, Victoria, Australia

.... 3   Christina Sophia Lowe b: 21 Sep 1877 in Sheffield, Tasmania, Australia, d: 23 May 1940 in Fitzroy, Victoria, Australia

....   +Thomas Henry Holmes b: 21 May 1874 in Tasmania, d: 05 Sep 1947 in Tasmania, Australia, m: 02 May 1895 in Deloraine, Tasmania

.... 3   Eva Grace Lowe b: 12 Apr 1879 in Sheffield, Tasmania, Australia, d: 05 Aug 1953 in Colac, Victoria, Australia

....   +George Percy Hillman b: 26 Jan 1866 in Camperdown, Victoria, Australia, d: 16 Apr 1948 in Colac, Victoria, Australia, m: 03 Aug 1899 in Launceston, Tasmania

....   +James Simmonds b: 28 Sep 1838 in Launceston, Tasmania, Australia, d: 16 Jun 1923 in Wyndham, Southland, Southland, New Zealand, m: 1859 in Longford, Van Diemen's Land, Australia, m: 01 Oct 1864 in New Zealand, m: 06 Jan 1892 in Roxburgh, Otago, New Zealand

.... 3   James Arthur Simmons b: 19 Jul 1859 in Cressy, Tasmania, Australia, d: 16 Jul 1945 in Tasmania, Australia

....   +Emily Wise Houghton Graham b: 03 Apr 1877 in Corindhap, Victoria, Australia, d: 21 Sep 1921 in Geelong, Victoria, Australia., m: 1899 in Victoria, Australia.

....   +Sarah Elizabeth Bott b: 27 Jan 1860 in Port Sorell, Tasmania, Australia, d: Tasmania, Australia, m: 01 Jan 1883 in Sheffield, Tasmania, Australia

.... 3   Edward Simmonds b: 1861 in Longford, Van Diemen's Land, Australia, d: 28 Jun 1862 in Longford, Van Diemen's Land, Australia

.... 3   William Henry Simmons b: 21 Mar 1863 in Tasmania, Australia, d: 04 Sep 1908 in Launceston, Tasmania, Australia

....   +Susannah Liberty b: 05 Apr 1864 in New Norfolk, Tasmania, Australia, d: 09 Apr 1954 in Carrick, Tasmania, Australia, m: 05 Jun 1886 in Northview, residence of C.Krushka, Ringarooma, Tasmania, Australia

....   +John Francis b: Abt. 1828 in County Armagh, Ireland, d: 1912 in Deloraine, Tasmania, m: Abt. 1897, m: 24 Dec 1860 in St Marys Church, Deloraine, Tasmania, Australia

.... 2   Hannah Wilcox b: 20 Nov 1845 in Longford, Van Diemen's Land, Australia

....   +George Smith m: 1886 in Victoria

.... 3   Olive May Smith b: 14 Aug 1894, d: Abt. 1969 in Mount Albert, Victoria

....   +Charles Henry Crouch m: 1924 in Victoria, Australia

.....   +William Graves b: 1791, d: 29 Mar 1876 in Depot, Tasmania, Australia, m: 24 Sep 1827 in Launceston, Van Diemen's Land

Elizabeth (Betsy) Barefoot

Elizabeth Barefoot was born around 1814 in Paramatta, New South Wales.

She married Thomas Bird on 31 October 1831 in Launceston. She then married William Black Smith on 25 Feb 1843 in St James Anglican Church, Melbourne.

Thomas Bird was tried in 1821 at the Warwick Assizes for disposing of forged bank notes. He was found guilty and transported for seven years. He was then transported on *Lord Hungerford* to Van Diemen's Land. When he obtained his freedom, he committed a further offence of stealing horses, as described. Again, he was found guilty and sentenced to life. He was sent to Norfolk Island, and there is some evidence that he was executed there[3].

Elizabeth then married William Smith with the service carried out by the Reverend Adam Compton Thomson, in the first church built in Melbourne. This was a "simple wooden structure used for both Anglican and Presbyterian services and as a school",[4] which stood on the corner of William and Little Collins streets. There is still a small street called St James Lane, which ran adjacent to the church's school on the next block to the north.[5] The foundation stone for St James was laid on 9 November 1839 by Charles La Trobe, the superintendent of the Port Phillip District (now the state of Victoria), in what was then still part of New South Wales.

Elizabeth had met Reverend Mr Thomson before …

---

3   Archer (2009), *The Scott Letters*, p. 278
4   Byrne (July 2008), 'Church lane' entry
5   See https://en.wikipedia.org/wiki/St_James_Old_Cathedral

From the Port Phillip Herald, 2 April 1841[6]:

For the last few days a female representing herself as the wife of a man called Boucher, now confined in the Gaol for sly grog selling, has been travelling through the town and extorting sums of money from our generous fellow townsmen, on the plea of extreme destitution. She yesterday morning called on the Rev Mr Thomson, who immediately had her taken before the Police Magistrate, who severely reprimanded her, and cautioned her how she followed such courses in future. To add to the grossness of her offence, it was proved that the wretched woman was Boucher's concubine, and not his wife. (PPH 2 April 1841)

And Elizabeth's outraged response[7], published in the Port Philip Patriot and Melbourne Advertiser on 8 April 1841:

THE Port Phillip Herald having falsely asserted that I was passing myself off as the wife of a man named Boucher, and that I waited upon the Rev. Mr. Thomson, " who immediately had her taken before the Police Magistrate, who severely reprimanded her, and cautioned her how she followed such courses in future." This so far is false as to the taking before any Magistrate, I positively declare that I was not taken before any Magistrate—therefore the Herald has told a direct falsehood, purposely to injure me, who am already labouring under a paralytic affection, and one whom the editor thinks is not likely to obtain redress—is this the conduct of a gentleman or of a blackguard, this I leave to the public to judge.

her
ELIZABETH ✕ BIRD.
mark

---

6   See https://residentjudge.com/2016/04/10/this-week-in-port-phillip-1841-april-1-7-1841/

7   See http://nla.gov.au/nla.news-article226509015

Descendant Report for Elizabeth Barefoot

..... 1   Elizabeth Barefoot b: 1814 in Paramatta, New South Wales, d: 11 Oct 1886 in Geelong,
     Victoria

.....   +Thomas Bird b: 1799 in Birmingham, Warwickshire, England, d: unkn in Norfolk Island, m:
     31 Oct 1831 in Launceston, Van Diemen's Land

.... 2   Zipporah Susan Bird b: 29 Aug 1832 in Launceston, Van Diemen's Land, d: 19 Jun
     1882 in Geelong, Victoria

....   +Frederick Charles Niblett b: 18 Sep 1816 in Dorking, Surrey, England, d: 17 Jan 1883 in
     Geelong Hospital, Victoria, Australia, m: 1849 in St James's Old Cathedral, Melbourne,
     Victoria

.... 3   Jane Elizabeth Niblett b: 08 Oct 1850 in Melbourne, Victoria, Australia, d: 1851 in
     Melbourne, Victoria, Australia

.... 3   Frederick Charles Niblett b: 1852 in Deniliquin, New South Wales, Australia, d: 15
     Jun 1943 in Kew, Victoria

....   +Mary Ann White b: 1854 in Bellarine, Victoria, Australia, d: 20 May 1930 in Fitzroy,
     Victoria, Australia, m: 09 Sep 1876 in St Mary's, Geelong, Victoria, Austra

.... 3   Alfred Edward Niblett b: 04 May 1854 in Germantown, Victoria, Australia

....   +Jane Radley b: 1858, m: 1880 in Victoria

.... 3   Thomas Bird Niblett b: 1858 in Geelong, Victoria, Australia, d: 1937 in Ballarat,
     Victoria, Australia

.... 3   Harriet Niblett b: 1860 in Germantown, Victoria, Australia, d: 1947 in Malvern,
     Victoria, Australia

.... 3   James Niblett b: 31 Aug 1863 in Germantown, Victoria, Australia, d: 30 Dec 1947 in
     Geelong, Victoria, Australia

....   +Margaret Beaton b: 1866 in Victoria, Australia, d: 18 Feb 1932 in Geelong, Victoria,
     Australia, m: 1890

.... 3   Henry Niblett b: 1866 in Germantown, Victoria, Australia, d: 1946 in Footscray,
     Victoria, Australia

....   +Eveline Hopkins b: 23 Dec 1871 in Queanbeyan, New South Wales, d: 30 Apr 1948
     in Victoria, Australia, m: 14 Sep 1904 in Hurstville, New South Wales, Australia

.... 3   Jane Elizabeth Niblett b: 1869 in Geelong, Victoria, Australia, d: 1870 in Geelong,
     Victoria, Australia

.... 3   John Niblett b: 1871 in Geelong, Victoria, Australia, d: 1947 in Cheltenham, Victoria,
     Australia

.... 3   Fanny Niblett b: 1874 in Geelong, Victoria, Australia, d: 19 Jun 1961 in Hawera,
     Taranaki, New Zealand

....   +Charles Dickens Martin m: Victoria, Australia

.... 2   Thomas Bird b: 17 Oct 1834 in Launceston, Van Diemen's Land, d: 09 Oct 1911 in
     Geelong Western Cemetery, Geelong, Victoria

....   +Mary Ann Martin b: 1845 in Rickinghall, Suffolk, England, d: 1915 in Geelong, Victoria,
     Australia, m: 06 Sep 1867 in Mount Duneed, Victoria,

.... 3   Elizabeth Bird b: 1866 in Paraparap, Mount Duneed, Victoria, Australia, d: 10 Jul
     1898 in Bairnsdale, Victoria, Australia

....   +John Taylor b: 1854 in Wandiligong, Victoria, Australia, d: 03 Jul 1921 in Geelong,
     Victoria, Australia, m: 1879 in Victoria

.... 3   Thomas William Bird b: 1878, d: 1896

.... 3   Walter Henry Bird b: 1882, d: 1882

.... 2   Ann Elizabeth Bird b: 1837, d: 15 Feb 1837 in Hobart

.....   +William Black Smith b: 14 Mar 1814 in Edinburgh, City of Edinburgh, Scotland, d: 19 Feb
     1881, m: 25 Feb 1843 in St James, Melbourne

.... 2   Theodore Bird (or John?) b: 1839 in Launceston, d: 27 Nov 1914 in Ballarat, Victoria,
     Australia

....   +Bridget Wilkinson b: 1841 in Liverpool, England, d: 1889 in Sandhurst, Victoria,
     Australia, m: 17 Jan 1859 in Geelong, Victoria, Australia

.... 3   Elizabeth Bird b: 1860 in Geelong, Victoria, Australia, d: Geelong, Victoria, Australia

....   +Henry Mead b: 05 May 1857 in Ballarat, Victoria, Australia, d: 1932 in Rushworth,
     Victoria, Australia, m: 27 Dec 1881 in Geelong, Victoria, Australia

.... 3   Bridget Bird b: 1866 in Mt Duneed, Victoria, Australia

.... 3   Emma Ellen Bird b: 1867 in Mount Duneed, Victoria, Australia, d: 22 Dec 1941 in
     Cheltenham, Victoria, Australia

....   +John Robertson b: 1866 in Durham Lead, Victoria, Australia, d: 20 Sep 1932 in
     Gardenvale, Victoria, Australia, m: 1891 in Geelong, Victoria, Australia

.... 3   Theodore Bird b: 1869 in Mt Duneed, Victoria, Australia

.... 3   Kate Bird b: 1874 in Mt Duneed, Victoria, Australia

.... 3   Catherine Bird b: 1877, d: 1917 in Meredith, Victoria, Australia

.... 3   William Bird b: 1880 in Charlton, Victoria, Australia

.... 3   Robert Henry Bird b: 1883 in Victoria, Australia, d: 1969 in Long Gully, Victoria,
     Australia

.... 3   Ada Bird b: 1885 in Victoria, Australia

John Barefoot Junior (Johnny)

John Barefoot (Johnny) was probably born around 1815 in Paramatta,
New South Wales, and died on 29 January 1905 at the Bendigo Asylum,
Victoria.

John was charged and convicted on the horse stealing charge. He was sentenced to life imprisonment. This article was published in the Hobart Town Courier on 8 December 1837[8]:

> **SUPREME COURT,**
> *Criminal Side.*
> Before His Honor Chief Justice Pedder.
> On Tuesday morning at 10 o'clock, the Criminal Sessions commenced, and on entering the Court House, we observed that great improvements had been made, both for the accommodation of the legal gentlemen and the Public. However we cannot exactly applaud the taste displayed, which seems rather heavy and ponderous.
> The calendar is heavier these Sessions than for many years past. In the Gaol are about 60 prisoners for trial, besides those out on bail, and some bills have been ignored.
> *Tuesday December 5.*
> *John Barefoot* and *William Lancaster* stood charged with stealing a mare, guilty, but not sentenced.
> This was a case of most atrocious character. The mare was taken away from the foal, which starved to death in consequence, and the mare was spoiled by being obliged to retain her milk.

While this mentions William Lancaster, it doesn't mention Thomas Bird, who seems to have been the ringleader. John may have been initially sent to Port Arthur but was assigned to Mr Jillett at Back River.

Young John's record does not read well ...

18 April 1838: Positively refusing to work in the mines this morning (This is the Coal Point Mine)[9] 25 stripes

3 July 1840: Gov house / Disorderly conduct in Gov house & being drunk, (?-id --) on the (?sds) 3 mos /Confined Glenorchy road (---) then New Norfolk for a fortnight vide Lt Gov Sec. 4 July 1840.

28 Dec 1841: Jillet / Misconduct reprimanded 8 April 1843. Neglect of duty 10 days hard labour.

8 April 1843: Jillett / Neglect of Duty 10 days hard labor.

 * 5 August 1843: Jillet / Drunk neglect of duty still beating his Master's Horse 3 Calendar Months. hard labor & referred Lt Gov

---

8   There is a much more detailed account of the trial available at http://nla.gov.au/nla.news-article8650440

9   More information about the coal mines can be found at https://coalmines.org.au/history/

directed not to be again assigned from this date / Ticket of Leave /
Long Hobart & not to be again assigned in the New Norfolk District
vide lt Gov Rec'd 11 Aug 1843.

1 March 1844: 2 Class

20 March 1844: Shannon / Drunk 14 days labor Certificate

6 September 1844: 3 Class. T of L.

8 January 1846: Recommended for a Conditional Pardon 31 Aug 1847.
Conditional Pardon

31 August 1847: Conditional Pardon granted to John BAREFOOT.

31 August 1847: Ticket of Leave 6.1.46 Received a conditional pardon
31/8/47.[10]

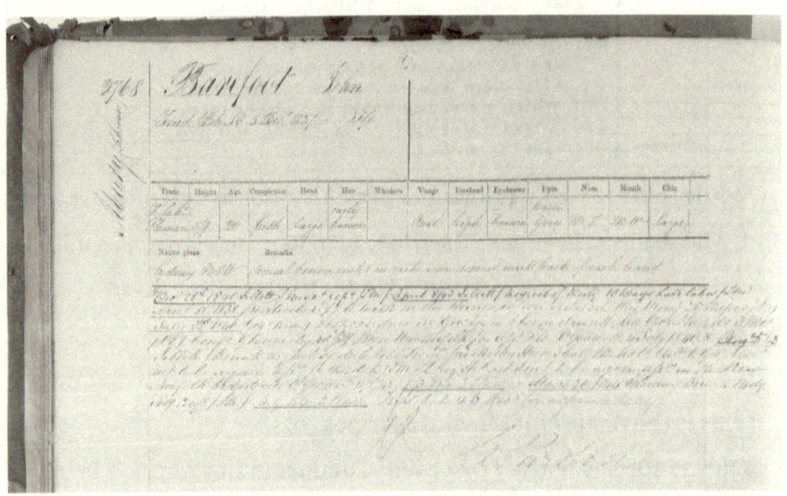

Johnny married Ellen McAnally on 29 May 1848 at St Josephs, Launceston.
He married Priscilla Wilde later on, date unknown.

Ellen McAnally was transported on *Mexborough* for seven years;
however, I have not been able to locate her on the shipping lists under
this name or any variant. She died in 1860 in Melbourne.

John came to Melbourne on *Shamrock* in April 1849.

---

10   John Barefoot's record: Tasmanian Archives, CON35-1-1 Image 52

Descendant Report for John (Johnny) Barefoot

..... 1   John Barefoot b: 1815 in Paramatta, New South Wales, d: 29 Jan 1905 in Bendigo Benevolent Asylum, Victoria

.....   +Ellen Mc Anally b: 1825 in County Armagh, Northern Ireland, d: 1860 in Melbourne, Victoria, Australia, m: 29 May 1848 in St. Josephs, Launceston, Van Diemen's Land

.... 2   Ellen Barefoot b: 11 Mar 1848 in Tasmania, Australia, d: 23 Jun 1913 in Launceston, Tasmania, Australia

....   +George Roe m: 1869 in Port Sorell, Tasmania, Australia

.... 3   Annie Perimer Roe b: 09 Jan 1870 in Port Sorell, Tasmania, Australia

.... 2   Mary Jane Barefoot (Jenkins) b: 29 Oct 1850 in Barrabool Hills, Victoria, Australia, d: 05 Oct 1884 in (Murdered) Castlemaine, Talbot, Victoria, Australia

....   +Duncan Lennie b: 1831 in Glasgow, Lanarkshire, Scotland, d: 22 Sep 1889 in Castlemaine, Victoria, Australia

.... 3   Mary Jane Lennie b: 17 Jan 1878 in Castlemaine, Victoria, Australia, d: 08 Oct 1935 in Royal Park, Victoria, Australia

.... 3   Ellen Victoria Lennie b: 1882 in Castlemaine, Victoria, Australia, d: 1949 in Bendigo, Victoria, Australia

.... 2   John Barefoot b: 25 Dec 1853 in Geelong, Victoria, Australia., d: 15 Oct 1920 in Carlton, Victoria, Australia.

....   +Bertha Ann Augusta Hiene b: 1858, d: 1952, m: 1874 in Victoria

....   +Isabella Ross b: 17 Jun 1844 in Yea, Victoria, Australia, d: 10 Oct 1939 in Carlton, Victoria, Australia., m: 1865 in Victoria, m: 23 Jan 1878 in White Hill, Victoria, Australia

.... 3   George Henry Barfoot b: 18 Dec 1879 in Stuart Mill, Victoria, Australia, d: 18 Jan 1956 in Kew, Victoria, Australia

....   +Ann Christina Fraser b: 09 Dec 1884 in Richmond, Victoria, Australia, d: 28 May 1951 in Preston, Victoria, Australia, m: 20 Dec 1905 in Methodist Church, Great Southern, Victoria, Australia

.....   +Priscilla Wilde

.... 2   Elizabeth Barefoot b: 06 Nov 1861 in Kyneton, Victoria, Australia, d: 1948 in Stawell, Victoria, Australia.

....   +George Gorman b: 1855 in Maryborough, Victoria, Australia, d: 1926 in Stawell, Victoria, Australia, m: 16 Oct 1882 in Murtoa, Victoria, Australia

.... 3   George Henry Gorman b: 19 Jul 1883 in Stawell, Victoria, Australia., d: 10 Oct 1910 in Stawell, Victoria, Australia.

.... 3   Maude May Gorman b: 20 May 1885 in Stawell, Victoria, Australia., d: 06 Mar 1961 in Flemington, Victoria, Australia.

....   +Amos Edgar Dans b: Abt. 1885 in Driffield, Victoria, m: 09 Dec 1909 in Stawell, Victoria

.... 3   William Arthur Gorman b: 1888 in Stawell, Victoria, Australia, d: 1891 in Stawell, Victoria, Australia

.... 3   Edith Louisa Gorman b: 1890 in Stawell, Victoria, Australia., d: Abt. 1890 in Stawell, Victoria

.... 3   Reuben Gordon Gorman b: 06 May 1891 in Stawell, Victoria, Australia., d: 23 Apr 1972 in Ballarat, Victoria, Australia

....   +Sarah Ann Dunn b: 1888 in Stawell, Victoria, Australia, d: 13 Nov 1976 in Stawell, Victoria, Australie, m: 1912 in Victoria, Victoria, Australie

.... 3   Adeena Elizabeth Gorman b: 1892 in Stawell, Victoria, Australia., d: 1976 in Murtoa, Victoria, Australia

.... 3   William Arthur Gorman b: 19 Feb 1894 in Stawell, Victoria, Australia., d: 11 Aug 1964 in Strathmore, Victoria, Australia

....   +Jessie Elliot b: 1893 in Brighton, Victoria, Australia, d: 1959 in Victoria, Australia

....   +Clara Beatrice Burke b: 1897 in Nirranda, Victoria, Australia, d: 04 Mar 1987 in Victoria, Australia

.... 3   Edith Lavinia Gorman b: 20 Nov 1895 in Stawell, Victoria, Australia., d: 26 Nov 1896 in Stawell, Victoria, Australia.

.... 3   Edwin Gorman b: 1897 in Stawell, Victoria, Australia., d: 1897 in Stawell, Victoria, Australia.

.... 3   Edward Harland Gorman b: 31 Dec 1899 in Stawell, Victoria, Australia., d: 13 Jun 1976 in Merlynston, Victoria, Australia

Michael Barefoot

Michael was the last child born in Parramatta, probably in 1819, but no birth registration has been located. He died on 13 January 1853 in Geelong, Victoria.

Michael came to Melbourne in 1840 on board the schooner *Gem*.

No record of a marriage has been found, however his relationship with Hannah Cronan/Cronin may have begun in 1843 when Hannah was one of the witnesses to Elizabeth Barefoot Bird's marriage to William Smith in Melbourne.

Descendant Report for Michael Barefoot

..... 1   Michael Barefoot b: 1819 in Paramatta, New South Wales, d: 13 Jan 1853 in Geelong, Victoria

.....   +Hannah Cronin b: 1818 in County Cork, Ireland, d: 24 Oct 1874 in Geelong, Victoria; Age: 56

.... 2   William John Barfoot b: 1844 in Geelong, d: 13 Apr 1894 in Geelong, Victoria, Australia

....   +Elizabeth Payne b: 1846 in Barrabool Hills, Victoria, Australia, d: 16 Apr 1917 in Geelong, Victoria, Australia, m: 1874 in Victoria

.... 3   William Colin Barfoot b: 1875 in Geelong, Victoria, Australia, d: 25 Sep 1877 in Geelong, Victoria, Australia

.... 3   Hannah (Annie) Barfoot b: 1876 in Geelong, Victoria, Australia, d: 08 Apr 1943 in Prahran, Victoria, Australia

.... 3   Frederick "Thomas" Barfoot b: 1877 in Geelong, Victoria, Australia, d: 21 Jul 1955 in Geelong, Victoria, Australia

....   +Tamzin Jewell "Tot" Hocking b: 23 Nov 1884 in Murgheboluc, Victoria, Australia, d: 09 Dec 1955 in Geelong, Victoria, Australia, m: 1911 in Geelong, Victoria, Australia

.... 3   James Henry Barfoot b: 1879 in Geelong, Victoria, Australia, d: 19 Feb 1942 in Geelong, Victoria, Australia

....   +Agnes McMillan Craig b: 1881 in Lismore, Victoria, Australia, d: 04 Jul 1961 in Geelong, Victoria, Australia., m: 1902

.... 3   William Edwin Barfoot b: 1882 in Geelong, Victoria, Australia, d: 02 Jul 1964 in Drummond, Victoria, Australia

....   +Ida May Nicholson b: 1886 in Hawthorn, Victoria, Australia, d: 1949 in Geelong, Victoria, Australia, m: 1914 in Victoria, Australia

.... 2   Michael Barefoot b: 1847 in Geelong, Greater Geelong City, Victoria, Australia, d: 1863 in Victoria

.... 2   Patrick Barfoot b: 1848 in Geelong, Victoria, Australia, d: 23 Oct 1849 in Geelong, Victoria, Australia

.... 2   Anne Honora Barefoot b: 1849 in Geelong, Victoria, Australia, d: 24 Jan 1854 in Geelong, Victoria, Australia

.... 2   Catherine Mary Barfoot b: 1851 in Geelong, Victoria, Australia, d: 23 Jul 1901 in Geelong, Victoria, Australia

....   +Anthony Berntsen (Bernsten Benson) b: 1844 in Christiana, Norway, d: 10 Oct 1928 in Bentleigh, Victoria, Australia, m: 1869 in Victoria, Australia.

.... 3   Ada Lydia (Sister Mary Winifred) Berntsen b: 28 Jun 1870 in Rokewood, Victoria, Australia, d: 23 May 1926 in Genazzano Convent, Kew, Victoria, Australia

.... 3   Edward James Berntsen b: 1872 in Rokewood, Victoria, Australia, d: 1877 in Melbourne, Victoria, Australia

.... 3   Annie Caroline Berntsen b: 19 Jul 1876 in Ballarat, Victoria, Australia, d: Melbourne, Victoria, Australia

....   +Charles Lawrance Gibson m: Victoria, Australia

.... 3   Eugene Albert Anthony Berntsen b: 1877 in Geelong, Victoria, Australia, d: 10 Jul 1942 in East Melbourne, Victoria, Australia

.... 3   William Aloysius Berntsen b: 1883 in Geelong, Victoria, Australia, d: Mar 1938 in Middlesbrough, Yorkshire North Riding, England

.... 3   Frederick Percival Berntsen b: 1885 in Melbourne, Victoria, Australia., d: 08 Sep 1944 in Randwick, New South Wales, Australia

....   +Ellen Mary O'Brien d: 29 Oct 1954 in Hurstville, New South Wales, Australia

.... 2   James Barefoot b: 1853 in Geelong, Victoria, Australia, d: 1855 in Geelong, Victoria, Australia

Ann Barefoot

Ann was born in Port Dalrymple in 1821, although no birth registration found. She died 9 October 1896 at Kyneton, Victoria.

She was married on 12 December 1838 to James Hockey, who applied to marry her, aged eighteen and "Free". They married on 1 April 1839 at St John's Church, Launceston.

James Hockey was transported on *Sir Charles Forbes* along with brother Samuel. James was tried at Bridgwater Assizes and was found guilty of stealing a gelding worth twenty pounds. He was sentenced to death on 22 August 1829, which was commuted to 14 years transportation. He arrived at Van Diemen's Land on 26 July 1830. While his record states he was single, James was married and had two children.

James married Rachel Bafue in 1820. His children were Louisa Hockey (1827–?) and Elizabeth Hockey (1829–1889).

While Louisa lived out her life in England, Elizabeth came to Australia in 1853 on board *Six Sisters*. She was living with her father, and an ex-convict called William Terry had proposed to her. William Terry murdered a loner called Peter Redyk, who was carrying both some cash and land deeds. Terry then came back to James Hockey and suggested that he Elizabeth get married immediately, which they did (in 1862) but under the name Peter Redyk, which he said was his real name ... At that time Redyk's body could not be found, so Terry was acquitted. However, five years later the body was found, Terry was charged again with the murder, found guilty and sentenced to death. He was hanged in Castlemaine Gaol.[11]

In the meantime, Elizabeth married Thomas Mobley in 1864 in Melbourne.

James' convict record was very spotty. He was assigned to Mr Wedge:

30 September 1831: D Wedge / Drunk & disorderly at Perth. Reprimanded.

---

11   For a full description of this case (with Hockey misspelled as Hockyn), see http://nla.gov.au/nla.news-article33030648

21 February 1833: Wedge / Insolence and indecent language, 25 lashes.

12 April 1837: Ticket of Leave. Out after hours & having firearms in his possession. Admitted having given a (un)satisfactory account of himself.

29 November 1838: TL / Absent from his authorized place of residence. Reprimanded.

12 February 1839: TL / Tippling in a public house on Sunday, 6 hours in the stocks.

29 August 1839: TL / Misconduct. Ordered to leave the district of Campbell Town & recommended to be ordered to the District of Hamilton to break his connection

17 December 1839: TL / Wilful prevarication, 6 months hard labour, to be removed from the District of Oatlands being badly connected there / TL / Town Surveyors Gang Hobart. Not ? then for asst. Vide Lieut Governor's Decision, 20 Dec 1839.

4 August 1841: Conditional Pardon No 3143.

7 December 1847: Certificate of Freedom.

Ann and James came to Victoria on 20 December 1847, and the family had a somewhat chequered life in Victoria[12].

DEPARTURES.
Vessels reported outwards during the week.
December 20.—Schooner *Will Watch*, 63 tons, M'Arthur, master, for Portland Bay ; R. Green, agent. Passengers—James Hockey, wife and 3 children, W. Howard, wife and child, R. Howard, Miss Thomas, John Murray, S.⸱Hockey, wife and child, J. F. Gilman, G. Stanley.

In April 1848, James and Ann were accused by Martha Silk of stealing a silver hunting watch. The text of the article is a bit of a hoot: "... she (Silk) had just gone out of her house for a minute, leaving her husband's silver hunting watch snugly resting on her downy pillow ..."[13] Mrs Hockey

---

12   See http://nla.gov.au/nla.news-article36253667
13   See account of theft at http://nla.gov.au/nla.news-article226355816

had been in their house during their absence. The watch was not found at their home, but was found later in the Silk's home, somehow hanging from the ceiling. All sounds very dodgy but there was no evidence, so they were acquitted.

In August 1850, Ann did a runner[14] ...

THE

Goulburn Herald

AND

COUNTY OF ARGYLE ADVERTISER.

Goulburn Herald and County of Argyle Advertiser (NSW) Saturday 3 August 1850, page 6

Hockey, residing at Mount Macedon, and employed as a splitter in the Mount Macedon Ranges, was astonished the other evening on returning from his work and finding that his wife, the mother of seven children, had absconded with a man named John Callendar, who occupied a hut in the neighbourhood. He soon learnt that the guilty parties had taken the direction of Melbourne, and following them, he arrived in Melbourne on Sunday morning. Immediately entering into communication with the Chief Constable, the retreat of Callendar and his paramour was quickly discovered, and Hockey with the Chief Constable entered the room which they occupied, and demanded the restoration of his wife, which Callendar resisted, and ultimately drove Hockey and the Chief Constable from the premises, overwhelming them with abuse for daring to invade his privacy. It was subsequently ascertained that Callendar's box had been deposited in a different house, to which, therefore, Hockey accompanied by a constable repaired, and prevailing upon the person in whose charge it was left to point it out, the box was broken open, and on being searched was found to contain several articles of wearing apparel belonging to Hockey's wife. Callendar was then apprehended on a charge of felony, and on being brought before the sitting magistrate at the Police Office, on Monday, Hockey stated he had got back his wife, and under these circumstances, Edmund Westby, Esq., did not deem it necessary to entertain the charge of felony that had been made against Callendar. Threatening language having been used by Callendar towards Hockey at the Police Office, in the hearing of the the sitting magistrate; Callendar was directed to find sureties to keep the peace for six months, himself in £20, and two sureties in £15 each, a mandate to which he was wholly unable to conform, and was therefore lodged in gaol, where it is very likely he will remain during the next six months.——It would appear that Governor

In 1858, Ann and James seemed to have separated (again)[15]:

---

14   See http://nla.gov.au/nla.news-article101728080

15   *Kyneton Observer*, 27 April 1858, see http://nla.gov.au/nla.news-article240789357

> **Caution.**
>
> THIS is to Certify that I will not be answerable for any Debts MY WIFE, ANN HOCKEY, may contract after this date.
>
> **JAMES HOCKEY.**
>
> Kyneton, April 26th, 1858.

Ann and James farmed and lived in the Kyneton area, and there were numerous incidents involving James and pigs or cattle running loose, and a number of reports of a horse stealing gang, consisting of James, John Barefoot (Junior), and sons-in-law Richard Cassidy, Joseph Allen, and Henry Allen.[16]

In 1859, Ann Hockey was committed to prison for one month for being drunk and disorderly and using obscene language. "Besides the positive evidence of the policeman, who had picked up the prisoner off the street from near the wheels of a bullock dray, her husband appeared to complain of her conduct, stating that 'she would sell the very clothes off her back for drink'."[17] She had been charged multiple times prior to this for the same offense. She was again charged with drunk and disorderly in February and fined.

In 1860, John was charged with vagrancy. From the Kyneton Observer: James Hockey, of Kyneton, was brought up by Detective Tuckwell charged under the Vagrant act with being the occupier of a house frequented by reputed and convicted thieves and vagabonds ...Witness in company with Constable arrested prisoner in a low brothel in Baynton street, kept by a Mrs Clarke, Witness has known the prisoner for nearly two months, during which time he has been the constant associate of convicted and reputed thieves ...Witness has also seen

---

16   *Kyneton Observer*, 21 June 1860, see http://nla.gov.au/nla.news-article240849126
17   *Kyneton Observer*, 25 January 1859, see http://nla.gov.au/nla.news-article240895569

at prisoner's house a notorious prostitute and reputed thief named Margaret Mahony ... Mrs Hockey was in Mrs Clarke's along with the prisoner when he was arrested.

... Witness believes Hockey's house to be the nursery of crime in the district. Every prisoner leaving Pentridge, witness knows by private information, is directed to call at Hockey's; with every case of burglary, robbery, and horse stealing, he is more or less connected.[18]

James was sentenced to 12 months' imprisonment in Melbourne Gaol (Pentridge), with hard labour.

In 1861, the family were living in Baynton Street, Kyneton, when the house was broken into and Elizabeth allegedly assaulted. The witnesses "were cross-examined, with the view of showing that Hockey's house bore a questionable character, and that complainant's father was in confinement under the Vagrant Act, for keeping a disorderly house"[19]. (See prior paragraph.)

The pièce de résistance has to be the Redyk murder in 1862, and after reading through everything, I am still not absolutely convinced he didn't have anything to do with it!

Ann died in 1896 in Geelong and James in 1870 in Elphinstone.

---

18 *Kyneton Observer*, 22 Dec 1860, p. 3, see http://nla.gov.au/nla.news-article240850810
19 *Kyneton Observer*, 12 June 1861, p. 2, see http://nla.gov.au/nla.news-article240852218

Descendant Report for Ann Barefoot

..... 1   Ann Barefoot b: 1821 in Pt.Dalrymple, Van Diemen's Land, d: 09 Oct 1896 in Kyneton, Victoria

.....   +James Hockey b: 20 May 1806 in Evercreech, Somerset, England, d: 29 Nov 1870 in Elphinstone, Vic, Aus, m: 1826 in Ashwick, Somerset, Eng, m: 01 Apr 1839 in Launceston, Van Diemen's Land

.... 2   Matilda Hockey b: 07 Jan 1839 in Snake Banks, Launceston, d: 20 Jun 1922 in Moorabbin, Victoria, Australia

....   +Henry Allen b: 23 Jan 1828 in Georgetown, Van Diemen's Land, Australia, d: 19 Mar 1911 in Ascot Vale, Victoria, Australia, m: 09 Apr 1857 in Kyneton, Victoria, Australia

.... 3   Joseph Henry Allen b: 24 Jul 1858 in Kyneton, Victoria, Australia, d: 20 Sep 1932 in Beechworth, Victoria, Australia

....   +Mary Younger b: 1860 in Shelbourne, Victoria, Australia, d: 05 Oct 1934 in Footscray, Victoria, Australia

....   +Elizabeth Jane McKenzie b: 28 Sep 1859 in Bacchus Marsh, Victoria, Australia, d: 04 Dec 1934 in Mildura, Victoria, Australia

.... 3   Mary Jane Allen b: 1860 in Blackwood, Victoria, Australia, d: 20 Dec 1907 in Melbourne, Victoria, Australia

....   +Charles Henry Chamings Lamb b: 03 Nov 1853 in Melbourne, Victoria, Australia, d: 08 Jul 1898 in Melbourne, Victoria, Australia, m: 1876 in Victoria, Australia

.... 3   William John Allen b: 1862 in Trentham, Victoria, Australia., d: 25 Aug 1947 in Beechworth, Victoria, Australia

....   +Susan Williams b: Australia, d: New Zealand

....   +Mary Shananhan m: 1905 in Victoria, Australia

.... 3   Ellen (Nellie) Allen b: 1864 in Trentham, Victoria, Australia, d: 10 Nov 1940 in South Melbourne, Victoria, Australia

....   +Samuel Taylor b: 1855 in Melbourne, Victoria, Australia

.... 3   Henry Bernard (Aka Harry) Allen b: 04 Jun 1865 in Trentham, Victoria, Australia., d: 01 Sep 1918 in Parramatta, New South Wales, Australia

....   +Fanny Ethel Veale (Brokenshire) b: 29 May 1878 in Sandhurst, Victoria, Australia, d: 15 May 1955 in Geelong, Victoria, Australia., m: 17 Nov 1900 in Broken Hill, New South Wales, Australia

....   +Henrietta May Davis b: 19 May 1884 in Wilcannia, New South Wales, Australia, d: 14 Jun 1957 in Parramatta, New South Wales, Australia, m: 30 Jun 1906 in Surry Hills, New South Wales, Australia

.... 3   George Allen b: 1867 in Kyneton, Victoria, Australia, d: 1917 in Moree, New South Wales, Australia

.... 3   Edward William Allen b: 1869 in East Trentham, Victoria, Australia, d: 14 Feb 1950 in Richmond, Victoria, Australia

....   +Mary Jane Hearn b: 18 Aug 1870 in Echuca, Victoria, Australia, d: 21 Apr 1956 in Parkville, Victoria, Australia

....   +Edith Mary Poole b: 1868 in Gloucestershire, England, d: 05 Aug 1946 in Richmond, Victoria, Australia, m: 1940 in Victoria, Australia

....   +Sarah Elizabeth Green b: 1863 in Warrnambool, Victoria, Australia, d: 1938 in Richmond South, Victoria, Australia

.... 3   Susannah Allen b: 1871 in Trentham, Victoria, Australia, d: 1876 in Trentham, Victoria, Australia

.... 3   Robert Allen b: 20 Feb 1874 in Trentham, Victoria, Australia, d: 06 Dec 1953 in Rotorua, Auckland, New Zealand

....   +Lillian Isobel Mills b: 18 Apr 1879 in Brunswick, Victoria, Australia., d: 02 Jun 1948 in Rotorua, Bay of Plenty, New Zealand, m: 07 May 1904 in Wellington New Zealand

.... 3   Samuel (Daniel) Allen b: 31 Mar 1876 in East Trentham, Victoria, Australia, d: 21 Oct 1947 in Yarrawonga, Victoria, Australia

.... 3   Matilda Teresa Allen b: 1879 in Trentham, Victoria, Australia, d: Sep 1946 in Melbourne, Victoria, Australia

....   +Alexander Hope Valentine Oliver b: 14 Feb 1870 in Melbourne, Victoria, Australia, d: 08 Aug 1944 in Newmarket, Melbourne, Victoria, Australia, m: 1910 in Victoria, Australia

.... 2   Ellen (Helen) Hockey b: 29 Apr 1841 in Launceston, Tasmania, Australia, d: 29 Oct 1927 in Footscray, Victoria, Australia

....   +Edward Herman Gustave (Gus) Aurish (Aurisch) b: 15 Jun 1834 in Gugelwitz, Kreis Lüben, Liegnitz, Provinz Breslau, Schlesien, Preussen, d: 29 Oct 1915 in Footscray, Victoria, Australia, m: 01 Feb 1874 in Kyneton, Victoria, Australia.

.... 3   Gustave Bernard Aurish b: 1874 in Trentham, Victoria, Australia, d: 1959 in Ballarat, Victoria, Australia

.... 3   Christina (Christine) Aurish b: 1876 in Trentham, Victoria, Australia, d: 11 Jun 1924

```
                in Melbourne, Victoria, Australia
............... 3  Ernest Benjamin Aurish b: 1878 in Trentham, Victoria, Australia, d: 1950 in Chelsea,
                Victoria, Australia
............... 3  Melvina Daisy Ellen Aurish b: 1880 in Trentham, Victoria, Australia, d: 1948 in
                Chelsea, Victoria, Australia
............... 3  Elizabeth Mary Jane Aurish b: 1881 in Trentham, Victoria, Australia, d: 12 Jan 1931
                in Yarraville, Maribyrnong City, Victoria, Australia
...............    +Michael James Moloney d: Abt. 1953, m: Victoria, Australia
............... 3  Laura May Aurish b: 26 Jan 1883 in Trentham, Victoria, Australia, d: 16 Jul 1979 in
                Footscray, Victoria, Australia
............... 3  Thomas Henry Aurish b: 19 Oct 1884 in East Trentham, Victoria, Australia, d: 1890
                in East Trentham, Victoria, Australia
..........       +Joseph Henry Allen b: 03 Feb 1830 in Georgetown, Van Diemans Land, Australia, d: 11
                Apr 1872 in Trentham, Victoria, Australia
............... 3  William James Allen b: 1859 in Clowes Forest, Victoria, Australia, d: 1860 in Clowes
                Forest, Victoria, Australia
............... 3  Jospeh Henry Allen b: 1866 in Trentham, Victoria, Australia, d: 1866 in Clowes
                Forest, Victoria, Australia
............... 3  Louisa Elizabeth Allen b: 20 Feb 1867 in East Trentham, Victoria, Australia, d: 1929
                in Albert Park, Victoria, Australia
...............    +John Brown b: 1866 in Queenstown, Cork, Ireland, d: 26 Mar 1926 in Footscray,
                Victoria, Australia
............... 3  Daniel William Allen b: 29 Mar 1869 in Trentham, Victoria, Australia, d: 18 Oct 1926
                in Footscray, Victoria, Australia
...............    +Elizabeth Mary Ann Morgan b: 01 Aug 1877 in Woodend, Victoria, Australia, d: 28
                Aug 1921 in Kinglake, Victoria, Australia, m: 01 Mar 1895 in Moor Street, Fitzroy,
                Victoria, Australia
...............    +Annie Thompson Burnett b: 1883, d: 1960 in Hopetoun, Victoria, Australia, m: 1924
............... 3  Matilda Jane Allen b: 1870 in Trentham, Victoria, Australia, d: 03 May 1948 in
                Seymour, Victoria, Australia
............... 3  Ann Allen b: 1873 in Trentham, Victoria, Australia, d: 17 Jan 1904 in Footscray,
                Victoria, Australia
............... 3  Gustave Barnard Aurish Allen b: 1874
.......... 2  Eliza Jane Hockey b: 20 Aug 1842 in Launceston, Tasmania, Australia, d: 07 Mar 1882
                in Trentham, Victoria, Australia
..........       +Richard James Cassidy b: 1838 in Tasmania, d: 1909 in Picton, New South Wales,
                Australia, m: 1859, m: 1888 in Victoria
............... 3  Melvina Ellen Cassidy b: 1860 in Kyneton, Victoria, Australia., d: 1861 in Kyneton,
                Victoria, Australia.
............... 3  Walter James Cassidy b: 1864 in Violet Town, Vic, d: 05 Jan 1936 in Collie, Western
                Australia
...............    +Elizabeth Jane Pascoe b: 1870 in Newlyn, Victoria, Australia, d: 14 Jul 1900 in
                Pinjarra, Western Australia, Australia, m: 22 Aug 1888 in Boho East, Victoria,
                Australia
...............    +Alice Amelia Garwood b: Apr 1875 in Kensington, London, England, m: 1902 in
                Perth, Western Australia, Australia
............... 3  Selina Jane Cassidy b: 1867 in Kyneton, Victoria, Australia, d: 1887 in Woodend,
                Victoria, Australia
...............    +Henry Bowyer m: 1886 in Victoria
............... 3  Elizabeth Rose Cassidy b: Aug 1869 in Trentham, Victoria, Australia, d: 23 Dec
                1869 in Trentham, Victoria, Australia
............... 3  Emily Eliza Cassidy b: 1871 in Trentham, Victoria, Australia, d: 09 Sep 1876 in
                Trentham, Victoria, Australia
............... 3  Richard Ernest Cassidy b: 1873 in Trentham, Victoria, Australia, d: 07 Aug 1876 in
                Trentham, Victoria, Australia
............... 3  Lillian Cassidy b: Jul 1874 in Trentham, Victoria, Australia, d: 26 Oct 1874 in
                Trentham, Victoria, Australia
............... 3  Annie Cassidy b: 21 Jul 1876 in Trentham, Victoria, Australia, d: 21 Jul 1876 in
                Trentham, Victoria, Australia
............... 3  George Albert Cassidy b: 1877 in Trentham, Victoria, Australia, d: 01 Sep 1879 in
                Trentham, Victoria, Australia
............... 3  William Cassidy b: Jun 1879 in Trentham, Victoria, Australia, d: 31 Jul 1879 in
                Trentham, Victoria, Australia
............... 3  Francis John (Frank) Cassidy b: 1880 in Trentham, Victoria, Australia, d: 31 Jul
                1941 in Fitzroy, Victoria, Australia.
...............    +Elizabeth Patricia Tickner b: 1894 in Winslow, Victoria, Australia, d: 1961 in
```

Wangaratta, Victoria, Australia, m: 1910 in Victoria, Australia
.... 3   George Cassidy b: 07 Mar 1882 in Trentham, Victoria, Australia, d: 07 Mar 1882 in
              Trentham, Victoria, Australia
.... 2   Annie Hockey b: 1843 in Launceston, Tasmania, Australia, d: 09 Mar 1930 in St Kilda,
          Victoria, Australia
....   +George William Dye Flack b: Jan 1841 in Chesterton, Cambridgeshire, England, d: 05
       Mar 1909 in Numurkah, Victoria, Australia, m: 1861
.... 3   Melvina Flack b: 1864 in Lancefield, Victoria, Australia
.... 3   Sarah Ann Flack b: 1865 in Rochford, Victoria, Australia, d: 08 Oct 1956 in Alberton,
              Victoria, Australia
.... 3   William George Flack b: 1867 in Lancefield, Victoria, Australia
.... 3   Harriet Flack b: 1869 in Lancefield, Victoria, Australia, d: 08 Jan 1905 in
              Strathmerton, Victoria, Australia
.... 3   Edwin Flack b: 1872 in Romsey, Victoria, Australia, d: 20 Mar 1886 in Numurkah,
              Victoria, Australia
.... 3   John Flack b: 1874 in Rochford, Victoria, Australia, d: 1874 in Melbourne, Victoria,
              Australia
.... 3   Rosena Flack b: 1876 in Toolern Vale, Victoria, Australia, d: 12 May 1908 in
              Queensland, Australia
.... 3   Mary Ann Flack b: 1880
.... 3   Annie Wilhemina Cecily Flack b: 1882 in Numurkah, Victoria, Australia, d: 06 Oct
              1958 in St Kilda, Victoria, Australia
....   +Edward John Reilly b: 1880 in Carlton, Victoria, Australia, d: 1954 in Elwood,
              Victoria, Australia, m: 1909 in Victoria
.... 3   Ada Beatrice Flack b: 1884 in Numurkah, Victoria, Australia, d: 1885 in Numurkah,
              Victoria, Australia
.... 2   Elizabeth Hockey b: 10 Jan 1844 in Launceston, Tasmania, Australia, d: 1924 in
          Maidstone, Victoria, Australia
....   +James Charles b: 26 Aug 1839 in Swansea, Glamorganshire, Wales, d: 03 Mar 1913 in
       Footscray, Victoria Australia, m: 1861 in Melbourne, Victoria, Australia
.... 3   William James Charles b: 1863 in Kyneton, Victoria, Australia., d: 1924 in
              Flemington, Victoria, Australia
.... 3   Walter Charles b: 09 May 1864 in Kyneton, Victoria, Australia., d: 1938 in West
              Footscray, Victoria, Australia
.... 3   Edward Charles b: 1867 in Kyneton, Victoria, Australia., d: 1885 in Footscray,
              Victoria, Australia.
.... 3   Elizabeth Jane Charles b: 1869 in Kyneton, Victoria, Australia., d: 13 Jul 1950 in
              Footscray, Victoria, Australia.
.... 3   Mary Alice Charles b: 1871 in Kyneton, Victoria, Australia., d: 1952 in Ormond,
              Victoria, Australia
.... 3   James Charles b: 1872 in Kyneton, Victoria, Australia., d: 1873 in Kyneton, Victoria,
              Australia.
.... 3   James Charles b: Abt. 1873 in Kyneton, Victoria, d: Abt. 1873 in Victoria
.... 3   Winifred Venita Charles b: 25 Sep 1874 in Kyneton, Victoria, Australia., d: Oct 1936
              in Sunbury, Victoria, Australia
.... 3   George Charles b: 1876 in Kyneton, Victoria, Australia., d: 1938 in Victoria, Australia
.... 3   Albert Edward (Berty) Charles b: 1880 in Kyneton, Victoria, Australia., d: Victoria,
              Australia
.... 3   Daniel Edward Charles b: 31 May 1882 in Footscray, Victoria, Australia., d: 22 Jan
              1959 in Lilydale, Victoria, Australia
....   +Frances Helena Little McCracken b: 28 Sep 1886 in Fitzroy, Victoria, Australia, d: 03
              Jun 1976 in Auburn, Victoria, Australia, m: 18 Apr 1908 in Melbourne, Victoria,
              Australia
.... 3   Evelyn (Eveline) Charles b: 1884 in Footscray, Victoria, Australia., d: 1956 in
              Footscray, Victoria, Australia.
.... 3   Edward Sirell Charles b: 1885 in Footscray, Victoria, Australia., d: 14 Mar 1887 in
              Footscray, Victoria, Australia.
.... 2   Alice Charlotte Hockey b: 1845 in Launceston, Tasmania, Australia
.... 2   Charlotte Jane Hockey b: 18 Feb 1847 in Launceston, Tasmania, Australia, d: 11 Apr
          1882 in Burwood, Victoria, Australia.
....   +John Lewis Hawkins b: 24 Aug 1847 in Melbourne, Victoria, Australia, d: 30 Nov 1925 in
       Echuca, Victoria, Australia., m: 09 Apr 1868 in Taradale, Victoria, Australia
.... 3   John Andrew Hawkins b: 1868 in Taradale, Victoria, Australia, d: 1869 in Melbourne,
              Victoria, Australia
.... 3   Sarah Jane Hawkins b: 1869 in Taradale, Victoria, Australia
.... 3   James Lewis Hawkins b: 1870 in Echuca, Victoria, Australia., d: 03 May 1951 in

.... Echuca, Victoria, Australia
.... 3   Charlotte Agnes Hawkins b: 1873 in Echuca, Victoria, Australia, d: 1948 in Coburg, Victoria, Australia
....   +William Henry FaulknerFawkner Gilbert b: 1860 in Sealake, Victoria, Australia, d: 1929 in Footscray, Victoria, Australia.
.... 3   John Adrian Hawkins b: 1873 in Echuca, Victoria, Australia, d: 1950 in Echuca, Victoria, Australia
.... 3   John Lewis Andrew Hawkins b: 1874 in Echuca, Victoria, Australia., d: 26 Aug 1908 in Weeta Waa, New South Wales, Australia
.... 3   Ellen Nelly (Helen) Hawkins b: 30 Mar 1876 in Barmah, Victoria, Australia, d: 31 Jul 1958 in Echuca, Victoria, Australia
....   +Walter Isaac Clifford b: 1862 in London, London, England, d: 30 Dec 1925 in Echuca, Victoria, Australia, m: 18 Feb 1892 in Echuca, Victoria, Australia
.... 2   Melvina (Phoebe) Hockey b: 03 Mar 1849 in Mt Macedon, Victoria, Australia, d: 03 Aug 1891 in East Melbourne, Victoria, Australia
....   +John Gardiner Starr SNR b: 1845 in Cheddar, Somerset, England, d: 11 Jul 1928 in Kew, Victoria, Australia., m: 22 Jul 1867 in Chewton Victoria Australia
.... 3   Lillian Louisa Starr b: 1868 in Chewton,Victoria,Australia, d: 27 Sep 1955 in Kew, Victoria, Australia.
....   +Jacob Schneider b: 1856 in Nunawading, Victoria, Australia, d: 05 Jun 1935 in Balwyn, Victoria, Australia, m: 1893 in Melbourne, Victoria, Australia
.... 3   John Alfred Starr b: 1869 in Chewton, Victoria, Australia, d: 1952 in Hawthorn, Victoria, Australia
....   +Dora Adine Starns Harding b: Abt. 1872 in Dexter, Penobscot, Maine, USA, m: 21 Jan 1908 in Millbury, Massachusetts, USA
....   +Blanche Edith Bond b: 12 Jun 1876 in Collingwood, Victoria, Australia, d: 06 Aug 1962 in Ivanhoe, Victoria, Australia, m: 1891 in Victoria, Australia.
.... 3   Bernice Malvina Starr b: 1871 in Chewton, Victoria, Australia, d: 1961 in Bendigo, Victoria, Australia
....   +Charles Boyle b: 1861 in Castlemaine, Victoria, Australia, d: 1947 in Bendigo, Victoria, Australia, m: 1891 in Melbourne, Victoria, Australia
.... 3   Leila Mary Starr b: 24 Jul 1872 in Chewton, Victoria, Australia, d: 29 Sep 1959 in Halls Creek, Western Australia, Australia
....   +Hamilton James Lillingston Nicholls b: 1872 in Ararat, Victoria, Australia, d: 10 Oct 1945 in Perth, Western Australia, Australia, m: 07 Feb 1895 in Surrey Hills, Victoria, Australia
.... 3   Cynthia Starr b: 1874 in Chewton, Victoria, Australia, d: 1952 in Perth, Western Australia, Australia
....   +Andres Jepsen Nielsen b: 20 Jun 1857 in Barde, Ringkobing, Denmark, d: 18 Dec 1903 in Malvern, Victoria, Australia, m: 1896 in Melbourne, Victoria, Australia
....   +Ernest William Terry d: Western Australia, Australia, m: 1905
.... 3   George Gardiner Starr b: 17 Aug 1875 in Chewton, Victoria, Australia, d: 22 Feb 1970 in Nedlands, Western Australia, Australia
.... 3   Joseph Henry Starr b: 1877 in Chewton, Victoria, Australia, d: 19 Jul 1926 in East Melbourne, Victoria, Australia
....   +Maude Sylvia Stewart b: 03 Jul 1878 in Ramsay, South Australia, Australia, d: 12 Apr 1951 in Mosman Park, Western Australia, Australia, m: 27 May 1903 in York, Western Australia, Australia
.... 3   Mina Starr b: 07 Apr 1879 in Mt Korong, Victoria, Australia, d: 28 Jun 1930 in Malvern, Victoria, Australia.
....   +James John Flynn b: 1881 in Melbourne, Victoria, Australia, d: Melbourne, Victoria, Australia, m: Mar 1901 in Hawthorn, Victoria, Australia
.... 3   Bertha Constance Starr b: 1880 in Mt Korong, Victoria, Australia, d: 20 Nov 1950 in Harbord, New South Wales, Australia
....   +Francis John Flynn b: 1885 in Woodend, Victoria, Australia., d: 1907 in Victoria, Australia., m: 1903 in Melbourne, Victoria, Australia
....   +Hilary Dormer Brown b: 1888 in Plymouth, Devon, England, d: 22 Apr 1946 in New South Wales, Australia, m: 1914 in Sydney, New South Wales, Australia
.... 3   Ella Starr b: 24 Apr 1881 in Mt Korong, Victoria, Australia, d: 24 Apr 1881 in Mt Korong, Victoria, Australia
.... 3   Wedderburn Starr b: 15 Dec 1882 in Mt Korong, Victoria, Australia, d: 15 Dec 1882 in Mt Korong, Victoria, Australia
.... 3   Ella Starr b: 1884 in Mt Korong, Victoria, Australia, d: 30 Oct 1918 in San Antonio, Bexar, Texas, USA
....   +Robert B Daugherty
....   +UNK

.... 3   Wedderburn Starr b: 1886 in Mt Korong, Victoria, Australia, d: 28 Feb 1887 in Mt
                   Korong, Victoria, Australia
.... 3   Malvina Phoebe Pearl Starr b: 1887 in Wedderburn, Victoria, Australia, d: 1973 in
                   Essendon, Victoria, Australia
....   +Frank William Rowe m: 1906 in Victoria, Australia
.... 3   Ruby Olive Starr b: 19 Jan 1890 in Box Hill, Victoria, Australia, d: 09 May 1979 in
                   Cheltenham, Victoria, Australia
....   +Francis George Voigt b: 1897 in Richmond, Victoria, Australia, d: 06 May 1962 in
                   Parkville, Victoria, Australia, m: 1925
.... 2   James Hockey b: 1851 in Mount Macedon, Victoria, Australia
.... 2   Jane Hockey b: 1853 in Kyneton, Victoria, Australia., d: 1896
.... 2   Daniel James Hockey b: 02 May 1855 in Kyneton, Victoria, Australia, d: 12 May 1933 in
                2 Argyle Street, St. Kilda, Victoria, Australia
....   +Annie Elizabeth Cassidy b: 12 Mar 1853 in Campbell Town, Tasmania, Australia, d: 11
                Nov 1922 in 25 Sterling St, Footscray, Victoria, Australia, m: 1877 in Kyneton, Victoria,
                Australia
.... 3   Ada Emily Hockey b: 1878 in Trentham East, Victoria, Australia, d: 1905 in
                   Melbourne, Victoria, Australia
....   +Charles William Carpenter b: Kent, England, m: 1901 in Melbourne, Victoria,
                   Australia.
.... 3   James Frederick (Alfred) Hockey b: 06 Oct 1879 in Irishtown, Victoria, d: 1942 in
                   Sunshine, Victoria, Australia
....   +Phoebe Adelaide Crassweller b: 01 Aug 1882 in Lexton, Victoria, Australia, d: 05
                   Jan 1940 in Melbourne, Victoria, Australia
.... 3   Clara Victoria Hockey b: 1881 in Trentham, Victoria, Australia, d: 21 Aug 1974 in
                   Alphington, Victoria, Australia
....   +George Arthur Loniollo Cain (Williams) b: 1875, d: 21 Jan 1945 in Richmond,
                   Victoria, Australia.
.... 3   Alfred James Hockey b: 1881 in Trentham, Victoria, Australia
.... 3   Florence Annie Hockey b: 20 Sep 1882 in Trentham, Victoria, Australia, d: 20 Sep
                   1953 in 3 Ellison St, Ringwood, Victoria, Australia
....   +Harry Greig Anstey b: 1885 in Ballarat, Victoria, Australia, d: 12 Jun 1958 in 6
                   Leopold Crescent, Mont Albert, Victoria, m: 22 Mar 1924 in Presbyterian Manse, 61
                   Curzon St, Nth Melbourne, Victoria, Australia
....   +Leonard Henry Morgan b: 22 Oct 1875 in East Trentham, Victoria, Australia, d: 21
                   May 1945 in Royal Melbourne Hospital, Parkville,Victoria, Australia, m: 02 Apr 1899
                   in 422 Queen St, Melbourne, Victoria, Australia
.... 3   Daniel George Hockey b: 1884 in Trentham, Victoria, Australia, d: 1884 in Trentham,
                   Victoria, Australia
.... 3   Edward George Hockey b: 1885 in Trentham, Victoria, Australia
.... 3   Elizabeth Mary Hockey b: 1885 in Trentham, Victoria, Australia, d: 1885 in
                   Trentham, Victoria, Australia
.... 3   Eva Margaret Ellen Hockey b: 1887 in Trentham, Victoria, Australia, d: 1972 in Glen
                   Iris,Victoria, Australia
....   +Pierre Frederick Eugene Janssens b: 1881 in Belgium, d: 1957 in Kew, Victoria,
                   Australia., m: 1913 in Victoria, Australia
.... 3   Alice Maud Hockey b: 1888 in Blackwood, Victoria, Australia, d: 01 Feb 1920 in
                   Leongatha, Victoria, Australia
....   +Herbert Alfred Bowler b: 04 Mar 1887 in Taradale, Victoria, Australia, d: 27 Sep
                   1951 in Melbourne, Victoria, Australia
.... 3   Lillian Hockey b: 1889 in Blackwood, Victoria, Australia, d: 1890 in Blue Mountain,
                   Victoria, Australia
.... 3   Arthur Richard Hockey b: 18 Jul 1890 in Blackwood, Victoria, Australia, d: 1945 in
                   Kyneton, Victoria, Australia
....   +Rebecca McKinley b: 31 Jan 1894 in Bullarto, Victoria, Australia, d: 15 Sep 1977 in
                   South Melbourne, Victoria, Australia, m: 12 May 1933 in Melbourne, Victoria,
                   Australia
.... 3   Daisy Violet May Hockey b: 1894 in Trentham, Victoria, Australia, d: 08 Mar 1937 in
                   Brunswick, Victoria, Australia
....   +Frederick James Hopgood b: 23 Jun 1889 in Kiewa, Victoria, Australia, d: 04 Sep
                   1954 in Brunswick, Victoria, Australia, m: 1912 in Victoria
.... 3   George Henry Hockey b: 1898 in Trentham, Victoria, Australia, d: 1898 in Trentham,
                   Victoria, Australia

Helen (Ellen) Barefoot

Helen was born around 18 June 1824 in Port Dalrymple and died on 30 October 1897 in Launceston. She married Edward Cassidy on 5 February 1839 in Launceston.

Even though it seems that the older Cassidy children stayed in Launceston, the younger ones did not, with Richard James and Annie Elizabeth marrying children of James and Ann Hockey.

Edward was not a convict but was in and out of orphan homes in New South Wales when he was young. As he had lost his father early in life and his mother had five other children, she ended up having to place him in an orphanage.

Descendant Report for Ellen (Helen) Barfoot

..... 1 Ellen (Helen) Barfoot b: 18 Jun 1824 in Port Dalrymple, Van Diemen's Land, d: 30 Oct 1897 in Launceston, Tasmania

..... +Edward Cassidy b: Abt. 1814 in New South Wales, d: 20 Jun 1891 in Launceston, Tasmania, m: 05 Feb 1839 in Launceston, Van Diemen's Land

.... 2 Richard James Cassidy b: 1838 in Tasmania, d: 1909 in Picton, New South Wales, Australia

.... +Eliza Jane Hockey b: 20 Aug 1842 in Launceston, Tasmania, Australia, d: 07 Mar 1882 in Trentham, Victoria, Australia, m: 1859

.... 3 Melvina Ellen Cassidy b: 1860 in Kyneton, Victoria, Australia., d: 1861 in Kyneton, Victoria, Australia.

.... 3 Walter James Cassidy b: 1864 in Violet Town, Vic, d: 05 Jan 1936 in Collie, Western Australia

.... +Elizabeth Jane Pascoe b: 1870 in Newlyn, Victoria, Australia, d: 14 Jul 1900 in Pinjarra, Western Australia, Australia, m: 22 Aug 1888 in Boho East, Victoria, Australia

.... +Alice Amelia Garwood b: Apr 1875 in Kensington, London, England, m: 1902 in Perth, Western Australia, Australia

.... 3 Selina Jane Cassidy b: 1867 in Kyneton, Victoria, Australia, d: 1887 in Woodend, Victoria, Australia

.... +Henry Bowyer m: 1886 in Victoria

.... 3 Elizabeth Rose Cassidy b: Aug 1869 in Trentham, Victoria, Australia, d: 23 Dec 1869 in Trentham, Victoria, Australia

.... 3 Emily Eliza Cassidy b: 1871 in Trentham, Victoria, Australia, d: 09 Sep 1876 in Trentham, Victoria, Australia

.... 3 Richard Ernest Cassidy b: 1873 in Trentham, Victoria, Australia, d: 07 Aug 1876 in Trentham, Victoria, Australia

.... 3 Lillian Cassidy b: Jul 1874 in Trentham, Victoria, Australia, d: 26 Oct 1874 in Trentham, Victoria, Australia

.... 3 Annie Cassidy b: 21 Jul 1876 in Trentham, Victoria, Australia, d: 21 Jul 1876 in Trentham, Victoria, Australia

.... 3 George Albert Cassidy b: 1877 in Trentham, Victoria, Australia, d: 01 Sep 1879 in Trentham, Victoria, Australia

.... 3 William Cassidy b: Jun 1879 in Trentham, Victoria, Australia, d: 31 Jul 1879 in Trentham, Victoria, Australia

.... 3 Francis John (Frank) Cassidy b: 1880 in Trentham, Victoria, Australia, d: 31 Jul 1941 in Fitzroy, Victoria, Australia.

.... +Elizabeth Patricia Tickner b: 1894 in Winslow, Victoria, Australia, d: 1961 in Wangaratta, Victoria, Australia, m: 1910 in Victoria, Australia

.... 3 George Cassidy b: 07 Mar 1882 in Trentham, Victoria, Australia, d: 07 Mar 1882 in Trentham, Victoria, Australia

.... +Amelia Broad NEE Chadwick b: 1862 in Melbourne, Victoria, Australia, d: 14 Aug 1942 in Maryborough, Victoria, Australia, m: 1888 in Victoria

.... +Amelia Broad NEE Chadwick b: 1862 in Melbourne, Victoria, Australia, d: 14 Aug 1942 in Maryborough, Victoria, Australia, m: 1888 in Victoria
.... 3   Beatrice Cassidy b: 1889 in Kyneton, Victoria, Australia, d: 1936 in Maryborough, Victoria, Australia
.... 3   Amelia Mary Ellen Cassidy (Nellie) b: 1892 in Adelaide Lead, Victoria, Australia, d: 1967 in Northcote, Victoria, Australia
.... 3   Elizabeth Myrtle May (Myrtle) Cassidy b: 1894 in Avenel, Victoria, Australia., d: 24 Aug 1978 in Geelong, Victoria, Australia
.... 3   William Henry Cassidy b: 1898 in Meredith, Victoria, Australia, d: 21 Aug 1990 in Maryborough, Victoria, Australia
.... 3   Clarice Isabel Rose (Dolly) Cassidy b: 1900 in Morrisons, Victoria, Australia, d: 10 Feb 1945 in Geelong, Victoria, Australia
.... 2   Elizabeth Celestine Cassidy b: 1843 in Launceston, Tasmania, Australia, d: 28 Oct 1932 in St Kilda, Victoria, Australia
....   +Alexander Henry Blair b: 28 Oct 1841 in Launceston, Tasmania, Australia, d: 13 Aug 1926 in Melbourne East, Victoria, Australia, m: 28 Aug 1867 in Launceston, Tasmania, Australia; BLAIR-CASSIDY.-On 28th August, at the Church of the Apostle, by the Very Rev. Dean Butler, Alex. Blair, to Elizabeth, eldest daughter of Mr. Edward Cassidy, both of Launceston.
.... 3   Elizabeth Eleanor Blair b: 12 Jun 1868 in Launceston, Tasmania, Australia, d: 19 Oct 1941 in Leichhardt, New South Wales, Australia
....   +Albert Edward Roberts b: 02 Feb 1864 in Hobart, Tasmania, Australia, d: 22 Jun 1928 in Annandale, New South Wales, Australia, m: 09 Feb 1898 in Brisbane, Queensland, Australia
.... 3   Richard Alexander Blair b: 11 Oct 1870 in Launceston, Tasmania, Australia, d: 05 Sep 1932 in Launceston, Tasmania, Australia
....   +Alice Amelia Ewart m: 20 Apr 1905 in Launceston, Tasmania, Australia
.... 3   Florence Mary Blair b: 26 Jan 1873 in Launceston, Tasmania, Australia, d: 28 Feb 1967 in Johannesburg, South Africa
.... 3   Edith Emma Blair b: 06 Jun 1875 in Launceston, Tasmania, Australia, d: 1959 in Caulfield, Victoria, Australia
.... 3   Teresa Annie Blair b: 24 Jan 1878 in Launceston, Tasmania, Australia, d: 1962 in Melbourne, Victoria, Australia
.... 3   Henrietta Myra Blair b: 20 Mar 1880 in Launceston, Tasmania, Australia
.... 3   Arthur Vernon BLAIR b: 13 Sep 1882 in Launceston, Tasmania, Australia
.... 3   Leslie John Blair b: 04 Apr 1885 in Launceston, Tasmania, Australia, d: 27 Jul 1899 in Launceston, Tasmania, Australia
.... 3   Basil Sydney Blair b: 12 Aug 1890 in Launceston, Tasmania, Australia, d: 1971 in Victoria, Australia
.... 2   Edward Herbert Cassidy b: 02 Apr 1845 in Evandale, Tasmania, Australia, d: 30 May 1918 in Evandale, Tasmania, Australia
....   +Emma Smithers Thompson b: 27 Mar 1852 in Chatteris, Cambridgeshire, England, d: 30 May 1891 in Evandale, Tasmania, Australia, m: 23 Sep 1870 in Evendale, Tasmania, Australia
.... 3   Ernest Alfred Cassidy b: 1869
....   +Catherine Brown m: 1891 in Launceston, Tasmania
.... 3   Alfred Edward Cassidy b: 20 Nov 1870 in Evandale, Tasmania, Australia, d: 11 Jun 1878 in Morven, Tasmania
.... 3   Lillian Ann Cassidy b: 18 Jun 1872 in Morvan/Evandale Tas, d: 21 Oct 1897 in Morvan/Evandale Tas
....   +Edward Merrington b: 03 Aug 1870 in White Hills, Tasmania, Australia, d: 31 Jan 1944 in Launceston Tasmania, Australia,, m: 21 Oct 1897 in Launceston, Tasmania
.... 3   Arthur James Cassidy b: 30 Aug 1874 in Evandale, Tasmania, Australia, d: 18 Nov 1876 in Evandale, Tasmania, Australia
.... 3   William Robert Cassidy b: 04 Nov 1876 in Morven, Tasmania, Australia, d: 21 Jun 1964 in Scottsdale, Tasmania, Australia
....   +Margaret May Owen b: 07 Sep 1886 in Morvan/Evandale Tasmania, d: 13 Oct 1973 in Scottsdale Tas, m: 1900 in Coombank Evandale
.... 3   John Cassidy b: 04 Oct 1878 in Morven, Tasmania, Australia, d: ?
.... 3   Marion Ellen Cassidy b: 19 Dec 1880 in Evandale, Tasmania, Australia, d: 26 May 1959 in Tasmania, Australia
.... 3   Edwin James (Ted) Cassidy b: 12 Nov 1882 in Morven, Tasmania, Australia, d: 18 Oct 1960 in Launceston, Tasmania, Australia
....   +Mary Ann Rigney b: 06 Aug 1879 in Evandale, , Tasmania, Australia, d: 1960 in Launceston, Tasmania, Australia
.... 3   Amy Violet Cassidy b: 14 Oct 1884 in Evandale, Tasmania, Australia, d: 25 Oct 1925 in Evandale, Tasmania, Australia
....   +Cecil James Cutler b: 10 Apr 1878 in Evandale, Tasmania, Australia, d: 27 May 1962 in Evandale, Tasmania, Australia, m: 29 Apr 1908 in Evandale, Tasmania, Australia

.... 3   Robert John Cassidy b: 09 Apr 1887 in Evandale, Tasmania, Australia, d: 12 Oct
              1887 in Evandale, Tasmania, Australia
.... 3   Edith Emma Cassidy b: 28 Jun 1888 in Evandale, Tasmania, Australia, d: 26 Feb
              1889 in Evandale, Tasmania, Australia
.... 3   Harold John Cassidy b: 17 Mar 1890 in Evandale, Tasmania, Australia, d: 14 Jul
              1974 in Evandale, Tasmania, Australia
....   +Ida May Allen b: 18 May 1902 in Barwon, Victoria, Australia, d: 1989, m: 22 May
              1922 in Kooyong, Victoria, Australia
.... 2   John Cassidy b: 24 Oct 1847 in Morven (Evandale), Tasmania, Australia, d: 18 Nov
          1847 in Morven (Evandale), Tasmania, Australia
.... 2   Mary Anne Cassidy b: 07 Feb 1849 in Morven (Evandale), Tasmania, Australia, d: 12
          May 1869 in Evandale, , Tasmania, Australia
....   +William Mathew Burley b: 1841, m: 25 Jul 1868 in Horton, Tasmania
.... 2   Francis James Cassidy b: 1850 in Evandale, Tasmania, Australia
....   +Ann Burly
.... 3   Mary Ann Cassidy b: 21 Dec 1869 in Horton, Tasmania, Australia
.... 2   Annie Elizabeth Cassidy b: 12 Mar 1853 in Campbell Town, Tasmania, Australia, d: 11
          Nov 1922 in 25 Sterling St, Footscray, Victoria, Australia
....   +Daniel James Hockey b: 02 May 1855 in Kyneton, Victoria, Australia, d: 12 May 1933 in
          2 Argyle Street, St. Kilda, Victoria, Australia, m: 1877 in Kyneton, Victoria, Australia, m:
          1870 in Victoria. Australia

.... 3   Ada Emily Hockey b: 1878 in Trentham East, Victoria, Australia, d: 1905 in
          Melbourne, Victoria, Australia
....   +Charles William Carpenter b: Kent, England, m: 1901 in Melbourne, Victoria,
          Australia.
.... 3   James Frederick (Alfred) Hockey b: 06 Oct 1879 in Irishtown, Victoria, d: 1942 in
          Sunshine, Victoria, Australia
....   +Phoebe Adelaide Crassweller b: 01 Aug 1882 in Lexton, Victoria, Australia, d: 05
          Jan 1940 in Melbourne, Victoria, Australia
.... 3   Clara Victoria Hockey b: 1881 in Trentham, Victoria, Australia, d: 21 Aug 1974 in
          Alphington, Victoria, Australia
....   +George Arthur Loniollo Cain (Williams) b: 1875, d: 21 Jan 1945 in Richmond,
          Victoria, Australia.
.... 3   Alfred James Hockey b: 1881 in Trentham, Victoria, Australia
.... 3   Florence Annie Hockey b: 20 Sep 1882 in Trentham, Victoria, Australia, d: 20 Sep
          1953 in 3 Ellison St, Ringwood, Victoria, Australia
....   +Harry Greig Anstey b: 1885 in Ballarat, Victoria, Australia, d: 12 Jun 1958 in 6
          Leopold Crescent, Mont Albert, Victoria, m: 22 Mar 1924 in Presbyterian Manse, 61
          Curzon St, Nth Melbourne, Victoria, Australia
....   +Leonard Henry Morgan b: 22 Oct 1875 in East Trentham, Victoria, Australia, d: 21
          May 1945 in Royal Melbourne Hospital, Parkville,Victoria, Australia, m: 02 Apr 1899
          in 422 Queen St, Melbourne, Victoria, Australia
.... 3   Daniel George Hockey b: 1884 in Trentham, Victoria, Australia, d: 1884 in Trentham,
          Victoria, Australia
.... 3   Edward George Hockey b: 1885 in Trentham, Victoria, Australia
.... 3   Elizabeth Mary Hockey b: 1885 in Trentham, Victoria, Australia, d: 1885 in
          Trentham, Victoria, Australia
.... 3   Eva Margaret Ellen Hockey b: 1887 in Trentham, Victoria, Australia, d: 1972 in Glen
          Iris,Victoria, Australia
....   +Pierre Frederick Eugene Janssens b: 1881 in Belgium, d: 1957 in Kew, Victoria,
          Australia., m: 1913 in Victoria, Australia
.... 3   Alice Maud Hockey b: 1888 in Blackwood, Victoria, Australia, d: 01 Feb 1920 in
          Leongatha, Victoria, Australia
....   +Herbert Alfred Bowler b: 04 Mar 1887 in Taradale, Victoria, Australia, d: 27 Sep
          1951 in Melbourne, Victoria, Australia
.... 3   Lillian Hockey b: 1889 in Blackwood, Victoria, Australia, d: 1890 in Blue Mountain,
          Victoria, Australia
.... 3   Arthur Richard Hockey b: 18 Jul 1890 in Blackwood, Victoria, Australia, d: 1945 in
          Kyneton, Victoria, Australia
....   +Rebecca McKinley b: 31 Jan 1894 in Bullarto, Victoria, Australia, d: 15 Sep 1977 in
          South Melbourne, Victoria, Australia, m: 12 May 1933 in Melbourne, Victoria,
          Australia
.... 3   Daisy Violet May Hockey b: 1894 in Trentham, Victoria, Australia, d: 08 Mar 1937 in
          Brunswick, Victoria, Australia
....   +Frederick James Hopgood b: 23 Jun 1889 in Kiewa, Victoria, Australia, d: 04 Sep
          1954 in Brunswick, Victoria, Australia, m: 1912 in Victoria
.... 3   George Henry Hockey b: 1898 in Trentham, Victoria, Australia, d: 1898 in Trentham,
          Victoria, Australia

..... 2   John Cassidy b: 08 Jul 1854 in Evandale, Tasmania, Australia, d: 09 May 1938 in
           Launceston, Tasmania, Australia; CASSIDY.--Passed peacefully away on the 9th May,
           1938, John, relict of the late Eliza Cassidy, of 81 Howick street, and loving father of Bert
           and May (Mrs. W. H. Edwards), in his 84th year. (Private interment Car: Villa Cemetery.
           Wednesday.-C. T. Fisney,
......   +Eliza Carter b: 29 Jul 1855 in Launceston, Tasmania, Australia, d: 02 Jan 1920 in
           Launceston, Tasmania, Australia, m: 04 Jul 1874 in Launceston, Tasmania, Australia
.... 3   John Bertram Cassidy b: 20 Jun 1878 in Kyneton, Victoria, Australia, d: 01 Dec
           1954 in Launceston, Tasmania, Australia
....   +Rose Ellen Small b: 1855 in Paddington, New South Wales, m: 1916 in Paddington,
           New South Wales
.... 3   Arthur William Cassidy b: 15 Apr 1880 in Kyneton, Victoria, Australia
.... 3   May Cassidy b: 28 Sep 1882 in Kyneton, Victoria, Australia, d: 12 Aug 1950 in
           Devonport, Tasmania, Australia
....   +William Harvard Edwards b: 05 Jul 1884 in Launceston, Tasmania, Australia, d: 26
           Jul 1955 in Devonport, Tasmania, Australia, m: 06 Jan 1909 in Launceston,
           Tasmania, Australia
.... 3   Harry Francis Cassidy b: 26 Jan 1886 in Tasmania, Australia, d: 17 Feb 1887 in
           Launceston, Tasmania, Australia
..... 2   Isabella Cassidy b: 22 Feb 1858 in Evandale, Tasmania, Australia

.... 2   Margaret Cecilia Cassidy b: 12 Nov 1860 in Evandale, , Tasmania, Australia, d: 06 Dec
           1876 in Launceston, Tasmania, Australia; CASSIDY-On 6th December, at her parents'
           residence, Howick-street, after a long and painful Illness, Margaret Cecilia, the fifth and
           dearly beloved daughter of Edward and Eleanor Cassidy, aged 16 years.
.... 2   Emily Cassidy b: 1862 in Evandale, Tasmania, Australia, d: 1948 in Launceston,
           Tasmania, Australia
....   +John Frederick Howell b: 28 Dec 1861 in Launceston, Tasmania, Australia, d: 07 May
           1889 in Launceston, Tasmania, Australia, m: 18 May 1884 in Tasmania, Australia
.... 3   Elsie May Howell b: 18 Sep 1884 in Launceston, d: 25 Feb 1970 in Preston
.... 3   Frederick Gordon Howell b: 29 Nov 1886 in Launceston, d: 01 Apr 1957 in
           Launceston
....   +Eliza Spiers Ingles b: 28 Oct 1892 in Launceston, Tasmania, Australia, d: 25 Aug
           1973 in Devonport, Tasmania, Australia
.... 3   Sydney William Howell b: 29 Jan 1889 in Launceston, Tasmania, Australia

Bridget Barefoot

Bridget was born around 1825 in Port Dalrymple, although no birth
registration was found. She died on 9 December 1896 at Mooroopna,
Victoria.

Samuel applied to marry Bridget and permission was granted[20], but
no record has ever been found of the marriage taking place.

Sam was tried at the Somerset Assizes on 22 August 1829, for stealing
two asses and sentenced to transportation for fourteen years. He was

---

20   Tasmanian Archives, CON52/1/1 p. 82, see https://libraries.tas.gov.au/
     Digital/CON52-1-1p039j2k

transported on *Sir Charles Forbes* and arrived in Van Diemen's Land on 26 July 1830.

Sam's convict record was … chequered, and punishments were harsh. He was assigned first to Mr J Bonney:

13 December 1830: Repeated insolence and disobedience of orders – 12 lashes on the breech.

2 April 1831: Repeated neglect of duty and insolence particularly yesterday – 25 lashes.

10 February 1832: Neglect of his Master's flock – 50 lashes.

29 May 1833: Disobedience, neglect and insolence – 10 days in a cell.

Then he was assigned to Mr Wedge—probably the surveyor:

23 February 1839: Out after hours – 3 days solitary confinement on Bread and Water.

23 August 1839: Ticket of leave. Suspicion of being an accessory to a robbery committed at Mr Wedges. Charge dismissed for want of evidence.

29 August 1939: T.L. Misconduct 3 months imprisonment and hard labour and recommended to be ordered to leave the district of Campbelltown after his punishment, the district of Bothwell. Recommended T.F./Spring Hill then if well conducted T.L. To be restored but to reside in Bothwell district. Vide Lt Govr decision 6 Sept 1839.

11 September 1839: Misconduct in having in his possession a one pound note contrary to the regulations. Discharged.

27 February 1841: T.L. Larceny discharged and let off.

6 January 1842: T.L. Misconduct in making use of threatening language to John Craven as he was going out of the Police Office - one month hard labour.

4 August 1842: T.L. Misconduct in having a piece of pork in his possession without being able satisfactorily to account for it - 12 months hard labour in chains.

Now ...[21] This piece of pork ...

> *Bridget Hockey*, a married woman, was indicted for stealing on the 3rd instant six pounds of pork, valued at 6d., the property of Mr. H. Cockerell, of Bothwell.
>
> The prisoner was defended by Mr. Macdowell.
>
> Mr. Cockerell stated, that on the morning of the day mentioned, and in consequence of information which he had received, he went with the district constable (Mr. Midgley) to the prisoner's house ; on approaching the house Mrs. Hockey ran away to the back of the house ; and Mr. Midgley afterwards produced a piece of pork, which the prosecutor immediately identified as a piece he had missed that morning.
>
> The pork was here produced, which was the skinny shank of the shoulder and had been spoilt in the curing ; the prosecutor valued it at 6d.
>
> On his cross-examination by Mr. Macdowell, Mr. Cockerell stated that the prisoner's husband, *being a ticket-of-leave man, had been sentenced to a year's imprisonment at Bothwell, for renting the house where this pork was found.*
>
> Mr. D.C. Midgley stated, that as he and Mr. Cockerell went towards the house of the prisoner, she ran towards the house, and afterwards came out with the pork in her possession.
>
> This being the case on the part of the prosecution, the Chairman said he did not see there was any case against the prisoner ; there were circumstances, perhaps, that might have rendered an enquiry necessary at the time ; for it was shown that her husband was now suffering punishment on account of that very pork.
>
> The prisoner, who was a free woman and a native of the colony, was immediately Acquitted and discharged.

Bridget and Samuel also came to Victoria on 20 December 1847[22]:

> DEPARTURES.
>
> *Vessels reported outwards during the week.*
>
> *December 20.*—Schooner *Will Watch*, 63 tons, M'Arthur, master, for Portland Bay ; R. Green, agent. Passengers—James Hockey, wife and 3 children, W. Howard, wife and child, R. Howard, Miss Thomas, John Murray, S. Hockey, wife and child, J. F. Gilman, G. Stanley.

Somewhere between then and 1840, Bridget and Samuel separated, and

---

21   *Colonial Times* (Hobart), 23 August 1842, see http://nla.gov.au/nla.news-article8752917

22   See http://nla.gov.au/nla.news-article36253667

Bridget started living as the wife of James Clover. Bridget was married to James Gladwin Clover maybe in 1850 in Kilmore, Victoria.

James Clover was born on 23 August 1818 in Writtle, Essex, England as James Gladwin, son of John Gladwin and Lucy Bright. He was an ex-convict, who was tried in Essex in 1838, age twenty-two, for house breaking. Had been convicted of a felony prior to this. He was transported for ten years and arrived in Van Diemen's Land in 1840 on *Mandarin*.

Descendant Report for Bridget Barfoot

..... 1 Bridget Barfoot b: 1825 in Port Dalrymple, Van Diemen's Land, d: 09 Dec 1880 in Mooroopna, Victoria

..... +Samuel Hockey b: 23 Jan 1811 in Shepton Mallet, Somerset, England, d: 02 Mar 1886 in Geelong, Victoria; Age: 75, m: Jan 1840, m: 1871 in Victoria

.... 2 Isabella Hockey b: 17 Dec 1842 in Launceston, Van Diemen's Land, d: 05 Oct 1904 in Staffordshire Reef, Victoria

.... +William Walter Guy b: 16 Jul 1830 in Stepney, Middlesex, England, d: 11 Mar 1917 in Staffordshire Reef, Victoria, Australia, m: 10 Dec 1855 in Geelong, VIC, AUS

.... 3 Emily Valeria Guy b: 10 Feb 1857 in Mt Misery Diggings, Vic, Aus, d: 11 Oct 1909 in Ballarat, Vic, Aus

.... +James Rosewarne b: 08 Apr 1858 in Ballarat, Ballarat City, Victoria, Australia, d: 21 Sep 1911 in Rokewood, Vic, Aus, m: 1880 in Victoria

.... 3 William Samuel Guy b: 18 Jan 1859 in Berringa, Vic, Aus, d: 11 Jun 1908 in Ballarat, Vic, Aus; Age: 49

.... +Blanche Margaret (Maggie) Causon b: 21 Jun 1871 in Smythesdale, Ballaarat, Victoria, Australia, d: 09 Jul 1952 in Melbourne, Vic, Aus, m: 28 Oct 1887 in Smythesdale, Vic, Aus, m: 1918 in Victoria

.... 3 Alfred Guy b: 01 Jun 1861 in Kangaroo Gully, Vic, Aus, d: 26 Mar 1907 in Staffordshire Rf, Vic, Aus

.... +Elizabeth Annie (Bessie) Causon b: 21 Dec 1866 in Smythesdale, Ballaarat, Victoria, Australia, d: 25 May 1926 in Kew, Melbourne, Victoria, Australia, m: 1916 in Victoria, m: 29 Jun 1885 in Pascoe Street, Smythesdale, Victoria, Australia

.... 3 Louisa Guy b: 08 Feb 1863 in Staffordshire Rf, Vic, Aus, d: Jul 1864 in Italian Gully, Vic, Aus

.... 3 Charles Henry Guy b: 27 May 1865 in Staffordshire Rf, Vic, Aus, d: Apr 1867 in Rokewood, Vic, Aus

.... 3 Walter Guy b: 15 Oct 1867 in Rokewood, Vic, Aus, d: 19 Dec 1929 in Staffordshire Rf, Vic, Aus; Police inquiry into death found cardiac failure - extra strain on heart by excitement of firing a gun ...

.... +Amelia Edith Laughlin b: 29 Aug 1876 in Springdallah, Vic, Aus, d: 18 Jul 1957 in Staffordshire Rf, Vic, Aus, m: 03 Aug 1899 in Italian Gully, Vic, Aus

.... 3 Lucy Guy b: 02 Apr 1870 in Staffordshire Rf, Vic, Aus, d: 24 Jul 1946 in Staffordshire Reef, Victoria, Australia

.... +John Williamson b: 1864 in Hamilton, Vic, d: 01 Jan 1927 in Geelong, VIC, AUS, m: 14 Dec 1894 in Staffordshire Rf, Vic, Aus

.... 3 Janet Rosina Guy b: 15 Oct 1872 in Staffordshir Rf, Vic, Aus, d: 04 Dec 1954 in Mildura, Vic, Aus

.... +Herbert Roscoe Hoyle b: 31 May 1871 in Richmond, Vic, Aus, d: 18 Apr 1940 in Mildura, Vic, Aus, m: 01 Feb 1895 in Staffordshire Rf, Vic, Aus

.... 3 Marion Isabella Guy b: 22 Apr 1875 in Staffordshire Rf, Vic, Aus, d: 22 Aug 1956 in Lilydale, Vic, Aus

.... +Albert Lovat Frazer b: 07 Feb 1877 in Seven Houses, IRE, d: 28 Dec 1939 in
         Lilydale, Vic, Aus, m: 05 Aug 1909 in Staffordshire Rf, Vic, Aus
.... 3 Albert Cecil Guy b: 05 Dec 1878 in Staffordshire Rf, Vic, Aus, d: 27 Jul 1957 in
         Ballarat, Victoria, Australia
.... 3 Florence Cecilia (Doll) Guy b: 21 Jun 1880 in Staffordshire Rf, Vic, Aus, d: 11 Mar
         1953 in Allendale, Vic, Aus
.... +George Scott b: 1877 in Smythedale, Vic, d: 02 Apr 1941 in Ballarat, Vic, Aus, m: 22
         Mar 1900 in Berringa, Vic, Aus
..... +James Gladwin Clover b: 23 Aug 1818 in Writtle, England, United Kingdom, d: 20 Jun 1881
in Mooroopna, Victoria, Australia, m: 1850 in Kilmore Presbytian Church, Victoria
.... 2 Sarah Clover b: 1854 in Sandhurst, Vic, Aus, d: 1855 in Sandhurst, Vic, Aus
.... 2 George Albert Clover b: 1855 in Heathcote, Vic, Aus, d: 02 Apr 1906 in Wangaratta,
         Victoria, Australia
.... +Sarah Ann Lakeman b: 1876 in Benalla, Victoria, Australia, d: 02 Apr 1903 in Benalla,
Victoria, Australia, m: 1896 in Heathcote, Victoria, Australia
.... 3 Alfred Lakeman Clover b: 1893 in Benalla, d: 1893 in Benalla
.... 3 Lily Elizabeth Clover b: 1895 in Victoria, Australia, d: 09 Jan 1965 in Newcastle,
         New South Wales, Australia
.... 3 Elizabeth Clover b: 1897 in Benalla, Victoria, Australia, d: 1909 in Stawell, Victoria,
         Australia
.... 3 Florence May Clover b: 1900 in Benalla, Victoria, Australia, d: 1901 in Benalla,
         Victoria, Australia
.... 3 Gladys Isabella Clover b: 1901 in Benalla, Victoria, Australia, d: 1982 in New South
         Wales, Australia
.... 2 James Clover b: 1856 in Heathcote, Victoria, Australia, d: 04 Dec 1868 in Avenel,
         Victoria, Australia
.... 2 Charles Clover b: 1859 in Seymour, Vic, Aus, d: 26 Sep 1932 in Tocumwal, New South
         Wales, Australia
.... +Lucy Haley b: 1865 in Broken Creek, Victoria, Australia, d: 22 Nov 1896 in Benalla,
Victoria, Australia, m: 1884 in Melbourne, Victoria, Australia
.... 3 Lucy Mary Clover b: 30 Apr 1885 in Benalla, Victoria, Australia, d: 04 Dec 1953 in
         Bendigo, Victoria, Australia
.... +John Thomas Reynolds b: 1881 in Youarang, Victoria, Australia, d: 22 Nov 1914 in
         Wangaratta, m: 24 Apr 1904 in St James Church, Yowrang Vic Bmd #3186
.... 3 Charles Henry James Clover b: 1888 in Maffra, Victoria, Australia, d: 1888 in Maffra,
         Victoria, Australia
.... 3 Herbert James Clover b: 1889 in Yea, Victoria, Australia, d: 11 Jul 1942 in Cobram,
         Victoria, Australia
.... 3 Ethel May Clover b: 29 Feb 1892 in Black Range, Victoria, Australia, d: 20 Aug 1922
         in Levin, Horowhenua, Manawatu-Wanganui, New Zealand
.... +Alfred James Mark b: 11 Jan 1884, d: 15 Sep 1974, m: 25 Nov 1913 in Levin, New
         Zealand
.... 3 Hector Albert Clover b: Oct 1894 in Benalla, Victoria, Australia, d: 04 Oct 1915 in
         Battle of Lone Pine
.... 2 Elizabeth Anne Clover b: 26 Aug 1861 in Seymour, Vic, Aus, d: 21 Jul 1923 in Eildon
         Weir, Victoria, Australia
.... +Carl Johann Rosenqvist (Charles John) Lond b: 01 Oct 1855 in Helsingborg, Sweden,
d: 08 Nov 1947 in Alexandra, Vic, Australia, m: 17 Sep 1885 in Benalla, Victoria
.... 3 Charles Johan Lond b: 1880 in Dooki, Vic, Australia, d: 1900 in Kilmore, Victoria,
         Australia
.... 3 Louisa Elizabeth (Cissie) Lond b: 1882 in Albury, New South Wales, Australia, d:
         1950 in Coburg, Victoria, Australia.
.... 3 William Olaf Lond b: 1883 in Benalla, Victoria, Australia, d: 1885 in Benalla, Victoria
.... 3 Elna Botilde Lond (Rosenquist) b: 1886 in Benalla, Victoria, d: 1948 in Alexandra,
         Victoria, Australia.
.... 3 Lucy Isabella Lond b: 18 Aug 1888 in Molesworth, Victoria, Australia, d: Dec 1941 in
         Whittlesea, Victoria, Australia
.... +Henry Baldwin Ovenden b: 21 Aug 1885, d: 19 Feb 1955 in Whittlesea, Victoria,
         Australia
.... 3 Florence May (Florrie) Lond b: 1890 in Yea, Victoria, d: 1912
.... 3 Olaf Leslie Lond b: 29 Apr 1893 in Gobur, Vic, Australia, d: Sep 1944 in Alexandra,
         Vic, Australia
.... +Hilda Harriet Roberts b: 06 Sep 1897 in Williamstown, Vic, Aus, d: 11 Aug 1983, m:
         01 Jul 1916 in Victoria
.... 3 Eileen Florinda Lond b: 1895 in Gobur, Victoria, Australia, d: 1915 in Alexandra,
         Victoria, Australia
.... 3 Eva Blanche Lond b: 06 Feb 1898 in Gobur, Victoria, Australia, d: 23 Jun 1957 in
         Thornton, Victoria, Australia

.... 3   Gertrude Victoria (Gertie) Lond b: 22 Mar 1900 in Benalla, Victoria, Australia, d: 26
            Mar 1988 in Victoria, Australia
.... 2   John James Clover b: 1867 in Avenel, Victoria, Australia, d: 31 Aug 1903 in Robertson,
            New South Wales, Australia
....   +Isabella McPherson b: 1873 in Berrima, New South Wales, Australia, d: 20 Mar 1903 in
            Bowral, New South Wales, Australia, m: 1888 in Molesworth, Victoria, Australia
.... 3   John Clover b: 1890 in Benalla, Victoria, Australia, d: 1964 in Newtown, New South
            Wales, Australia
.... 3   Oliver Ernest Clover b: 1892 in Mansfield, Victoria, Australia, d: 1977 in Fitzroy,
            Victoria, Australia.
.... 3   Rosie (Rose) May Clover b: 1895 in Mansfield, Victoria, Australia, d: 23 Jul 1979 in
            Molong, New South Wales, Australia
.... 3   William Joseph Clover b: 1897 in Benalla, Victoria, Australia, d: 1899 in Benalla,
            Victoria, Australia
.... 2   Joseph Clover b: 10 Nov 1868 in Seymour, Victoria, Australia, d: 31 Aug 1903 in
            Robertson, New South Wales, Australia
....   +Maria McPherson b: 1873 in Berrima, New South Wales, Australia, m: 1896 in Victoria,
            Australia
.... 3   Ellen McPherson Clover b: 1888 in Yea, Victoria, Australia
.... 3   Daisy Dilla McPherson Clover b: 1892 in Strathbogie, Victoria, Australia, d: 1912 in
            Sydney, New South Wales, Australia
.... 3   Joseph John Clover aka Theo Zoloff b: 1895 in Benalla, Victoria, Australia, d: 23 Oct
            1958 in Newcastle, New South Wales, Australia
....   +Ethel Veage b: 1889 in County Cork, Ireland, d: 30 Dec 1973 in Lake Macquarie,
            New South Wales, Australia, m: 1941 in Katoomba, New South Wales, Australia
....   +Mary Gwendoline Bennett b: 14 Aug 1892 in Paddington, New South Wales,
            Australia, d: 24 Nov 1968 in Cronulla, New South Wales, Australia

William Barefoot

William was born in maybe 1826 in Lodden Vale, although no birth registration has been found. He died on 22 September 1856 in Melbourne.

William married (date unknown) Mary Ann Steele (b. 1839, d.1911) and had two children: Mary Ann Barfoot (b.1854, d.1854) and Mary Ann Ellen Barefoot (b.1856, Collingwood, d.1904 in Melbourne),

Mary Ann Ellen Barefoot was adopted by Patrick and Elizabeth Brogan but married as Mary Ann Ellen Barfoot to Charles William Ridley (1860–1936) in Melbourne.

Descendant Report for William Barefoot

.... 1   William Barefoot b: 1826 in Lodden Vale, Van Diemen's Land, d: 22 Sep 1856 in
         Melbourne, Victoria
.....   +Mary Ann Steele b: 1839, m:, d: 06 May 1911, m: 1857 in Victoria
.... 2   Mary Anne Barefoot b: 1854, d: 1854
.... 2   Mary Ann Ellen Barefoot (adopted by Patrick and Elizabeth Brogan) b: Abt. 1856 in
             Collingwood, Victoria, d: 17 Feb 1904 in Melbourne, Victoria
....   +Charles William Ridley b: 08 Nov 1860 in Vaughan, Victoria, Australia, m:, d: 14 Aug
             1936 in Northcote, Victoria, Australia, m: 1887 in Victoria
.... 3   Francis Patrick Edmund Ridley b: 1888 in Richmond, Victoria, Australia, d: 28 Dec
                 1935 in Kensington, Victoria, Australia
....   +Minnie Isabel Thayer b: 1887, m:, d: 1949
.... 3   Herbert Joseph Henry Ridley b: 1890 in Richmond, Victoria, Australia, d: 10 Dec
                 1890 in Richmond, Victoria, Australia
.... 3   Leonard Henry Ridley b: 20 Feb 1892 in Richmond, Victoria, Australia, d: 29 Oct
                 1956 in East Kew, Victoria, Australia
....   +Violet Mary Irene (Irene Violet May) Stevens b: 31 Mar 1892 in Hotham West,
                 Victoria, Australia, m:, d: 30 Jun 1989 in Thornbury, Victoria, Australia, m: 1918 in
                 Victoria
.... 3   Elizabeth Gertrude Ridley b: 1894 in Richmond, Victoria, Australia, d: 06 Dec 1900
                 in Carlton, Victoria, Australia

George Barefoot

George was born in 1829 in Launceston and died in Launceston in 1897.

He married Louisa Soden in 1866 in Torquay, Tasmania.

Descendant Report for George Barefoot

..... 1   George Barefoot b: 1829 in Launceston, Van Diemen's Land, d: 02 Dec 1897 in Tasmania
.....   +Louisa Soden b: 14 Apr 1850 in Launceston, Tasmania, Australia, m:, d: 04 Dec 1914 in
         Emu Bay, Tasmania, Australia, m: 28 Mar 1866 in Torquay, Tasmania
.... 2   George Frederick Barfoot SNR b: 04 Feb 1867 in Port Sorell, Tasmania, Australia, d: 08
             Apr 1950 in Mirboo North, Victoria, Australia
....   +Florence Sophia Millington b: 1869 in Coghills Creek, Victoria, Australia, m:, d: Nov
             1929 in Morwell, Victoria, Australia, m: 1899 in Ballarat, Victoria, Australia
.... 3   Florence Louisa Barfoot b: 1900 in Mirboo, Victoria, Australia, d: 14 Feb 1986 in
                 Melbourne, Victoria, Australia
.... 3   Emily Amelia Barfoot b: 1902 in Mirboo, Victoria, Australia, d: 05 Apr 1974 in
                 Preston, Victoria, Australia
....   +Lawrie Milne Hatch b: 1898 in Melbourne, Victoria, Australia, m:, d: 25 Jan 1977 in
                 Heidelberg, Victoria, Australia., m: 25 Apr 1925
.... 3   Annie Isobel Barfoot b: 1903 in Mirboo North, Victoria, Australia, d: 1979 in
                 Parkville, Victoria, Australia
....   +Norman Clifford Palmer b: 1901, m:, d: 1983
.... 3   Mary Eliza Barfoot b: 1905 in Mirboo, Victoria, Australia, d: 1979 in Malvern,
                 Victoria, Australia
.... 3   George Frederick Barfoot JNR b: 1906 in Mirboo, Victoria, Australia, d: 08 Apr 1978
                 in Castlemaine, Victoria, Australia
.... 3   Ethel Amy Barfoot b: 1907 in Mirboo, Victoria, Australia, d:
.... 3   Robina Barfoot b: 1909 in Mirboo North, Victoria, Australia, d: 1982 in Castlemaine,
                 Victoria, Australia
.... 2   Eliza Emma Barfoot b: 11 Aug 1868 in Port Sorell, Tasmania, Australia, d: 11 Jul 1941 in
             Zimbabwe
....   +Thomas Andrew Ferguson b: 1866 in Australia, m:, d: 22 Apr 1939 in Zimbabwe, m: 13
             Aug 1889 in Ulverstone, Tasmania, Australia
.... 3   Thomas Andrew Ferguson b: 20 Aug 1890 in Strahan, Tasmania, Australia, d: 28
                 Oct 1890 in Strahan, Tasmania, Australia
.... 3   Elsie Myrtle Mayger b: 21 Sep 1891 in Strahan, West Coast Council, Tasmania,
                 Australia, d: 12 Feb 1939 in Bulawayo, Zimbabwe
.... 3   Percy Albert Ernest Ferguson b: 12 Nov 1892 in Strahan, Tasmania, Australia, d: 19
                 Mar 1954 in Kilburn, South Australia, Australia
.... 3   Annie Louisa Ferguson b: 23 Jan 1895 in Dongara, Western Australia, Australia, d:
.... 3   Ruby Edith Honey b: 07 Nov 1895 in Dongara, Irwin Shire, Western Australia,
                 Australia, d: 06 Nov 1965 in Bulawayo, Zimbabwe
....   +Honey b:, m:, d:

.... 3   Andrew Thomas Ferguson b: 1899 in Yunndaga, Menzies Shire, Western Australia,
Australia, d: 03 Mar 1962 in Bulawayo, Zimbabwe

.... 3   Grace Adelaide May Ferguson b: 1900 in Kurrawang, Coolgardie Shire, Western
Australia, Australia, d: 30 Aug 1972 in Bulawayo, Zimbabwe

.... 3   Emily Pauline Ferguson b: 1902 in Kurrawang, Western Australia, Australia, d:

.... 3   Pearl Ethel Ivy Emil Ferguson b: 1902 in Kurrawang, Western Australia, Australia, d:

.... 3   Joy Ferguson b: Tasmania, Australia, d: Bulawayo, Southern Rhodesia, Eastern
Cape, South Africa

.... 3   Elizabeth Ferguson b:, d:

.... 3   Jake Ferguson b:, d:

.... 2   William Thomas Barfoot (aka Kelly) b: 05 Feb 1870 in Port Sorell, Tasmania, Australia,
d: 1933 in Longwarry, Victoria, Australia

.... 2   Albert Edward Barfoot b: 1874 in Don, Tasmania, Australia, d: 15 Nov 1952 in
Somerset, Tasmania, Australia

.... 2   Sarah Ann Barfoot b: 17 Feb 1876 in The Don, Barrington, Tasmania, Australia, d: 1876
in Tasmania, Australia

.... 2   Alfred Ernest Barfoot b: 12 Jan 1878 in Port Sorell, Tasmania, Australia, d: 1958 in
Warragul, Victoria, Australia

.... 2   Annie May (Mary Ann) Barfoot b: 28 Dec 1879 in Port Sorrell, Tasmania, Australia, d:
1933

....   +JohnIsaac Moss b: 1876 in Glasgow, Lanarkshire, Scotland, m:, d: 19 May 1952 in
Perth, Western Australia, m: 25 Nov 1913 in Leederville, Western Australia, Australia

.... 3   John George Moss b: 03 Nov 1913 in Perth, Western Australia, Australia, d: 06 Oct
1999 in Manly, New South Wales, Australia

....   +Joyce Dardanelle Grier b: 1915, m:, d: 2013

.... 2   Caroline Jane (twin) Barfoot b: 28 Dec 1879 in Port Sorell, Tasmania, Australia, d: 17
Mar 1880 in Port Sorell, Tasmania, Australia

.... 2   Matilda Isabella Barfoot b: 03 May 1882 in Port Sorell, Tasmania, Australia, d: 25 Jan
1936 in Wivenhoe, Tasmania, Australia

....   +Walter Byron Mitchell b: 03 Dec 1882 in Ulverstone, Tasmania, Australia, m:, d: 07 Jan
1963 in Launceston, Tasmania, Australia, m: 1904 in Tasmania, Australia

.... 3   Coral Vera Mitchell b: 1902, d: 04 Jun 1907 in Emu Bay, Tasmania, Australia

.... 3   Myra Elma Edna Mitchell b: 1905 in Emu Bay, Tasmania, Australia, d: 27 Jun 1968

.... 3   Crofton Byron Henry Mitchell b: 1909 in Tasmania, Australia, d: 27 May 1971 in
Wivenhoe, Tasmania, Australia

....   +Elsie May Lynch b: 1911, m:, d: 1998

.... 3   Lionel Clarence Mitchell b: 1909 in Wivenhoe, Tasmania, Australia, d: 12 Jan 1993
in Tasmania, Australia

....   +Mirabel Molly Diprose b: 12 Aug 1916 in South Burnie, Tasmania, Australia, m:, d:
03 Jun 2008

...... 2   Emily Elmore Ellen Barfoot b: 09 Nov 1883 in Port Sorell, Tasmania, Australia, d: 09 Ap
1898 in Devonport West, Tasmania. Australia

...... 2   Myrtle Mary Barfoot Bedford b: 1884 in Launceston, Tasmania, Australia, d: 12 Nov
1939 in Merredin, Western Australia, Australia

Bibliography

Alexander, A. (Ed.). (2014). *Convict lives at the George Town Female Factory*, Convict Women's Press, Launceston.

Archer, D. J. L. (2009). *The Scott letters: VDL & Scotland 1836–55*/transcribed by D. J. L. Archer, Regal Publications, Launceston, Tas.

Boyce, J. (2023). *Van Diemen's Land*, Black Inc., Carlton, Vic.

Byrne, E. (July 2008). *Church Lane*, Encyclopedia of Melbourne, School of Historical Studies, University of Melbourne, https://www.emelbourne. net.au/biogs/EM01741b.htm, retrieved 23 September 2024.

The Cornwall Chronicle (12 December 1846). 'Country Intelligence, Longford: Coroner's Inquest', *The Cornwall Chronicle*, p. 660, http://nla.gov.au/nla. news-article65942716.

Costello, C. (1987). *Botany Bay: the story of the convicts transported from Ireland to Australia, 1791–1853*, Mercier Press.

Daniels, K. (1998). *Convict women*, Allen & Unwin.

Frost, A. (2019). *Botany Bay and the First Fleet: the real story*, Black Inc., Carlton.

Frost, L., & Hodgson, A. M. (Eds.) (2011). *Convict lives at the Launceston Female Factory*, Convict Women's Press, Launceston.

Heney, H. (1978). *Australia's founding mothers*, Nelson, Sydney.

Hirst, J. (1983). *Convict society and its enemies: a history of early New South Wales*, George Allen & Unwin, Sydney.

Karskens, G. (2010). *The colony: a history of early Sydney*, Allen & Unwin, Sydney.

Marr, D. (2023). *Killing for country: a family story*, Black Inc., Carlton.

Oxley, D. (1996). *Convict maids: the forced migration of women to Australia*, Cambridge University Press.

Reynolds, J. (1969). *Launceston: history of an Australian city*, Adult Education Board, Tasmania.

Robson, L. L. (1994). *The convict settlers of Australia*, 2nd edn, Melbourne University Press.

Shaw, A. G. L. (1977). *Convicts and the Colonies: a study of penal transportation from Great Britain and Ireland to Australia and other parts of the British Empire*, Melbourne University Press, Melbourne.

Tardif, P. (1990). *Notorious strumpets and dangerous girls: convict women in Van Diemen's Land, 1803–1829*, Angus & Robertson.

About the Author

An uncle once warned Sue that she should not research her family history, as "the secrets of our ancestors should stay buried with them". Of course that sparked a curiosity about what these secrets were, and a forty-year journey to find out as much as she could! The story of her convict fourth great-grandmother has always intrigued her, and after retiring from a role as an internationally recognised educational researcher, she set her sights and research skills to writing *Fighting the shadows: The story of Elizabeth Welborn.*